GW00469506

Rattle of Bones

HARRY Walton is a journalist who lives with his wife, Hazel in Weymouth, Dorset, on the sunny south coast of England.

Rattle of Bones is the sequel to his first novel, The Rusting Shires.

His interests include travel, books, gardening, rock music and real ale. When not enjoying the fruits of his home-made blackberry wine making, Harry is a volunteer at the historic Victorian Nothe Fort near his home documenting everything from gas mask spectacles to U-boat propellers.

ACKNOWLEDGEMENT

MY grateful thanks go to Kevin Frost for his atmospheric front cover, for checking the book and for general technical advice and suggestions. I'm also grateful to my family for putting up with me while I followed the apocalypse, a writing theme I have long been interested in.

This novel is entirely a work of fiction. The names, characters and incidents portrayed in it are either the work of the author's imagination or are used fictitiously. Any resemblance to actual persons, living or dead, organisations or events is entirely coincidental.

Rattle of Bones

Harry Walton

<u>CHAPTER ONE</u>

HE ran for his life, boots thudding through a thin skin of snow on the forest track, the sound of pursuing dogs in his ears.

One hand held a shotgun and the other a brace of pheasants which might yet cost him dear.

Foraging was one thing but he'd been foolish enough to stray on to land claimed by the so-called laird of Loch Lomond Castle, a bitter foe of his own laird who ran Callander Castle.

No excuses would be accepted and it could be death if he was caught which looked likely now as the baying of hounds got closer.

Still Duncan Weir kept his head, running but looking sharply about at his surroundings which suddenly presented him with a possible escape route.

Ahead of him the trees thinned a little and exposed a steep rocky outcrop rising to the mountainside above. It would have to do.

Putting on a burst of speed, Weir reached the first boulders and ledges no more than a hundred metres ahead of a pack of five rangy dogs which yelped in eagerness as they caught sight of their quarry bounding up across the treacherous rock face.

Weir held his nerve and took care that while he could only climb slowly it was up the worst of the slope too steep for the dogs to follow.

Their rage at being baulked of their prey soon translated into frustrated barks and growls as they arrived at the base of the rock face to find Weir tantalisingly out of reach and getting further away all the time.

Ten minutes of climbing left the dogs a hundred metres below him but Weir had not entirely escaped retribution and the sound of angry voices alerted him to the arrival of the dog pack's masters.

He risked a glance down and saw two men. One spotted him and pointed up while the second man unslung a rifle, briefly aimed and fired.

The bullet pinged off a rock a few metres to Weir's right. He hastily crabbed across the rock face to where a gully partially shielded him from view, infuriating the rifleman who poured shot after shot into the gap. Most dissipated but a couple whanged around, the ricochets buzzing nastily as Weir redoubled his efforts to get clear.

He eventually succeeded and lost no time in heading east across rugged country towards Callander.

With safety in his grasp he berated himself for taking the risk. It wasn't that two pheasants weren't worth his life although the food would be welcomed back at the castle. It was more that he felt alive again when he was out hunting, that he somehow recovered some of the feel for life that he'd lost as a city had died around him when the Red Plague killed millions and brought the world to its knees.

Out here in a world reduced to an empty shell he felt more in his element than he ever had as a taxi driver in Glasgow.

He'd watched as the city was swamped by death and anarchy. Streets became battlegrounds, supermarkets became violent flashpoints as first one gang took control only to be ousted by the next.

Slowly the city withered away. Once more than 700,000 people had lived there but the rampaging virus reduced the population to a few hundred hardy souls, scavenging during the day and hiding away at night.

He knew other cities in every country had gone the same way, a feast of life reduced to desperate surviving scraps in just a few short years.

Weir was nothing if not a survivor and he finally decided that Glasgow life had become so dangerous that he was prepared to take his chances in the countryside.

Getting there was itself an exercise in survival. Cars were always a target even if they could somehow negotiate streets choked with vehicles, so Weir had slipped away on a bicycle as dusk fell and spent his first night in a garden shed behind a row of terraced houses, jumping at every night noise he heard.

By mid-morning he was miles away, pedalling aimlessly but with some idea of finding a lonely house and holing up there until the authorities took over the area or the virus threat faded.

This he did, moving in to a stone cottage where a burn ran under a small road bridge. He rightly guessed that anyone living in such a remote place would have to have food supplies to hand and he was fortunate. The location was so lonely that looters had yet to discover it.

Weir found a large stock of tinned food, quite a bit of dried goods and enough fruit and vegetables to keep him going for months.

A couple had lived there but the man had died in a back bedroom and Weir found the remains of the woman rotting on the ground near the half open door to a large shed. Inside among lawnmowers, cultivators and a white Range Rover car was an electric Honda 125cc motorcycle and a small petrol generator.

He buried the couple in a flower border and put up a simple cross over them, feeling it was the least he could do if he was taking over their home.

Months went by and when his own food ran out Weir used the bike to visit other remote cottages and scavenge what supplies he could, bringing them back to his base.

In all this time he never heard or saw another human being. Twice there were distant sounds of vehicles but none came past his cottage.

Eventually his foraging brought him in contact with two men stood near a small flatbed truck where a switchback road snaked up a hillside.

Weir had the benefit of the high ground, something he was grateful for when he saw both men had a rifle slung over their shoulder.

Surprise was his and when he shouted down at them both men visibly jumped and reached for their weapons but they didn't raise them.

There was a brief conversation below then one man gave the other his rifle and began to slowly climb towards Weir who waited for him but kept the Honda's engine running just in case escape was needed.

When the man got within a hundred metres he began a conversation which left Weir both wary and full of hope.

The man invited Weir to come and live with their group. The only proviso was that he obeyed the orders of the laird and that he contributed towards the community's food stocks. There were no passengers, he was told. If he didn't like the idea then he was free to just ride away but the offer would not be repeated.

By now Weir was fully aware of the risks and demands of trying to survive alone and he reasoned that joining the group wouldn't prevent him leaving quietly one night if he didn't like the set-up.

So he agreed and rode down to join them, noting that the rear of the little truck was piled with cases of alcohol, boxes of tinned food and various other foodstuffs.

The two men saw where he looked and said they had "liberated" the supplies from a small village shop a few miles away.

Weir followed the two men as they took the truck away and drove for nearly an hour to Callander Castle whose rugged beauty couldn't be dimmed by once beautiful grounds now becoming shaggy and overgrown with saplings seeded from surrounding trees.

He was quickly introduced to about a dozen men and women who lived there and told he would meet the laird that night. He was then shown to a tower room he was informed was now his accommodation.

After a simple but solid evening meal of venison and root vegetables he was shown into a small library and introduced to the laird, Andrew McCain, who said life here was hard but no-one went hungry and everyone pulled together to survive.

He was scathing of a rival laird about thirty miles away, one Ewan Fraser, who he warned Duncan to be on his guard against. He said Fraser and his men were involved in a feud with everyone at Callander over foraging rights.

Weir learned later that, like so many feuds, antagonism had flared over food the McCain's group had found and taken but which Fraser and his group claimed was in their area.

Over the next few months he learnt the ropes and was involved in several clashes with men from Loch Lomond Castle although no-one was killed on either side.

He joined foraging parties and also did some hunting on his own which proved so successful that McCain gave him licence to roam the area claimed by Callander and bring back whatever he could find or shoot.

The problem was, thought Duncan, that the border between the two rival lairds was pretty vague and included a sort of no-man's land where patrols often clashed.

He knew only too well that the deer, pheasant and other game he hunted had no idea of boundaries, so he adopted the same approach. If a plump bird fell to him on the edge of land claimed by Loch Lomond then he wasn't too bothered although he took as much care as possible to dodge detection by using snares whenever he could to avoid the noise of shotgun fire.

It had just been bad luck that a Loch Lomond hunting party and their dogs crossed his scent on land they felt was theirs and pursued him.

Now he had won clear of that pursuit he turned north and east and soon collected his bike left near a tumbled down hut in a break of trees

Within an hour he was turning his Honda up the driveway to the castle and parking it in a stone-built garage behind the main imposing building.

He then took his pheasants in through a rear entrance and left them in the kitchens, putting his shotgun in a hallway rack before going into the living room where he found the housekeeper, Matilda , talking with David Allan who acted as a sort of head keeper for those who lived at Callander.

"Any luck?" asked Allan.

"A little," replied Duncan. "Got a brace of pheasants but I had to work for them. A hunting party from the Loch took a pot at me."

"Were you on their patch?" said Matilda.

"Difficult to tell," said Duncan. "If I was then it was marginal and I wasn't hanging around to chat. It's difficult to explain the niceties of boundary lines when you're being shot at!"

"David, you'll have to talk to Mr McCain about this," said Matilda. "That Lomond lot, they're getting more and more aggressive."

"Aye, but you know the laird's policy. No contact unless absolutely necessary."

"It may soon become necessary," she replied. "That's the second exchange of fire in a month."

"A dispute's one thing but a war is quite another and we have a way to go before we reach that state of affairs. I'll have a word but I doubt he'll change his mind."

"Try," said Matilda . "I've a feeling that Fraser might fancy his chances a little less if we showed a bit more willingness to stand up to him."

Allan nodded and left in search of the laird while Matilda asked Duncan about what game he'd seen.

"A few deer at distance," he replied, "a good few grouse and pheasant, some partridge, the usual rabbits and hares and I noticed a few cattle. Might be worth seeing if we can herd any of them into some pastureland with the others we've got."

"Have a word with Allan about it tonight. It's winter, so we need all the livestock we can get. Anything still running around out there won't survive long if we get heavy snow. Now sit yourself down and I'll get you a cup of tea."

She left and Duncan briefly stepped across to bookshelves lining the walls, searched for a few minutes and then took down a volume on Alaska which he brought to an armchair. Pheasants hadn't been the only creatures he saw today. He slowly turned the pages feeling that, if he could identify the glimpse he'd had of a large animal, then Fraser and his roughnecks might not be the only menace out there in the wild.

CHAPTER TWO

CHRISTMAS Day began crisp and cold at Waterfall Manor in Cornwall where newly married John and Dawn Kane were woken by the muffled shrieks of excited children.

John moaned in pretended anguish as the youngsters tore down the corridor outside their bedroom heading for the staircase and the drawing room where their presents were laid out under a Christmas tree ready to be opened after breakfast.

"You'd better get used to noise," said Dawn. "In six or seven months time you'll have plenty of it when we have our own baby to look after. There'll be no lying late in bed for you after that."

"Best I make the most of it now then!" said John, drawing a mock cry of shock from his bride when he put a cold hand on her hip and pulled her to him.

They kissed and then laughed at returning footsteps, more shrieks and the sound of adult voices shushing the children and telling them to be quieter.

"Perhaps breakfast won't have so many interruptions!" said John, swinging his legs out of bed and shivering as he fumbled for pants and socks.

"Don't think you've got away with avoiding your husbandly duties," said Dawn. "I shall expect extra effort from you tonight!"

"I'd better make sure I get an extra helping of turkey then!" said John, doing up shirt buttons before pulling on cord trousers, a thick pullover and a pair of slippers.

"I suppose you'll be starting our married life by getting up at your leisure."

Dawn laughed throatily and stretched, her heavy breasts revealed as the sheet slipped back.

"I'm sleeping for two now. You could always come back to bed" she said, patting the sheet next to her.

"Oh no you don't!" said John. "If I do that we'll be here all morning!"

"Promises, promises" said Dawn. "Just make sure you keep them tonight!"

John became a bit flustered and hastily left the bedroom closing the door behind him to the sound of her delighted laughter.

By the time he got downstairs and into the kitchen the children had almost finished their breakfast.

"Anything left for me?" he asked Janice who was bustling about near the aga.

"Plenty," she said. "Sit down and I'll bring you a plate."

John did so just as Jed appeared in the doorway, the two bridegrooms greeting each other with happy grins.

John said: "Sleep well?" and both men grinned again since sleep hadn't figured prominently in either of their wedding nights.

Jed had married Becky at the same time John married Dawn in a double ceremony performed by Captain Tolly Harcourt who had flown in specially by helicopter from his fission-powered container ship.

It was a surprise wedding certainly for both brides who hadn't been told of the event!

Captain Harcourt even stayed on after for some of the celebrations. He commanded one of two container ships sent to England after Dawn and John managed to make radio contact with Australia where a Recovery Council was operating to run the country.

His ship and a second commanded by Captain Finn Stapleton were loaded with soldiers, equipment, food and power sources including generators and half a dozen portable nuclear power units to help survivors start to try and get the country back on its feet.

A base was set up in Plymouth before both ships left on Christmas Eve to take Leo Anderson, the Recovery Council's lead representative, to London.

Jed pulled up a chair and sat down with John, both men looking tired.

"Here you go," said Janice, placing huge plates of fried breakfast in front of them. "You two look like you need to keep your strength up!"

Both men flushed at her sally as she broke off to hastily stop Becky's son, Kevin, from leaving table, telling him there would be no present opening until he had finished his food.

Others began to drift into the kitchen including chef, Victor, and his wife Norma, who began to help Janice prepare more breakfasts.

"When you and I have finished eating we'd better check those turkeys are ready for the oven or our names will be mud come lunchtime," said John.

Jed nodded and replied: "We'll need to check the animals as well. Better do that this morning before lunch so we've got a bit of time to relax this afternoon."

"Agreed," said John, adding that he wanted to make sure everyone enjoyed themselves at what would for many be the first proper Christmas celebration they'd had for five years.

More and more people began to arrive for breakfast including Roy, Mike and Evie and then Donna who saw the two men and came over to join them.

"Morning husbands!" she began, laughing when John and Jed studiously looked at their plates.

They were just finishing and had begun to chat with her about the chickens and bees when Becky and Dawn came in. Dawn had warm clothing on but Becky was still in her dressing gown which accentuated the bump of her pregnancy.

A ripple of applause broke out for the two brides who joined in the fun by giving exaggerated curtsies to the room.

"I thought the newly-weds would have had a lie in!" said Mike to much laughter.

"We would have," shot back Becky, "but Dawn and I have been sadly led down by our husbands. Perhaps a good Christmas dinner will help them get their strength back!"

Cheers greeted that effort and John and Jed, their faces red with embarrassment, hastily finished their food and practically fled out to the porch.

"Blimey!" said Jed. "This married life thing's got a bit of cut and thrust to it."

"I think we may have got off lightly," said John. "I feel like I'm being stalked! Come on, it's time to talk turkey."

The two men put boots on and made their way behind the manor to where an impressive range of stone barns and other outbuildings lay.

Several had already been converted into accommodation for their growing community while others were still being worked on. Still more had been given new leases of life as everything from chicken houses to storage for freezers.

It was to the latter that the two men made their way, removing a padlock to get into the gloom of a long narrow building lined with freezers which held a large part of their supplies of food.

The nearby town of Launceston had been a thriving community before the Red Plague virtually wiped out human life across the country. Part of that life had been a turkey farm and, while most of the birds had perished through deprivation or lack of care, a few dozen had survived and now lived wild in the area. John had caught and killed two for Christmas and, when Donna heard about the surviving turkeys, she immediately got John to agree to snare two or three so they could be added to the poultry flock they already had.

The two Christmas turkeys had been taken out of their freezer on Christmas Eve and were now sufficiently thawed to be collected and brought to the kitchen for Victor to work his magic.

Both birds stood on separate trays in the building and John and Jed worked together to lift them and empty the trays of melted ice water. Each then took one tray and carried it back to the manor kitchen where their arrival was cheered by the excited children who had begun to open their presents.

Victor swiftly took over and placed both turkeys on a large work surface, before checking that the giblets and any remaining feathers had been removed. He then used strips of John's bacon to cover the turkey breasts, carefully wrapped them in foil and put them in two aga ovens before carrying on with other preparations for the meal.

By now Maisie had come down for breakfast, her walking stick thumping on the floor. She sat nursing a mug of tea, talking with Janice about the pies she was going to make for everyone's desert.

She teased John and Jed about their wedding night which only hastened their departure, both men taking bicycles and firearms before pedalling off to check on their animals. Their breath plumed in the cold morning air as they rode a couple of miles to the farm, a sack of vegetable peelings strapped to the rear panniers of John's bicycle.

All seemed well and they forked a few bundles of hay for the cows, sheep and goats together with several handfuls of grain as a treat for the chickens who clucked appreciation as they pecked up their own Christmas meal. The two men collected more than a dozen eggs to take back to the manor.

It was cold and there was much clumping of gloved hands together to try and keep warm as they moved on and checked the pigs which were already out foraging in the fields. They soon came closer when John tipped the vegetable peelings into several troughs.

Again all seemed well and discussion turned to raiding Launceston's industrial estates for a few miles of security fencing to strengthen the fields' perimeters and those of the manor.

"Shouldn't be too hard," said John. "Grind the supports off and roll the fencing up. There's plenty of unused posts lying about to put the fencing up. It will be a long job but we need to protect the animals."

"We also need to check surrounding fields first," said Jed. "If we are going to fence a perimeter then we need to widen the area we enclose to allow for growth. There'll be more animals this Spring and summer and more people as well. Becky's baby is due in a couple of months or so."

"Keep it quiet for a while," said John, "but Dawn is pregnant as well. We think she'll have the baby sometime around July or August."

"That's great news!" said Jed, clapping him on the back. "Now let's get back in the warm. I'm sure there'll be jobs waiting for us."

And with that they made their way back to the farm buildings, retrieved their bicycles and pedalled slowly away.

Meanwhile behind them, lower down where the fields ran into woodland, water was beginning to seep into large fresh tracks on the edge of a stream.

CHAPTER THREE

SNOW was falling slowly on Loch Lomond Castle where furious laird Ewan Fraser had just been told of the abortive chase after Duncan Weir.

"So two of you and a pack of dogs couldn't catch one man?" queried Fraser in a dangerously calm voice.

"The pack chased him for more than a mile," said one of his staff, a man called Brennan with a red face and greying stubble. "By the time we caught up he was near the top of a mountainside."

"I did take a shot at him," said his colleague, Ross, "but it was distance and I was shooting uphill."

"You mean you missed him," said Fraser, at which the two men shuffled uncomfortably and tried not to look at him.

"And he was definitely on our land?"

"Aye, that he was," said Brennan. "He may have got away on to Callander land but the dogs picked up his scent on your land."

"You're sure?" said Fraser.

"As sure as we could be," said Ross.

"Which means not very sure and McCain has beaten us again. Do I have to do everything myself? Is it beyond your feeble abilities to catch just one of his men? Go on, get out of my sight."

The two men hastily paid their respects and left the drawing room where Fraser stepped across to a small gate leg table with a tray of bottles and glasses on it and poured himself a whisky.

This couldn't go on, he thought, as he stood beneath a huge pair of antlers mounted high above him on the wall.

Pin prick incident after pin prick incident, each estate needling the other with incursions. It was wasting the time of his staff to constantly be on the look-out for foragers from Callander. But what to do?

If they could catch or even kill one or two of McCain's men it would only spark reprisals and there were barely thirty people on both sides put together. Neither laird could afford to lose a single person. It was hard enough to survive with current staff never mind coping with casualties.

No, it grated but some sort of compromise had to be reached. Fraser was a ruthless man. He'd run a security business before the Red Plague came and was no stranger to Scottish estates. When he survived the devastating virus he swiftly realised that safety lay away from built-up areas. He knew the Castle and brought the remains of his staff there together with a few people he found along the way. It was deserted except for two or three bodies which were quickly removed and buried well away from the house.

Then it was a question of running the place which was not much different from running his former business. You just needed to stay on top of situations.

They had solar and water power as well as generators so electricity wasn't a problem. The accommodation was enough for the people he had, food wasn't plentiful but they got by and there was a chance for some sort of life out of the ruins of the plague, but not if this feud with McCain continued.

He wasn't even sure how it had started, just a minor tit-for-tat which escalated. The question was, how could things be smoothed over without either side losing face?

A sip of whisky rolled slowly across his tongue and he mused on the problem, eventually deciding that some sort of approach would have to be made for a meeting with McCain.

Perhaps the old hunting lodge in Queen Elizabeth Forest Park might do, he thought, taking another sip of whisky.

It was roughly half way between the two of them, was barely twenty miles away and easily reached yet was off the beaten track to allow a quick withdrawal if necessary.

The more he thought about it the more the lodge idea seemed to work. Even if McCain rebuffed a truce then at least Fraser would know where he stood and could decide whether to take their antagonism up to another level.

Yes, it just might work, and he smiled at a decision made and the prospect of action.

*   *   *

There was no smile from Duncan Weir as he thoughtfully tapped a finger against pictures in the book on Alaska he had taken down from a shelf in the library at Callander Castle.

What he was looking at were photographs of grizzly bears, but he wasn't interested in the ones showing them fishing, fighting or foraging. It was a single distance photograph of a bear entering a belt of trees which held his attention because it so closely matched what he had just seen that day.

Could it be possible that the wilds of Scotland were now home to a grizzly bear? It didn't seem likely but Weir had seen some strange things in recent years. He knew and had visited several wildlife parks, zoos and attractions in his time, some of which had displayed grizzly bears. Could one of them have escaped?

Again his finger absently tapped the picture. The book wasn't putting his mind at rest as he read that grizzlies could run up to 35mph and weigh as much as a third of a ton. One of McCain's hunting rifles might stop it but you'd need a lot of luck to kill a grizzly with a shotgun, particularly one with the sort of light shot his weapon had.

It might den through most of winter, but what happened in the Spring when it woke full of life and with a big appetite? Weir didn't like the prospect of stumbling across a hungry grizzly.

Still, he might be wrong and what he'd seen at distance might be something else. Perhaps he'd glimpsed the rear of a deer or cow, but he didn't think so. Caution might be the best course of action, keeping his mouth shut until he had a bit more evidence. No point in starting a panic for nothing. He'd keep his eyes open and report when he had something more substantial to back up his concerns.

With a nod at a decision reached, Weir got up and put the book back before turning round at the clink of crockery as Matilda carried in a cup of tea for him.

"Drink it while it's hot," she said, putting cup and saucer down on a small oak table whose legs had thistle heads carved on them.

"Thank you," said Duncan, giving her a smile and an appreciative glance which she took in her stride. Being one of the few women in the castle she was used to being eyed up by the men and it didn't bother her.

Matilda Patterson had been the madam of a very successful brothel in Glasgow and knew what men liked and how best to keep them sweet, so she simply smiled back at Duncan and briskly left the room.

Very nice, he thought, but he didn't want to rock the boat by making unwanted advances. She didn't seem to be interested in anyone except McCain and he wasn't about to start risking his berth at the castle by sparking the boss's woman if that was the way it was. He'd wait and see. Weir was good at waiting.

Instead he decided to occupy himself by going to check the cellars which no longer just contained spirits and wines.

He strode along a corridor full of gold framed paintings showing dark scenes of heather, mountains, rivers and deer until he came to a sturdy oak door set with metal studs. He reached up and took down a key from the architrave before unlocking the door and stepping carefully inside.

Dim conditions made him fumble before he found a dusty switch which he flipped to flood a heavy banister with light.

Stone steps led down into the cellar whose low vaulted roof was supported by stone arches. When he reached the bottom of the steps a series of arched alcoves stretched away from him on either side of a stone-paved walkway.

A lot of work had gone into rearranging contents and all the wines and spirits had been shifted to the furthest alcoves to empty those closest to the steps for use as food storage.

Duncan shivered. The cool conditions might be ideal for food and wine but they didn't do a lot for him.

In front of him were dozens of fridges and freezers, most in use but some empty and disconnected. Those humming away contained everything from meat joints, poultry and game to hams and salami. There were also brine barrels full of meat which could last for years and smoked meat hanging on hooks which could also last a long time before having to be eaten.

The little community's weakness lay in vegetables. They had some in frozen store, but fresh vegetables were in short supply. The castle gardens supplied a little and more was gained by foraging, but unless more people joined them and more land was opened up for cultivation then they faced a growing health problem.

What he was after was potatoes. There were sacks and sacks of them in one alcove and Weir lost no time beginning to sort through them.

First he sifted through the remains of one sack, keeping only a few small potatoes, but then he began to sort through some of the other sacks, retaining only very small potatoes while replacing them with larger ones from the nearly empty sack.

When he'd finished he had a quarter sack of small potatoes for seed which he carried to the back of the alcove before tying it up and suspending it from a ceiling hook.

Before the plague Weir had broken the monotony of taxi driving in Glasgow by looking after an allotment where he'd grown a whole range of vegetables.

Now he could indulge what for him had been a hobby and put it to proper use for the benefit of the castle.

Its gardens were still cultivated but large areas were starting to become overgrown and, once the weather warmed up a bit, Weir planned to bring them back into use and try and grow some potatoes and a few root vegetables such as carrots, parsnips, swedes and cooking onions.

The castle also had a perfectly good greenhouse which had been used for cultivating flowers. Weir planned to use it for tomatoes and to try and find enough seed to bring on runner beans and French beans if he could, perhaps even chillies if he could find the seed. The more food choices they had the better and he might even score a few housekeeping brownie points with Matilda.

Starting all that was at least two months away while winter gripped the land so fiercely, but he could make preparations and he was sure McCain would approve of the work to boost their food supplies.

But it was that memory of the animal he had seen at distance that nagged at his mind as he climbed the steps back out of the cellar and switched off the lights.

Perhaps it was nothing, but if what he'd seen did turn out to be a bear then foraging was going to have to be a lot more cautious and he'd need to carry a weapon which packed a lot more punch than a shotgun.

Weir relocked the cellar door, replaced the key and headed for the kitchens where Poppy Moore was busy plucking the pheasants he had brought in.

"What are you planning with them?" he asked.

"Once they're plucked I'm going to braise them slowly and then strip the carcasses for meat for game pies with a bit of venison and rabbit. They freeze well and I can make an easy meal wi them and a few tatties."

Weir nodded. Poppy might not be the best cook but she was reliable and what she produced stuck to your ribs. Everyone needed a full stomach to be able to cope with the conditions outside which were currently hovering around zero with a bitter wind.

Next stop was the log house where Weir stripped off his jacket and put half and hour's work in with an axe, building up a wall of billets for the castle fires before spending a few minutes with a hand axe chipping away to produce several armfuls of kindling for the fireboxes in the main rooms.

Finally he went up to his room and changed into more comfortable clothing for their main meal and the evening ahead.

The laird demanded no formality at dinner but everyone had to be as clean and presentable as possible because "without standards we are nothing".

Weir had a pair of comfortable brogues, corduroy trousers and a rust-coloured pullover on when he descended the stairs to the dining room.

He joined Andrew McCain and a number of others round a massive oak dining table gleaming with polish and laid with cutlery and glasses. Soon tureens of vegetables were being brought in by Poppy followed by two large game pies, a gravy boat and two carafes of wine. Everyone lost no time tucking in.

McCain took time during the meal to talk with a man called Alec Wilson whose main duty was to lead trips out foraging for supplies.

Duncan's former hideaway had already been cleaned out of anything useful and Wilson was advocating trips out further west and north to try and locate similar isolated properties as well as hamlets and villages which might still have properties and gardens containing food capable of being used.

"It's getting harder," said Wilson. "Every now and again we find a cottage which has been missed, but much of the food is unusable. In another six months I doubt five percent of the supplies we find will be edible. We're still having better luck with vegetables in gardens, but even that is starting to dwindle. Everything is becoming overgrown."

Duncan saw his chance and said: "I've been down in the cellar and sorted out some of the smallest potatoes to chit and use to grow our own potato crops.

"I think we not only need to bring back more of our gardens into cultivation but to check every garden we visit for vegetables gone to seed. Everything we can find and sow back here can only benefit us in the long run. We might even create our own seed store. One of the sheds would do for that."

"Are you volunteering?" asked McCain.

"In a way, yes," replied Weir, "but as many people as possible need to be involved, either collecting seeds or clearing ground ready for planting once the weather warms up a bit. There's no point having seeds with no available ground to put them in. Some of our walled garden is still dug, but a lot of it is just overgrown. We need to bring the whole garden into production. You found me and two more like me in the last year.

"People will continue to trickle in and you're going to need more and more food. Make the numbers work. Get a rota system going for the gardens. Clearance, digging, weeding, planting. Make the greenhouse earn its keep. We can't eat flowers but we can eat tomatoes, chillies and sweet peppers and the glasshouse can be used to bring on vegetables early so they have the best chance when we come to planting out."

McCain put another forkful of game pie into his mouth, chewed thoughtfully for a while and then stabbed his knife towards Weir.

"You're elected then. In addition to your foraging duties I want you to rough out a rota duty for me which will bring the walled garden up to speed.

"Alec? You heard what Duncan said. Can you keep your eyes peeled on your travels for any vegetables gone to seed?"

"I don't see why not," said Alec. "Makes sense to me and most of us have a rough idea of what to look for. Some of the village shops might have seed stands with packets still on them and Duncan can give us a crash course on what particular seeds look like so we don't waste time on weeds."

"That's fairly easy," said Duncan. "I've already been through gardening books in the library and whoever grew flowers in the greenhouse also did a bit of vegetable gardening as well because there are old seed packets in there. Some still have seed in them. They're way out of date, but a seed's a seed whether it's useless to plant or not and I can show people what to look for.

"Also, if you find vegetables in a garden then don't pick them all. Leave some, tell me where they are and we can harvest the seeds in the autumn."

Weir turned back to his meal which suddenly tasted a lot sweeter. It was a small step but he felt it was an important one. Granted it might be a while before they saw the fruits of their labours, but the prospect of a regular supply of fresh vegetables would be crucial for everyone's health. And what about apples and plums? He'd have to investigate what types of tree did best so far north and whether any of the derelict garden centres in the area still had fruit tree stocks that they might bring to the castle.

He was full of enthusiasm, but he'd have been a lot less enthusiastic about the future if he could have seen a woman with two antique silver baby rattles slung round her neck.

Her rag-tag band of survivors had left a trail of murder and destruction behind them when they left Edinburgh. They were now chugging towards Callander in a battered double decker bus...and they were hungry.

CHAPTER FOUR

BACK at the manor breakfast was over, the children had dispersed to play with their new toys and other presents and the kitchen was a hive of activity.

Maisie had flour up to her elbows as she made the pastry for three of her famous apple pies.

John and Jed had barely got into the kitchen before she chimed out: "Now I don't want you two under my feet. Go and chop firewood or something. We'll call if we need you."

"Nice to feel wanted!" said Jed as they moved through into one of the sitting rooms.

There was no escape there as the floor was covered in toys and makeshift wrapping paper while children created their own dramas and stories to suit whatever they were playing with.

John looked at Jed and rolled his eyes before saying: "I thought the manor would be ideal for a community but we're already getting cramped!"

Nearly forty people now lived at Waterfall and, while its bedrooms housed quite a few of them, it had become an urgent matter to create new accommodation in some of the many sturdy outbuildings which included a number of stone barns.

John, who lived in his family's semi-detached house a few miles away in Launceston, had hoped to start married life there and then move to the manor when there was room. At this rate, he thought, it could be years before he could do that because of the needs of the Leeds group he and Dawn had brought down to start a new life in Cornwall.

Jed cried off and said he was going for a bit of peace and quiet in the library, so John found himself wandering back outside and up to the outbuildings.

Seven of the smaller stables and barns had been or were in the process of being converted to accommodation with footings already dug to extend the ground floor and add extra storeys. Most hadn't been completed although some were occupied because of the pressure on space in the manor. Fortunately John's house and a neighbour's he used for storage afforded heated accommodation for most of the Leeds party with John and Dawn sleeping in the Morelo motor home he used for foraging round the country.

Everyone hoped the new accommodation at the manor would be completed in time to move in before next Christmas but that still seemed a long time away.

Some of the larger agricultural buildings were jam packed with building materials from beams and supports to roof tiles. Great heaps of cement bags lay sheltered ready to be mixed with mountains of sand outside ready for foundation work to get new walls up in the Spring.

John was idly kicking at some weeds near a huge open-sided building full of bricks, doors and windows when an arm went round his waist and he was hugged.

"A penny for your thoughts husband....as if I couldn't guess," said Dawn.

"I was just thinking about where we might set up home if we came to live here permanently. The way things are going we'll be lucky to be within a hundred metres of the place. Everything seems taken."

"Which is no bad thing," said Dawn. "Gives us a bit of privacy at your place. We don't have to move immediately and, when we do, who says it has to be to the manor? I was wondering what you thought about taking over that farmhouse with the dairy up near where you've got all the animals?"

He went thoughtful at her words and she could see the wheels of consideration and planning turning in his mind. She loved it when she saw him focus on anything. It was like watching something inevitable and reliable happening.

She gave him another hug and said: "Come on. There's a glass of sherry and an apple turnover waiting for you in the sitting room. Maisie says it will be a while before we see proper mince pies again."

And with that they strolled back to the manor to be enfolded in warmth and the smell of cooking.

Inside work forces had been divided between the two kitchens with one group concentrating on preparing all the vegetables and the other focussing on the meat, setting tables and helping Maisie with her pies.

Bruno, tail wagging slowly, wandered hopefully about until he was shooed out of the main kitchen, the huge mastiff flopping down disgustedly in the small sitting room where some of the children were playing.

Both kitchens gradually became like saunas with clouds of steam eddying everywhere while Mike, Roy and Noah made sure there was no shortage of beer and wine to help the celebrations along.

Finally the meal was ready and everyone took their places in the dining room and drawing room where tables had been laid and decorated with holly and candles.

There were cheers when John began to carve the first turkey and he was kept busy for some time putting slices on plates which were swiftly ferried away to bowls loaded with vegetables before being handed to an appreciative audience, each waiting hungrily for their turn.

Soon all were served and the hum of conversation was replaced by the clink of knives and forks as everyone did justice to their Christmas feast.

Maisie's pies soon followed to widespread acclaim before the adults sat where they were and chatted over wine or a beer or moved away to relax and let their meal go down in one of the three sitting rooms.

Becky said she was heading for a nice settee and Mike and Evie opted to go with her while Dawn said she'd try and make radio contact with the Recovery Council in London to wish Leo Anderson and everyone else a Merry Christmas.

When she came back from her call she went to the sitting room overlooking the courtyard and told everyone there that both ships had arrived and docked at Tilbury and that the port had seen some fires but was generally still useable.

"Over the next few weeks they're going to establish themselves and try and get into the city," she said.

"Mr Anderson plans to send out loudspeaker vans to as wide an area as possible explaining they are there to help and inviting survivors to meet them, perhaps at the London Stadium. He thinks there could be several thousand people still alive in the city. He wants to reach as many as possible and encourage them to set up their own Recovery Council to help co-ordinate survivors."

She paused here and looked around until she saw John, then continued: "He also wants to check on other parts of the country, to find out how they have fared. To do that he'll be sending one helicopter party to the north, Wales and the Midlands and another to Central Scotland to check on major population centres. He wants John and I to be his representatives on the trip to Scotland."

Up to now there had been keen interest in what she was saying, but all conversation died away when they heard that she and John might be leaving them.

Roy said: "We can't afford to lose John as a mechanic. Jed's searching for farm machinery and the like. That will be useless if what he finds won't start or won't work

properly. Only John knows how to puzzle out what might
be wrong. What are we supposed to do while he's away?
How long's he supposed to go for? And what about the
protection we lose if Dawn goes? She's the only one with
weapons training."

His questions opened a buzz of comment until John
clapped his hands and said: "Very kind of you, but I'm
not indispensable.

"Most machinery just needs clean fuel and Jed knows
how to fit a battery. You could quite easily carry on
sourcing what we need. If it works when you try it then
great, otherwise just store it until I get back and I'll deal
with it then. The sort of trip Mr Anderson is talking about
won't last more than a week."

"You'd go then?" asked Donna.

"They're helping us," said John. "It would be a bit
churlish if I said I wouldn't help them. And as I've said,
this is only likely to be a short trip. We'll be back before
you know we've gone."

There was a more subdued hum of conversation at that.
Then Jed said: "Come on everyone! A while ago we were
all on our own fighting to stay alive. Then a few of us
came together at Plymouth, a few more at Leeds and now
we're all here. There will be others just like us scattered
about the country, particularly in the cities, and something
has got to be done to start knitting the country together
again. It won't happen in our lifetimes, but there are the

children to think about. If they are to have any sort of a future life then we have to work for it now. That's what we are starting to do here, but there's the whole country to think of. If they need John and Dawn to help set up other recovery councils then they should go. It's not as if we're losing them forever."

There was a thoughtful air in the room after he finished speaking and a little of the Christmas atmosphere seemed to have been lost, but the children soon became noisy again and there were shrieks of excitement when Mike and Evie led a game of hide-and-seek.

A light tea brought Christmas Day to a close, the children were slowly put to bed despite their protests and the adults relaxed in front of blazing log fires in two of the sitting rooms or helped clean up in the kitchen.

Dawn lazily reclined on a big cushion which allowed her to rest her head on his legs where John sat in a wingchair, one hand gently stroking her hair.

"Come on, out with it," she said.

"What do you mean?" he replied.

"I can tell when something's bothering you," said Dawn."What is it?"

There was a brief pause and then John said: "I was wondering whether it was a good idea for us both to go to Scotland, what with the baby and everything."

Dawn sat up and looked at him, then said: "You're serious aren't you? In case you haven't been listening, I'm not due for six or seven months and this trip will only take six or seven days. A more suspicious person might think you were just trying to get rid of me!"

"No, no!" said John, hastily shifting in his seat. "It's just that we can't be too careful and...."

"Oh come on John! I'm not going to have to watch what I do for months yet. It took a long time for us to meet and I'm not letting you out of my sight now I've got you."

And with that she settled back against him, John warily relaxing himself although he still looked worried.

They chatted about various things including a possible move to the farmhouse and dairy near the animals, but Dawn could tell his mind was only half on what they were talking about.

"Are you going to be like this all the time until the baby's born?" asked Dawn.

"Probably," said John with a smile. "It's not just a new experience for you but for me as well."

"Best we enjoy ourselves while we can then," said Dawn giving him a wicked grin. "I was short changed this morning so I expect a bit more effort from you tonight!"

"Good job I had that extra helping of turkey then wasn't it!" replied John, smiling as Dawn got up, grabbed his hand and pulled him to his feet.

"Let's wish everyone good-night," said Dawn.

"But it's not even 9pm yet!" said John in mock complaint.

"I'm sure I can think of something to while away a bit of time before we sleep!"

"I'm sure you can," said John. "That's what's worrying me. At this rate I won't be able to get up in the morning!"

"Now there's a thought!" purred Dawn, pulling him to the door past grinning faces and a chorus of "good-nights".

They climbed the stairs together and once inside the bedroom they slowly kissed, Dawn stripping off his shirt and fumbling at the belt of his trousers in her eagerness.

He began to breathe heavily as she undid the zip and slipped one hand down inside his shorts, John responding by urgently tugging her blouse free and sliding his hands up her back to unclip her bra.

They practically fell on the bed, John's legs tangled in his trousers as he overbalanced trying to pull down her leggings.

They kissed again and Dawn slowly stroked him until they both lost control.

John's hands were shaking as he began to undo the buttons on her blouse, Dawn tearing the rest of the garment off as they came together in a flurry of discarded clothing. When he rolled on to his back Dawn was quick to straddle him, John thrusting inside her again and again until her thighs clenched as they climaxed together and collapsed in each other's arms, kissing slowly and with great passion.

A while later John asked: "So, have I fulfilled my husbandly duties to your satisfaction?"

Dawn smiled at him and said: "For the moment, for the moment."

The two of them drifted off into sleep and the next thing John knew was morning light beginning to seep through the curtains.

Dawn was still sleeping and he spent some time lying beside her just enjoying the pleasure of her presence until she eventually woke up, stretched lazily and said: "Good morning husband!"

"Good morning wife. Happy Boxing Day!"

She laughed as she gently twisted and curled a lock of hair on the side of his head, John becoming lost in the wonder that such a beguiling woman was his wife.

He dragged himself reluctantly back to reality and said he was going to take a shower, getting out of bed and padding across to the ensuite bathroom which included a large glass walled shower.

Hot water was soon cascading down on him as he poured shampoo into his hands and lathered his hair clean before rinsing his head clear of soap. The noise of falling water disguised Dawn's approach and the first he knew that he wasn't alone was when her soapy hands slid along his shoulders making him jump.

She continued to soap lower and lower until she embraced him, her breasts pressing into his back as her hands drifted round and cupped his swelling erection.

"Can't a man even take a shower without demands being made on him?" he asked.

"You want me to be happy don't you?" said Dawn, beginning to soap and stroke the whole of his groin.

"Yes, but it's very hard to concentrate on anything when you're doing that!" he said, turning to face her.

"So concentrate on me," she said and he did, her nipples coming erect as he soaped her slowly to moans of encouragement. They were soon making love and, when their passions finally cooled, the two of them just stood there, the shower cascading down one side of their bodies, as John kissed and gently nibbled at one of her ears causing Dawn to wriggle in appreciation.

"Now I'm happy!" she said.

"You'd better be!" said John. "I haven't had breakfast yet and I need to keep my strength up with you around."

They turned fully into the shower jets and removed the last traces of soap from their bodies, drying themselves with fluffy cream towels before returning to the bedroom to get dressed for the day ahead.

When they descended to the breakfast room they made short work of toast, fruit preserve and hot tea before retiring to the library as the children arrived to loudly demand something to eat.

John swiftly tracked down what books there were about Scotland and then asked Dawn if Leo Anderson had given any date for their trip.

"No," she replied. "All he said was that it had to be early in the New Year so he could try and judge the number of survivors and what needed to be done as soon as possible."

"Not sure I like the idea of Scotland in winter," said John. "No crops and if you can't kill something or you haven't got food put by then the odds are stacked against surviving until Spring. Who knows what we'll find....or who."

CHAPTER FIVE

SHOULD he live or should he die? That was the question vexing a furious Emily Riddle as she drove a ramshackle Leyland Olympian bus along the M9 out of the barren remains of Edinburgh.

The capital of Scotland had once been called home by more than half a million people. Barely five hundred survived the Red Plague but even that dispirited and downtrodden remnant had somehow rallied, taken on a new lease of life and banded together to counter-attack her gang which had been preying on anyone they thought might have food. Riddle and the remnants of her pack of cutthroats were forced to leave the city one jump ahead of a lynch mob.

Now she was grinding slowly along a motorway littered with abandoned vehicles, drifts of debris and the occasional fallen tree.

There were also bodies, some in cars but others just lying in the roadway where their last moments of life had flickered away in a choking stumble and collapse as death swiftly took them.

Emily was no stranger to death. In the early years of the pandemic she had lost her husband and faced the harrowing task of trying to keep herself and two young children alive in the teeth of looting, rape and murder.

Her privileged life in a five-bedroom detached house in the sought after area of Morningside rapidly meant nothing and she was barely able to grab the children and hide in their summerhouse when looters came and smashed their way in through the front door.

A night of terror followed huddled together as they listened to screams, drunken singing and the occasional gunshot. When morning came her cautious return revealed the body of a man in the kitchen while every crumb of food in the house was gone. All a distraught Emily had to give the children was a sweet packet with five sherbet lemons in it.

Her daughter died three weeks later after falling down a flight of stairs as they scavenged flats in a half-wrecked tower block and when her little son just faded away and died from some sort of infection Emily's mind went completely.

She wandered aimlessly for days until one afternoon the sound of breaking glass under her shoes seemed to bring her round and she realised she was outside the remains of an antiques shop.

Any weapon or anything useful had been taken, but the sunshine streaming through the smashed plate glass window reflected off the remnants of a display cabinet. When she bent over and tentatively picked up the shiny objects she had found Emily realised she was holding two antique silver baby rattles.

Her muddled mind somehow associated the rattles with her dead children and she soon had the noisy playthings slung round her neck on a piece of string like some sort of macabre keepsake. How macabre they became was due entirely to Emily.

Survival saw her become brutal. When a drunk tried to rape her in the ruined cafe of a ransacked store she killed him with a shard of glass as he tore at her trousers. She then rifled his pockets and found a kitchen knife.

With a measure of protection came a measure of power. Within a month she bossed three men. Each had been drawn into her web by promises of food as she sought to expand her scavenging success.

The first joined her for half a rat. She became aware of him one afternoon as she cooked over a small portable gas cooker in a deserted terrace house kitchen with a smashed window. He just appeared and stood looking at her through the jagged glass hole.

"Smelt your food," he said. "Could do with some if you've any to spare."

Wordlessly Riddle opened a few cupboards, found a bowl and spoon and ladled some of the rat stew out before handing the bowl to him through the hole in the window. He kept a respectful distance and by morning he was still with her. When she moved on so did he.

A second man bought his way into her graces. He had some cans of Irish stew but was having trouble opening them up. Riddle had a can opener. He stayed too.

The final member of her embryonic gang hailed them one day as they crossed an overgrown public garden. He wanted to trade whisky for food.

Riddle didn't drink, but they'd caught and killed a spaniel dog that day. The two men with her glanced at her for permission and, when she nodded, they eagerly invited the man to join them.

It was a beginning and the four of them began to work as a team to target any home which showed a light after dark.

Any occupant they caught was given a chance to reveal where their food was. If they refused then Emily noisily shook her silver baby rattles, listened to what they said and passed sentence on the spot. The sentence was usually death.

Her band grew as opportunists, the desperate, the selfish and the plain criminal joined her gang, Emily leading them with a cold carelessness which made them wary but quick to obey.

At first they had it all their own way. They never acted during the day, living in a couple of large town houses in a street with views of most of the city.

Binoculars were in constant use, sweeping the landscape for movement or smoke. Then, once night fell, they drifted down on any promising area and took what they could find, by force if necessary.

Emily scarcely cared if they found food or not. Only the rattles mattered and what they seemed to tell her.

Sometimes she felt the rattles were ordering her to spare someone. If it was a man she offered them a choice – join or die. If it was a woman she was handed over to the men to be used as they wished. Some killed themselves but others, dulled by the carnage all around, chose life albeit a brutal one.

Their downfall came when the gang's night-time raiding took them to a hall in a terraced area of the city. During the day they had seen occasional movement there, so that night they struck.

Surprise was complete when they surrounded the hall and Emily walked inside with six men at her back.

In front of her was a mixed group of people including one child huddled round a large hall stove being stoked with what looked like planks from a garden fence. On top was a big cooking pot with tendrils of steam rising from a tasty smelling stew.

"Well, good evening!" said Emily, stepping forward. She made an elaborate pantomime of sniffing the air before turning back to the men and saying: "Smells good doesn't it boys?"

The men grinned while the hall group watched her with horrified fascination the way a bird watches the approach of a snake.

Her face hardened and she said: "Now then. Such a fine soup must have had some fine ingredients and I'm sure there's more left to share with us. Where is it?"

The hall group just stared at her, frozen in fear, and Emily slowly nodded in disappointment before stepping to where an old man and a young woman sat on iron framed chairs at a trellis table near the stove.

Turning back to the men she said: "Take her and find out where their supplies are."

A tattooed man wearing a trilby hat at a jaunty angle stepped up and grabbed the woman by her left arm. When she tried to slap his face he simply twisted her arm high up her back to a cry of pain from the woman which brought the old man to his feet.

"You leave my grand-daughter alone!" he shouted, shuffling forward only for Emily to calmly intercept him and stick her kitchen knife deep into his stomach.

It was a killing wound and the woman screamed her shock and outrage as she was dragged towards a door leading to a room behind the hall stage.

Two men from the hall group got to their feet as the grandfather slid moaning to the floor and Emily wagged her bloody knife at them in the manner of a headmistress telling her pupils not to be naughty.

A woman near her suddenly spoke up and said: "The food's in boxes in a cupboard under the stage. Take what you want but leave us alone."

"Oh we will take what we want," said Emily, "and perhaps a bit more."

She barely finished speaking when a scream came from the room behind the stage, then another one. Shortly afterwards the man with the trilby returned and said: "Food's under the stage."

"We know," said Emily, ordering several of the men to get it. They walked to the stage and opened the cupboard door. What they brought out was so little that they carried it easily between them in two thick cardboard boxes."

They took their finds outside, part of a familiar process which now centred on Emily. She faced the horrified group of people in the hall and slowly took out first one and then the second antique silver baby rattle, shaking them several times while she listened to their sharp noises, her head cocked to one side in concentration.

When she finished she looked round the hall until her eye was caught by the woman who'd revealed where the food stores were.

She pointed at her and said: "You can come with us if you want."

The woman replied: "I'd sooner die!"

Emily nodded, turned to the remaining men behind her and said: "Kill them all." Then she walked out of the entrance.

Behind her there were first shouts of outrage and then screams and isolated gunshots. Eventually all was quiet and the men began to wander out of the hall, some of them with blood on their clothes.

"Back to Brixton Street everyone," said Emily, beginning to stride away from the hall.

The area outside the building slowly fell silent, but inside the hall there was movement as the grand-daughter, Lauren Fane, cautiously peered out of the door of the room behind the stage.

She had seized brief moments to open a window before the men came then hide behind some scenery showing a large tree with a Cheshire cat in its branches. She heard footsteps approaching, the cursing as men thought she'd escaped through the window followed by the sound of them leaving. She then heard the screams and the shots. Only when she was sure the gang had gone did she painfully drag herself to the door and survey the massacre which had taken place in the hall.

Her grandfather lay unmoving where he had fallen, eyes open staring at the ceiling, four men lay jumbled together in a corner while the women were crumpled in various places, their clothing torn. They appeared to have been raped before they were killed. The solitary child, a boy, almost seemed to be sat asleep near the stove, his back against a wall with hands clasped across his stomach as if to hold in the red mess he was cradling.

Tears rolled down Lauren's face as she staggered into the hall, moving from one body to the next before ending up at her grandfather's side. Her face grim as she gently closed his eyes and then slowly walked to the stage where the food cupboard door lay open.

Reaching inside and up she brought out a shotgun and a bag with five cartridges in it. The gang had missed the weapon and it would cost them dear.

Lauren took the shotgun and retreated to the stove with its pot of stew still bubbling away. Food was food and she was hungry, so she retrieved her bowl and spoon from the floor near an overturned table and carefully lifted the pot off the stove.

Rat wasn't her favourite meat but in these times you had to take what you could get. She thought it tasted a bit like chicken as she carefully spooned out a bowlful and sat down to eat surrounded by bodies. The shotgun lay to hand on the table and she never took her eyes off the entrance door.

There was no-one to share with and she took two big portions, leaving the remains of the stew for breakfast. It should be enough to get her across the city to where she'd heard of another group of survivors living in two flats above a wrecked cafe.

She stoked the stove with a few more pieces of fence and retreated behind its bulk so she was shielded from the entrance and had the hall wall at her back. She then dragged a rubber exercise mat into the angle between stove and wall, made sure the shotgun was to hand and lay down to get what sleep she could.

Someone screaming in a nearby street woke her during the night, but the sound was quickly cut off and she heard nothing more as she pulled her clothes tightly about her and struggled to find a comfortable position as close to the dying warmth of the stove as possible.

Morning light slowly seeped into the hall and Lauren lost no time getting up, adding wood to the stove and reheating the last of the stew for her breakfast.

By the time it was bubbling, steam swirling above the pot, she had put on a heavy coat stripped from the body of one of the women and retrieved a large backpack to store away her few belongings. She emptied the pot, scraped it clean and roughly washed it as best she could before setting a metal teapot of water to boil on top of the stove.

Already hungry, she lost no time then in tucking into the stew before cleaning her bowl and cutlery and stowing them away in the backpack with the stew pot. A used teabag then went into the teapot to produce a weak brew which she poured into an enamel mug. She cradled it in her chilled hands, blowing on the contents and taking an occasional sip until the mug was empty. It went into her backpack which she slung over a shoulder. Then, with one last tearful look at the body of her grandfather, Lauren picked up the shotgun and stepped cautiously through the doors into the hall's small foyer.

One of the main entrance doors had been left half open by Riddle's departing gang, but she made no attempt to step out until she had cautiously checked as much of the street outside as she could see. It was lifeless, a jumble of cars and vans with one body lying in the road some distance away half hidden by a battered estate car.

Over the next three hours she flitted across the city. Each street corner was carefully approached and the route ahead checked before she moved on. Lauren didn't hurry and if she was the slightest bit suspicious of anything, if she thought she saw movement ahead, then she backed up and went a different way.

Midday brought her to the cafe she sought, its frontage crumpled by the remains of a car which had been reversed into the front doors. The building looked long deserted.

She hadn't been here before but others had told her that entrance to the flats was gained via a fire escape at the back, so she slipped across to the far side of the road using abandoned vehicles for cover and was soon opposite an overgrown lane. It acted as the access to tiny gardens backing along the terrace, several houses of which showed fire damage.

Some of the gardens had rubble or were concreted over for parking, some had decking and others had the remains of flower borders and vegetable plots. Lauren's gaze focussed on the third garden along which contained a rusting staircase leading up to flat balconies, two on either side of the steel landing.

There was nothing to indicate any life but Lauren wasn't taking any chances, so she moved back a few yards and crossed the road at a point where a garden fence shielded her approach. When she peered round its corner she saw the fire escape close by and, more importantly, evidence of footprints on the edge of a muddy puddle near its base.

The flats were clearly still in use, but she was nervous about just walking up and knocking on the door. There were few friendly visitors these days and she might get shot for her trouble, so she decided to try and find an abandoned vehicle nearby with its doors open and watch for a chance to make contact.

She withdrew and quickly found a Ford Lunar with its passenger window smashed. The seat was soggy with rain, but the driver's seat was dry and offered a view of the lane.

An hour passed and then two men and a woman cautiously appeared in the road and looked warily both ways before edging out and beginning to walk down the street. She let them get fifty metres away and then got out and hailed them.

The three scattered and took cover among other vehicles, occasionally bobbing up and down to try and spot her.

"What do you want?" yelled one man.

"A talk and to give you a warning," Lauren shouted back.

"A warning about what?" the woman shouted.

Lauren moved her position further away and then shouted: "There's a big gang just killing people. I want to do something about it."

She spotted movement on her side of the street and smiled. It was an old tactic. Keep the speaker talking while someone else crept closer. They'd have to do better than that and she quietly moved even further away.

"How many of you are there?" asked the man.

"Enough," said Lauren. "Do you want to talk or shall I just let you find out for yourselves?"

There was a pause and then a hissed conversation she couldn't catch followed by the woman slowly stepping out into view.

"I'm trusting you," she said. "Now you'll have to trust us."

Nothing ventured nothing gained, thought Lauren, and she slowly stepped out into the road ready to dive back into cover if needed.

"Who are you?" she asked.

"I'm Carol," said the woman. "These two shy gentlemen are Robbie and Cooper. And you are...?"

"Lauren. Pleased to meet you although you may not be pleased to meet me."

"Go on," said Carol.

"Last night a strange woman brought a gang to our hall. They killed everyone except me. From what they said we weren't the first group of survivors they'd raided."

At this point Robbie and Cooper walked out from the vehicles they'd been hiding behind and joined Carol.

"This strange woman," said Robbie. "Did she carry two silver rattles?"

His question startled Lauren but she was quick to recover.

"Sounds like my woman. You've heard of her then?"

"Oh we've heard of her," said Robbie. "Mad as a hatter but ice cold with it. Shakes those rattles, listens to them and then issues her orders. Not a nice person."

"She's a murderer," said Lauren fiercely. "She killed my grandfather right in front of me. He was seventy-eight."

Her words seemed to freeze her listeners and when Carol spoke again her attitude was friendlier.

"So what have you got in mind?" she asked.

Lauren had thought about this all morning and she had her answer ready.

"I want to sit down with you and see what we can tell each other. I want to find other survivor groups and tell them about this gang and then I want to get as many people together as I can and either kill this scum or run them far, far away."

"Easier said than done," said Cooper. "Murder might be second nature for them but most people we meet have never hurt a fly. How are you going to get them to actually kill these people?"

"I won't have to," said Lauren. "You've heard of this gang, other people will have heard of them as well and when I tell them what they did at our hall they'll be under no illusion about what's necessary. It's kill or be killed, live or die. If we don't then sooner or later it will be another group's turn to be wiped out. These people are animals and I don't intend to just sit still and do nothing."

There was another whispered conversation between the three and then Carol stepped closer and said: "If you trust us we can stand you a cup of tea while you talk. We live in some flats over the back there."

"Fair enough," said Lauren. "Lead on, but you might want a drop of something stronger when you hear the tale I've got to tell."

CHAPTER SIX

NEW Year came and went at Waterfall Manor with Mike, Roy and Noah masterminding celebrations at the Manor Arms.

Weeks went by and there was an air of expectancy in the little community as everyone waited for Becky to give birth.

She seemed in no hurry and there was plenty of time for John and Dawn to chat with Leo Anderson in London where plans for a Recovery Council there were well advanced.

Anderson said that several thousand people had already come forward, lured by the promise of food and help, with more trickling in every day.

He was keener than ever for John and Dawn to make a survey of Scotland as part of wider checks embracing Wales, the Midlands and the north of England and he wanted to know if they could be ready to go by late February.

They said they could and Anderson said he'd despatch a helicopter to pick them up in a fortnight's time.

He was very specific about what he wanted them to do. Contact any authorities or groups still trying to operate, get a picture of what life and infrastructure was like in the big cities and try and establish a holding authority which he could liaise with by radio from London.

"Promise them help," he said. "Tell them we can supply power, technicians and some food but that they've got to band together to help themselves as well. Isolated groups are no good. There are so few people left that they need to come together to form viable communities. It is the only way people will be able to survive and move forward."

He had plenty more to say and John and Dawn had their brains buzzing with his ideas by the time he signed off.

"Doesn't he ever take a break?" asked John as Dawn handed him a spanner while he worked on one of two quad bikes stored in a small stone barn.

"I guess that's why the Recovery Council in Australia chose him to come here. They knew he was what we'd need to organise things and start to get the country back on its feet."

"Maybe," said John, cursing as he banged a knuckle, "but he's piled so much on us for this Scotland trip that I can't think straight. I feel like I've just got out of a tumble drier!"

Dawn laughed and said: "I know what you mean. Still, someone's got to go there and we've both experience of travelling long distance through some pretty nasty countryside. Who else does he know that he could ask?"

"True," said John, "but I'm still not happy about going up there in winter. That's why I never explored anywhere in Puffin later than early November. Too risky with the weather. You need to be tucked up warm somewhere with all the food you can find for winter. No chance of popping down to the takeaway for a Chinese if supplies run low. Run out of food up there and you die."

"Well I don't think we'll run out of food in a week and that's all Leo is asking us to spend up there. Glasgow, Edinburgh and a quick tour of the countryside to spot any outposts. That's all he's asking to start with."

"Yes. It's that "to start with" that I'm worried about. I'm just a simple mechanic who wants a quiet time. I'm not cut out for the life of a jet-setter!"

"Don't worry country boy," said Dawn. "The straw in the corner of your mouth let's people know who you are!"

She then skipped out of the way of his attempt to grab her and sauntered back towards the manor, aware that his eyes were following her and delighting in her ability to tease him.

John shook his head as she disappeared round the corner of a building and turned his attention back to the quad bike. Rodents had been at the wiring which he'd had to strip and reconnect, the tyres were flat and the seating was torn with most of its stuffing gone, but generally it was in good condition and he'd already been able to get the engine started. If they were going to bring more fields back into use then the quad bike would be handy for hauling.

Fuel was fairly precious despite large numbers of untapped silent garage forecourts and everyone was being encouraged to use mountain bikes to get about.

John agreed with this, but carrying trailers loaded with metal posts and security fencing was no job for a mountain bike. You needed power for that, perhaps more than even a quad could offer, so he was also on the look-out for a grab attachment for his tractor but he hadn't seen one yet.

The weather was still way too cold to get on the land, but Jed was already hustling the men into working on the accommodation.

Timber baulks were being cut to support floors, wiring was being sourced and installed and some rough plastering done when temperatures allowed, but Jed was also looking to the future.

Plaster boards could still be found easily in deserted builder's merchants, but Jed was also experimenting with lath and plaster. Boards would eventually run out and it could be many decades before they were in production again, so he wanted to try out a fall-back method of completing walls while it wasn't an urgent problem. This involved experimenting with the old lath and plaster method of nailing strips of wood across wall studs or ceiling joints before coating them in lime plaster.

John admired his approach. Jed was always looking ahead, always trying to find a sustainable way of doing things and he seemed almost as tireless as Leo Anderson.

An hour later and he had the quad bike ready to go, but he limited his test run to a few hundred metres to conserve fuel before storing the machine back in its barn and hungrily walking back to the manor for lunch. He arrived inside to bedlam.

There was much shouting, the kitchen was full of steam and Evie, Donna and Janice were bustling about with several other women including chef Victor's wife, Norma, and Hannah.

John joined a slightly wild-eyed Jed near the main staircase up which women moved briskly carrying towels, sheets and pans of hot water, scolding both men to keep out of their way.

"Is this what I think it is?" asked John.

Jed nodded and said: "Becky went into labour half an hour ago."

He was creasing and uncreasing a sheet of paper, seemingly unaware of what he was doing. Suddenly there was a bellowed scream from upstairs at which Jed's hands convulsed and tore the sheet of paper in half. He looked dazed and appeared to be about to climb the stairs, so John put one hand on his shoulder and gently guided him into the sun room and outside towards the Manor Arms. It might be a bit early for a drink but these were special circumstances.

One of the outbuildings had been converted into a small pub nicknamed the Manor Arms and Evie's partner, Mike, had enthusiastic plans for brewing their own beer. For the moment they were using scavenged bottles and cans of beer, a small mountain of which was stacked at the back of the building and upstairs in a loft seating area.

Mike said it would all be undrinkable before spring was out and everyone was enthusiastically making use of stocks before they had to be thrown away. John intended to do his bit to help.

He sat Jed on a bar stool and then walked round behind the bar to find two glasses and a couple of cans of beer, the Beast of Bodmin for Jed and some chocolate stout for himself.

After a few seconds watching Jed look nervously at the door he opened a can, poured it into Jed's glass and then pressed the glass into his hand all with the father-to-be only vaguely aware of what he was doing.

"Cheers!" said John, taking a sip and then halting with glass halfway to his mouth as Jed mumbled "Cheers" back at him before emptying his glass in one go.

"Another then," said John, putting several more cans on the bar top before taking a seat. He again had to fill Jed's glass as the former farmer nervously plucked at the buttons on his coat, his breath wisping in the chilly air.

"First birth I've actually been around for," said Jed, emptying half his glass. "You read about these things, but do women always scream like that?"

"I don't think it's anything personal, just part of motherhood," said John, reaching for another can as Jed drained his glass and stared absently at the door.

"No pleasure without pain I suppose," said Jed, accepting a refill for his glass. "I liked the pleasure bit but I'm not so sure about the pain. I can't even share it for her."

"She knows that," said John, refilling his own glass. "Just make a fuss of her once the baby's born."

"Oh I will, I will," said Jed, taking several nervous gulps of the Beast, gripping his glass so hard John was afraid it might shatter.

"She's had one child already you know," said Jed with the penetrating knowledge of a father-to-be.

"Yes," said John. "I've met Kevin, quite a bit actually."

"So do you think it will be easier for her the second time around?" asked Jed.

Just then a faint scream reached them from the manor and John hastily splashed some more beer into Jed's glass to distract him.

Jed shakily raised his glass, took a great mouthful and emerged with a frothy tide mark on his upper lip which he absently licked at.

"Do these things go on for very long?"

John bit back a reply that sometimes labour could last for many hours and instead opted to say that it differed from woman to woman.

"Some women have their baby in just a few minutes," he said," while others can take several hours to give birth."

"Several hours?" said Jed. "Yes, I seem to remember reading about that somewhere. Let's hope it's as easy for her as it can be."

They drank on together, the line of empty beer cans slowly growing. Then Lydia, one of those who made the trip down to Cornwall after John freed a group of survivors being held in Leeds, came in with a big plate of sandwiches.

Jed didn't seem to notice them and immediately asked: "How's Becky doing?"

"Very well," said Lydia, eyeing the mass of cans with a certain amusement.

"She's well dilated and Dawn thinks it won't be too long now, probably before teatime."

"Teatime?" said Jed nervously. "That's hours away. Are you sure she's all right."

"Perfectly sure," said Lydia. "You just stay here out of the way. The last thing we want is an expectant father getting under our feet. She's in good hands. We'll give you a call when she's getting close."

She left and Jed didn't take his eyes off her until she was out of sight as if she was some sort of physical link between himself and Becky.

John made him take and eat a sandwich but it was mechanical, not something Jed seemed aware of. His thoughts were elsewhere, but the level of beer in his glass still sank steadily.

Two hours later they heard another dim scream and shortly after that Lydia returned to say Jed could come now if he wanted to.

His stumble for the door was slightly spoilt by falling over a stool, but John and Lydia helped him to his feet and piloted him towards the manor.

"I just hope my Lucas isn't like this if we have a baby," said Lydia.

John rolled his eyes in agreement and then realised that a few months down the line he'd be the nervous one waiting for Dawn to give birth. All of a sudden he had real sympathy for Jed rather than amused support and he hurried the tipsy man along as best he could.

The stairs to Becky's bedroom were a bit of a trial. More than once Jed swayed and threatened to totter backwards but they kept him upright and steered him from the landing along to the bedroom as another scream split the air followed by female words of encouragement.

Jed weaved into the bedroom just as Dawn said she could see the baby's head emerging. Everything then got a bit chaotic.

Becky saw Jed come in and gave him a tired smile before a contraction took her and she screamed again. Jed took one look at the baby arriving, his eyes rolled up into his head and he crashed to the floor. There was a different sort of screaming from Becky as she tried to see if Jed was all right, Dawn ordered John to drag him out of the bedroom and flustered women tried to step round the father to be and help with the birth at the same time.

John bent and grabbed Jed under his arms, the baby arrived and began to cry lustily, delighted women congratulated Becky and Jed woke up long enough to see a bloody bundle being swathed in a towel only to promptly collapse again.

Mumbled apologies from John were greeted with a fierce look from Dawn as she helped clean up Becky and put the baby in her arms. Jed would need some fast talking to get out of this one, thought John, as he hauled the comatose father out of the bedroom, sat him in a landing chair and cracked open a window to let in a gust of wintry air.

Within a minute or two Jed regained consciousness and immediately asked how Becky and the baby were.

"Never mind their health," said John. "I'd give it a minute or two for your own health. Get yourself sorted out or you're in big trouble."

Jed stared at him blearily, nodded with difficulty and began to take in gulps of fresh air. It seemed to work and he soon pronounced himself fit enough to meet his first child.

John was taking no chances and supported his friend back into the bedroom to be met by a forest of backs. Everyone in there was grouped round the bed looking at the new baby.

"Make way, make way!" said John as cheerily as he could. "Give the happy father a look in."

That drew several sharp glances including one from Dawn who stayed right where she was, tucking sheets round Becky as John edged Jed forward.

"Hello love. How did it go?" asked Jed.

"You have a beautiful daughter!" said Becky, her proud face still grey and sweaty with pain as she carefully parted a fold of sheet to reveal a tiny screwed up red face with wisps of hair on its head. The baby welcomed him with a slow yawn and a mumble of its lips.

Jed swayed a bit and was steadied by John before he said: "She's so lovely. What do you think we should call her?"

"I think Tilly is a nice name. It was my grandmother's and she lived a long and happy life. Hopefully this little one can do the same."

"Tilly it is then," said Jed rocking on his heels and blinking as he briefly saw twins. He leaned over and parted the sheet a little further and the baby squirmed and then made some gurgling noises. The watching women were delighted, but Jed snatched his hand back as if he had somehow injured the baby.

"She's all right, isn't she?" he asked nervously.

"Tilly is fine," said Dawn, "which is more than can be said for you. Wetting the baby's head is supposed to be done after the birth not before!"

"Yes! A celebration, we must have a celebration," said Jed, swaying in a half turn and making an extravagant gesture with one arm which nearly took John's head off.

Dawn glared at John and sweetly said: "Perhaps you could take the happy father away. He must be exhausted by his efforts and we need to wash Becky and the baby and get them settled in together."

John recognised a dismissal when he saw one and hastily steered his friend towards the door. Jed did really well and only knocked over a pile of towels and a tin of talcum powder on his way out.

The two men got out on to the landing and John guided Jed across to and down the main staircase. When they reached the safety of ground level they were greeted with a chorus of questions from more than two dozen people waiting for them in the hallway or peering from nearby doorways.

Everyone wanted to know whether the baby was a boy or a girl, how big it was and whether Becky and the baby were doing well. Jed's answer fell somewhere between being informative and bewildering.

"She's had a girl!" he said and then beamed happily at everyone as if his words answered all their queries.

"Blimey John! What have you done to him?" asked Matthew, another one of those who had made the trip from Leeds.

"Anything that's been done to Jed he's done to himself," replied John tersely. "Now help me pilot him to the kitchen and get some tea down him or he's a dead man when Becky recovers."

There was much laughter at this as Peter joined Matthew to help steer Jed away to the kitchen while everyone else grouped round John.

"Before anyone asks, Becky has had a lovely baby girl they've called Tilly and they are both doing a lot better than Jed is!"

More laughter burst out together with questions about hair colour and whether the baby looked like Becky or more like Jed.

"Give it a while and I'm sure you'll all be able to judge for yourselves," said John. "In the meantime I'm going to have a small whisky for my nerves!"

There were cheers at this and people began to drift towards the kitchen and living rooms to arrange their own celebration drinks.

Over in the kitchen Jed cradled a steaming mug of tea in his hands and was repeating his penetrating comment that Becky had had a baby girl. Victor and Norma gave him amused glances but didn't stop their preparation of the evening meal which they were busy putting together amid clouds of steam and enticing aromas.

John had been into the library to find his whisky which he brought into the kitchen where he sat down with Jed who shuddered at the sight and smell of the pungent spirits.

"I think I've done my celebrating," said Jed. "Just at the moment I don't think I could face another drink."

"You weren't being offered one!" retorted John. "You've already drunk half your own weight in beer so piling whisky on top of that isn't a good idea. Becky will be hoping you'll call on her again once they've been cleaned up and she's had a rest. You don't want to arrive unable to stand up like last time or she'll never let you forget it."

There was a pause while John took a sip of his whisky and Jed a gulp from his mug of tea. Then a look of cautious puzzlement came over Jed's face.

"It was just the one baby Becky had wasn't it?" he queried warily. "Only I swear I saw two at one point."

"That would be the barrel of beer you drank," said John. "I thought you told me you weren't a big drinker?"

"I'm not usually," said Jed. "Just the occasional weekend pint and perhaps a few flagons of cider at haymaking time, but seeing Becky in pain made me nervous. Did I really have a lot to drink?"

A startled John said: "Well you didn't get like this from tap water! Look at you. Your hands are shaking!"

And they were, so much so that Jed had to carefully put his mug down on the kitchen table before he spilt tea everywhere.

"That's it for me then. No more beer for a good while."

"I'm sure everyone else will be very pleased to hear that! At the rate you were knocking it back there'd soon have been none left! What you need is some proper food inside you. You've only had a couple of sandwiches since breakfast."

"I'm not sure I could eat anything," said Jed.

"You'd better," said John. "A crowd of people have just seen your famous impression of a falling tree and I don't think they want to see it again. I certainly don't!"

"No, no. I won't fall over again. I just don't want to be sick over Becky and the babe."

John choked on his whisky as he produced a vivid mental picture of such a disaster and he hastily turned to Victor and Norma.

"What can this monument to sobriety safely eat without getting himself into any more trouble than he already has?"

Victor smiled as he chopped vegetables and said: "Keep it simple. Boil him an egg and give him a slice of bread to go with it. His stomach has to have something to work on. Just don't let him boil the water. I don't want any accidents in our kitchen!"

John nodded and did the necessary, grabbing a saucepan, filling it with water and putting it on the aga. When it boiled he added an egg, buttered a slice of bread and then spooned the egg into an eggcup once it was cooked.

The simple result was placed in front of Jed who looked at it warily.

"Well go on then!" said John. "It isn't going to eat itself."

When Jed shakily picked up a knife John hastily took it away and sliced the top of the egg off for him.

"I'm not eating it for you as well," he said.

Jed slowly dipped a teaspoon into the egg and spooned out yellow yolk and white surround which he tentatively placed in his mouth, bit off a small piece of bread and began to chew.

John watched him like a hawk in case he was going to be sick but the food seemed to do the trick and Jed rapidly polished off the rest of the egg and the bread.

"Just sit there for a while and let it go down," said John. "Then we'll think about going back up to see Becky and the baby."

Mention of the baby seemed to sharpen Jed's brain and he was about to ask a question when Dawn came into the kitchen.

"Well, a bit of common sense at last," she said. "If you feel up to it you can go and see them whenever you're ready."

Jed got to his feet and swayed a bit, but this time he was able to stabilise himself without help although John followed behind to prevent a fall on the stairs, Dawn quietly mouthing a warning to John for him to stay close.

Upstairs they reached the bedroom without incident to find Becky and the baby quietly dozing. There was a small armchair near the bed and John shooed Jed into it where he sat and watched mother and baby with a wondering expression on his face. Within a few minutes

Jed slipped into a doze himself, his breath whistling in his nose and John tip-toed out and left them to it. Sleep was the best thing for the three of them.

Hundreds of miles away in Edinburgh sleep was about to be very rudely interrupted.

CHAPTER SEVEN

IT was several days after the hall massacre and Emily Riddle was deep in a dream about dying children, her body twitching in the big double bed as her tortured mind lived the nightmare.

Snores rumbled through the house and the property next door where her gang had taken up chilly residence and all was still in the early morning mist shrouding the city in a ghostly pall.

Emily didn't bother with guards or they might have alerted her to the steady arrival of more than two hundred people on a small green at the bottom of the street. Vengeance had arrived.

Lauren Fane had been busy since she'd seen her grandfather murdered in front of her by Riddle, a kitchen knife thrust indifferently into his stomach.

She had tracked down one group of survivors and used their knowledge to find and make contact with others. To each she made the same pitch. There was safety in numbers.

Most knew about Riddle and warily stayed out of her way, but when they heard what had happened in the hall they needed little encouragement to agree to band together and deal with her gang once and for all before they became her next victim.

It took just two days to pinpoint where Riddle and her thugs were living and to co-ordinate a plan of attack.

All through the night small groups of people had filtered through the city to a meeting point in a disused bus station littered with drifts of debris and smashed glass.

As they arrived they were assigned to one of two groups making a frontal assault or a third blocking any escape from the rear of the properties. People had brought some food with them but Lauren made sure everyone was given a hot drink just before they left the bus station to make their attack.

She also moved quietly among them, talking to a clutch of people here, a group there, explaining that this was their chance to rid themselves of a violent parasite which was sucking what little life there was left out of remaining survivors. There was grim approval for what she said and what they were doing because several groups had had skirmishes with Riddle which had cost them precious food and lives.

When it came time to move, the mass of determined people flowed quietly out of the bus station and made their way as silently as they could through deserted misty streets littered with abandoned vehicles and the debris of looting.

When Lauren arrived at the green she had selected near Riddle's base she halted the drift of people, had one final chat with fellow group leaders and sent them on their way, the crowd of people seeming to melt away in the early morning light.

Lauren led her group forward and up a road which curved and climbed past mansion-like houses, their frontages a sad display of dirty ornate stonework, smashed windows and piles of rubbish. A few skeletal bodies dressed in clothing tatters lay in front gardens.

The two buildings they were after projected out in a bulge where the road dog-legged round and then began to descend.

The second frontal assault group could now be seen quietly coming towards them from the other direction and Lauren knew the third group should by now be in position at the back, lower down the hill where a road provided a boundary to stone walls which guarded the bottom of gardens belonging to the mansions.

The two properties they were targeting commanded seventy metres of street. Each had a drive-in and drive-out entrance through stone gateposts and short driveways flanked by overgrown shrubbery leading to front doors beneath faded and peeling porticos.

Some had felt that Riddle should be told to come out and surrender, but Lauren fiercely opposed this. She argued that Riddle had no defence for her crimes and would simply use any warning they gave to strengthen her defences and make their task even harder.

She favoured an all-out frontal attack with the rear group mopping up any gang members who tried to flee down through the gardens, but they were in for a lesson in tactics.

Surprise was complete when Lauren's group and the second led by a man called David Curtain timed their approach to simultaneously storm both front doors.

Riddle might have been overconfident by not posting guards but she didn't entirely trust her own followers and so had taken crude precautions to guard the main entrance. She used the simple expedient of pushing a heavy oak hall cabinet up against the front door.

The result saw Curtain's group meet no opposition when they poured into the mansion they were attacking whereas Lauren's group lost precious seconds forcing their way in past the cabinet. For some the delay proved to be the difference between life and death.

Those in the first mansion, particularly gang members sleeping on the first floor, had little chance. One minute they were deep in slumber and the next they were being charged by screaming attackers.

Many gang members had firearms but they were outnumbered three to one and often didn't get a chance to use them.

Curtain, armed with a garden fork, killed two himself, stripping one body of a shotgun and a handful of cartridges which he then used against surviving gang members.

His group swept up through the building, meeting stiffer and stiffer resistance the higher they climbed. Landings and stairs had to be paid for in blood. Gang members refused to surrender and at the end even tried an abortive counter charge which ended with four of their number tumbled in a bloody heap on the stairwell.

Within fifteen minutes the building had been taken. Twenty-three gang members lay dead together with five of the attacking force while there were a number of wounded who might not survive. It was a different story at the mansion attacked by Lauren's group.

Getting past the oak cabinet and into the hallway took enough time to wake Riddle and alert her to what was happening.

When the attackers began to fan out through the ground floor and climb the stairs they were met with concerted resistance from the defenders.

Riddle's bellowed orders had wakened gang members on upper floors and brought them stumbling down to join a crude barricade set up on the first floor landing.

The air became thick with the sound of combat. People screamed as they were injured, others swore and there were shouts and cheering as the attackers pressed forward up the stairs.

Riddle had grasped the situation she faced immediately and the first thing she did was to send a dozen gang members out on to the rusting fire escape and down to the ground to secure a line of retreat.

The first attacker to open a rear door near the base of the fire escape almost had his head blown off by gang members sheltering in an overgrown laurel hedge bordering a stone terrace. He hastily slammed the door again.

Sheer weight of numbers was beginning to tell in the attackers' favour who were covered by colleagues as they forced their way close to the barricade. Once there the heavy pieces of wood furniture hastily dragged out to block the attackers worked in their favour by affording some protection from the guns and knives of Riddle's gang. The defenders had to expose themselves more and more to inflict any casualties on those they faced and

Lauren's force picked off several of the gang as they tried to lean over the barricade to fire or slash at those below.

But the delay posed by the barricade enabled Riddle to slowly reduce her force on the landing, sending men and women out on to the fire escape and down to ground level. When only a few were left she skipped out herself and shouted for the last defenders to follow her.

They needed no second urging as the attackers toppled a chest of drawers back on to the landing and began to thrust and fire at the remaining defenders.

Those in the forefront of the attack saw their hated opponents slipping away through a sash window, but when they sought to follow them there were several shots from the laurel hedge below which shattered glass and peppered the landing walls with pellets.

Quickly the attackers flattened themselves to either side of the window, returning fire so effectively that they killed the last two gang members running for cover below and injured a third.

The hedge shook and wavered as Riddle's gang used its cover to slip away but a few remained to cover the back door and prevent the attackers from following.

Frustrated at the delay, Lauren grabbed two men and raided the mansion's kitchen, tipping up a huge oak table to send dirty crockery and empty tins cascading to the floor. They then opened the back door, used the table as cover and forced it out on to the terrace.

The remaining gang members realised they were about to be overwhelmed and hastily fled into the heavily overgrown garden. By the time the attackers warily fanned out across the terrace they had gone leaving three bodies behind them. Lauren grabbed a fallen shotgun and quickly searched the bodies which yielded three cartridges which she handed to a balding man in a camouflage jacket.

At this point David Curtain's group began to arrive behind her and Lauren cautiously pushed down off the terrace and led the way into the gardens.

It was impossible to move silently as progress was hampered by drifts of dead leaves along paths where shrub branches clutched and tore at clothing.

Lauren fully expected to hear shots from the road below where the third group of attackers was waiting to mop up any gang members who escaped but there was only silence.

They briefly forced their way clear near a derelict summerhouse where a fallen gang member lay clutching the bloody remains of his stomach, but there was no trace of Emily Riddle and the surviving members of her gang. Where had they gone?

With great caution they continued to make their way down through the garden, making sure they shouted their identity when they got close to the road. The three groups then merged and Lauren discovered that the blocking group had heard a lot of noise but hadn't seen a single gang member.

Everyone slowly returned to the houses to discover the gang had somehow clambered into the next garden and doubled back to the first mansion where they'd grabbed what they could and left.

A man with his left arm swathed in a bloody bandage came forward and said he'd caught a glimpse of at least twenty men and women running away up a side road.

Missed them, thought Lauren, who immediately talked with David Curtain about following the fleeing gang members to keep track of them.

She volunteered to lead the pursuers, an image of her dying grandfather still firmly in her mind, and a hasty conference with Curtain and several others agreed to her plan. They would stay, treat the wounded and salvage what they could from the gang's headquarters while Lauren shadowed the gang to see if they continued to flee or if they were trying to regroup.

Lauren selected six men to go with her and talked briefly with her little group as Curtain set up a crude treatment centre for the wounded in the faded grandeur of a living room where a painting of cows in a field stood tilted to one side on a wall pockmarked with mould.

The butcher's bill could have been worse. Sixteen had died in the assault on the second mansion with another score or so suffering a variety of wounds while a similar number of gang members had died. In all the combined assault had cost them twenty-one dead but the gang had lost at least forty killed and a number wounded.

Unknown to the attackers, one of those wounded was Riddle herself, her left hand pierced by a carving knife as she helped with the barricade defence.

She knew there was no going back as she hastily tore a piece of material from her grimy blouse and wrapped it round the wound in her hand. Mentally she was very confused as she led a stumbling retreat away from their defeat. Where had so many people come from?

Riddle continued to jog and walk without once checking to see if gang members were following her. She now led about thirty people several of whom struggled with wounds. There was nowhere to go, she didn't know this part of the city and it was now imperative that they broke clear of their pursuers who she had no doubt would try to follow up and finish them off.

What they needed was some sort of transport and they found it quite by chance, abandoned in a tourist point lay-by next to a battered rusting sign which proudly announced that historic tours of the city left from that point every hour on the hour.

The Leyland Olympian still had two passengers on board who seemed to have crawled inside to die and Riddle would have ignored the bus had she not seen keys still dangling in the ignition.

She called a brief halt, gang members sinking panting to the rubbish-strewn pavement which was starting to dry in patches. Emily used the breather to climb into the cab and try the keys. Her reward was a brief flicker of needles but no firing of the engine. She didn't care. She had the manpower to achieve that and shouted for everyone to get behind and push when she said so. There was much grumbling and cursing which died away at one fierce look from the deranged leader.

A few seconds finding and releasing the handbrake and checking the road ahead was clear enough for what she had in mind allowed gang members to group at the rear of the bus. When she shouted for them to push they soon had the bus rolling on mostly inflated tyres, its engine bucking and then catching with a roar and a cloud of blue smoke when Riddle released the clutch and engaged second gear.

She gently coaxed the bus to a halt, carefully keeping the spluttering engine going, and saw the fuel gauge registered a quarter full. Not much but it would have to do. They needed to get away.

There was still the question of the wounded and what should be done about them. Perhaps the rattles would have an answer.

There was a brief murmur of elation from the tattered remnants of her gang at having started the bus, but that died away when they saw her take out the two antique silver baby rattles. They knew what that meant and looked fearfully at her.

Emily gave the rattles a shake and then held them to her ear, listening attentively to what they might say. After a while she nodded twice and then moved forward to where three of her number lay beside the layby sign. All had been wounded and Emily knelt by the first man with a hand pressed to his bloody chest to ask him how he was.

He began to reply that he was not too bad when Emily simply leaned forward and thrust her kitchen knife deep into his heart. The man's face took on an expression of surprise as his breath whistled and slowly died away.

The other two casualties, a man with a lower stomach wound and a woman with a knee injury showing bone, both tried to scramble to their feet, but the woman with the injured leg was too slow to avoid a second thrust from Emily's knife and she subsided with a gurgle by the side of the man with a chest wound, his eyes now staring at the grey sky.

She turned to follow the third casualty, but he stood his ground and said: "I'm fine. It's just a flesh wound."

Emily hesitated and looked at him closely. Perhaps he was telling the truth and perhaps not. She would watch him and she gave a quick nod before turning back to the rest of the gang.

"Those who are coming get on board," she said. Then Emily looked down at the two bodies and added with a giggle: "Those who aren't....you're on your own."

There were many wary looks at her but no-one lost any time in hastily clambering aboard the old bus which Emily clashed into gear and began to drive slowly away towards the M9 while the last of her gang were still scrambling on board.

Back at the mansions Lauren was mounting a pursuit. She'd already found a bicycle propped against a scullery wall. Its tyres were flat but they inflated when she used a pump unclipped from its frame. The problem was that they needed to leave now, so they'd have to take it in turns to ride the machine as they set off after Riddle.

She had personally chosen the men who would come with her. All were armed, all were young and all looked reasonably fit. She didn't need to worry about motivation as they'd lost friends in the attack.

"Now listen to me," she said quietly as they grouped round her. "No heroics. We want to keep an eye on these animals but only from a distance. If they're planning to attack us then whoever is on the bicycle when we find them must ignore us and ride straight back here to warn David and the others. Clear?"

There were several grim nods. They were under no illusions as to what Riddle would do with anyone she caught. The trick was not to get caught.

Lauren spoke briefly with David Curtain and then returned to lead her little group through the battered hall, past the oak cabinet and out of the front door down to the street.

She took the bicycle first, riding ahead of her group who followed at a slow trot. Lauren pedalled along the direction taken by the fleeing gang, tracking their passage by occasional discarded pieces of clothing or equipment and a flurry of empty shotgun shells where several gang members appeared to have paused to reload their weapons. It was a warning to the pursuers that the shaken gang was recovering.

The bicycle was soon passed to a man called Ashley who weaved away up the road, his posture strengthening as forgotten talents were dusted off and brought back into use.

By now they were more than a mile from the mansions and Lauren varied their progress with jogs followed by brisk walking to conserve their energy. Along the way they found half a dozen more bicycles but only two were just about useable. It was as they coaxed the second machine to work that Ashley shot back to them and said he'd heard an engine.

The news galvanised the pursuit and everyone followed him back to the top of the road as quickly as they could, trotting past abandoned cars, burnt out houses and the remains of several bodies lying in the street on a surface which sparkled with broken glass in the weak midday sunshine.

They reached the remains of a small shopping precinct which had been widely looted. A wheeled rail from a charity shop lay half in and half out of its smashed front window and numerous items of soggy clothing just lay rotting on the pavement. An estate agency was virtually untouched apart from smashed windows while a fish and chip shop, a greeting card outlet, a baker's shop and a pub called the Dirk and Sporran all showed evidence of looting. A fire had charred displays in a second hand furniture shop where the body of a man lay against a wall and Lauren saw two more bodies in a newsagent's shop which had been practically torn apart by looters, its sweet shelving ripped down and the floor covered in smashed jars and a mess of confectionery, newspapers and magazines.

Ashley called out and pointed to a wide parking area with overgrown flower planters by a big sign advertising that historic city tours left from that point every hour. Nearby lay two bodies and a brief check revealed them as gang members who had died very recently, blood still being wet on their grubby clothing. It was Lauren who spotted the tyre tracks.

They curved out of the lay-by and headed away up the road, splashing through puddles to leave a clear but staccato track of the vehicle's passage. She pointed them out to the group.

"Look at this," she said, indicating a large oblong of dirt, leaves and detritus which lay near the sign.

"You can see where the tyres stood for a long time. Whatever was here was very big. You don't suppose Riddle's taken a bus?"

"No doubt about it," said Griff, a heavy-set bearded man with a small shoulder pack slung at his side.

"Look at the size of the tracks," he said. "They are wider than a car and the tread is much thicker. "If it's not a bus then my bet would be a lorry of some description."

"You're right," said a small man called Ricky. "We know several dozen of them got away but there's no-one here. They all left together and they couldn't really do that in a lorry. It has to be a bus."

Another man called Jack said they'd have trouble following a bus for any distance while Roddy and Steve, who rode the other two bicycles they had found, said they had to find more bicycles or those on foot just wouldn't be able to keep up.

Lauren kicked idly at a toy car lying in the gutter and made a decision.

"Roddy. You and Steve go on. Follow those tracks as far as you can and leave an arrow to show us which way to go at every turn and junction. We can't rely on wet tyre marks for ever.

"There are no more than a few hours of daylight left and they'll have to stop somewhere soon for the night. Don't get close but, when you do come near them, one of you must come back and tell us if we haven't caught up. We'll keep the other bike and follow as quickly as we can."

Steve and Roddy nodded and swiftly rode off following the tyre marks from the bus while Lauren turned to the remaining four men.

"Right," she said. "Spread out and search. We need more bikes or something like a van we can carry us all in. Anyone know anything about cars?"

No-one really did, but Jack claimed to have done some of his own repairs before the Red Plague came, adding that any vehicle they found would either need little work to get it going or too much.

"Look at garages, covered forecourts, anywhere with a bit of shelter," he said. "If it's just got a flat battery we might be able to bump start it, but if it's been out in the open for years then the chances are the electrics will be buggered."

"That's a technical expression is it?" said Griff with a smile.

"It's about as technical as I get!" Jack replied with a grin. "I'm strictly an oil, tyres and hit it with a hammer if it doesn't work sort of man."

"Always like someone who knows his limitations," said Griff, hitching his pack and beginning to walk away.

Everyone spread out and Lauren shouted for them all to meet back at the tour sign in half an hour, no more.

When the appointed time came their search had produced one more useable bicycle. They then discovered that their group was missing a member.

"Where's Ashley?" asked Lauren looking about.

"Last I saw he was pedalling off that way," said Jack, pointing off to his left.

He no sooner spoke than Ashley appeared in the distance, rode towards them and pulled up with a hesitant grin on his face.

"I've found something driveable," he said, "but you may not like it."

"If it works we like it. Lead on," said Lauren and, with a shrug, Ashley turned his bicycle round and pedalled slowly away as they followed. They didn't have far to go and one street over he pulled up on a small sloping forecourt beneath a sign which said "J.G.Goddard & Sons, Funeral Directors".

The group stared at him as he parked his bicycle and walked over to peeling white paint doors before simply forcing them to one side, the doors grating a little in their runner as they reluctantly slid back into the building. With mock drama he spread his arms towards a dusty hearse parked next to a row of coffins stood against a wall.

CHAPTER EIGHT

THERE was no rush to take advantage of his find and Ashley was forced to continue with his pitch.

"Your chariot awaits," he said. "One careful owner, a spacious boot and only fifty funerals on the clock!

"The keys were in the office, no-one seems to have bothered searching the place and there's a full tank of petrol. Even the tyres are half inflated and there's a foot pump in the workshop. I checked."

"What else was in the workshop?" asked Roddy warily.

"There are a couple of bodies in storage but they're nothing new. We've all seen enough bodies to last us a lifetime. What matters is that the ignition lights up. It may not start but the electrics work and there are enough of us to give it a shove and get it going. I'll drive if you lot don't fancy it."

No-one did indeed fancy it and Ashley quickly pumped up the tyres and then organised everyone in the storage area behind the hearse ready to push hard when he gave the signal. He then dusted off the windscreen before clambering behind the wheel and giving a shout, the group hurling themselves against the rear of the hearse which swept silently out and down the forecourt slope. Ashley had barely turned into the road when he engaged gear, the engine catching with almost no noise much to the group's surprise.

He halted and everyone caught up and crowded round the driver's window.

"Where to Lauren?" he grinned.

Lauren recovered swiftly and got all the bikes piled into the back of the hearse where the coffin was usually placed before climbing into the front passenger seat. Ricky, Jack and Griff got in behind her and Ashley drove slowly away heading back to the tour sign lay-by.

When they got there the wet tyre tracks from Riddle's bus had either faded or evaporated altogether, but they set off hopefully along the line taken by Steve and Roddy.

All trace of tyre tracks soon vanished in the afternoon sun, but a series of arrows left at junctions by the two cyclists ahead kept them on course at a steady 10-15mph, weaving in and out of rusting abandoned vehicles and the occasional skeleton cloaked in rags.

They found both men waiting for them several miles ahead near the entrance to Edinburgh Zoo. The arrival of a hearse left them speechless.

Eventually Steve managed: "What the hell is that?"

Griff replied: "It's a steamroller! What the hell do you think it is?"

"Just checking," said Steve. "We've been able to follow the bus quite easily. Every time they go through any water they leave tracks and if it's dry then they leave tyre traces every time they have to steer round something. We only stopped on account of the noise."

"What noise?" asked Lauren.

"The roaring," replied Roddy.

His words created a silence broken only by the quiet purr of the hearse and a whispered oath from Ricky.

"What was it?" asked Jack.

"I don't know," said Roddy, "and I'd rather not hang around to find out. I've been to the zoo with my family. We saw a load of animals including lions and tigers. Take your pick, but whichever it is then I for one don't want to be within a country mile of this place when night falls."

Another silence followed broken by Lauren telling the riders to load their bicycles into the hearse. Roddy then got in the back while Steve squeezed into the front passenger seat with Lauren.

They set off and daylight was beginning to fade when they reached the M9 interchange. The sporadic abandoned vehicles they had passed soon increased until smashes, crashes and snarled tangles of cars and lorries became a serious problem.

It was not one for Riddle and her bus whose passage could be easily plotted by its mangled route across grassy hard shoulders and verges as the fleeing gang churned their way through or round various jams and obstructions including a caravan which had crashed and partially blocked passage under a bridge.

By the time the hearse joined the M9 and crossed over the River Almond, Lauren decided to call a halt for the night rather than risk missing any sign that the bus might have left the motorway and taken a slip road.

They had food and water for several days but Lauren saw the wisdom of not condemning them all to a cramped night in the hearse and she asked Ashley to bump across to a small exit road flanked by saplings to see if they could find somewhere to put a roof over their heads.

Within a mile they saw a cottage nestled beneath hills which they were able to reach via a short lane where hedges were encroaching on the highway. They forced their way through and arrived at a half-open wooden gate into a weed-choked area which had once been gravelled parking. A battered Landrover with flat tyres stood to one side.

Lauren got out and walked across to the front door but it was locked, so she went down the side of the cottage through a little gate and out on to a paved terrace overgrown with weeds. It was overlooked by French windows and when she tried them they were open. Returning to the front, she had everyone bring their gear with them, made sure the hearse was locked and then led her group back and inside the cottage.

They found the desiccated body of a man lying on blood-stained carpet just inside the doors and quickly removed him to the garden below the terrace. A rotting shed gave them a spade to make a hasty shallow burial in a withered and overgrown flower border.

The cottage was deserted and seemed to have been completely missed by looters, so Lauren's brief exploration turned up some useful items in the kitchen.

There were tins of meat, fruit and butter, sealed plastic bags of pasta, jars of honey and mustard and even jars of coffee, tea and dried milk. A veritable feast, she thought, although cooking might be a challenge.

Even that problem faded away when Griff came and found her to say the sitting room had a wood burning stove.

"If the man we found has a stove then he must have a supply of logs to go with it," said Lauren, "See if you can find them and get a fire going. And check outside to see what smoke you're making. I don't want to bring Riddle and her boys down on us."

Griff nodded and left and Lauren began to arrange what food she'd found on the kitchen table. It would be a scratch meal but it would be a welcome and very unexpected addition to their supplies.

By the time she'd got things together and put a quantity of pasta in a large saucepan of water drawn from the top of a water butt, Griff had found a lean-to stacked with dry logs and got a fire going in the stove which he said was burning with almost no smoke.

Lauren put the saucepan on top and followed that with another filled with meat and tinned vegetables. A nice stew would be a godsend on what promised to be a freezing cold night.

Meanwhile the others had explored and moved their packs into three bedrooms. They were a bit musty but otherwise habitable. Blankets found in a cupboard and in drawers under the beds ensured they'd be as warm as possible in the circumstances. Lauren said she'd sleep on the settee once they settled down for the night.

Everyone then relaxed a bit in the sitting room or helped Lauren by finding cutlery and plates for the food. Griff browsed shelves packed with books, selected one and settled down in an armchair to read.

"What you got?" asked Ricky.

"Home Doctor," said Griff, without taking his eyes from the book.

"Anything in it about stomach troubles only my guts have been giving me some awful gyp."

Griff sighed and flicked to the index before making a show of turning some pages and then highlighting one paragraph with his finger.

"Is it the lower stomach, is the pain persistent or does it come and go?" he asked.

"Well it's sort of down here," said Ricky indicating an area near his belly button. "As for the pain, it does come and go. Does the book say anything about that."

Griff rolled his eyes and tutted then said: "Could be quite serious. Seems that the most severe cases can lead to death unless the sufferer regularly takes two acetylsalicylic acid tablets. Looks like you could be in a bit of trouble here."

Lauren let him have his fun for a few seconds and then told Ricky that the tablets were actually aspirin and Griff was teasing him!

There was much laughter at this and a gentle smile from Griff who resumed reading his book. Ricky gave a grimace but took the hint and left him in peace.

Soon the meal was ready and the seven of them crowded round a small dining table to enjoy the hot food. When they finished there were sighs of satisfaction and a general move back to the sitting room to slump on the settee or in armchairs. When people began to drift off to bed Lauren made sure furniture was barricaded in front of the French windows as a simple safety measure before popping a few logs into the wood burner and settling down to sleep on the settee under a couple of blankets.

*   *   *

FIVE miles ahead of them prolonged screaming from inside the bus had forced Emily Riddle to halt her battered Leyland Olympian in the pull off lane to a caravan park on the edge of a loch.

Once she had clambered out and made her way back and inside the bus she found that the screaming was coming from the man with the wound in his lower stomach who'd said earlier that he hadn't been seriously injured.

Now he writhed on the floor having slipped down between two seats, both hands held to his stomach where blood drenched his shirt and the front of his trousers.

So, thought Emily. He had been lying about how badly he'd been hurt. No-one could fool the rattles and she had been wrong to ignore their advice to kill him. She reached forward with her kitchen knife and rectified her mistake, the man's screams suddenly changing to a gurgle as life bubbled out of his slashed throat.

When she looked up it was to see a clutch of faces frozen in fear. Her stare broke their shock and people looked away.

"Get this rubbish out of here," she said, gesturing at the man's corpse. "And don't any of you try to lie to me again!"

She glared at them for a few moments and then said: "We're clear of the city now and those bastards who attacked us are miles behind. They're going to stay miles behind because we're not going back. Now let's see if this fleapit of a place can put a roof over your miserable heads for the night."

And with one more glare she returned to the driver's cab and took the bus a few hundred metres to a small car park with a scattering of abandoned cars and camper vans. Saplings were springing up on what had been lawns and play areas and carefully snipped hedges between caravans had gone wild, sprouted and begun to close round each caravan.

As the gang exited the bus and began to wander about it didn't take them long to find out that the cafe had been looted and the administration building ransacked.

Ever shrewd, Emily ordered everyone to spread out and make the best of it for the coming night. The bus would go on in the morning, she said, and if anyone was late they'd be left behind. No time was specified for leaving and there were a few worried glances at the chance of being cut adrift in the middle of nowhere.

Some of the caravans were locked but many were open and the tide of people visibly thinned as claims were staked for a bed for the night. An hour later and some caravans actually sported wisps of steam from vents as gas bottle cookers warmed caravan interiors. Some were even lucky enough to find a little food in storage cupboards but this was very scarce. There was no sharing and most went hungry.

Emily had taken one look at her motley crew competing for caravans and immediately decided to sleep on the back seat upstairs on the bus. At least that way she could feel and hear anyone or anything trying to sneak up on her.

Her rucksack yielded a shrivelled apple and the remains of a foil-wrapped cereal bar. Hardly a feast but better than most ate that night.

Her sleep was tortured by dreams of children pleading for help, but she couldn't understand what they wanted and every time she tried to ask they looked at her reproachfully and faded away.

When she finally woke in the dim light of early morning it wasn't the dreams which were responsible but a series of distant roars. She listened carefully but they weren't repeated and no-one else in the gang seemed to have heard them. She stayed right where she was until the light improved and she could see clearly for at least a hundred metres, then she got up, stretched and descended the staircase.

Outside nothing moved and Riddle wiped the core of her apple over her teeth before throwing it into the car park. That would have to do for breakfast and oral hygiene.

She was short on patience and after a brief walk to exercise her legs she returned to the bus impatient to be off. They'd been lucky to escape. She knew that. A more ruthless opponent would have scouted the area, seen the fire escapes and realised their significance as she had. She now wanted a new base which was impregnable and she had one idea for that firmly in her mind.

As birds began to sing so her gang began to arrive in ones and twos, dishevelled and looking pretty miserable with life. She did a brief head count.

They'd fled with a mixed bag of followers, stunned by the attack but grateful to escape and still be alive. Injuries and death had thinned that group out to barely thirty. They had some pistols and shotguns but ammunition was low and she saw more than one sword while a man called MacGregor wielded a viciously thick blade as long as his arm with a grip bound in copper wire. He could often be seen whetting its edge.

Emily's cursory count revealed nearly twenty gang members at or already in the bus with stragglers arriving all the time. When the number rose to twenty-nine she would wait no longer and waved those still outside on to the bus before taking the wheel and starting the engine. An indifferent glance back at the silent caravan park revealed no-one else trying to join them and she gave a nod and pulled slowly away back towards the M9.

As she jerkily engaged third gear a glance in her mirrors revealed a lone man running up the road behind them waving frantically. She ignored him, increased speed to 15 mph and he slowly fell behind. Eventually he gave up and just stood in the road and watched the bus disappear from sight. Maybe next time he'd pay closer attention to what she said....only there wouldn't be a next time.

*   *   *

Lauren's group enjoyed a quiet night broken only by the occasional owl hoot or fox scream and everyone awoke in the morning refreshed and ready to go.

Lauren coaxed the fire to life in the wood burner and put a saucepan of water on the top for coffee which the group really appreciated as it had been so cold in the bedrooms that they could see their breath.

Everyone was keen to get going, Jack and Roddy bagging up what useable food they could find and taking it out to the hearse before everyone took their back packs outside. Lauren was the last to leave. She pulled the French windows closed behind her, giving one final look towards the grave of the man they'd buried in the garden before joining the rest of the group at the hearse which Ashley turned round before they all climbed inside. Ten minutes later and they were back on the M9 but it was slow going.

All traces of wet tyre tracks from the bus had long since evaporated. They were forced to check every road exit in case the gang had left the motorway and every clump of abandoned vehicles they met to discover scrapes where bus tyres had bit into the road as the vehicle was driven round the obstacle.

They'd been going nearly an hour when they reached the caravan park pull-off lane and saw a hint of tyre tracks through a drift of weeds, leaves and mud near a kerb.

There was nothing definite to show that a bus or the gang had been here and Lauren was beginning to wonder if it might just have been a toilet stop when she suddenly saw something out of place in a large empty area of the car park.

She asked Ashley to stop, got out of the hearse and walked over to the object which she picked up. It was an apple core.

Someone had clearly been here recently because the core hadn't rotted, but was it Riddle and her gang?

She had her answer when there was a sudden shout from the ruined cafe to her right. She barely had time to un-sling her shotgun as a man in a torn blue anorak and dirty trousers stumbled towards her, angry words spilling from his mouth.

Lauren quickly noted that she could see both his hands and that he appeared unarmed but she didn't drop her guard. Trust had to be earned.

The man paused a short distance away from her and said: "So can you help me?"

Lauren realised she had missed the sense of what he was saying and said: "Help you what?"

He stared at her for moment then said: "I've been dumped. Riddle just drove off and left me all because I was a bit late getting to the bus. You won't leave me here will you?"

His nervous plea was barely registered by Lauren who was busy scanning the cafe and administration building in case all this was the prelude to an ambush.

Satisfied that she could see nothing threatening, she said: "Why should we take you with us? A few hours ago you were trying to kill us."

The man looked down, aware of his weak position, then said: "I didn't kill anybody, but you'd be killing me if you left me here with no food and no weapon."

He didn't know it but Lauren immediately had a vision of the big cats that Steve and Roddy said they had heard roaring. If she left him and he ran into a lion or tiger it would be a death sentence without her firing a single shot. She had no choice, but she made him sweat while she appeared to consider his request.

"We may help you and take you with us," she said eventually, "but not unless you help us first."

"Anything," the man said fervently.

"Firstly, how many does Riddle have with her?"

"We lost a lot," the man said immediately, "but I'd guess there's about thirty people left including Riddle."

"Where is she going?" asked Lauren.

"Nobody knows," the man said: "We got this old bus going, she drove and everyone else just piled inside to get away. She never said where she was going, just away from Edinburgh."

"So she's not said anything about coming back to attack us?"

"No, nothing like that. She's got those damn silver baby rattles that she listens to. Got a screw loose if you ask me."

Lauren was confused and said: "Whoah! What's this about baby rattles?"

The man said: "Seen her use them several times. She's got these antique silver baby rattles. She shakes them, listens to the noise and then makes some decision, usually to kill people."

Lauren wondered if Riddle had used them at the hall massacre but that was somehow in the distant past. This was here and now. She made a decision.

"What's your name?"

"Richard, ma'am," he said.

"Forget the ma'am. I'm Lauren. The others you'll get to know if you stay with us long enough."

"We going to Edinburgh?" Richard asked.

"No, we're following Riddle to make sure she really has left Edinburgh and isn't just regrouping for another attack."

Richard looked dubious at that and said: "Have to be mad to do that. You killed more than half of us."

"What she has left is still more than enough to massacre any smaller group she finds. I intend to make sure she leaves the area or stays here permanently and I'm prepared to dig the grave myself."

Richard swallowed nervously at that and said: "I've had enough of fighting."

"Haven't we all," said Lauren, "but sometimes there's no choice. What happens now depends on Riddle."

She looked past him back at the ruined cafe and said: "You got any belongings? If you do then get them now. We leave in a few minutes."

Richard turned hastily and began to jog back to the cafe before suddenly stopping and turning round.

"You won't just drive off and leave me will you?" he said.

"Not unless you smell as bad as you look," said Lauren. "Try and clean yourself up a bit. You'll be travelling in a confined space and my companions are particular."

Richard nodded and then trotted back out of sight into the cafe while Lauren strolled back to the hearse where Griff had got out and covered her with his shotgun as soon as he saw the man emerge from the cafe.

"What was that all about?" he asked.

"His name's Richard. Seems he's been cut adrift from Riddle's gang. Says she's got about thirty people with her and they're in an old bus. We were right about that."

"What are you going to do with him?"

"Take him with us. All we can do bearing in mind there are lions or tigers roaming around out there. If we left him he's got no weapon that I've seen. He wouldn't last a week."

Griff looked dubious at her decision but nodded and climbed back inside the hearse as Lauren went round to the back and opened the boot where she shoved bicycles to one side and made a space for their new passenger to sit.

When Richard appeared from the cafe Lauren saw the dirt had gone from his face and he had made some attempt to clean himself up, so she simply waited until he got close to the hearse before gesturing for him to climb inside with the bicycles. This he did, tossing a small pack on top of the mass of wheels and frames.

"What you got in there?" asked Griff, indicating the pack.

"A little food," said Richard, "a change of clothes and a picture of my children."

Griff's face went neutral at that. His own children had died early on with his wife, so he understood why this man might keep a picture with him of his children. Griff had his own picture in a wallet and he didn't show it around. It was too personal.

Lauren got in the front passenger seat with Steve before Ashley drove them all slowly away from the caravan park.

Richard said that Riddle's gang had disappeared up the M9, but the group still had to check every junction in case the bus had left the deserted motorway so progress was very slow.

They drifted past everything from battered signs for kilt outlets to paintballing sites advertised on giant gap-toothed displays missing several boards which appeared to have been torn off by storms.

Infrastructure was breaking down everywhere and the group had to negotiate several spots flooded by blocked culverts, cope with drifts of debris and rubbish and edge their way through snarls of abandoned vehicles dotted with the remains of bodies.

Through all this the bus tyre tracks went serenely on and Lauren began to wonder just how far Riddle was prepared to travel in her flight from Edinburgh.

She knew a little about the area they were driving through and realised they were heading towards the port of Grangemouth.

Lauren warned Steve and Ashley to keep a close eye ahead in case the bridge over the River Carron had collapsed forcing the bus ahead of them to take a different route, but everyone soon had eyes only for the Kelpies.

The towering steel sculpture of two horses' heads dominated one side of the approach to the bridge and it almost seemed incidental that the road bridge was intact despite large amounts of debris lining the river banks beneath them.

They stopped a mile further on for a brief toilet break and a snack during which Ricky raised a concern that hadn't escaped Lauren.

"If they go on much further we're going to have food problems," he said, chewing slowly on a handful of dried stale pasta.

It was a worry for Lauren. Edinburgh lay a good few miles behind them now and alerting David Curtain and the other city survivors to Riddle's whereabouts was a task which was becoming increasingly difficult. Their only positive was that whoever cycled back to inform Curtain could do so without constant stops to keep track of the bus. Even so they were reaching the point where it might take at least a day to cycle back to the city through all the many obstacles.

Almost to underline the need for them to stay alert, they nearly missed the bus leaving the motorway.

Roddy had got out to check yet another slip road only this time he came back to report that there were signs the bus had left the motorway. He pointed behind him to where a carriageway rose among a series of routes and bridges at the Bannockburn Interchange.

Lauren had read the history books about Robert the Bruce's famous victor over Edward II at Bannockburn. More than seven centuries had passed since then and she wondered what Bruce would have made of their own recent battle in Edinburgh.

She was more concerned now with avoiding any repeat of violence especially as she was heavily outnumbered, so she ordered Ashley to take it steadily until the motorway fell away behind them and she called a halt.

"Griff, you've got the best eyes," she said. "Come with me and we'll see what we can see."

He got out and followed her forward past the remains of an entire family in a Subaru Lightning which stood slewed on the slope with the driver's door open. The driver's skull lay on the steering wheel as if he was somehow resting but neither Lauren nor Griff paid the grim scene the slightest attention. They had both seen far worse and at the moment were much more interested in avoiding the living than the dead.

Cautiously they advanced, being as careful as possible not to silhouette themselves against the skyline, until they could see the A872 stretching away from them across a bridge over the motorway.

There was not a living thing to see except occasional birds, no movement and no colour except white banks of snow drifted into sheltered spots. Spring was coming but it wasn't here yet and the flat steel grey skies promised flurries to come.

Lauren was wary and she made no move to go on. The question was, why had Riddle suddenly chosen to leave the motorway at this particular point? She knew there was a Bannockburn visitor centre because she had been there, but Riddle wouldn't be interested in that. It had to be something else and she couldn't for the life of her think what it might be.

Fading light brought her thoughts back to more immediate problems. They needed shelter before it got dark and a big sign bent over by the wind offered a possible solution, its words pitched to entice motorists into a simple hotel.

She and Griff returned to the hearse and told the others there was still no sign of Riddle and her gang. Then Lauren told Ashley to drive on a little further and try the hotel as a camp for the night.

When they got there they found half the hotel had burnt to the ground some time ago, ash washed clean by past rain into grey mud which clung to their feet when they got out and explored.

The whole of reception was a charred ruin together with all nearby rooms, but the remains of a corridor led to an intact wing of bedrooms some of which proved habitable if damp.

Beggars couldn't be choosers, thought Lauren looking around and getting organised. For safety's sake she got Ashley to disable and lock the hearse before they took their packs into the ruin and set themselves up in two family rooms with an interlocking door they forced open. There was enough bed space for everyone to be comfortable and blankets would keep some of the cold away, but it was still pretty miserable until Ricky found a small portable gas heater in one of the other bedrooms. The unexpected warmth swiftly cheered everyone up.

There was some food and they shared what they had and chatted for a while before settling down for the night.

The early hours found Lauren restless and she quietly got up and slipped out to check the hearse. She was enjoying the crisp night air and the wheel of the stars above her when she became aware of a light in the distance. It was clearly visible and came from several miles away. Could it be Riddle and her gang and, if it was, what had brought them off the motorway at this specific point? The answer might come in the morning and, after watching a while, she returned to bed and this time managed some sleep.

She was woken by movement nearby as her men began to stir and collect their things including the heater which was small enough to fit in a gap inside a bicycle frame.

No-one made a move to get in the hearse, Lauren having explained that she wanted to scout the light she had seen that night.

"You aren't going on your own," said Griff. It was more in the nature of a statement than a question, but it made sense to take back-up with her in case it did turn out to be Riddle.

She chose Ricky and Jack and left Griff in charge of the hearse with strict instructions to post a look-out near the bridge to warn of any trouble. Then she unloaded three bicycles and they set off cautiously towards the outskirts of the city of Stirling.

Only a fraction the size of Edinburgh, Lauren knew that the Red Plague would have decimated its population the same as any other city to the point Stirling was likely to have less than a hundred survivors. Less than half might have lived through the murder, injury and disease which followed, so she didn't expect much help if the gang were here.

They rode on, steering their way round abandoned vehicles or avoiding the rubble of collapsed and burnt out buildings.

Jack spotted several glimpses of recent tyre marks so they appeared to be on the right track, but it wasn't until she saw the smoke that she realised she had her answer to why Riddle had chosen to leave the motorway at this point.

Stirling Castle dominated the city, rising proudly against a backdrop of mountains still dusted with snow. No wonder Riddle had come here. They might have forced her out of a couple of mansions in Edinburgh but it would take an army to storm the castle which Riddle could easily defend with the people she had against all but the most overwhelming force.

A thin wisp of smoke was rising from one section and Lauren guessed that the gang had set up quarters in that part of the castle. She still had to be sure and she was in no hurry for the three of them to risk getting seen which would tip Riddle off that she was being followed.

After a while she sent Ricky back to tell Griff what was happening then she and Jack drifted closer to the castle until they had a view of the walled entrance. The battered bus left outside ended any doubts she had. They had found Riddle.

She and Jack slipped back away from the castle and retraced their steps, cycling quickly back to her anxiously waiting group. There were grim faces when she told them Riddle had stopped at Stirling Castle. It was more than forty miles from Edinburgh but still within striking range should Riddle decide on a revenge attack.

Lauren had a brief chat with Griff and they decided to send Ricky cycling back to tell David Curtain in Edinburgh what they had found and that they were staying for a while to see what Riddle was doing. With luck he could be back in Edinburgh by nightfall.

They gave him some food and water, checked his machine was the best they had and sent him quickly on his way. Lauren then sent out Steve and Ashley to keep watch on the approaches to the castle and report back if there was any concerted movement to leave. She had to know if this was a temporary stop or the base for another Riddle reign of terror.

CHAPTER NINE

THE clatter of rotor blades overhead brought people spilling out of Waterfall Manor.

They looked to the sky as the machine turned towards the back of the buildings and began to descend into a field which had hosted another helicopter arrival before Christmas bringing Captain Tully Harcourt to perform a double wedding.

This time people would be leaving the manor not arriving as the Lockheed Arapaho had come for Dawn and John.

The countryside was trying to convince itself that the time had arrived for an English Spring but there were still only a few fresh hints of green as John came out carrying two bags, one for himself and one for his new wife who he hoped would produce their first child in late summer.

Other people came out to see them off as a young Lieutenant in the Australian Army appeared from the direction of the helicopter landing and made his way towards them where he saluted John.

"Good morning sir. I'm Lieutenant Mayhew" he said: "Are John Kane and Dawn Sutton here?"

"You've found him," said John. "And Dawn Sutton is now my wife. She will be along in a moment...I hope."

Dawn stepped out into the courtyard a few seconds later and walked towards them with a smile on her face.

"What a lovely morning for a helicopter flight!" she said, taking her bag from John.

The lieutenant seemed slightly startled at such a non-military remark and gave her the sort of glance reserved for civilians who couldn't be expected to know any better.

He gestured for them to follow him and, with Bruno's barks and everyone's best wishes ringing in their ears, they walked away from the manor, through its numerous outbuildings and out over a stile into a meadow where the helicopter waited for them.

John immediately saw other figures and when they reached the machine and climbed inside he counted five more soldiers as well as a pilot and co-pilot. Leo Anderson was taking no chances with his emissaries to Scotland.

"Sir, if you and your wife would sit in these seats and strap yourselves in then we'll be off," said Lieutenant Mayhew climbing in after them.

There was then some fumbling with webbing and metal locking devices as one of the soldiers made sure John and Dawn were snugged tightly into their seats before he gave a nod to the pilot and resumed his own seat.

The note of the engine then changed, John and Dawn experiencing a moment's disorientation as the Arapaho lifted into the air before climbing into a turn with the ground falling away beneath them.

Waterfall Manor became a doll's house far below and they got their first real appreciation of just how much the countryside was changing.

The clean line of roads had been blurred by hedge growth, cultivated fields had gone wild and there was evidence of extensive sapling growth, flooding and scores of fallen trees.

As they headed north they passed over many towns and villages. Some showed traces of smoke from chimneys but the vast majority stood silent as if they had fallen asleep in some gigantic fairytale.

Some population centres appeared untouched while others had whole areas destroyed by fire and everywhere they went there were brutal scars or traces of digging to mark hasty efforts to dispose of countless dead struck down by the Red Plague.

They flew across the Bristol Channel, its coastline dotted with wrecks, and then up through Wales where snow still cloaked the top of the mountains.

Snowdonia fell behind them at which point the pilot leaned across and held a brief helmet microphone conversation with Lieutenant Mayhew who glanced back at John and Dawn and then hastily looked away.

John gave Dawn a questioning look and she just shrugged her shoulders, as mystified as he was.

By now the helicopter was heading out over the Irish Sea and John was soon amazed to realise that they were approaching the coast of Scotland barely two hours after they had left Cornwall. He'd become so used to a different life post-plague that getting a reminder of the mechanical power most of the world no longer saw was a bit unsettling. If he'd been on the ground travelling in his motor home, Puffin, it would have taken him weeks to reach Scotland if indeed passage there was still possible by road. Many bridges were down across the country and John knew it might be several generations before the country even approached the previous level of infrastructure which had been devastated by the greatest pandemic the world had ever seen.

As they watched they saw the Scottish coastline arrive and drop behind them, the land rising and a forest appearing. At this point the pilot again leaned over to talk with the lieutenant, this time making a forceful point which the officer nodded at.

The carpet of trees beneath them thinned and then faded away as they flew towards and past Kilmarnock, reaching the edge of Glasgow in early afternoon.

Views from 2,000ft revealed the River Clyde and its estuary choked with ship wrecks as the helicopter looped first north-east and then to the south of the city.

Several wisps of chimney smoke could be seen at various points within the city, but it was a fraction of the life expected from a major conurbation. More than one and a half million people had lived in this area before the plague, but John knew they'd be lucky to find a thousand people left alive from the disease and the mayhem that had followed. He doubted Edinburgh would be any different but managed to get Lieutenant Mayhew's attention long enough to ask for the pilot to fly east to see the other city.

He looked wary but went forward and tapped the pilot on the shoulder. There was a brief exchange and the pilot showed a marked lack of enthusiasm at the idea. Mayhew seemed to press and after a brief hesitation the pilot shrugged and swung the helicopter to the east.

Within twenty minutes they were approaching Edinburgh and John and Dawn could see the same hints of smoke but the same lack of general life and movement that Glasgow had displayed.

They turned and curved to the south of the city before swinging up to the Firth of Forth, heading along the coast to the Forth Bridge.

The great structure still stood but there was wreckage or entire ships littering the shoreline for mile after mile as they sped up the coast for a short while before turning west for a look at Perth.

It was as they continued west towards Loch Lomond and the Trossachs National Park that the pilot became animated.

He began to take the helicopter down and when a worried Lieutenant Mayhew slid next to him he stabbed a finger at the control panel and practically shouted into his helmet microphone, Mayhew nodded understanding and made his way back down between the seats to where John and Dawn sat before leaning over and shouting in John's ear.

"The pilot thinks there may be a problem with the engine and he wants to take us down to check."

He was then forced to turn his head as John shouted back: "What sort of problem?"

Mayhew turned back and said: "He doesn't know for sure but it may be a fuel problem. Make sure your harness is tight."

With that he turned away and resumed his seat as John passed on what he'd said to Dawn and checked both their harnesses.

The pilot began to descend, gently slowing their rate of progress as he clearly sought to place as little stress as possible on the engine which still seemed to be performing normally to John.

Suddenly the engine bucked and the next three minutes were a cacophony of shouts, gut-wrenching drops in height and the liquid fear which comes when facing a situation over which there is no control.

Rugged mountainside beneath them quickly got a lot closer and suddenly changed to lochs and forest as the helicopter's engine failed and then bit, their progress being reduced to a series of swoops and darts as the pilot fought the controls and desperately attempted to keep them in the air long enough to find a safe landing spot.

When they were down to barely a hundred and fifty feet the co-pilot shot one arm out pointing down and to their left. John barely had enough time to glimpse an area of grass near a small river before the pilot acted and brought the helicopter round in a stoop ending with a howl of power which sent stomachs sinking into boots.

A split second passed before the helicopter skids slapped the ground and slewed the machine round, grass and dirt flying through the air as the pilot tried to control and shut down the rotors.

Harnesses kept everyone in their seats except the co-pilot who was somehow torn sideways to crumple against the control panel.

The pilot still focussed intently on his controls as the helicopter again slammed into the ground before the machine came to rest, the pilot hastily flicking switches to cut fuel and reduce the risk of a fire.

John found Dawn's right hand had gripped his left one so hard that her nails had driven through the surface of his skin.

Mayhew issued a stream of orders and there was a volley of metallic clicks as the soldiers unlocked their harnesses and bulled their way out through the helicopter door.

John and Dawn followed suit, hastily clambering out and down to the ground where they saw that the soldiers had formed a distant cordon round the helicopter and were peering this way and that as they assessed the terrain they had landed in.

It was remote almost threatening countryside under a dour sky, the small river carving a bend to the left beneath them which had created a bar of pebbles leading up to the grassy bench the pilot had landed on. Pine trees appeared all round the site and grew denser the further away John looked, but there was no sign of habitation. John turned back to Dawn.

"You all right?" he asked, putting a hand on her arm.

"A little shaken," she said, "and I seem to have picked up a bruised arm. Apart from that I'm fine."

John turned back to the helicopter at a shout from the pilot who was beckoning him and Mayhew over.

When they reached the doorway the pilot had taken his helmet off and was looking grim. One gesture from him and they could see why. The co-pilot was dead, his neck broken in the landing.

John took one look and quietly said: "Welcome to Scotland."

Mayhew remained detached and was all business, asking the pilot, Church, if he was still able to fly.

Church replied: "It's not me you've got to worry about. It's the Rap. I still think we may have fuel problems and the landing won't have helped. I can't tell if anything's been damaged without a full check and that will take hours. I may also have to drain the fuel."

"Do we carry spare fuel?" John asked looking inside.

"Enough to do the trip twice over," said Church, "but if it is a fuel problem and the reserve is affected as well then we are going nowhere without fresh uncontaminated supplies and that might be rather hard to find out here in stick land."

John nodded and said: "Do you know where we are, roughly I mean?"

"Well, we don't have GPS or satellites any more, but I know precisely where we are," said Church. "We flew over the A84 a few miles back and we are now about a mile south of Loch Ard."

Mayhew consulted his map case, made a brief calculation and said: "That puts us nearly thirty miles west of Stirling and at least that north of Glasgow."

"No place of size nearby?" asked John. "No regional airports where we might find av gas?"

Church looked sharply at him. Civilians didn't tend to know much about helicopters.

"There may be some private strips but I don't know any. How do you know about av gas?" the pilot asked.

"I'm a mechanic," said John. "I've never worked on a helicopter but I know what fuel it uses and a bit about engines."

"Do you indeed," said Church. "I may yet need your help. Consider yourself promoted to co-pilot."

"Just as long as he doesn't have to fly the thing," said Dawn which drew a smile from Church.

Mayhew issued more orders and two of his men came and removed the co-pilot, gently carrying his body back into the trees where they dug a grave and buried him. Rocks were piled on the site into a small cairn with a crude cross. It was the best they could do.

Meanwhile the chain of command had swung. Technically Mayhew led the mission, but he was wise enough to realise he was a stranger in a strange country. Yet in front of him he had two people who had somehow survived the last five years here, one of whom was a corporal in the British Army. The situation demanded he be flexible and he was a good enough officer to realise it.

"Well Mr Kane," he said, taking his helmet off and wiping the inside of the rim. "You know this country, you know what we're here for. What do you recommend?"

John looked at him a moment and then said: "I don't know this part of the country but there are only two things we have to worry about – shelter and food.

"At a pinch we can use the helicopter for shelter, but that achieves nothing unless Captain Church here can somehow find out what's wrong. If he's right about the fuel then there's more chance of me taking to the air than getting this machine off the ground without fresh av gas. Now there are airports at Glasgow, Edinburgh and Perth where we might find replacement fuel but don't bet on it.

"About a third of the petrol tanks and garages I've found across the country have been useless. Looted, polluted or both. On the other hand, we may get lucky and it's not the fuel but something the good captain can fix.

"That means we stay put until Captain Church gives us the word on the Arapaho. If it was me I'd put a couple of men out there just to be on the safe side so we don't get any nasty surprises. No telling what's out there. The rest of us should be able to put up a shelter for the night. If it rains then there's always cover in the helicopter."

Mayhew nodded, already appreciating John's advice. It was pretty much what he'd considered doing, but he still asked a question.

"We're in the middle of nowhere here miles away from people," he said. "Why the need for guards?"

John smiled and replied: "It's not people I'm worried about."

Mayhew stilled a little at that, so Dawn put her hand on his arm, smiled at him and said: "Let's just say the local wildlife has suddenly had to welcome a few foreign imports."

"And what might they be?" queried Mayhew.

Dawn looked across at John who gave her a slight nod which wasn't lost on Mayhew.

She continued: "In the last year or so we've seen signs of or met everything from tigers and wolves to bison and lions. Admittedly that was much further south, but

Glasgow and Edinburgh both had zoos and Scotland's got a number of wildlife parks.

"I'm not saying all their animals have escaped, but the odds are that some have got out and there are only nine of us for guard duty so no-one's going to get comfortable tonight. We need a secure place where we can sleep and that won't be all cramped together in a broken helicopter."

John chipped in and asked: "What's the food situation like?"

Mayhew replied: "Field rations for ten days. We didn't think we'd need even that."

"Any emergency rations in the helicopter captain?" asked John.

"None," said Church. "This was supposed to be a hop, skip and a jump trip, back within a week, not camping out under the stars."

"In that case let's get to it. I saw a fire axe inside and that's going to be worth its weight in gold," said John, climbing inside the helicopter and undoing the straps and clips which held the axe in place.

When he jumped down he said: "I'll get some firewood while the lieutenant sets up some sort of perimeter.

"Dawn? Can you start putting a meal together? I don't think we've got much more than an hour of daylight left and I want to be dug in here while we can still see what we're doing. We'll pull the guards in closer when we've got a fire going."

Mayhew nodded and issued orders to collect and purify water and set up tarpaulin shelters while John strode off to the closest pine and began knocking off some of the lower dead branches. He stacked them in a neat pile ready to be dragged into their camp before moving away to the next tree and repeating the procedure.

Mayhew watched him go and Dawn said: "Don't worry. He's not being disrespectful. He's just thinking ahead."

"Oh I'm not complaining," said Mayhew. "I thought it might be us looking after you and now I'm not so sure it might not be him looking after us. He must have seen and done a lot of difficult things over the last five years."

"You wouldn't believe how much," said Dawn. "Now show me where the rations are. I've a meal to prepare and not much daylight left to do it in."

*   *   *

HUNDREDS of miles to the south Jed had seen John and Dawn fly off before beginning his now daily jobs with the animals and fields.

He had much more help than in the beginning as the community's numbers had increased sharply, but it was still work he had to organise and oversee.

Today he and Asher, Lucas and Noah were beginning to put up security fencing along the edge of their livestock fields using sections cut from some of the many miles available on deserted local industrial estates.

He'd already dug post holes round one field and it was simply a matter of concreting in the uprights ahead of unrolling and securing metal mesh to keep out deer, foxes and some of the more dangerous animals which had escaped from zoos and wildlife parks.

Jed knew John had had encounters with wolves, that he'd seen a tiger and that the group he'd brought down from Leeds had fought off an attack by lions, so he was under no illusions how necessary the fencing was if he hoped to keep his animals alive as a source of meat and milk for the manor.

A portable diesel cement mixer did the hard work and he made sure that once the concrete was poured and the post inserted that each one was secured with a bracer until it was solidly in position.

Lunchtime had come and gone by the time they finished and Jed knew he had similar work planned for the next day.

Already the manor was using a dozen fields for livestock and for crops which wouldn't last long in the face of hungry deer and rabbits unless it was protected.

Tomorrow's work would be to fence in some rich pastureland which gently sloped down to woods and a stream and as they packed up their tools for the day Jed wondered if it might already be time to consider bringing even more fields into use.

He was mulling over the intricacies of crop rotation when he saw their small herd of bullocks was bunched together in a corner of the next field. They were all stood facing down towards the woodland and they appeared agitated.

Jed walked down a short way and then climbed over a crude stile and began to cross grassland dotted with cow pats towards the animals. He spotted the churned ground when he was about fifty metres from the bottom hedge next to the stream.

Puzzled he diverted to where clumps of grass and earth had been torn out of the ground. He saw the blood and the drag mark at the same time and immediately unslung his shotgun and called urgently to the other three men who came running.

They arrived panting and Jed just pointed at the ground. All of them unslung their weapons and they spread out in a line to follow the drag mark down to the stream where it went through a gap in the hedge, down one bank and up the other before disappearing into the woodland.

The men looked at each other, none too keen on crossing the stream to go into the silent trees, but Jed didn't hesitate. He took a grip on his shotgun stock and began to follow the dragline through the hedge. After a brief hesitation the others bunched behind him to splash through the stream before spreading out on the other side to form a rough search line as they warily began to climb up through the wood.

They crunched through fallen branches and leaves as the ground rose and then folded at a gentle ridge where the woodland dropped away to another stream running through dense thickets of hazel. Half a dozen crows flapped hastily into the air below them.

Jed paused and considered the situation. It seemed one of their precious bullocks had been killed and then dragged some distance, possibly by the tigers whose tracks John had reported seeing the previous year, but crows were unlikely to be on the ground if a tiger was still on its kill.

He again gripped the stock of his shotgun and began to edge down the slope into the thickets, the others following very warily with tense looks about them. There was nothing to see, but the undergrowth and fallen trees were getting denser.

Suddenly Jed caught a splash of black and white. It was the body of the bullock partially covered in branches. There was no sign of whatever had killed it and, after circling the site to make sure he wasn't walking into the predator, Jed approached and checked the carcase.

The bullock's neck had been broken and a substantial part of the body had been eaten and the rest covered. That's what had attracted the crows.

The men talked quietly and everyone agreed to retreat back to Waterfall and discuss what to do next. They had hunting rifles back at the manor and the heavier calibre would be more than enough to kill a tiger, but they'd never attempted anything like this before and there was a lot of wild talk as they trudged back to the quad bikes.

Their return to the manor sparked consternation with widespread concern for the children who were promptly ordered to play only within the courtyard and complex buildings.

Becky cradling new baby, Tilly, was also concerned that Jed didn't act hastily.

"I don't want you going off half cocked and getting yourself eaten," she said. "I'm still getting used to being married again!"

"I'll bear that mind," said Jed drily. "What I had planned on doing was taking the Rigby back to the woods, building a platform and sitting up over the kill for a few nights to see if I can get a shot at whatever did it. We can't stay close to the manor forever. The animals and crops need us. Life must go on, so the sooner this is sorted the better."

"You know that and I know that," said Becky, "but does the tiger know that?"

"I'll ask it when I see it," said Jed. "Now, if you'll excuse me, I've got a bit organising to do."

He turned away and sought out Roy who, after a brief chat, left and headed for the building stores area. By the time Jed, Asher, Lucas and Noah had grabbed a bite to eat and returned to the quad bikes they found Roy had been busy. Stacked in the back of the machines were two metre sections of timber, some plywood, lengths of rope, a hammer and some nails.

"That ought to do it for you," said Roy. "Use as much rope as you can. That way we can dismantle the platform when you've finished with it and reuse the materials."

Jed nodded his agreement and thanked him before the men climbed on to the quad bikes and drove slowly away back to the field with the bullocks in it. The animals were now grazing but they were staying well away from the woodland end of the field.

The men parked and unloaded the quadbikes before laboriously carrying the wood and tools down to the stream, cursing when hawthorn spiked them as they clambered through the hedge.

When they reached the ridge and descended the other side they cautiously took time to make sure the tiger hadn't returned before Jed climbed about thirty feet into a tree overlooking the kill and began to haul up the baulks of timber and rope them to convenient branches.

When he had a crude platform Asher passed up several plywood sections and Jed nailed them in place to form a floor. He then cut a section of rope, attached it to a tree fork above the platform and then simply dropped it over the edge. He'd need that to climb the overhang to get on the platform.

Everyone was mightily glad when they finally retreated to the quad bikes and returned to the manor.

Dinner was a subdued affair. The children sensed something was wrong because all the grown-ups were very quiet, so they seized the moment to be even noisier than usual, adding to the tension.

Darkness began to fall and Jed made his preparations. He collected a Rigby rifle, a dozen rounds of ammunition, a venison sandwich and a flask of coffee before kissing Becky good-bye and heading back out to his quad bike, "good lucks" ringing in his ears from worried community members.

The drive back to the field didn't take long and Jed took it as good luck that some of the bullocks were grazing while others were lying down chewing their cud. They would not be doing that if there was a tiger nearby.

He walked into the field, bullock heads swinging to look at him, and angled down to the hedge which he clambered through before sloshing across the stream.

Jed was soon drifting as quietly as he could through the gloom of the wood until he came to the tree with the platform in it that they'd built that afternoon.

Slinging the Rigby over one shoulder and putting flask and sandwiches in his coat pockets, Jed carefully climbed up beneath the platform and then used the rope to brace and haul himself past the overhang and on to the platform.

He made himself comfortable and checked that he could see the splash of white and black from the dead bullock before settling down to wait, the Rigby rifle cradled in his arms pointing towards the carcase.

Slowly the sounds of the wood he had disturbed began to come back. There was the squeak of bats, an owl hooted and there were several small rustling sounds as rodents explored the floor of the wood for food. Of the tiger, if tiger it had been, there was nothing.

Several hours passed during which Jed ate half his sandwiches and gratefully sipped at hot coffee. Then, just after midnight, he slowly became aware that he wasn't alone.

He felt a tremor in the tree trunk his back was resting against and there was a sort of slapping sound. Moonlight made dead leaves gleam while the white hairs on the dead bullock stood out brightly, but when Jed tried to scan below he couldn't see a trace of the tiger.

Branches shook again and to his horror Jed realised that whatever it was had climbed into the tree below him.

CHAPTER TEN

RECOVERY council lead representative Leo Anderson had gone into the banking business.

Once a base had been established at Tilbury he had moved into the eastern edge of the city near the London Stadium and set up his operations in a bank with ornate stonework and two Ionic columns either side of the entrance. It was solidly built on a corner plot with good lines of fire, there were offices at first floor level and even a small kitchen which his team swiftly brought into use with a portable generator.

In a few weeks his patrols had made contact with hundreds of people only too eager to accept his authority and the security that went with it.

There was no charity. People were bluntly told that they would all be fed but that they would all have to work in some way towards the goal of setting up a government which could eventually run the country and get it back on its feet.

More than two thousand people attended a Stadium meeting to hear Anderson talk about power plants, growing food, recycling useable transport and machinery, a score of different topics which confused many but which did have the effect of generating hope where there had been no hope before.

Work gangs were created. Some foraged for food, others worked on clearing overgrown gardens and parks ready for Spring planting of crops using seeds brought in the ships and still more gangs worked under the guidance of Anderson's experts to pool expertise with a view to establishing ten community hubs across London.

Each community would make use of what its area might have, all would be linked to a single portable nuclear power source being set up and run by Anderson's men and each community would be required to draw up a list of its possible assets so any obvious shortfalls could be dealt with.

Anderson told the sea of Stadium faces looking expectantly at him that he was now the law for the next five years. After five years he would review the situation with the hubs and after ten years he hoped to withdraw and leave them to run the city themselves and, hopefully, the rest of the country with the help of the Plymouth base and others he hoped to set up in Wales, the Midlands, Manchester and Scotland.

There were whistles, cheers and enthusiastic applause when he finished before the crowd began to slowly filter out of the stadium past wooden table checkpoints which collected details of where they were living and what they could do.

Those details were sifted through in the days that followed and Anderson realised that he had enough medically qualified survivors to consider trying to open a hospital.

In the end his choice was easy. The Royal London Hospital was chosen because it had been a teaching hospital and they'd need to train up as many new staff as possible. It had also been a children's hospital, a major Air Ambulance base and a busy accident and emergency centre as well as a top class dental centre.

So far they had found nearly forty doctors, nurses or specialists which Anderson augmented with his own medical experts and a team of twenty soldiers to protect and help them. It was only a fraction of the hundreds who used to work at the hospital before the Red Plague struck but they had to start somewhere. Anderson knew that having a recognised hospital re-open, no matter how reduced the service, would act as a focal point for those still alive in the city, something they could relate to and cling to as evidence that not everything they knew had been destroyed.

Anderson and his team drew up a seemingly impossible list of major infrastructure tasks which needed to be tackled from getting sewerage dealt with to restoring fresh water and making sure each hub cleared at least one main road route through its area to begin linking different communities within the remains of London.

And as he paused for a cup of coffee and a sandwich Anderson pondered his progress further afield.

His mission despatched to Wales, the Midlands and the North had already achieved some minor success. The helicopter team sent to Wales had found a few small communities, landing long enough on the edge of Cardiff to meet one leader of a large group who was given a radio and encouraged to pull together as many scattered groups as he could for support.

When they flew on to the Midlands they found the makings of an almost Middle Ages war between rival groups both claiming to control Birmingham. One side operated from a fortified bullion depot in the Jewellery Quarter of the city and the other from a warren of lorry containers in a half derelict jam factory in Scattertown. Neither seemed willing to give up power and work with the other and both were cool towards the helicopter mission as if they were in no hurry to be saved. Anderson was radioed that it might take troops to make both sides see reason.

The story was very different in the North where they were practically greeted as heroes when they landed in the centre of Manchester. A single day was all it took for a rough council operating there to agree to making contact with as many groups of survivors as they could and to try and start organising the city. The promise of a portable nuclear power station, food, help from infrastructure experts and some military protection against gangs of looters actually saw them cheered and Anderson took some comfort that, while things were bad, there was enthusiastic support for his recovery plans.

His main worry was that Scotland was proving something of an enigma. He knew John Kane and Dawn Sutton – who he understood were now married -- had arrived there safely because Lieutenant Mayhew had radioed as much, but since then he had heard nothing.

It was entirely possible they could have been attacked by survivors desperate for food but Anderson didn't think so because Mayhew would have radioed the discovery of any large group of survivors before he allowed the helicopter to land. No such message had been received. In fact they had heard nothing for days.

He pondered the advisability of sending a second helicopter group to Scotland but decided against that for now. It could just be a mechanical problem and his resources weren't bottomless. He had to conserve what he had and use assets wisely. London was his main focus followed by a link-up between Plymouth, Wales, the Midlands and Manchester. It would be nice to add Scotland but not immediately vital since he could concentrate more on the Highlands once he'd got the plan started for England and Wales.

His latest task on a seemingly endless list was bringing back into use equipment to create a chain of petrol stations and electric points across the city so his taskforce didn't have to keep returning to Tilbury to refuel.

On top of that he had people looking at trying to bring a Thames refinery back on line but it was very early days there and he had more immediate problems.

There were still gangs of looters out there because not everyone welcomed the arrival of authority. They had to be dealt with and he also had to keep an eye on how his resources were being used up so he could liaise with Canberra and Sydney to arrange resupply.

It was his technical people who were most in demand particularly those expert in restoring infrastructure. Some areas were almost as they were pre-Red Plague, but others were badly looted, burnt to the ground or simply suffering from storm damage and years of neglect.

The intricacies of restoring power and drainage weren't lost on him and he had to focus first on those areas being considered for hubs. They were the key to unlocking recovery for London.

If he could make the hubs work then recovery would slowly spread to embrace other areas.

Anderson privately believed that it would take two generations to get the country back even remotely close to what it had been, perhaps fifty years to tackle decay which had happened in just five years.

It was a daunting prospect but he had no family and, as he joked with his subordinates, "I've got nothing else to do at the moment!"

He brought his thoughts back to the present and the first floor bank office in which he sat compiling a list on the back of a sheet of paper about something to do with overdrafts.

Among his "to do" ideas was to check on the possibility of bringing a north-south and east-west Tube line back into use. It might be possible, he thought, and would help movement of people until a main route could be cleared across the city.

Then there was the question of Heathrow. He had no idea what state the airport might be in. The runways might be intact but were they blocked? It was barely twenty miles away and if he could get a scouting party there to assess whether flights might be able to land then he might only have to wait days for essential supplies and equipment to be flown over from Australia, New Zealand or Japan instead of the many weeks it was taking by sea.

Another issue was water. Everything had to be boiled at the moment but Anderson had staff checking pumping stations to investigate if a central area could be reconnected to supplies that all the hubs would be able to access.

He faced a thousand and one tasks, one of which was unfortunately keeping law and order.

Even in the short time they had been in London there had been incidents and today he would have to deal with the most serious of them, the murder of a man and the serious injury of a soldier.

The dead man had been killed in a dispute over a bag of food tins. A patrol of soldiers had intervened and one nearly died when the surviving looter slashed him with a knife before being overpowered.

It was a clear cut incident. In normal times the murderer would have been given a life sentence but these weren't normal times and Anderson had sentenced him to be hung. A life for a life and perhaps the example would deter similar violence.

Whatever the circumstances, Anderson was determined to see this through to the end, so at 11am he left his commandeered office and walked a few hundred metres to a small church.

Almost the entire burial ground showed evidence of being dug up as people desperate to bury loved ones had torn at the earth. Even old graves had been opened to deal with new corpses and it had taken a while to find ground capable of accepting one more body.

The pathway entrance to the front doors of the church had an oak beamed gateway and a rope had been tossed over it, the noose swaying in a slight breeze.

Four soldiers brought the condemned man to his death, his arms bound tightly behind him and his thinning hair tumbling over one eye. There was no priest so Anderson read out details of the man's crimes, his sentence and asked mercy for his soul He then ordered sentence to be carried out.

All through this the man didn't so much as twitch but when the soldiers brought out a small stool from the church he refused to climb on to it and began to struggle violently but in complete silence.

It took three of the soldiers to lift his kicking form up on to the stool while the fourth soldier held the rope as the noose was looped round the man's neck. All three soldiers then rejoined their colleague, took hold of the rope and simple marched briskly away with it. There was a horrible gagging noise but the only other sound was a thud as the man's flailing legs kicked over the stool on to ancient flagstones.

When the man finally fell still Anderson gave it a short while and then ordered his body lowered to the ground. The entire execution had taken three minutes and the body was carefully checked to confirm death before it was carried behind a stone cross and placed in a shallow grave which the soldiers filled in. There was no marker.

The soldiers saluted Anderson who thanked them for doing a difficult duty. The corporal in charge then marched them away for other tasks while Anderson retraced his steps back towards his office in the former bank, but when he got there he couldn't go inside. Instead he walked on past where soldiers were billeted in first floor flats, past where half a dozen flatbed lorries were parked and in to a small square where he swept rotted leaves off a bench and sat down.

He'd seen as many dead bodies as the next man but it was the first time he had ever ordered someone's life to be taken. He didn't like the way he felt because he felt nothing. It was a job and he had done it. There had to be respect for law and order and people had to see that those who wantonly broke those rules would be punished, but still he thought he should feel some regret at the passing of another human being, some sorrow or sadness, but there was nothing. It had been a necessary action but still just a job and Anderson was a little alarmed at how easy it had been.

He watched as a sparrow fluttered to the ground near him and began to hop about looking for seeds.

What other distasteful tasks lay waiting for him as he tried to rebuild the life of this country? Would he feel so little for them as well or was there some action which would generate an emotional response in him? Anderson didn't know but he hoped there was because he didn't like this empty feeling he had.

The sparrow flew up into a tree when he finally stood and began to walk slowly back to the office. Several members of staff were waiting for him when he got back.

He made them wait while he checked with the radio room, but there was still no message from the group in Scotland. Frustrated, he returned to his office and began to deal with a sheaf of issues.

Washing facilities so the troops could have clean clothing, decisions on where hub headquarters should be sited which he delegated so the people in each area chose their own base, fuel storage points, hooking solar power linkups to battery banks to eke out their generators. He even found time to discuss a four-week menu with Army chefs. The demands on his time were endless.

By the time he finished for the day and grabbed a hot meal he was ready for a rest which he took in the foyer of a small boutique hotel housing some of the Recovery force.

Already the bar area had been cleared of broken glass and debris left by looters and it was with a sigh of relief that he made his way to a deep armchair and ordered a shot of rum from a mess orderly.

At some point he fell asleep, his rum only half drunk, and when he woke and looked at his watch it was nearly 1am and he had a crick in his neck from the awkward position he had dozed off in. Getting up and stretching, Anderson made his way across the foyer and out on to front entrance steps where he was stopped by a sentry.

"I wouldn't go out there if I was you, sir," the sentry said.

"What do you mean?" Anderson asked, glancing out into the night.

"Patrols are keeping an eye on things," said the sentry, "and there's been a few brushes with the locals."

"Anyone hurt?" asked Anderson.

"Not on our part," said the sentry, "but we've had to lasertaser a few bright boys trying to help themselves to our stores."

"Did they get anything?" asked Anderson.

"Only a headache," said the sentry. "Two in custody. The rest legged it."

Anderson nodded and was about to turn back into the hotel when there was a horrible giggling laugh which rose into the night and then fell away into silence.

"What on earth was that?" said Anderson.

"Hyena we think," said the sentry. "Called a few times tonight but no-one's seen it yet. No-one wants to either."

As if there wasn't already enough out there for him to worry about. Now they had a hyena. Anderson wasn't surprised. There were so many wildlife sites in the London area that escapes had been bound to happen and John Kane had already warned him about wolves, lions, bison and even a tiger. He'd just add the hyena to the list. Still, there must be food about for the hyena to subsist on and Anderson had a nasty suspicion what the animal might be eating.

But he was tired and he needed his bed after a long and difficult day, so he bade the sentry good-night and trekked up to his room. Fifteen minutes later he was fast asleep.

It wasn't daylight filtering through curtains which woke him in the morning but a series of sharp raps on his door.

Blearily he swung his legs out of bed, went to the door and opened it to see one of the soldiers from the radio room outside.

"Good morning, sir. We have received a message from Scotland."

"I'll come at once," said Anderson. The soldier saluted and left, Anderson closing the door and giving a huge yawn as he walked over to where his clothes lay on a chair.

Five minutes later he was in the radio room looking at a message sheet from Lieutenant Mayhew which read: "FORCED LANDING AFTER ENGINE FAILURE. CO-PILOT DEAD. SOME LIFE GLASGOW EDINBURGH. WILL UPDATE WHEN POSSIBLE."

Anderson now faced a dilemma as he absently creased and recreased the message slip in his hand. Eventually he decided not to reinforce the Scotland mission. The other helicopter had to return to London when its work was finished. It was needed for operations around the capital and Anderson wanted it thoroughly checked as soon as possible. Having one machine down was bad enough. He couldn't afford to lose his second. It was early days so those in Scotland would have to fend for themselves until they told him different or actually called for help.

His grumbling stomach alerted him to the need for breakfast and Anderson took himself and his problems off to the kitchen where he enjoyed a simple fry-up, toast and a cup of black coffee.

It was while he was eating that his mind drifted not to the problems in front of him but those he had left behind in Australia.

The Red Plague had struck the country hard but then faltered and died out. There seemed no rhyme or reason for that but Anderson knew his country's virologists had welcomed the respite to try and find a vaccine to take the country back from the brink.

It was the same story in New Zealand and Japan. Horrific numbers of dead followed by the plague fading.

All three countries had seized on the lull to band together, pool resources and throw everything they had into finding a vaccine which they had managed to do. Then they slowly realised there was no plague left to fight, just ravaged cities and communities battling to get back on their feet.

Barely one in a thousand people survived in most countries but the trio of Recovery councils fared much better with survival rates of perhaps one in thirty. They had forged a new future for themselves and were generous enough to realise what it could mean for other less fortunate nations able to receive their help. The problem was that so few countries had anything like a viable population.

Great Britain was a small nation best able to make the most of what the Recovery councils could do for them, but many of the worst hit countries were just open graves which might take a century or more to stage even the crudest of restoration programmes if they ever did.

It was a grim choice and Anderson appreciated the fine lines between being helped and being left alone. A single radio call made by Dawn Sutton had sparked the response to England, a piece of pure determination and skill backed up by a hefty slice of luck. Few had been so fortunate.

He finished his last mouthful of breakfast and put his knife and fork together on his plate. Another day faced him, another step forward up the long climb to give this country a chance of getting back on its feet and he wouldn't achieve that by sitting here dwelling on the size of the task he faced.

*   *   *

FAR to the north of them in Birmingham two rival gangs were heading for a showdown in a vicious turf war.

The Wolves from their headquarters in a fortified bullion depot in the jewellery quarter proclaimed rulership of the city.

Their claim was hotly disputed by the Blues from their complex of lorry containers stacked in a half derelict jam factory in Scattertown.

Now they were on a violent collision course, each determined to wrest control of the city from the other.

CHAPTER ELEVEN

SOMEONE else was combining breakfast with some serious thinking and Ewan Fraser had finally reached a decision.

Any truce with Callander Castle and Andrew McCain had to be watertight. There would be no second chance because McCain would only come to the table once. If anything happened to wreck the meeting then McCain would be so suspicious that he'd never agree to another one and the chance of a wary peace would be lost.

Fraser spread a tiny bit of marmalade on his toast. Stocks of the treat were now very low and he wondered how long it would be before anyone would be able to rely on regular supplies of oranges to produce more. He'd savour it while he could and he took an appreciative mouthful before chewing it slowly.

He'd send Ross to make contact and give McCain his offer to meet and discuss a truce at the old hunting lodge in Queen Elizabeth Forest Park. Three men on each side, no more.

Fraser felt McCain would consider the offer even if he didn't go along with it. Neither side could afford to continue skirmishes which wasted time, manpower and assets. The question was, would McCain turn up? He'd have to wait and see.

With that in mind he wiped his mouth with a knapkin, got up and went to the dining room door which he opened and shouted for Ross before returning to table to finish his toast.

A few minutes passed then there was a brief knock at the door and Ross entered.

"Sir?" he said.

"Sit down," said Fraser, gesturing to a dining chair. "I've got a little job for you. I want you to take a letter to Andrew McCain at Callander Castle. Wait there while he reads it and bring any reply from him straight back to me. Have you got that?"

Ross nodded and Fraser dismissed him, saying he would give him a call when the letter was ready.

The laird popped the last of the toast into his mouth as Ross left and then moved from the dining room through into the main sitting room and on into his study where he sat at a heavy ornate desk and took out paper and an envelope from one of the drawers.

He unscrewed a gold-nibbed fountain pen, thought for a moment and then dashed off three lines written in a tight crabbed style before signing it. He waved the paper about for a few seconds to dry the ink and then folded and inserted it into the envelope, writing McCain's name on the front before sealing it.

With the envelope in his hand, he went out into the corridor and again shouted for Ross. When he arrived Fraser gave him the envelope and said: "Try not to get yourself shot delivering this. Just drive up to the main entrance and wait for someone to come to you."

Ross took the envelope and looked at it warily, turning the paper back and forth before sliding it carefully into an inside pocket of his heavy wax jacket.

"When would you like me to deliver it?" he asked.

"Now if you please," said Fraser. "I'd like to know McCain's thoughts on this matter by this evening."

Ross looked dubious but left the room and a few minutes later Fraser heard the sound of a vehicle leaving the castle. Now it was up to his rival, he thought.

He'd have been a lot less certain of getting a reply if he could have known Ross's thoughts which were chaotic. The man was afraid. Afraid of what might happen to him at Callander Castle and afraid of what Fraser might do to him if he failed to deliver the letter.

It was more than a two hour drive to Callander and there were enough hazards along the way to keep Ross from dwelling too much on his instructions.

Once he had to pause and drag a small tree off the road and he met another delay at a landslip caused by a stream overflowing a blocked culvert. Ross cleared the blockage and then drove his 4 x 4 slowly over a mound of stones, dead branches and mud to reach clear road beyond.

It was nearly lunchtime when he arrived at Callander where he had barely pulled up on the gravel frontage than he was approached by head keeper David Allen. He carried a shotgun although it wasn't pointed directly at Ross.

"And what might you be doing?" asked Allen when Ross dropped the driver's window.

"Got a letter for Mr McCain," said Ross. "I've been told to wait for any reply."

"Have you now," said Allen, taking the letter and giving it a cursory glance.

"Well, you just stay here laddie while I deliver it. Don't get out. Someone will bring you a hot drink."

Ross nodded his thanks and sat still. He had no intention of risking his neck any more than he had to for a letter.

It was Matilda who brought him a mug of what tasted like coffee and he was quick to thank her. She raised an eyebrow, smiled at him and then sauntered back through the entrance.

Inside Andrew McCain also had his eyebrows raised but in shock not amusement. Just to be sure, he read the letter Ewan Fraser had sent him again and then for a third time. Even then he didn't feel he had grasped its contents as if some hidden meaning was there if only he could fathom it out.

The letter read: "NEITHER OF US CAN WIN BUT IF WE ALLY OURSELVES THEN NEITHER OF US CAN LOSE. IF YOU ARE INTERESTED IN WHAT I PROPOSE THEN MEET ME IN THREE DAYS TIME AT MIDDAY IN THE OLD HUNTING LODGE IN QUEEN ELIZABETH FOREST PARK. I WILL BRING THREE MEN. SO SHOULD YOU. " The message was simply signed "FRASER, LOCH LOMOND CASTLE."

McCain blinked to break the spell of the letter then turned it over to see if anything more was written on the back. It was blank.

He rubbed his chin and thought furiously. Either Fraser had taken leave of his senses or he was serious and, whatever else McCain thought of his opponent, he grudgingly accepted that the man wasn't stupid or rash.

If he wanted contact it was for a reason, but was it the one the letter hinted at or was there a hidden agenda? The answer was obvious. He would have to go and find out.

Briskly he walked to the library and across to a writing desk where he took a sheet of paper, penned a few words on it and inserted it into an envelope which he sealed and put Fraser's name on the front. He hesitated briefly, tapping the envelope on his fingers, then shook his head and went in search of Allen. When he found him he handed over the envelope and instructed him to give it to Fraser's man.

Matilda saw the exchange and went over to him as Allen hurried out to the forecourt.

"Is there a problem?" she asked.

A thoughtful McCain replied: "Not yet there isn't, not yet, but there will be a meeting in the drawing room in an hour. Could you please arrange it?"

"Of course," said Matilda and then watched as McCain returned to the library and began to sort through a shelf of maps.

She heard the sound of a car engine as Ross drove off and then was lost in busying herself reaching as many people as she could to alert them about the meeting.

When the appointed hour arrived there were more than a dozen people assembled, waiting expectantly to hear what McCain might say.

When he walked in it was Matilda who spoke first, telling him: "I've reached everyone I can. Poppy can't come because she's in the kitchen and there are two men out foraging. Everyone else is here."

McCain nodded, turned to the group and said: "Thank you for coming. I felt it right to update you since all our lives may be affected by what I have decided.

"As you know, Fraser and I haven't seen eye to eye for some time and there has been....how can I put it....a bit of friction between us.

"This morning one of his men brought a letter to me from Fraser proposing a sort of truce, even an alliance if I've got it right.

"Both of us have been lucky so far. There have been a few injuries but no-one has been killed, so halting the hostility between us does have the obvious advantage of preserving our numbers to build on for the future.

"Between us I estimate we might have thirty or more people. Now if we continue the way we are as two separate communities sniping away at each other then it is only a matter of time before numbers fall and threaten the continued existence of everyone.

"I believe that what Fraser may be proposing is an alliance. At the very least this might involve leaving each other alone and at best it might even see us work together, a sort of pooling of resources.

"In three days time he has suggested a meeting in the old forest hunting lodge. He'll bring a few men for security and I'll be taking Duncan and two others with me. It is remote and fairly open so, if Fraser does what he says, there should be little likelihood of any unpleasantness.

"That merely tells you the "why" of why you are here. I am more interested in the "how". How should I approach this meeting and what should we be looking for from it?"

Allen said he gave any alliance a cautious welcome because it would stop wasting a lot of the manpower spent on guarding their borders.

He added: "If you can get Fraser to agree to leave us alone, even pool resources and help each other, then both sides would benefit. We have enough people here to make our lifestyle much more secure than it is. We are only prevented from that at the moment because we can't afford to drop our guard."

Alec Wilson agreed and said: "From what I know of Loch Lomond Castle it has similar greenhouses to ours as well as a walled garden. If they are constantly watching out for us the way we are watching out for them then I doubt they've done any more towards food production than we have. If we could change that we'd all be better off."

Duncan couldn't wait to chip in and said: "I'd advise extreme caution. If this leopard is going to change its spots then I'd want a lot more information than a few vague hints of a ceasefire.

"That said, you know my views on our own greenhouse. It needs overhauling and turning to food production. So do the gardens and if Fraser means what he says then the possibilities are endless. They have a walled garden which we don't. If we discuss what each community is trying to plant then we can trade and swap our surpluses. It would mean a better diet for everyone not to mention that having two separate food sources guards against one being lost."

McCain stood and heard several more suggestions, some of which he wrote down including one from Alec that he discuss drawing up a map with McCain to detail places which had been cleaned out, gardens which might produce seeds and other sites which might contain equipment they both could use.

At the end of the meeting McCain had a page and a half of suggestions to take with him and a host of other ideas from the unworkable to the possible.

When he called a halt he said: "Thank you for your thoughts. I value them all. Now, Poppy will be serving our main meal soon so I suggest we get washed and changed. Matilda? Could you spare me a minute in my study?"

"Of course," said Matilda as everyone began to drift away. She followed McCain away to a room at the base of a turret which was lined with books and files above a sturdy if battered desk which had a well used chair on castors in front of it. A single armchair lay over near an ornate fire grate where a whisky decanter and a glass stood on a small sturdy table.

McCain waited until Matilda closed the door and came over to him before saying: "Please, sit down. This shouldn't take long."

Matilda did so, crossing her legs and waiting, aware that McCain's eyes had followed the way her skirt rode up. Men were such simple lambs, she thought, smoothing a non-existent crease in her skirt.

McCain seemed to gather himself and then said: "What did you make of all that."

Matilda had already guessed why he wanted to talk and she had her answer ready.

"I don't think it's a trap. If it was then Fraser would want as many of us as he could get in one spot. Equally I would urge caution. Three men gives you enough protection but only if Fraser doesn't bring more."

"My thoughts exactly," said McCain beginning to pace up and down. "It is an opportunity but one I need to be sure of before I commit, so when I leave I'll want you and Allen to organise a lockdown until I return. If I'm taken or killed then at least any attempt to overrun Callander won't catch you cold."

Matilda nodded and said: "Well and good. And if Fraser's offer is genuine?"

"Then it could be the first real hope of a prolonged future we've had. We can't afford to continue these skirmishes."

He came over and stood behind her, Matilda allowing him a few seconds to glimpse her cleavage before she slowly got to her feet and turned to move in close and face him.

"Don't you go taking any stupid risks now," she said, straightening the collar of McCain's shirt. "We all need you to come back. This place won't run without you."

He smiled, placed his hands on her hips and said: "I doubt that. You organise everything. I have ideas but you make them work."

"You seem to like some of my ideas too!" she said archly at which there was a sharp intake of breath from McCain as her hand dropped and gently brushed the front of his trousers. He made a clumsy attempt to lean in and kiss her but Matilda swayed out of his reach and reminded him that they were all due to eat soon.

"Perhaps later," said McCain as he attempted to get close to her again, Matilda evading him and saying: "Perhaps. We'll see." She then flowed invitingly to the door, giving him a smile as she went out into the corridor.

McCain released breath he hadn't realised he'd been holding and found himself looking forward to the evening with an enthusiasm he'd almost forgotten.

Callander was his family home and before the Red Plague came he'd commuted every day into Glasgow for his work as manager of a network of Scottish estates with absentee owners.

When the city began to fall apart with death and looting everywhere he had decided to return permanently to Callander and take his chances there.

He'd grabbed a few treasured belongings from a flat he kept and been on his way north out of the city when he came across the incongruous sight of a well dressed businesswoman walking along pulling an expensive wheeled leather suitcase.

On impulse he had stopped to ask if she was all right and found himself offering her a place of safety at Callander. Matilda had been with him ever since.

He'd always been aware of her as a woman but up to now had never sought to take their relationship any further. However, the adrenalin rush from the planned meeting with Fraser seemed to have heightened his senses and he began to have some very different thoughts about her, feelings he hoped she might return. Down the corridor Matilda was making some plans of her own.

Everyone was full of praise for Poppy after she conjured up venison steaks, potatoes and a few scarce vegetables, but for Duncan Weir it only underlined how much they needed to bring the gardens and greenhouse into the full production of food. He didn't think the isolated towns and villages around them would continue to supply wild vegetables and seed for much longer. They either put the effort in now or the chance would be lost forever.

So he spent the next couple of days ahead of the trip to the hunting lodge checking what materials might be needed. Glass to replace several smashed panes in the greenhouse was a priority and some of the main beams were showing signs of rot and might need new ones. He also checked their meagre supply of tools and made notes that they needed at least a dozen more spades and forks, some trowels, loppers, a bow saw and a crow bar.

Privately he'd been impressed by Alec Wilson's news that Loch Lomond Castle had a walled garden. As soon as he heard that he realised just how much sense it made. The protective walls would give them a head start in Spring and Weir was determined that Callander would have a walled garden too to help its own food production. They couldn't afford to miss a trick and he already had in mind a spot not far from the large greenhouse. There was plenty of stone to be had, he was pretty sure he could lay his hands on a small digger and a cement mixer and if he got his way when he suggested his idea to Andrew McCain then Weir planned to have the garden built by the end of summer and the ground inside dug before winter began to sink its claws into the earth.

The meeting day finally arrived and Weir joined two other men, Barnard and Page, as escorts for McCain when they all set off for the lodge in an old-style battered Land Rover which had done duty at Callander for years.

They drove for more than an hour, passing several deserted villages and homes many of which showed severe damage. There were occasional bodies to be seen.

One in Doon-on-Tay appeared to have died in an old red telephone box converted into a community book swap point, the collapsed decaying skeleton slumped against the windows.

The road became a growing problem, sides crumbling and sections entirely gone where streams had sought new courses when culverts or small bridges became jammed with debris.

Eventually they reached Tarranbrae where the road they were on seemed like a motorway when compared with the track they now took into Queen Elizabeth Forest Park.

Large sections were overgrown with bright green moss through which not a single tyre track showed. Initially trees were visible but set well back from their way but this slowly changed until their route was overhung with pine and oak and the Land Rover rolled slowly forward through a silent world where the only sound was occasional birdsong.

The hunting lodge when it appeared seemed part of the forest itself, backed by mature trees with saplings striving for a foothold in front of the building on what once was a border and gravelled drive. The front door was gained from a large railed veranda. Three or four reclining chairs had been blown together in a heap, acting as a trap for drifts of leaves.

Barnard pulled just past the lodge and turned the Land Rover so it was pointing back the way they had come for their return journey, then everyone got out and stretched their legs.

Andrew McCain strode briskly up wooden steps and immediately learned caution when one snapped beneath his feet, the rotten board throwing him sideway so he had to make a grab at railings to save himself from a fall.

Shaken, he dragged himself erect and carefully tested the remaining two steps up on to the veranda floor which looked damp but intact. When he reached the entrance and tried to twist the deer horn handle the door resisted briefly before opening with the grinding noise of long unused hinges.

Inside his nostrils sucked in a cloying smell of damp. There was mould on the gloomy walls as he stepped forward to a small reception area at the bottom of a short staircase which led to upstairs rooms. Beyond reception were two glassed swing doors into a bar which, when he pushed them open, contained an unexpected benefit. The whole place was exactly as it must have been pre-plague. No looting had been carried out here and the small counter flap was still raised to allow access to a short row of bottle optics, three shelves of bottled beers and one of mixers.

He looked briefly round the small bar, coughed then took a handkerchief from his pocket and held it over his nose and mouth, gagging on the dusty air with its overpowering smell of rot.

At that moment he heard the sound of an engine and hastily retraced his steps back to the veranda to see a white 4 x 4 pull up near the Land Rover. Two armed men got out of the back and immediately looked over McCain's group and scanned the trees surrounding the lodge. Satisfied, they gave a nod and Fraser got out of the front passenger seat and strolled to the bottom of the steps where he thrust his hands into his jacket pockets and looked up at McCain.

"Good of you to come," he said.

"I can go just as easily," said McCain. "Why have you called this meeting?"

"You know why," said Fraser. "We've been walking a tightrope that neither of us can afford to fall off. Limited personnel, limited prospects and the possibility – even the likelihood – of things getting a whole lot worse if we start a war. And that's what things are heading for, a war and one that neither of us can win."

McCain stared stolidly at him and then said: "Come on in. This place is mouldering away but it hasn't been smashed up yet by looters. It'll do for a chat."

He turned away and went back through the entrance. Fraser followed, negotiating the broken step on the way. By the time he joined McCain in the little bar the other man had found glasses and put shots of whisky in them both. He handed one to Fraser and gestured to a table and two upholstered chairs, all covered in a film of dust.

When Fraser tried to flick his chair clean he only succeeded in creating a cloud of dust which made him cough.

McCain said: "When I came in first I had to cover my nose and mouth with a handkerchief. The cleaners don't seem to have been in for a while."

Fraser nodded and took a hasty swig of whisky which only made him cough more, McCain waiting until his throat cleared.

"So what exactly are you proposing?" he asked, taking a sip from his own glass.

Fraser replied: "What I'm proposing is an alliance of necessity. You've got your patch and I've got mine. We each agree to stay within our own borders, to help each other when needed and to pool our resources."

"Look," he said, taking a cautious sip of whisky. "I used to run a security business and I learnt how many men I could get away with as the minimum level needed for a job. Too many and the costs were too high, too few and you risked trouble. What I'm seeing right now is that we are both risking trouble. We only have small workforces which we can't afford to reduce, certainly not to fight a private war when we're both bound to take casualties.

"The intelligent thing to do is to put our differences to one side and take the long view. We've two communities barely clinging on. Working together instead of against each other gives both of us a better chance of surviving and growing.

"I'll keep out of your hair if you'll keep out of mine and we both might find a bit more co-operation to be useful and mutually beneficial."

He paused there, taking another sip of whisky while waiting for the other man to reply.

McCain finally said: "I've spent some time thinking about what your letter suggested. I believe it has merit if – and I say if – we both agree to some sort of truce.

"As for co-operation that, too, has merit. Both of us know how to run a large organisation, but neither of us can do so without the talent and skills to go with it. I don't know how you are fixed but I have a few rough diamonds with surprising skills. Unremarkable a few years ago, they are vital now when we have no schools, no apprenticeships and no craft workshops."

"I see what you mean and feel the same way myself," said Fraser. "I can safeguard Loch Lomond without a second thought. It's what I do, but don't ask me how to grow a potato or milk a cow."

"Well I don't know about cows," said McCain, "but I've got one man who seems to have green fingers. A lot of ideas about growing a lot more vegetables and fruit to improve our diet."

"Sounds interesting," said Fraser. "Perhaps we can use his advice to get our own gardens going again. Nothing much growing there at the moment except weeds."

They talked on and agreed to keep in touch by messengers to start with, Fraser promising to investigate some sites he knew which had long range walkie talkies. Using a supercharge relay might mean being able to communicate between the castles without the need of a journey although a short wave radio would be better, he said. McCain welcomed the idea which between them they broadened out into everything from game drives to foraging circuits.

They sat together for a while longer, finishing their whiskies, then got up to leave. When Fraser offered his hand there was a brief hesitation then McCain took it and they shook. Each seemed stunned at what he was doing.

Outside the two rival groups had kept apart, each staying by their vehicle until Fraser and McCain suddenly appeared and walked down the steps, McCain pointing out where his foot had gone through a rotten board. There was an air of expectancy when they walked towards their men.

McCain spoke first and said: "Mr Fraser has come up with a suggestion that I feel could benefit us all. We are going to try and run a co-operative together. Callander Castle and Loch Lomond Castle will each retain its independence but each will have access to the skills of the other to try and improve everyone's lot."

Fraser then said: "We have agreed to respect our borders, pool our resources and each to help the other when we can. Divided we are small and vulnerable but together we are much stronger and can look to the future. It may not be the future we want, but it will be a better future than the one we have at the moment."

To underline their points the two men shook hands again and this time the gesture seemed a little more natural.

It still mystified John Kane who was cautiously watching the exchange through field glasses two hundred metres away as he lay in undergrowth on an earthen bank.

He and Lieutenant Mayhew had been alerted by the distant sound of an engine. It came from south of their position and they spread out towards the vehicle to try and find it. When a second engine was heard coming towards them from the west they homed in on it and had been observing the meeting from a distance ever since.

What confused John was the way there were clearly two groups of people yet they didn't mix. Why was that? And why were all the men armed and clearly in a state of nervous readiness?

If he was confused before then he certainly didn't know what to make of things when two men came out together from what seemed to be a hunting lodge and proceeded to make little speeches.

John heard castles mentioned and something about working together, but that was all. The two men shook hands and both groups seemed to relax a bit before climbing into their respective vehicles. However, they didn't leave together but in opposite directions, the Land Rover grinding away to the north-east while the 4 x 4 hummed away to the south-west.

When all was quiet John turned to his right and saw Lieutenant Mayhew busy with his field map. It was displayed in a clear plastic map case which Mayhew had drawn one cross on and was now drawing a second.

"What do you make of that?" he asked, handing the case across to John.

"Where are we on this?" asked John and Mayhew pointed to a spot in an area of forest roughly half way between the two crosses.

The officer then explained that the westerly cross was Loch Lomond Castle and the cross to the east was Callander Castle, the two names mentioned in the get-together they had just witnessed. Why then, thought John, had two groups chosen to meet in the middle of nowhere well away from where they came from?

He put this to Mayhew who immediately said: "Has to be because this place was neutral ground. If two sides who are wary of each other want to hold a meeting then they'd have to choose a spot where neither felt threatened. I'd pick a place like this. It's deserted, off the beaten track yet still accessible and you could withdraw smartly if you had to without the risk of being pinned down."

John nodded in agreement and then said: "So what was that all about."

"If you're asking me," said Mayhew, "then my best guess is that we've just seen the local big wigs reach some sort of agreement. You heard that speech about being much stronger together? That can only mean they were divided before, perhaps even opposed to each other. Not many of them on this showing, so it makes sense to work together and not waste manpower. What do you think?"

John nodded in agreement and said: "I can't think of anything else which makes as much sense. I agree everyone was on guard, but you saw how everyone relaxed when those two men shook hands. Looks like an alliance to me, but an alliance of what? If it's two separate communities then how many more people are involved with this?"

"If they think they run this area then they probably do," said Mayhew. "God knows we saw precious little activity during the flight and none at all in this area."

"I think we may have to pay both of them a visit if we can get our machine into the sky again."

And with that they withdrew back to their camp where they were met by a grim faced pilot who told them that tainted fuel was the problem with the helicopter. Captain Church added that it extended to their reserve cans as well.

"Great!" said John. "On foot in the middle of nowhere. Can you radio for more fuel and get us resupplied with some which isn't polluted?"

"Oh I can radio," said Church, "but it does us no good if there's nothing available to fly it up to us."

"Better and better," said John. "Why no back-up?"

"Because I gather that the second machine is needed for urgent tasks in the London area. They'd come if our lives were in danger but I had to tell them they weren't....unless you know different."

John looked across at Dawn who gave him a shrug before he turned back to Church and said he was forced to agree with him. They weren't in immediate danger and the helicopter was safe where it was.

He told everyone what they had just seen and then said: "Now what do we do?"

"Go and make contact with one or other of the two groups you've just watched," said Dawn. "We know where they appear to come from."

John thought about it for a moment and then turned to Lieutenant Mayhew and said: "Which of them appears to be closest to our current position?"

Mayhew consulted his map, made a brief calculation and said: "Callander is a little closer to us but there's not much in it."

"That settles matters. Callander it is. We'll leave first thing in the morning. And if that lodge is good enough for a meeting it is good enough to give us a roof over our heads for tonight. Let's set up camp there."

The group broke up and began to collect equipment and food to take to the lodge as John joined Dawn and said: "Not the start we wanted."

She replied: "At least you know there will be people where we're going and our instructions were to make contact where we could."

John nodded and said: "Let's hope they are friendly."

CHAPTER TWELVE

EMILY Riddle was lost in thought as she sat before a smoky fire in one of five fireplaces in the Great Hall at Stirling Castle.

Her two antique silver baby rattles had told her to come here. She always did what the rattles wanted, but it was more than that. She felt safe here, as if it were her home.

There had been some dissent in the battered old Leyland Olympian bus when she pulled off the motorway and headed for Stirling Castle and even more when they arrived and found the grim structure deserted except for a few bodies.

All anybody seemed able to see was that the place was cold and had no food, the kitchens having been looted. Emily knew food was important, but the castle interested her greatly because it offered a strong defensible base which was just what she'd been looking for. The rattles had looked after her again.

What she was mulling over now was how to feed everyone. They might find some caches of food in Stirling but the sooner they got to widespread foraging the better. A log collapsed in the fireplace and a little shower of sparks went up the chimney but Riddle barely noticed.

Food was power, she thought. Control the food supplies and you controlled everyone who wanted to eat. Sacrifices would have to be made and she was prepared to make them or she was prepared for other people to make them. The silver antiques were clear that nothing would be right again until they were given new life.

She didn't quite understand that part but was sure the rattles would tell her when the time was right. She just needed to do their bidding until then. Right now she needed some sleep. Everyone else had spread out through the castle, taking bedrooms or just curling up to slumber wherever was comfortable enough to do so. Riddle was happy to stay put in her fireside chair. She craved oblivion and hoped the screaming children would stay out of her dreams....but they didn't.

A procession of sobbing youngsters reproached her for letting them down without ever allowing her to find out what mistake she had made. The result was gritty eyes and a drained feeling when her tortured dreams finally left her and she got up shortly after it was light.

She walked slowly to the kitchen and found a dusty mess with broken glass and crockery everywhere, but she saw a range and set to in an attempt to get it going. After twenty minutes she had a lot of smoke but not much fire, struggling to use the remains of smashed chairs and other furniture to coax the range to life. There was some anthracite in a bag but not much and Riddle realised that fuel would also be a consideration if they were to stay here. For the moment she just wanted a little hot water, so she scooped up a discarded saucepan with a dent in one side and went outside into a small courtyard.

A silent ornamental fountain contained rainwater and she dipped some up before returning inside where she put the saucepan on a hob which spluttered, turning stray drips of water into steam as the range heated up.

Riddle explored all the kitchen cupboards while she waited for the water to boil and managed to find a half used packet of herbal teabags and a battered tin of cocktail sausages. Hardly a feast but it would do for a meagre breakfast and she searched the wreckage to try and find an unbroken mug, settling for a bone china teacup with lily-of-the-valley painted on it.

Clouds of steam were soon pouring off the bubbling saucepan and Riddle snatched her hand away from the handle before picking up a grubby tea towel to grasp the metal and pour a stream of water into her cup.

Immediately the kitchen filled with the fragrance of herbs which Riddle sniffed at appreciatively before pulling the ring top off the tin and beginning to munch several sausages.

There was still no sign of life from gang members by the time she finished and Riddle decided to explore and see what else the castle might have to offer her.

She wandered down corridors full of dust, rubbish and fallen paintings before finding a small library. Riddle barely gave the books a second glance but she was drawn to one wall which displayed a giant framed map of the immediate countryside.

A vast area of forest dominated land to the west and north west and she swiftly saw that the countryside surrounding Stirling was made up of a network of small inter-linked communities. So much the better.

Riddle already knew that the Red Plague had reduced teaming cities such as Edinburgh to the level of a village. If the same attrition rate were applied here then they should have little trouble looting what they wanted from small towns and villages where few if any people had survived. It would take time to build up useable stores, but winter was coming to an end and they had more than enough time to loot what they needed to survive the next winter. Her thoughts were a little vague as to what to do after that, but she was sure something would come up.

Time to get to work and she began to roust out members of her gang, coaxing some and threatening others but always getting them moving towards the kitchens. The range now had two saucepans and a jam kettle steaming away and the first thing Riddle did when everyone had gathered was to approach a man with a bushy moustache and a bloody bandage on his left arm.

"You," she said. "Your only job today is to collect wood, see if you can find some more anthracite and keep this range going. If it goes out, so do you."

He gave a frightened nod and she turned her attention to the rest of the gang.

"Everyone else, you'll be split into two. Half will come with me in the bus while we prospect further afield and the rest of you will start to comb the town to see what you can find.

"I want food cans, dried goods, blankets and mattresses so everyone has a bed to sleep on. Look for dynamo torches and batteries, oil lamps, anything we can use.

"Those staying here, I want the castle cleared of any bodies. Take them down and throw them in the river. Find out how many bedrooms there are here and don't use the bathrooms too much until we find out if the sewers still work. And we'll need a dustbin of water in every toilet. I don't want to stink the place up before we've even settled in."

"So we're staying here then?" asked Derby, looking doubtfully around at the gloomy kitchen.

"Yes, we're staying," said Riddle. "Let's see anyone try and take a castle away from us. We could hold off an army and there probably aren't enough people left alive round here to make up a football team. Of course, you could go back to Edinburgh if you want."

"No," said Derby hastily. "Here is just fine."

"Good," said Riddle. She then raised her arm to roughly divide everyone into two groups and said: "Now, this half is coming with me. Get yourself a cup of tea and meet me at the bus in fifteen minutes. The rest of you are with Squirrel."

She pointed at a small nervous man wearing a tweed cap and continued: "Don't think that just because I'm gone you can loaf about all day. I'm expecting results when I get back. Don't disappoint me."

With that she gave a nod and began to walk back to the Great Hall leaving behind a small scrum of people trying to find any receptacle capable of holding tea. There was a lot of grumbling from Squirrel's group who were forced to wait their turn at the boiling water, but they knew better than to make an issue of matters. Previous complainants had developed a nasty habit of dying suddenly.

Outside the castle walls Riddle had climbed into the bus cab and switched the ignition on to check fuel levels. The gauge said they had used half their available fuel just to get here. They urgently needed more diesel or a new form of transport and Riddle decided that a couple of large vans would have to be found with the bus kept for emergencies.

She got out and walked over to a point where she could see the city laid out beneath her. A cold wind tugged at her clothing and made her hair swirl across her face, but she made no move to brush it away.

More and more Riddle appreciated what the rattles had done for her. Here was a place which a few dozen could defend against hundreds, but it would do her no good if they couldn't establish themselves in the castle and to do that they need food and warmth.

Her keen eyes swept the area immediately below the castle and she reached a decision as those chosen to accompany her began to arrive.

When the last member of her search party had reached the bus she turned and went back to them.

"Change of plan," she said. "We need diesel for the bus."

She pointed at two men and said: "You two won't be coming with me. I want you to find some fuel cans and spend the day tracking down diesel wherever you can find it. Nothing polluted. Only use pure fuel. When I get back

I want to see a full tank and enough spare to refuel when needed.

"The rest of you are on foot with me. The bus can't be used yet, so I want two large vans. There must be some still useable here. Find them and bring them back here. We can afford one hour for this, no more. Fire one shot when you find a van you can get going. Everyone back to the castle if they hear two shots."

The group just stared at her until Riddle barked: "Well, get going!" at which there was a stumbling rush through the gateway and down into the city. Riddle followed but walked off at an angle on her own. She had something else she wanted to find.

Searching for vans proved both easier and harder than they had anticipated. One street yielded three vans on its own, but the first had a buckled front offside wheel after smashing into a wall and a second van had jammed itself between a street lamp and several abandoned cars. The decaying skeleton of the driver was still behind the wheel.

Only the third van left on a sloping driveway was intact. Its doors were unlocked but the battery was dead and the three men who found it wasted some time debating the best way to get it started. They couldn't push one way because the street was uphill. The other way made the incline work in their favour but the street was blocked by vehicles slowly rusting in the drab morning light.

They eventually decided to try and start the van by
running it down towards the barricade of vehicles. If this
worked they would reverse back and simply drive away
up hill. If it worked.

A small man called Bentley was elected driver while a
slow-thinking giant called Oggie and a bearded man
called Burton provided the pushing power.

All four tyres were almost flat, but a tool kit in the rear of
the van yielded a foot pump and a few minutes work
inflated them again.

Keys had been found tucked behind the sun shield but
first they rocked the van to free the brakes. Bentley then
turned the ignition to the "on" position, selected second
gear and yelled at the other two to push as he released the
handbrake. All went well as the van rapidly gathered pace
down the driveway, but Burton lost his balance and fell
over as Bentley heaved the wheel left to direct the van
down the road. Oggie couldn't keep up and panted to a
halt, watching as the van gathered pace until there was a
bucking roar as Bentley engaged gear and fought to keep
the van in a straight line as the engine bit and the
barricade rushed towards him.

Somehow he was able to steer, rev the engine and brake
all at the same time as the van came to a spluttering stop
almost touching a crumpled Nissan Javelin with a
smashed passenger window.

Bentley kept the engine going, glancing at the fuel gauge which showed a nearly full tank, and then very carefully engaged reverse gear and slowly pulled back up the sloping street until he was able to turn back into the driveway he had just rolled out of.

He was winding down the driver's window when Burton and Oggie appeared beside him with grins on their faces.

"Who's got the gun?" asked Bentley.

Burton fumbled in his coat pocket and produced a battered automatic pistol which he waved about.

"Right," said Bentley. "Fire one shot and let's get this show on the road and back to the castle."

Burton flinched as he fired the pistol then both men lost no time in climbing into the front where, after some confusion over seatbelts, neither decided to wear one.

When they arrived back at Stirling Castle and parked next to the bus they got out and waited for the others to return. They didn't wait long as another shot rang out in the distance and within fifteen minutes a second van arrived. This one had a smashed nearside headlight but apart from that looked serviceable.

The remaining van searchers dribbled back to stand around chatting and looking at the vehicles but there was no sign of Riddle. All talk died away when she eventually arrived on a bicycle.

"Not bad," she said, looking at the vans and then at two men pushing a wheelbarrow full of fuel cans up to the group.

"And we even have fuel for the bus. Have you checked that the diesel is pure?"

Both men with the wheelbarrow hastily nodded and one said: "Came from a little back street garage. Used tubing to get it out of the tanks and there's more where this came from."

"Did you seal the tanks again?" asked Riddle.

Yes," said the man, "and we even pushed a car over them to hide the entry."

"Good work. Fill the bus and put any spare cans of fuel in the gatekeeper's office over there," she said, pointing at a door in the archway wall leading in to the castle. "Then you can join us in the vans for a bit of foraging. The rest of you, into the vans. And put my bicycle in the back as well."

It didn't take long to refuel the bus and both vans were soon edging out of the city where they reached a roundabout littered with abandoned vehicles and a number of bodies, tattered clothing fluttering over exposed rib cages through which dead grass poked.

One way led back on to the M9 while another exit headed off up the A84. Both vehicles halted and Bentley in the lead van looked at Riddle sat beside him, waiting for her to choose which way they were to go.

She didn't hesitate, taking out the antique silver baby rattles and giving them a shake before holding them to her ear as the men around her stared in horrified fascination at what she was doing. Then Riddle gave a nod, pointed to the A84 and said: "That way."

The road angled north-west and proved to be very slow going with several blockages caused by crashed vehicles to negotiate and a flooded area which fortunately proved to be passable with care.

Both vans made several miles in the first two hours until Riddle called a halt by a sign with a huge roaring lion on it advertising a turn-off to a safari park about half a mile ahead.

"We'll try here first," she said. "Lions need feeding but so do visitors and this far off the beaten track maybe looters have passed the place by.

This proved to be the case when they arrived and pulled up close to the park entrance where shrubs had gone wild and grown partially across turnstile kiosks.

Riddle got out and had taken several steps towards the entrance before she realised that no-one else had moved.

"Come on!" she shouted back at the vans. "We haven't got all day. An hour here and then we move on. Everyone spread out and collect any food they can find particularly canned goods."

Again there was no movement and Riddle became angry.

"What's the matter with you all?"

"Maybe the lions are still here," ventured Bentley, his gaze darting about.

"And maybe they're all long since dead with no-one to feed them," hit back Riddle.

Slowly the vans emptied until more than a dozen very reluctant foragers assembled and joined Riddle on her walk into the overgrown attraction.

Her observation about dead animals proved prophetic and there was no sign of life wherever they went. All the fences and barriers were intact while inside enclosures there were only heaps of bone to show where once lions, tigers, giraffes and even elephants had provided excitement for visitors.

Indoor cafe areas were littered with dead flies, dust and cobwebs but the kitchen areas yielded industrial tins of everything from beans to burgers which were gleefully carted away to the vans.

By early afternoon the vans were back on the road, continuing up the A84. They made occasional stops to check and ransack isolated homes they saw from the road, but their crude searches turned up little they could use as previous looters had virtually picked them clean.

They had just driven past a barn missing half its roof and were driving through the small town of Callander approaching a junction when Riddle's hand suddenly slammed down on the dashboard. She shouted for Bentley to stop and he hastily complied to the sound of skidding behind them as the second van slid on gravel. Its driver had been caught out by the unexpected halt and narrowly missed colliding with the back of the lead van, something which earned him a glare from Riddle when she got out and stood in the road.

A moment later and she had walked forward to the junction where she squatted and looked at the road.

Mile after mile they had travelled with never a sign of another human being yet here, in a remote area, was a junction with not one but several clearly visible tyre tracks and scuffs in the road surface.

The road they came from was signposted "A81", but it now had its sides choked with grass while undergrowth slowly spreading out into the highway showed evidence of where a vehicle had recently mangled the more adventurous plants. In the distance she could see the loom of high ground and a vast spread of trees back as far as the eye could see.

Riddle turned away and looked ahead up the A84 where the main street continued with a mixture of sturdy stone-built homes and businesses. She bit her lip in thought and then made a decision before walking back to the van and round to the side door which she slid open to reveal half a dozen men inside, their eyes blinking at the sudden light.

"Pass me out my bicycle," she said, holding out one hand.

The men made haste to comply and Riddle took the machine, twirled the pedals to a comfortable position and eased the bicycle forward to the driver's window where Bentley looked out expectantly.

"Stay here," she said. "I'm going to take a ride ahead for a little look and I don't want engines to tip anyone off that I'm coming. Turn the vans round and wait for me. I'll be no more than half an hour. Then we go back to the castle."

Bentley nodded his understanding and leaned back in his seat to watch Riddle ride slowly off up the road until she dwindled from sight.

A man called Brody wandered over from the second van, leaned against the window and said: "What's happening?"

"Her ladyship is going for a look-see," said Bentley. "We have to turn the vans round and wait which is fine by me. I'm hungry and I want to get back."

Up ahead Riddle was in the heart of the little town with cars abandoned everywhere and a few bodies lying in its single main street which boasted pubs, several shops and a small supermarket. All of them had smashed windows and seemed to have been roughly looted.

Further on the town quickly petered out as the road sloped slightly upwards revealing a single huge industrial building up a lane off to the right bearing a large sign, Museum of Toys. No children left to enjoy that, she thought, and cycled on past the empty museum car park, the land quickly curving over a ridge before sweeping down away from her towards what looked like a little chocolate box fairy castle, but Riddle had no time to admire the view. She had spotted movement down near the castle.

Hastily she got off her bicycle and dragged it into the cover of a straggly hedge from where she watched for a quarter of an hour, seeing people come and go but not in numbers. There were several vehicles including a large lorry but none in use, smoke wisping from a single chimney. So a small community but apparently a viable one.

She noted how there were no obvious defences, how the road curved down to an overgrown gravel driveway which swept up to the castle and how there was plenty of cover for an attacking force. They were almost asking to be raided, she thought, eventually edging away before turning her bicycle round and quickly freewheeling back to town and the two vans waiting for her at the crossroads.

When she arrived she went straight to the side of
Bentley's van, handed her bicycle inside and hopped into
the front passenger seats.

"Back to Stirling," she said, "and nice and slowly for the
first few miles. I've found a fat plum for us to visit and I
don't want them to have the slightest hint we're even in
the area."

Bentley nodded his understanding, started the van's
engine and carefully pulled away down the A84, quickly
leaving behind the junction where Riddle had spotted the
tyre tracks. When they passed the empty barn Bentley
accelerated a little to more than 15mph, watchful for road
collapses and fallen branches as the two vans slowly
faded into the distance.

When all engine sound had gone, a grubby hearse
appeared from behind the barn and Lauren Fane got out,
shading her eyes to look down the A84 after Riddle's
vans.

Now what had they seen which had made them suddenly
turn round and retrace their steps, she thought? What so
interested Riddle that she would drive away instead of
towards it?

Lauren decided to take a look herself and instead of
following the vans she ordered Ashley to turn right and
continue on up the road, quickly calling a halt when they
reached the junction and saw the same tyre tracks that
Riddle had.

They came from a seemingly remote area but the road ahead was also marked, so she decided to go on and check it herself, hopping back in the hearse which whispered away.

They soon reached the little town that Riddle had found and drove up through it, past the Museum of Toys to the ridge crest where a sharp command from Lauren saw Ashley stop and allow the hearse to coast back off the skyline.

They parked and Lauren took Steve with her, inching forward by a hedge until they could look down on the little castle Riddle had spotted.

They saw movement as a man came out of some rear buildings and disappeared towards the back of the main building.

So this was what Riddle had spotted! And it didn't take rocket science to work out why she was interested. Her gang needed food and this place looked in decent order. They must have stores.

Almost without thinking Lauren decided she would warn the castle occupants that they had been spotted by a gang which violently took what it wanted. Then she slowed, realising that even if she was believed, what could they do against the sort of force that Riddle was bound to bring back?

Thoughtfully she edged back to the hearse and directed Ashley to turn round and go back to the junction where they'd seen the tyre tracks. They must have come from somewhere.

Perhaps there was another community in the area in which case they might be encouraged to join forces against Riddle, especially once they knew it was fight or die. It wouldn't hurt to drive a few miles down this minor road and see what they could find.

CHAPTER THIRTEEN

LIGHT was beginning to fade as the hearse continued on, Ashley being teased with much laughter by the other men when he flicked on the vehicle's side lights.

"Don't want to get stopped by the law!" said Roddy as Jack made sounds like a police siren.

Lauren smiled and said: "Leave him alone. It will be dark soon and we need somewhere to stop. You lot might want to keep your eyes open for a house or a building of some sort we can camp in."

They continued on for a while and the countryside changed, becoming more rugged as forest appeared and closed in around them.

Ashley switched on the main headlights but they revealed nothing except the flash of tree trunks and the road ahead winding and dipping as it dropped down inclines, crossed small stone bridges and climbed up to the next ridge.

Soon it was pitch dark and they hadn't seen a single building. Lauren was beginning to think of turning round and taking their chances in the barn they had hidden behind to avoid Riddle when the headlights showed up a great smear on the road ahead.

She got Ashley to pull up and then carefully got out, looking warily at the surrounding trees before advancing towards where the forest curved in to reveal a muddy track disappearing into the darkness.

The dark smear on the road had been caused by tyre tracks depositing earth and leaf mould as the vehicle swung out of the forest track and on to the road. Lauren relaxed a bit as she reasoned that whoever had been here was long gone or they would have met them on the lonely road they had just driven along. She noticed a similar smear coming on to the road further ahead and fading away in the same direction they had been travelling.

So two vehicles, each using the forest track but each departing in a different direction. Intrigued, she decided this track might be worth exploring to see what it held that was of such interest in the middle of nowhere.

Lauren got back in the hearse and said: "Two sets of tyre tracks, each coming out of this track and leaving in a different direction. Let's have a little look and see what's important enough to attract people, but let's go nice and slowly eh?"

Everyone nodded, took a firm grip on their weapons and looked a little less relaxed. This was wild country and anyone they met might not exactly welcome visitors.

The hearse humped and bumped its way along the track, Lauren noting where a fallen tree had been dragged to one side, and they were soon turning slightly as the track curved round and then ended in an open area with a darkened building set back among several large trees.

There were no lights and the place looked deserted as Ashley turned the hearse in a circle until it was pointing out back down the track to the road. He kept the engine running as Lauren and Griff got out and began to walk towards the dilapidated hunting lodge. They didn't get far.

"Can we help you?" came a voice from the darkness.

Lauren and Griff clutched their shotguns and looked wildly about, unable to see a single person in the gloom.

"Please keep your weapons pointing down while you tell us what you are doing here," said the voice.

The whole place still seemed deserted and Lauren and Griff realised that they were completely at the mercy of whoever was out there.

"We don't want any trouble," said Lauren, turning first one way and then the other. "We were only looking to put a roof over our heads for the night."

"Well you've found a place," said the voice, John stepping slowly into view. "The question is, should we share?"

"It's always nice to share," said Lauren facing him and John smiled at that before raising his voice and saying: "What do you think?"

A voice from the darkness behind Lauren said: "There are four more in the hearse. What is this? An undertakers' convention?"

"As long as they're not looking for customers," said John.

"We're not," said Lauren, "but we know someone who might be."

John looked at her for a moment and then said: "You'd all best come inside. The least we can do is give you a cup of coffee."

Lauren and Griff looked slightly startled at that. It had been a while since either had tasted proper coffee yet these people made it seem an everyday drink they talked so casually of it.

Griff gave a shrug, still scanning the darkness, so Lauren said: "Coffee would be nice."

She carefully returned to the hearse, kept her shotgun but told the others to leave their weapons inside when they got out. All the time she watched the clearing dimly lit by the hearse's headlights. Two smaller lights suddenly winked on, a lantern at the top of the lodge porch steps and a second larger one inside the lodge.

Lauren led her group towards the steps and was warned about a broken one as she began to climb to the entrance. At the top she found a battery-powered lantern while inside there seemed to be the softer glow of an oil lamp. She had still to see a single person. These were very cautious people, Lauren thought, but they must be reasonable or she and everyone with her would have been dead by now.

Inside there was a woman waiting for them and off to her right two soldiers in uniform casually covered the reception area from the doorway of what looked like a bar. Curiouser and curiouser, thought Lauren, wondering how these people came to be here.

The more she looked the more she saw. There was a row of back packs against the far wall of the bar together with a neat stack of steel boxes with recessed handles and she could smell cooking.

"Bit much to take in all at once, isn't it?" said Dawn, stepping forward with a smile. "I'm Dawn and the dishy one behind you is John, my husband."

Lauren introduced herself and turned to see a stockily built man in a wax jacket over thick trousers thrust into laced boots. He was carrying a rifle which looked heavy and nasty. Behind him was some sort of officer and another soldier. So at least four of them, thought Lauren.

As if he could read her mind John said: "There are a few more of us out on perimeter duty, so we saw your headlights coming. We don't like surprises. Best you come on in and tell us why you are here."

He stepped past Lauren and led the way into the dusty bar, gesturing at sofa seating for Lauren and her men who warily took places either side of a long low table, aware that the soldiers were behind them stood back to command a good field of fire.

John and Dawn settled into armchairs with the officer behind them who instructed one of the soldiers to bring coffees.

"Now what brings you calling on us in the still watches of the night?" asked John.

Lauren looked at Griff and then said: "We've been tracking a mass murderess."

Now it was John's turn to be startled and he glanced at Dawn to see that she, too, was taken aback.

"Go on," said John.

"She and her gang terrorised Edinburgh. God knows how many they killed including my grandfather. We decided she needed stopping and ran her out of the city. We're tracking her to make sure she goes and keeps going, but I fear she may have decided on a new headquarters."

"And where might that be?" asked Dawn.

"Stirling Castle," replied Lauren. "We followed her up here today. She seems interested in a smaller castle north east of here and she may be planning to raid it."

John and Dawn both turned and looked at Lieutenant Mayhew who said: "It could be Callander Castle. It's in the right direction."

"How many men does this mass murderess have?" asked John.

"Perhaps a dozen or more up here in two vans today, but they had at least the same number out foraging in Stirling this morning. I'd say about thirty in all, some women."

John whistled quietly as the soldier returned with a tray of coffees and handed them out.

This gang outnumbered them at least three to one and, while John hoped their weapons were much better, it would be best to stay out of their way until he had a lot better idea of what they faced. There was no chance of taking on such a large group yet his brief had been to explore Scotland and make contact with any decent sized groups he could find. If Lauren's guess was right then one of those groups might soon be on the receiving end of a raid. Would it really happen and, if it did, could he afford to stand by and see innocent people killed when Anderson had stressed how important his mission was?

He put this thought to one side and asked: "You mentioned Edinburgh. What's the city like now?"

"People measured in hundreds where there used to be hundreds of thousands," said Lauren. "We brought together a dozen of the biggest groups we could find and still barely mustered two hundred people. It comes to something when I say we won but perhaps ten percent of the surviving population in the entire city died. Most still alive exist in different areas in one or two buildings at most. They're surviving but not for much longer without a source of regular food. A lot died this winter and a lot more will die next winter. They need domestic livestock such as chickens and pigs to grow for meat, cows to raise for milk and enough concentrated hands to clear and farm land. Do that and in a century's time you may have a pale shadow of the Edinburgh that was. Don't do that and in five years time there will be no Edinburgh."

She fell silent and a grim faced John looked at Dawn who said: "What if we were to help you? Food to tide you over, a guaranteed source of power, experts to help with the infrastructure. Would that interest you?"

Lauren looked at Griff and the rest of the men who seemed stunned. She asked: "You can't do that. There are only a few of you. So where are you from and who do you speak for?"

John dropped his bombshell: "We're from Cornwall but the help would be coming from Australia, maybe New Zealand and Japan as well."

Even Lauren was stunned and silenced by that, but she pulled herself together and said: "I always wondered what had happened in other parts of the world, whether anyone had survived, whether a city somewhere had been spared."

She paused here, her mind struggling to embrace a narrow world of survival which had just expanded out of all recognition.

"It sounds fantastic," she said, "but nobody does something for nothing. What do you want from us?"

"To help set up Recovery Councils for Scotland," replied John. "To bring survivors together as a group where their numbers will count and mean something for a recovery. If they stay divided in isolated pockets there will be no future. It has to be a community effort."

"Sounds good, but if things are so bad here then how come Australia, New Zealand and Japan have survived so well?"

"They didn't," said Dawn. "They lost millions, but they found a vaccine and then the plague just seemed to wither and millions survived. No-one knows why. Now those countries which can support themselves are trying to help those who can't. Most of Europe is in a bad way apart from a few Mediterranean sites, but Australia has brought two nuclear container ships to Plymouth and London loaded with food, equipment and staff. Their brief is to set up recovery councils in London, the South West, Wales, the North and Scotland. We're the advance party, a sort of whistle-stop tour to see where survivors are and what they need."

John nodded and said: "From what you say Edinburgh would be a good place to start. You already seem to have drawn people together to defend themselves. Perhaps they can be encouraged to pull together to build a new life."

"Perhaps," said Lauren, "but not while the likes of Riddle and her gang are out there. No-one would ever be safe and we couldn't build for the future constantly looking over our shoulder with one hand on a gun."

"Then we'll have to do what we can to protect people," said John, "and it seems that a visit to chat with whoever's at Callander Castle might be top of our list of things to do. They need to know about this gang. If they have people in numbers at the castle then they may be able to defend themselves, but if they are only a few then they'll have to find others to band together with or risk being overwhelmed."

"If Riddle is thinking of an attack on this castle then she'll come quickly," said Lauren. "Everything she did in Edinburgh was brutal and fast. Strike, kill, loot and leave.

That's what she did then and she's not a leopard which will change its spots. She'll do it again here."

"Sounds like we may not have much time," said John turning to Lauren. "Are you willing to help us?"

"Of course," said Lauren, "but if it comes to a fight we only have a few pistols and shotguns with not a lot of ammunition."

"Let us worry about any fighting," said Lieutenant Mayhew. "Hopefully it won't come to that, but we'll be prepared. Numbers are not on our side, but let's see how many people Callander has to offer."

John looked round at everyone then said to Lauren: "Right, all this talking has made me hungry. Let's eat. Care to join us?"

"Sure," said Lauren. "This lot never turns down a meal."

There were smiles from Griff and the rest at that before everyone got up and went over to where small field stoves heated a thick ham and chorizo soup. There were biscuits and cheese to go with it and packaged slices of fruit cake for desert.

"Been a while since we've tasted anything like this," said Griff, blowing on a spoonful of soup.

There was rumbling agreement at that, but everyone was too focussed on the food to actually speak. When the meal was over John served whisky to those who wanted it while Lieutenant Mayhew sent those soldiers inside the lodge out to relieve the perimeter guards so they could come in and eat.

John settled back in an armchair and told Lauren: "There are rooms upstairs. Dawn and I are in one, Lieutenant Mayhew and his men are in three others but there are still some empty rooms, plenty for you. This place was used to coping with hunting parties so there's a lot of accommodation. Get your heads down when you want. Dawn and I are on first watch."

Lauren offered herself and her men for sentry duty but was politely turned down.

John said: "Lieutenant Mayhew has got a rota and the men know each other and us. Wouldn't want you getting shot because you're mistaken for an intruder. You're best to get some sleep while you can. We'll look after security."

With that Lauren sent Ashley and Steve out to get a few things from the hearse and they all said their good-nights and trooped upstairs by the light of a dynamo lantern.

The hunting theme was less pronounced upstairs, but the landing they reached still had a corridor lined with paintings and prints as well as several sets of antlers. A stuffed Scottish wildcat snarled at them from a large glass case with gold lettering on it which revealed the animal had been shot in 1911 by an A.McTavish.

Several rooms had doors open through which army kit could be seen, but the rooms at the end of the corridor all had doors closed. When Lauren opened the first one she could see why.

A powerful musty odour of damp, decay and disuse assailed her nostrils and she hastily stepped past an ornate double bed in search of a window which she forced open, cold night air flooding in but soon banishing the stale smell in the room.

"Help yourself everyone. This one's mine," said Lauren as her men trooped further along and began opening other doors.

Each room contained either a double bed or two singles, dark furnishings and more hunting prints and trophies lending an almost funereal air to the accommodation.

There was a knock on her open door and Griff stepped in.

"We're in the next three rooms," he said, "two of us in each. You be OK in here?"

"I'll be fine," she said. "Makes a change not having to watch our own backs."

"You trust this lot then?" asked Griff.

Lauren smiled and said: "Everything they've got is new, no hand-me-downs, no torn clothing, their faces aren't pinched from having to scavenge and above all else they are squeaky clean. Now, does that sound like anyone you've met recently from round these parts?"

"Not really, now you put it that way," said Griff.

"They could have killed us but they didn't. Instead we've been fed and watered and given beds for the night. Now they're doing guard duty. No, wherever else this lot comes from it's not Scotland."

Then she came up close to him and said: "I think we might be being rescued!"

Griff looked startled and then gave a short laugh. "Been a while since I was rescued!" he said. "You've a candle by the bed. Sleep tight and we're all just down the hall if you need anything."

"Thanks," said Lauren, putting a hand on his arm at which Griff gave her a nod and left, closing the door behind him.

Lauren took a cigarette lighter from her pocket and lit a short thick candle which showed evidence of having been lit before. There was the crackle of dust and then the candle began to burn brightly.

Clouds of dust roiled up when she pulled back the bed coverlet and she coughed, hastily stepping close to the partially open window until the dust settled. The bed had a blanket and a pillow but no pillowcase or sheets and a cursory search of a dark oak wardrobe and chest of drawers didn't reveal any.

Lauren shrugged and began to take off her boots. A bed was a bed and she was tired. She'd have liked a wash but she'd make do until the morning. With that she climbed into bed, pulled the blanket and coverlet over her and blew out the candle.

Downstairs all the soldiers had been fed and John and Dawn had gone outside with one soldier to take first watch while everyone else bedded down.

The area was remote and the likelihood of anyone paying a visit even remoter, but they took no chances and stationed the soldier at the back of the lodge while John took Dawn over to a group of three large trees and settled down for their three hour shift.

Leaves under cover were largely dry and John swept an area clear so they wouldn't give their position away when they moved. They then began to chat quietly as they watched and listened.

"What do you think of Lauren and her boys?" asked Dawn.

"They're a unit," said John. "You can see they've fought together and they're close."

"But are they the stuff of a Recovery Council?"

"Perhaps, perhaps not," said John. "Only time will tell but right now they can really help us. I can't just approach whoever's at Callander and say they're about to be attacked by a mass murderess and a bunch of thugs.

They'd laugh at me. But if I say that and then produce Lauren to tell them about what might be heading their way they'll be a lot more likely to consider what we say and do something about it."

"And you, of course, have a few ideas about that!" said Dawn.

John smiled in the darkness and replied: "I do have an idea or two but it will depend on what this castle looks like."

He refused to be drawn more and they moved on to chat about the baby Dawn was expecting in July.

"What shall we call him?" asked Dawn.

"Or her," said John.

"I don't care what we have as long as the baby is healthy. Do you think we can trust Jed with being godfather? He was all over the place when Becky gave birth."

"That's because it was personal to him," said John. "When he has to tackle ordinary situations he's totally reliable. No better man to have at your back. He asked me to be godfather to their daughter, Tilly, so the least I can do is ask him to be godfather to our child."

"We're going to have to find somewhere to live. Launceston is fine but it's really too far from the manor if we need help," said Dawn.

"I always said I'd mothball my house at some stage but, with a baby to consider, I don't want to give it up until we've definitely got a place to live at Waterfall."

"Fair enough," said Dawn. "Then you'd better get building. You've only about six months until baby arrives and you don't want me to say that Daddy's doesn't care enough to build us a home!"

"Very funny," said John. "Bit difficult to build anything from the wilds of Scotland. That's one job I'm not thinking about now."

Their conversation turned to other things. There was talk of the survivors Lauren said existed in Edinburgh, what they would need and how to get it to them.

Almost before they realised it their three hours were up and there were sounds of soldiers coming up behind them. They said they'd heard nothing and left them to it, walking back to the lodge and quietly climbing the stairs to the bedroom containing their packs.

Dawn lit a candle. She had earlier given the bed coverlet a good shaking out of the window, so the worst of the accumulated dust had gone, but there was still a small cloud generated by John hastily climbing into bed and pulling the blanket and coverlet over himself, teeth chattering and his breath visible in the room's musty air.

"Hurry up!" he said. "It's freezing in here."

Dawn quickly took off her coat and boots, shivering as she did so, before she blew the candle out and clambered hastily over him into bed, yanking her share of the blanket and coverlet to her side.

She then drew the bed coverings over her shoulders, snuggled up and hugged him to her.

"Well as long as you are warm and comfortable!" said John, trying to cover himself with the remaining blanket and coverlet.

"Think of the heat I'm providing for you!" said Dawn, rubbing her breasts slowly against him.

John tried to turn and face her to better appreciate what she was doing but Dawn held him close and stopped him.

"Oh no you don't!" she said. "I need sleep and if you turn round we both know what will happen next."

"I thought you liked what happens next," said John.

"I do," said Dawn, "but I like it too much. Once you start touching me I'm practically cheering you on, so let's just try and sleep. It's really too cold for anything else."

So they did try to sleep and at some point they drifted off, waking only once in the early hours when the next shift of sentries went out to keep watch.

By the time morning came the heat from John and Dawn's bodies had dragged up their room temperature to the point where it was cold but they could no longer see their breath.

Dawn turned half on her back and stretched so John turned to face her and rested his head on her breasts.

"Now who's getting comfortable," said Dawn. She stretched again and John could feel her muscles tauten beneath him.

"We should really get up," he said, rubbing his cheek over her nipples so the stubble made them come erect to a hiss from Dawn.

"Maybe in a while," she said throatily, lightly raking her nails down his back which made him shiver, but the sound of boots in the corridor outside made them laugh, banishing any lusty thoughts, and they relaxed.

"Who's getting out first?" asked John.

"You can," said Dawn. "Tell me if it's really cold," and she drew the covers more tightly around herself.

"Thanks," said John, tensing himself before swiftly throwing the blanket back and reaching for his boots. A few clumsy moments trying to do up the laces and he stood up.

"Your turn next!" he said nastily.

When she showed no signs of getting up he reached his cold hand under the covers and grabbed warm flesh, her gasp of surprise sending her bolt upright. John dodged the pillow she threw at him.

"Rise and shine," he said, putting distance between them. "We've got a busy day ahead."

She gave him a sultry pout, aware of its effect on him, but John was immune to her wiles, tossed her coat on the bed beside her and said: "Your boots are here. I'll go down and see about something hot to drink."

Dawn stuck her tongue out at him, John grinning back before opening the door and leaving her to get up as he descended to the reception area and walked into the bar where Lieutenant Mayhew stood drinking coffee next to two trays of boiling water full of small oblong tins.

"Coffee?" he asked John who nodded in appreciation. "And I'd better get one for madam as well," he added.

"Coming up," said Mayhew, dipping mugs into the trays and putting them to one side where he simply ripped the tops off two plastic sachets and poured out powdered coffee from each.

"Sugar?" he asked, but John shook his head and said: "Sweet enough."

He took the mugs Mayhew offered, spooned half a measure of powdered milk into each and had it stirred and ready when the doors opened and Dawn walked in. He handed her a mug and she thanked him before noticing the trays and asking Mayhew what was cooking.

"The breakfast of champions, bacon roll," he said. "At least I think it's bacon roll. We also have bacon steak, bacon and sausage compress, bacon fritter and bacon and egg full English. They're all in tins and they all look the same to me. Probably taste the same as well."

"That's reassuring," said Dawn. "At least it sounds filling."

"It is," said Mayhew. "One tin per man – and woman – plus two hardtack biscuits. We share the strawberry jam. It's in a tube."

"Sounds delicious," said John a little doubtfully. "No smoked salmon then?"

"You missed it," said Mayhew. "Sold the last just before you came down."

John nodded and said: "I'll have the bacon roll then."

"Me too," said Dawn.

"Be right with you in a moment. Chef's a perfectionist and feels the tins need a minute or two more."

Dawn and John took their coffees back out to reception and on to the veranda. They righted two of the recliners blown into a heap by storms and carefully checked they would still take their weight before sitting down, steam eddying from their mugs in the cold morning air.

"So," said Dawn, taking a sip of coffee. "How are you going to approach Callander?"

"Noisily," said John. "I don't want to surprise them and I don't want any accidents. I doubt they get many visitors."

"Who goes and who stays?" asked Dawn.

"Good question," said John, taking a sip of his own coffee.

"There's Lauren and her man to drive the hearse. Myself, Mayhew and two soldiers. That's six. The hearse won't take much more and if we hit trouble I don't want it overloaded. We may need to get out fast if they pick a fight. If they're friendly we'll take the bikes out and send the driver back for the rest of you."

"What if they don't go along with what you've got to say?"

"Then we pull out back to the lodge, but if they've got a grain of sense they'll appreciate our help. Maybe this lunatic won't attack them, but Lauren thought it pretty likely. She has some nasty previous."

At that moment Mayhew stuck his head outside and said: "Breakfast is served."

They needed no second telling and followed him back into the bar which was now rich with the smell of cooking. Three soldiers were already finishing their meal and they left to relieve the sentries so they could eat.

John and Dawn took the meal they were given, grabbed an Army issue field cutlery set each and sat down to eat. When they finished they washed their plate and utensils in some of the spare boiled water from cooking and handed them to a soldier packing up the mini kitchen into two small aluminium cases.

Lieutenant Mayhew came over to them as they finished and they discussed with him what they planned to do. The only change he made was to increase the number of soldiers they were taking from two to three.

"Better too much firepower than not enough," he said and John nodded agreement.

"Choose your men then Lieutenant," he said. "The sooner we are off the better. Daylight's wasting."

Mayhew nodded and moved off to talk with one soldier while John collected his gear from upstairs and brought it down to reception.

Ten minutes later those who were going had packed themselves into the hearse and Ashley had pulled away from the lodge, driving slowly and carefully along the undulating track until they turned on to the A81 and headed back towards the crossroads, the forest eventually falling behind them as the land changed towards Callander.

This time they turned left and continued on along the A84 through the little town. Sightless windows watched them pass, some broken in small shops and homes lining the street but most intact and reflecting the broken sky above them.

John slowed their progress to an almost silent crawl as the hearse climbed up the main street, weaving round crumpled cars and the remains of several bodies.

Lauren pointed out the Museum of Toys to their right at the top of the town and said the land would soon drop away to the castle. When they crested the rise and could clearly see the castle below John instructed Ashley to blow three sets of three blasts on his horn which he did.

Before the second set had even been completed there was movement below them, two men racing to a small group of buildings to one side of the castle. When the third set of horn blasts had been completed John ordered the hearse forward until they had descended to the gravelled weed-choked driveway leading to the castle. They went up it but John told Ashley to stop a good hundred metres short of the main castle structure.

Lieutenant Mayhew and his three soldiers flowed out of the hearse and deployed into positions enabling them to cover the driveway and that section of the castle it led to. Then John and Lauren got out with a small white flag on a stick and began to slowly walk towards the building. When they reached half way a man stepped round the corner and began to walk towards them, stopping a dozen metres away.

"Can I help you?" asked Andrew McCain.

"Yes," said John. "We've come to bring this community a warning."

"We don't like threats here. You've come under a white flag so you may safely leave under it."

"The warning isn't from us," continued John. "We believe you may be facing an attack from a large gang."

McCain's face tightened at that but he remained urbane and said: "So who does the warning come from?"

"It comes from me," said Lauren. "This force has already killed my grandfather and scores of other people. We were hoping to have a chat to prevent you being the next community to be attacked."

McCain looked at her briefly, then nodded and asked: "And the soldiers?"

"They're from Australia," said John.

Now McCain looked first startled then incredulous.

"Just like that, from Australia?" he said. "We've seen no planes for years. If they came at all it had to be by ship."

"Two ships actually," said John, "and they're enormous, fission powered and packed full of experts, equipment and food to try and help us get this country back on its feet."

Again McCain was amazed but he reached a decision and said: "Attack or no attack, this I've got to hear. If you trust me you may come inside. I'll send hot drinks out for your soldiers."

"Agreed," said John. "Give me a moment to explain to them what is happening."

He walked away and Lauren and McCain saw him start a conversation with Lieutenant Mayhew that became animated. It ended with Mayhew staying where he was but John returning with one soldier at his back.

"I understand my safety requires one soldier to accompany us," said John.

McCain looked at him briefly, said "Agreed" and turned away to start walking back to the castle. He didn't look back and, after a moment's hesitation, John and Lauren followed him, the soldier trailing a few metres behind them, scanning everything around carefully for signs of an ambush.

When they got close to the castle John could see several gun barrels poked through windows and he saw two more from buildings at the back of the castle. Not entirely a toothless community then, he thought, following McCain as he rounded the corner and strode in through the main entrance. He didn't stop and John and Lauren had a few seconds to take in dark oil paintings of Scottish scenes, a giant pair of antlers and a suit of armour as they walked through a wide hallway and into a drawing room where light streamed in through tall windows.

McCain gestured to a sofa and several armchairs before seating himself as a tall, regal-looking woman came into the room.

"Ah Matilda ," said McCain. "Could you please arrange some coffee or tea for our guests, unless they'd like something stronger?"

He looked at them and Lauren said tea would be fine while John and the soldier opted for coffee. Matilda nodded and left after which McCain was all business.

"Now, which should I hear first? This rescue bid of yours for a possible attack on us or the rescue bid for the country?"

"I think it more pressing that we talk about the possible attack on you. I speak for Leo Anderson of the Recovery Council of Australia which sent the ships, but you should hear Lauren first because she speaks for communities in Edinburgh which have been preyed on by this gang."

"Edinburgh?" said McCain. "That's more than fifty miles away. What has Edinburgh got to do with us?"

"Nothing," said Lauren, "because surviving groups in the city banded together, fought the gang and drove them out. We think they've now set up home in Stirling Castle and that's less than twenty miles from here."

"Stirling Castle you say," said McCain thoughtfully.

"And they've already been to Callander and know you are here," said Lauren.

That brought McCain forward to the edge of his seat and he could scarcely restrain himself as Matilda brought in a tray of steaming drinks, handed them out and took a seat slightly away from their debate.

"When were they here? We've seen and heard nothing, no vehicles, nothing," said McCain.

"Nor would you," said Lauren. "Their leader is a monster and she went ahead to scout on a bicycle. When she came back they were at some pains to drive their two vans off as quietly as possible. No need to do that unless they knew you were here.

"Riddle knows she needs to find food to feed her men. What better place to find food than somewhere other people have done the finding for her?"

"They're leader is a woman?" asked McCain. "Must be a very strong willed woman to keep control of a large number of men."

"It can be done quite easily," said Matilda with a small smile, "if you give those men what they want."

Everyone looked thoughtful at that until McCain said: "So what are you proposing?"

When John told him what he had in mind McCain said that such a place might exist some miles to the south west, but he was incredulous of the idea while Lauren actually spoke out against his plan and the soldier they had brought with them looked dubious. His only support came from Matilda.

She gave him an appraising look and said: "It might work and, if there is an attack, then it's possibly the only chance we might have. We've barely a dozen people here."

"Even if you ally with us we'll still be outnumbered," said John. "There's no guarantee we'll win. All we'll have in our favour is surprise and our few soldiers."

"This is the second proposal I've received in 48 hours," said McCain. "Perhaps I can use the first to help us."

John hazarded a guess and said: "You mean your meeting yesterday at the lodge?"

Now McCain was really startled and he said: "How on earth do you know about that?"

"We watched it take place, from a safe distance of course."

"Well, if you saw that you know about Mr Fraser and his crew at Loch Lomond Castle. We've shaken hands on an agreement to help each other although I never thought we'd be asking for help quite so soon. If he agrees to send his men it could be crucial."

"If he agrees and if he comes in time," said John. "In the meantime, while you approach him, I suggest we send the hearse back to the lodge for the rest of us. We've got a lot of work to do and possibly not much time left to do it in."

CHAPTER FOURTEEN

AGAIN the tree shook and again the platform Jed had constructed in it overlooking the dead bullock prevented him from seeing directly below for a clear shot.

Whatever was climbing up through the night darkness was big and heavy because Jed could feel the trunk next to him shudder at the pressure being put on it.

If it was the tiger then the overhang meant the animal couldn't easily get at him, but that same overhang denied Jed the chance of a kill and he couldn't afford to shoot down blind and risk only a crippling injury. A wounded tiger would be ten times more dangerous than a healthy big cat.

When he'd built the platform high up in the tree it had seemed the perfect spot, but he'd lost sight of the possibility of the hunter becoming the hunted.

Now the tiger had turned the tables on him, hunting a hunter who could neither advance nor retreat.

There were more slapping sounds and the trunk swayed again, shredding Jed's nerves as he desperately tried to work out just how close his stalker was.

This time, however, the tree trunk gave an even more violent heave and then stayed still.

Every muscle in Jed's body was taut as a bowstring as he strained his hearing to try and locate the tiger, but all was quiet with no hint of movement from below.

It stayed that way for three more agonising hours. Every creaking branch, every time the wind caused the tree to sway convinced Jed the tiger had come back. By the time it began to get light enough to see he was mentally and physically exhausted.

He gave it another half an hour to be sure, carefully scanning the area immediately near his tree to make sure nothing was lying in wait for him in the clumps of undergrowth, but still there was no sound or movement.

It was Mike and Roy who came for him and saved his sanity. He heard the quad bike arrive in the distance. The engine cut out and a few minutes later he saw the two men, both armed with hunting rifles, making their way warily towards him.

"Jed?" shouted Mike. "Jed, you OK?"

"Never better," Jed croaked back.

Mike and Roy made no attempt to approach the tree. Instead Mike called again.

"Any luck?" he said.

"Yes," Jed managed. "I'm lucky to still be here. The bloody thing came up the tree after me. It's still out there somewhere. Didn't get a single shot."

His words saw Mike and Roy take an even firmer grip on their weapons and look nervously about.

"Have you seen anything at all since then?" shouted Roy.

"Not a damn thing," said Jed. "I'm cold and I'm busting for a pee! Didn't want to go until now."

The two men grinned at that, watching as Jed got shakily to his feet and relieved himself in a great streaming arc which hit the ground with a spattering rustle.

"Is that what Big White Hunters do?" teased Mike, never taking his eyes off the nearest undergrowth.

"Bugger what Big White Hunters do!" said Jed. "I need a cup of tea and a hot bath. Look sharp now, I'm coming down!"

Mike and Roy half raised their rifles, scanning the area, as Jed laboriously slung his Rigby over one shoulder and stiffly descended the rope until he could clamber down to ground level.

He paused at the bottom and looked grimly at the tree trunk which was shredded in several places. He also saw that brush and leaves had been pulled off part of the dead bullock and that the tiger seemed to have eaten more of the carcase although not as much as before. Jed then slowly climbed up to meet his friends.

"Boy am I glad to see you two!" he said. "Must have taken a lot of guts to come down here not knowing what you were walking in to."

"Oh yes," said Mike cheerfully. "A lot more guts than a man who's just spent a dark night on his own up a tree with a tiger trying to get at him."

His eyes were laughing at Jed but his mouth was drawn in a rictus snarl.

The tenseness of the moment was broken by Roy, the gentle giant just saying: "Morning Jed!"

There was a moment's silence then all three men burst out laughing before cautiously making their way back to the quad bike which purred to life and took them back to the manor.

Many people were up and Jed got a warm welcome. Becky looked like she was going to say something to him but then burst into tears and hugged him as she took his coat

Maisie handed over a hot cup of coffee and when Jed took it and lifted it to his mouth he was practically knocked off his feet by the powerful aroma wafting into his nostrils. It seemed that a drop of something stronger had been added as well. He smiled and took a mouthful, the brew searing his throat as he swallowed to send warmth flooding into his body.

"Did you get it?" Donna asked, everybody nodding their interest with her.

"Afraid not," said Jed, "but if you're interested, it nearly got me."

There were sharply drawn breaths and cries of shock at this until Jed raised a hand to quiet them and said: "Don't worry, I won't be going back to the platform. It knows about it now and I may not be so lucky next time.

"What we're going to have to do is a sort of game drive, flush it out so we can get a clear shot at it and that is going to take every gun we've got. Make no mistake. It's already killed once. If we're to survive here then we can't allow it to kill any more of our livestock."

He took a mouthful of coffee, wincing at the strength, as he looked at the faces in front of him. There was apprehension but no fear and he was proud of them for that.

"Right, I need a bath and a look at my lovely daughter," he said. "When I come down again I want to organise a drive for tomorrow and end this before it kills again."

There were murmurs of agreement as Jed took himself away with Becky, left his boots in the hall and climbed the stairs to their bedroom.

"Leave your clothes by the door while I run the bath," said Becky, Jed nodding before he slowly took off a thick pullover and wandered over to the crib where Tilley lay fast asleep on her back. He smiled down at her and then turned back to sit on the double bed and remove his trousers, socks, shirt and pants all of which he put in a pile by the door.

The bathroom was filling with steam when he went in and Becky said: "Just you get in and soak for a while. I'll put out a change of clothes for you."

She bustled off and Jed sank back as the bath water slowly rose over him. When it was deep enough he switched off the taps and lay back to think.

From what he'd read a tiger might roam ten miles in a night. That posed a problem because the countryside had become a lot denser in the years since the Red Plague struck and cross-country travel had become much harder.

It had killed once and returned again to feed, so it might stay in an area where it knew there was food to be had. He reached for soap and considered what he knew of the terrain surrounding Waterfall Manor.

The woodland where the tiger had dragged the bullock was dense but not extensive and its far side included fields Jed had already checked with a view to bringing them back into cultivation. They'd even crudely cut two fields for hay last autumn, so Jed knew there was a narrow road there for access.

It would take too long to ask for Recovery Council help from Plymouth even if it was available, so Waterfall had to solve this problem on its own. They could probably muster thirty to forty people now. If they started the drive from the manor and put their best shots in the hay fields by the lane and a few guns on the flanks then it might be possible to drive the tiger out of the woods and into the open where it could be killed. If it was still in the woods and if it didn't do something Jed hadn't thought of. He soaped a leg and continued to think.

They had a nurse and a dentist but no doctor although there was a Recovery Council doctor in Plymouth. They'd have to make do with what they'd got as he didn't feel comfortable radioing Plymouth to ask the doctor to attend the drive when he was needed more where he was. Their nurse, Lydia, would have to do the best she could. Hopefully she wouldn't be needed.

He continued to refine a plan of action in his mind until the bathwater became cold and forced him to pull the plug and get out. He made sure he cleaned the enamel and washed it down before he dried himself and went out into the bedroom to put on the fresh clothes Becky had left him. Tilly was still asleep and he smiled when one of her legs kicked.

Jed left and went downstairs where he grabbed some breakfast before pulling Mike, Victor and Matthew into the library for a chat.

He said: "We need some luck for this to work, luck that the tiger hasn't left the area of its last kill. Early tomorrow morning I'm going to take our three best shots with me and drive round to the hay fields, set up there and wait. I want you, Mike, and you, Matthew, to each take two guns and parallel opposite sides of the wood to scare the tiger back if it tries to break away. Finally I want you, Victor, to muster everyone else we can spare with pots, pans, anything metal they can bang, string them out in a line and walk them slowly through the wood, shouting and making as much noise as they can. We'll be in position by 7.45am. I want you to get everyone over to the wood in time to start the drive at 8am. Any questions?"

Victor thought a moment then said: "The script is perfect in theory, but has the tiger read the script? What if it didn't like finding you in a tree and has simply moved its hunting ground a few miles to somewhere more peaceful?"

"That's why it has to be tomorrow," said Jed. "Our only hope for a quick solution is if it hasn't moved yet. Leave it just a day and we might miss even that one chance. If we don't kill it tomorrow then we'll have to set up several hunting groups of at least four men each and try and track it down which could take days even weeks. We can't afford that coming into Spring. We need that manpower to work the land if we are going to produce enough food to get through next winter comfortably. We have to get rid of it as soon as possible."

"And what if it turns on the beaters?" said Matthew. "Parts of that wood are still pretty dense even if leaves haven't come out yet."

"We're taking ten guns for the flanks and the killing zone," said Jed. "That still leaves at least another twenty for the beaters to carry. The tiger's first instinct will be to slip away from the noise not go towards it. That means the flanks are likely to see it first. I'm hoping you can keep it running towards us. There'll be four good shots waiting. One true hit is all we'll need."

Mike had been quiet but now he grinned and said: "I've always said the main hearth needed a decent rug. Now we can try and get one!"

"The boy's mad!" said Victor with a smile, "just like the lady from Niger."

"The lady from Niger?" queried Mike.

"Yes," said Victor. "It's a rhyme. There was a young lady from Niger, Who went for a ride on a tiger, They came back from the ride, With the lady inside, And a smile on the face of the tiger!"

"That's not funny," said Matthew as Victor got up and turned to leave.

"Whoever said hunting a tiger was funny?" replied Victor as he left and headed for the kitchen.

The other three watched him go and Mike said: "I hope he takes beating seriously or we're in a lot of trouble."

"Oh I think we can rely on Victor to help kill it," said Jed. "After all, John said he killed the man running Leeds. Stuck a kitchen knife right through him."

Mike and Matthew looked a little sick at that and glanced the way Victor had left.

"You wouldn't think it of polite, measured Victor would you," said Jed, "but the quiet ones are always the ones to watch. He'll stand."

The rest of the morning and part of the afternoon was spent choosing the shooters and the beating party, drilling into them what they had to do and making sure the beaters had something to take with them that would make a noise when they banged it.

By late afternoon the light was starting to go and Jed ordered everyone engaged in building work or the gardens to come inside for the night for safety reasons.

"No point in taking chances," he told Becky.

"Says the man who spent last night up a tree trying to shoot a tiger!" she replied. "Think of our daughter and try and stay alive tomorrow."

Inside in the kitchen Maisie was folding and kneading dough for a batch of bread watched by two of Evie's children, Nancy and Robert.

"Why are you putting flour on the table?" the little boy asked.

"To stop the dough sticking to the wood so the fairies can work their magic and give us bread."

"There aren't any fairies," said Nancy who was older than Robert.

"Then how does the dough rise?" asked Maisie. "It can't do it by itself. The fairies have to give a bit of help."

"What help do they give?" asked Robert.

"They put their trumpets in the dough and blow them," said Maisie, giving the dough a final press before putting it in a large glass bowl and covering it with a damp tea cloth.

"Are they doing it now?" asked Robert.

"Don't be silly!" said Nancy. "If they were we'd hear them."

"I thought you said you didn't believe in fairies?" said Maisie.

"I don't," said Nancy, "but I love bread, so I'm prepared to believe a little bit."

"Very wise," said Maisie. "Fairies like children, especially those who believe in them. Now run along and play. I've still got more cooking to do."

The children clattered out boisterously and went to look for the others to tell them about the fairies.

Maisie smiled again and was turning towards the stove when a stabbing pain caught her in the right hip. She managed to stop her fall by grabbing the table, hastily looking to see if Victor and his wife, Norma, had spotted anything but they had their backs turned.

This was the second time the pain had come and it was much worse than the first. Her knuckles turned white as she held herself up by sheer willpower, but the pain began to fade and Maisie was able to slump into a chair just as Victor turned to face her.

His gaze sharpened and he came over to her and asked: "Everything all right?"

"Yes," said Maisie hastily. "Hip's just giving me a bit of gyp, but it's gone now. I'm not as young as I was you know!"

"Aren't we all," smiled Victor, opening a cupboard and taking out a canister of salt. He shook a little into his hand and tossed it into a bubbling saucepan before returning the canister to the cupboard.

"You take it easy for a while," he told Maisie. "You've been in here for hours. We can't afford to have our top chef going sick."

Maisie scoffed at that but privately she had a warm glow. Cooking was her love and she was always pleased when anyone praised her efforts.

As always, the main evening meal was served in both dining rooms to cope with numbers in their growing community.

Becky had already told Jed that she thought at least two of the women who had come down from Leeds were pregnant, perhaps more. It increased the pressure on their building work.

"If we go on like this," she said, forking mashed potato into her mouth, "then the accommodation we have here will be tight even with the new building work. We're at Waterfall to focus our efforts as a community. It won't be much longer before we need to spread that community out, perhaps even move in to Launceston."

"John will be pleased to hear that," said Jed putting his knife and fork down on an empty plate. "I had to talk fast even to get him to consider a move to the manor. If he thinks we're starting to groan at the seams then he'll stay put in Launceston and let people come to him no matter what he and Dawn have talked about taking over that farmhouse and dairy."

"They could do both," said Becky. "Keep the house going in Launceston and still run the dairy. The farmhouse could go to some other couple and we'd have a viable base in Launceston that we could expand from."

Jed looked at her, a little surprised at his wife's appreciation of the wider picture.

"What happened to all your talk of keeping everyone together for security?" he said.

"That was before the Recovery Council sent those ships," she said. "Now they've arrived and we've got hundreds of their soldiers in Plymouth and London. It's not law and order but it's a lot better than it was a few months ago."

"I suppose so," said Jed, "but we still have a few local troubles, the tiger to name but one."

Becky's face grew concerned at that and she said: "You take care tomorrow. I know you've got some of the men with you but don't take chances. Just kill the thing and there's an end to it."

She took their plates to the kitchen before the two of them adjourned to a small sitting room with a settee, three armchairs and a shelved alcove lined with books and a white marble bust of the Roman general, Scipio.

"I can't be long," said Becky. "Tilly's due a feed soon and I should really help with the washing up."

"Tilly comes first," said Jed. "You look after her, I'll help with the washing up. I'll be ready for bed by then."

"I'm not surprised," said Becky. "You can't have got a wink of sleep last night."

"Yes, well last night I was counting stripes not sheep."

Becky took his hand as they sat in the settee and said: "Don't talk about it. It makes my blood run cold thinking of you in a tree with that thing creeping up on you. Just get rid of it so we can all sleep easy."

When they later went up to bed together Jed undressed and climbed between the sheets as Becky laid Tilly in "jail", a small cushioned bed crib with rails and bars that Jed had put together. She then switched out the bedside light and climbed in beside Jed.

Becky felt tingles go up her spine as Jed shifted slightly and the rough hairs on his leg scraped across the outside of her thigh. She turned in to him and gently nibbled the lobe of his ear.

"She's out for the count," whispered Becky, snuggling closer and sliding one leg over him, but the only response she got from Jed was a gentle snore.

"Or we could just go to sleep," said Becky, as she relaxed her head on Jed's chest. Five minutes later she was snoring too.

Morning came with a hint of rain in the air. The kitchen was already filling early when Jed came down at 6.15am, the room packed with people talking too loudly and nervously sipping hot drinks.

Jed got his own drink while he waited for the other three men he was with to turn up including Conrad and Noah. The last to arrive was Roy who stooped to kiss Janice and then stepped over to join them.

"You picked a nice day for it," he said, his looming bulk shrouded in a large wax jacket. He wore a flat cap and wellington boots, looking like some dour sheep farmer about to start a day's work. All four men carried heavy calibre hunting rifles.

Jed looked about then shouted through the clamour which fell away into silence.

"Everyone knows what they've got to do. We're off now and the far wood guns will follow. In a few minutes the near wood guns will leave, but you beaters mustn't start moving into position for at least fifteen minutes to give the rest of us time to get into place. Remember, you start your drive at 8am on the dot. We'll have daylight by then. Good luck everyone."

There was a chorus of murmurs at his words including several "good lucks" and a "shoot straight". No-one was under any illusion about the danger they faced and the tension could be cut with a knife.

The entire manor community was turning out. Only Maisie was staying behind to take charge of baby, Tilly, and the children.

Jed stepped out into the courtyard, gave Becky a wave and then led Conrad, Noah and Roy round to the extensive outbuildings where he unlocked a small barn containing their two quad bikes and a sturdy Landrover spotted with mud.

"We'll take the Landrover," he said, moving round to the driver's door. "That leaves a quad bike each for Mike, Matthew and their men. They'll need the quads, particularly Mike. He's on the far side and there's some rough ground over there."

The men busied themselves getting into the Landrover and, when everyone was seated, Jed started the engine in a cloud of blue smoke which eddied round the vehicle as he slowly pulled out of the barn and headed down to the road.

They got waves from Mike, Matthew and their men who they met just coming out of the manor and a volley of barks from Bruno, but Jed took care to concentrate on the lane they turned in to. The sides had roughly been clipped back close to the manor, but they were soon back among hedgerows trying to spread into the carriageway, branches scraping on the side of the vehicle. They really had to find a hedge cutting flail, thought Jed.

Ten minutes later they had reached the hay fields, opened a gate and driven inside, Jed facing the Landrover towards the exit before switching off as the other three stepped out on to rough grass soaked with dew.

"Space yourselves out, thirty metres between us. I'll take this field with Noah. Conrad, you take that field with Roy and for God's sake don't both shoot towards each other. We're here to kill a tiger not start a graveyard."

With that he gestured Noah off to his left and followed Conrad and Roy as they opened another gate, stepped across a small wooden bridge over a busy stream and walked away from him into the second hayfield.

Soon all was quiet, the only sound coming from crows and rooks in trees where the wood ended at the top of the fields.

Jed cradled his rifle and pushed back the cuff of his coat to look at his watch. Nearly 8am. He licked his lips, his throat dry, hoping everyone would be in position on time.

Smack on 8am there was suddenly a distant racket of shouts and bangs as the beaters began their drive.

Jed looked to his left and saw Noah take a tighter grip on his rifle while he could see Conrad and Roy to his right doing the same. No going back now and he took a tighter grasp on his own weapon, checking the safety catch was off.

Out of their sight the line of beaters led by Victor had
spaced themselves out between the livestock fields on the
near side of the wood and rough pastureland on the far
side, walking slowly forward making as much noise as
they could while each end of the line kept in sight of the
flanking marksmen.

The line wavered at times as those in the centre coped
with dense brush or the stream running into a deep pool,
but they maintained steady progress and after twenty
minutes began to see the trees thinning towards the top of
the hayfields.

 Each end had been joined by the flanking marksmen by
the time the line emerged into the hayfields, everyone
looking keenly ahead to see if the tiger had broken cover
yet towards the road.

All the beaters stopped fifty metres into the fields, Bruno
running about excitedly, and Victor shouted down to
Jed:"Have you seen it yet?"

"Not a whisker," Jed shouted back. "Any joy your way?"
he shouted to Conrad and Roy who both shook their
heads.

"Nothing in the other field either," shouted Jed to Victor.
"Did you see anything when you came through the
wood?"

"Just trees and a few rabbits and birds," Victor shouted
back. "Either it's somehow slipped by or that tiger of
yours has moved on."

Jed's face was grim. They'd missed their chance. Now he'd have to contact Plymouth and ask for help in numbers. The tiger had to be found and found soon before it killed again.

Almost as the thought came into his mind there was the distant blast of a shotgun followed almost immediately by a second shot.

It could only be one person.....Maisie! And she was on her own back at Waterfall.

Frantically Jed bellowed: "Everyone back to the manor. Stay together as a group. Those with weapons take the front."

He was already turning to run back to the Landrover as Conrad and Roy arrived and hurled themselves into the back with Noah.

Jed dived into the driver's seat and started the engine with a roar. His door swung open crazily as he fishtailed down and through the gate, but he was able to grab a handle and heave the door closed.

He just managed to correct the Landrover as it tried to snake into an overgrown ditch and then they were off, engine screaming as Jed threw caution to the winds and clashed through second gear into third. Pray God they were in time, he thought.

CHAPTER FIFTEEN

WHEN Riddle and the two vans full of her followers arrived back at Stirling Castle she was annoyed to find that everyone there had already taken full advantage of what the scavenging group had found.

The smell of cooking wafted from the kitchen and when she finally got there it was to find a jumble of dirty saucepans, plates and cutlery carelessly dumped in a sink with no attempt made to clean them.

Boxes, tubs and crates roughly stacked against the walls showed the foraging group had enjoyed a productive day but hadn't thought to prepare food for her return.

Her lips thinned and she went to the Great Hall where most people lounged about smoking and chatting.

"Right! You, you and you outside and bring water to the kitchen!" she shouted, stabbing a finger out at a group near Oggie.

"But it's dark," said a man called Sprague. "How are we supposed to find water in the dark?"

"There's a courtyard fountain. Use water from that until we can fill jerrycans and bring some in.

"You over there," she said, pointing at a different group. "Get yourselves into the kitchen, boil some water and wash those dishes. And you others, if you can't be bothered to have a meal ready for me when I come back then you can put one together now."

She stood there, hands on hips, as the men she had selected grumbled and slowly got to their feet before trudging out towards the kitchens with surly faces.

Sheep, she thought, all of them were sheep incapable of constructive thought. The meal had better be edible or she'd have words.

Riddle then calmly strolled through a now silent Great Hall and out to the little library she had found that morning where she lit a candle and approached the giant map.

Her finger came out and laboriously traced the line of road north-west until she came to a small castle symbol on the map marked "Callander Castle" which she gently tapped.

The map confirmed what she'd seen. A castle below a ridge above the town with open countryside around it. If she was lucky this raid could set them up for autumn, perhaps even into winter as well.

She smiled and patted her breast pocket containing the two antique silver baby rattles as she picked up the candle and turned to leave the library, missing shadowed words at the bottom of the map which read "Bartholomew 1937". The map was more than a century out of date and didn't show new roads to the north of Callander!

She returned to the Great Hall until the men from the kitchen came out and nervously served a crude sort of stew with a few tinned vegetables to her and others from the scavenging vans. Not great but not worth making a scene over. She was in a good mood at the prospect of the raid.

When she'd eaten and warmed herself a bit in front of a spluttering fire she decided to share the good news of what she'd found.

So she stood up, turned to face everyone in the smoky hall and said: "Your attention please! Today we had a little luck with our foraging and brought back enough stuff to keep us going for a while, but I've found somewhere which may keep us going for months, perhaps until winter."

Those in front of her stirred in interest. One wag even shouted out: "Any beer?", but laughter froze at the glare Riddle gave him.

She continued: "There is a small castle on the far side of a town we went to today and it has people, not many just a few. They couldn't exist without food and I'm sure they'd love to share it with us!"

There was more general laughter now. This was familiar territory to them, veterans of a dozen smash and grab pillaging attacks on defenceless communities.

"We've always attacked at night before," she said, "but this is different, much further away than we usually go, so we're going to hit them mid-morning tomorrow. We'll go in the bus, so everyone be ready to leave by 8am. That will give us time to get there and those at the castle time to thin out a bit so they're not grouped against us.

"We'll take the usual measures. Get control of the site and then chat to our hosts about their food supplies, but this time I want to keep at least one prisoner for a bit more questioning about the area. Who knows what other communities may exist that they can tell us about."

There was more smiling at this. Everyone knew that the antique silver baby rattles would be asking the final question and no prisoner they had taken had managed to survive that yet.

Riddle gave them all one last sweeping glance and then strolled back to her armchair by the fire, putting a few pieces of a smashed up wooden box on the fire to try and coax a little more warmth.

Her thoughts turned to getting herself a room. She couldn't continue just falling asleep in the armchair. She needed a bit of privacy, but that would have to wait, she thought. The raid took precedence.

With that she settled back in the armchair and gazed at the tiny flames beginning to lick and crackle round the fresh wood she had added.

Behind her the number of people began to thin out as some sought their beds early, determined to get what sleep they could ahead of what would be the last day some of them would ever see again.

By midnight there were barely a dozen people left in the Great Hall, some lying on cushions, others huddled under blankets and a lucky few asleep on settees.

Riddle was curled in the fireside armchair, her dreams once again wracked with torment. This time her tearful children were reproaching her for causing their deaths and Riddle couldn't seem to explain that she loved them and that it hadn't been her fault. Just when she reached a point in her dream where the anguish made her want to scream she woke up.

The luminous dial of her watch told her it was 5.45am. It was still pitch dark and the only sounds she could hear were snoring and the occasional blustery gust from the chimney.

There were a few embers visible so she got up and added several shards of wood to the grate more for the comfort of a fire than because she was cold.

Eventually there was just enough light to see by and she picked her way carefully to the kitchen where she stoked the stove and set a pan of water to boil while she hunted for the last of the herbal teabags. By the time she found one and had identified a small tin of pineapple for her breakfast there was steam coming from the pan. When it boiled she again enjoyed the teabag's fragrance and took her mug and the hacked open tin out of the main building and across the castle's Outer Close to the gateway near the remains of the gift shop.

There she slowly chewed chunks of pineapple, savouring the sweetness while she looked out at the city below and took sips from her mug of tea. No sign of life showed, no lights and not a trace of smoke as grey light strengthened and picked out distant rooftops. Stark though it was, Riddle felt somehow settled here, grateful to the silver rattles for their advice on where to go when she was chased out of Edinburgh.

They had given her a home. Now it was up to her to make that home work so she didn't let them down. With that she swallowed the last of the pineapple, raising the tin to drip juice into her mouth before casually throwing the empty tin as far as she could.

When she returned to the Great Hall her first task was to take her knife in to the kitchen and sharpen it, but no sharpener could be found. Riddle solved that by opening a courtyard door and whetting the blade on a stone doorstep before sliding it carefully into an inside pocket of her jacket.

Others were awake now, stumbling blearily in to the kitchen in search of something to eat and drink before they left on the raid.

Riddle ignored them and went back outside to the old Leyland Olympian bus which she climbed in to, switching the ignition on to make sure her men had filled the tank properly. The needled hovered at "F" and she immediately switched off, climbed out of the cab and went round to the front where she carefully wiped away some mud splashes and blemishes on the windscreen.

She was impatient to go and took to pacing up and down as her men slowly began to arrive and get on the bus. As 8am loomed close she climbed on board and did a head count, noting around thirty people on board including several women. Her usually dour group seemed in high spirits at the prospect of action and there was some nervous chatter and crude jokes.

So much the better, she thought. Her crew were no shrinking violets and they weren't on a Sunday School outing. With that she gave one last glance at the gateway, but no-one else was in sight and she nodded before walking round to the cab, climbing in and driving the bus slowly away.

Riddle had cause to thank her foresight in allowing plenty of time to get to Callander as the bus hit problem after problem.

No sooner had she eased on to the A84 than she had to stop. The snarl of abandoned vehicles at a junction where the vans had snaked their way through the previous day proved too tight for the bus to get by.

She had to get out and organise teams with ropes to open a wider passage by sheer brute force and there was subdued grumbling at the effort required so soon into their journey.

They finally got the bus through only to find the road partially blocked further on by a giant rusting sign which had advertised cut-price tourist flights into space. Its steel skeleton had come down while large metal panels showing sling-shot trips round the moon lay scattered up the carriageway like huge leaves.

The vans had got through but the bus couldn't and again Riddle organised a system of ropes to pull the structure clear of the road and get the panels slung on to an embankment.

The high spirits generated by the prospect of a raid had gone now and there were a few glances darted at Riddle as the men got back inside the bus.

She managed to raise a smile here and there by using the intercom system to tell them what a ripe plum this might be as she drove along and the miles fell slowly behind them.

However, the fizzing air of excitement had gone to be replaced by an altogether darker atmosphere as if those on board had been cheated out of something.

By the time they reached Callander many just wanted to get the job done and go back to Stirling, but Riddle's microphone voice warning them to get ready had the desired effect.

Backs straightened as gang members reached for weapons and prepared for an attack they believed would be easy pickings.

There was no delay from Riddle, no checking out the lie of the land, and she simply drove the bus up to the ridge where she cut the engine and allowed the vehicle to coast down towards the small castle below.

She had seen it before but no-one else on board had. Their cries of wonder seemed to fire everyone's blood up again.

When they reached the overgrown driveway they poured out of the bus in a wave and quickly spread into a skirmishing line and advanced on the castle in a blustery wind which tugged at their clothing.

Riddle was immediately suspicious. Despite their numbers and sudden arrival there was no sign of life from the building ahead as she and her men got closer and closer until she could see something which completely mystified her. The large rear entrance door was open and all was quiet.

*   *   *

A few hours earlier it had been bedlam. Andrew McCain and John were everywhere, goading people to greater efforts as they piled a lorry high with sacks and casks of food and other stores.

Part of John's plan involved stripping the castle down to the last crumb. He reasoned that if the gang expected to loot food from them then they probably hadn't brought much if any with them.

Most of the castle's freezer food was transferred to a freezer van John had found in town the previous day and been able to start. The rest he asked to be cooked for their evening meal, breakfast and the journey ahead. All weapons were put in cars and vans together with people's personal belongings and Dawn managed a few seconds with her new husband.

"Don't get heroic," she said. "Baby and I need you back in one piece," she said patting her stomach before giving John a hug.

Lauren, too, was saying her goodbyes as she hugged Griff who was staying with John and the soldiers.

"Let the professionals guide the fighting," she said. "I don't want you needlessly hurt," and she hugged him again, almost lost against the powerful bulk of his body.

Griff's bushy beard split in a slow smile and he said: "You know me. I'm a coward!"

She punched him gently as they parted before she went over to make one last check on the lorry loading.

The small group of vehicles left the castle soon after breakfast, but they didn't head towards town. Instead Dawn and Lauren joined McCain who, with one last anguished look at the home he was leaving behind, led them north west away from Callander for nearly three miles until they reached a junction.

There they turned left to follow a road along the shores of two lochs and down to Aberfoyle where they joined the A81, went past the old hunting lodge and prepared to execute the second part of John's highly risky plan.

Behind them there was a hive of activity to sweep away any trace of the convoy's departure on the driveway and road before John and the soldiers raced to take up positions on the hillside among trees and undergrowth leading to the ridge.

Barely twenty minutes later one of the soldiers whistled and John saw an old double decker bus make a ghostly appearance and glide silently down the road towards the driveway to the castle. He waited until the bus was nearly there and then signalled two of the soldiers up to the ridge while he turned back and gave his whole attention to the castle.

The gang he saw spill out of the bus was slightly larger than he had anticipated which made things even tighter, but he compressed his lips and concentrated on what he wanted to do.

He watched as the gang swept towards the castle and then hesitated, wary at the complete lack of opposition. A woman stepped forward from their ranks when they rounded a corner of the castle and it was she who cautiously disappeared through the rear entrance doors which John had deliberately left open.

A few minutes later and there was a screech of fury as Riddle realised the cupboard was bare and the castle occupants had fled. She boiled out of the back entrance and her gaze raked the surrounding area at which point John fired. His bullet hit the ground near Riddle, spattering her and nearby gang members with gravel.

They scattered and began to fire wildly at the slope above them at which point two of the soldiers followed instructions and broke cover, zig-zagging up the slope to new positions near the crest.

John then broke cover with Griff, Mayhew and the final soldier, all four of them dashing towards the ridge and on to the Museum of Toys while the soldiers behind them ducked as a fusillade of shots from the gang tore into the slope around them.

Riddle appeared incensed and was urging gang members across the driveway and up a bank at the bottom of the slope, her men using bushes and the occasional boulder for cover as they began to climb towards the ridge.

They met little resistance, but when they gained the ridge and began to spread out across a car park area towards the Museum of Toys they were fired on from both sides.

Some stood still, some even tried to retreat but the vast bulk of the gang charged forward towards the only shelter available to them, the Museum entrance.

Riddle took stock of the situation as they gathered panting in the foyer beneath a giant clock with teddy bears for numerals.

One body lay in the carpark and several of her men had flesh wounds. She had no idea if they had killed any of the retreating riflemen but she doubted it. Riddle was used to dealing with ordinary people. Some were tough but none had the calculated efficiency she had just witnessed. So where had they come from?

Some were still outside but the bulk of them seemed to have fled into the museum. She urgently needed fresh information.

When she'd warily stepped inside the castle a knocked over chair and a broken box saw her rightly guess the castle occupants were gone. One look at the kitchen stripped bare, its food cupboards wide open and empty, brought the situation home to her and the empty cellar merely underlined the urgent need to find food.

Those who had fled had clearly taken their food with them, so all was not lost. Find them and find their food, she thought, as she stood by a ticket kiosk where ornate gold lettering revealed that a family ticket to the museum cost £39. But the only way to find out where the fleeing castle residents had gone was to capture one and encourage them to talk. Oh how she'd encourage them to talk!

Her eyes like flint, Riddle turned to her expectant followers sheltering from occasional shots and gestured for them to follow her deeper into the museum.

She led off down a short corridor lined with glass display cases full of Corgi and Dinky toys which emerged into a small hallway at the foot of a wooden staircase. The hallway had a sign guiding visitors to what was on each of two floors, all the details being spelt out in thousands of marbles.

Riddle realised that the museum had been designed on a one way basis with visitors coaxed to follow a set route from one display area to the next. Upstairs apparently lay model railways, dolls, model soldiers, board games and game consoles

She nodded and began to climb the stairs, her knife in one hand. After a brief moment of uncertainty her men began to follow her, more than a few pausing here and there to look at exhibits displayed on the staircase walls from toy drummers to mechanical acrobats. There were even aircraft suspended above them on wires.

When they reached a first floor landing the whole of the top floor opened out before them. Thousands of dolls lined the walls and early examples of board games such as Monopoly, Scrabble and Ludo were pinned to display boards while rank after rank of lead soldiers were on parade in the musty atmosphere, but one thing dominated the whole floor.

It was a gigantic model railway layout which started in front of them with a line following a river, the track then rising through forests into a range of mountains. Closer inspection revealed different gauges of line for different eras of model railway with great attention to detail from bridges to stations and from tunnels to trees.

Riddle only had eyes for the fact that the enormous room stretching away for nearly forty metres was empty of life. Nothing moved and there was no sound although she realised that there were enough hiding places up here to conceal a dozen marksmen, so she was in no hurry to venture out into the open.

She was surrounded by very nervous men and didn't fancy getting shot by some carelessly jerked trigger...so she sent one of the men forward to reconnoitre. His eyes darted everywhere as he crept forward further and further into the room, diving to the floor at a sudden regular clacking noise which came from the far end of the room and moved towards him.

Flickering movement drew Riddle's eye and she saw the clacking noise was linked to some sort of train briefly glimpsed as it passed across small open areas while pulling several carriages through a mountain tunnel.

The train quickly swept into sight as it left mountain scenery behind and crossed a great viaduct, Riddle shouting at her scout that it was only a toy train.

The man looked sheepish and got back to his feet just as the train turned into a forest area above the river and began to clatter noisily towards them. He looked at it uncertainly as the engine approached and then saw a wagon attached to the last carriage had a grenade in it!

It was the last thing he ever saw as the grenade exploded just as he turned to shout a warning.

Shrapnel cut him apart, but his advance half way into the giant room meant Riddle and the rest of her gang were far enough away from the blast to escape with cuts and bruises although they were blown off their feet in a cacophony of whirling metal and shattered glass.

When everyone climbed back to their feet, coughing and knocking dust and glass from their clothing, Riddle saw that her scout had been reduced to a bloody corpse. Damn them! They'd pay for this, she thought, peering fiercely through dying swirls of dust.

She ordered another man forward, this time following several yards behind so she could try and spot any traps. Her foot turned over on an object and she stumbled, looking down to see the toy train which had pulled the grenade. It was an old Hornby with a clockwork wind-up key mechanism. No electricity needed but still effective as her dead scout knew only too well.

Caution warred with the need for haste as she picked her way through the debris of smashed dolls and board games, finally reaching the top of another staircase surrounded by glass cases of Star Wars figures. A window half way down revealed stairs descending into gloom, the walls decorated with picture frames containing completed jigsaws.

Riddle ordered the man with her to stop while she listened carefully but there was no sound, so she turned back and beckoned the rest of her gang forward. They reluctantly complied as she cautiously began to descend the staircase, pausing some time on a landing to allow her eyes to get used to the poor light on the ground floor.

This part of the museum contained corridor sections with dozens of glass cabinets full of antique toys from early tin-plated soldiers and spinning tops to more modern examples of Action Man, Barbie, beanies and Rex Rocket.

Again Riddle halted, the only sound being shuffling noises as members of her gang began to descend the staircase after her.

She could see nothing but sent the scout forward again just to be sure, his figure first fading in the darkness and then being highlighted as he went through a shaft of daylight from a grubby window.

At the bottom of the corridor was an open area with a padded floor lined with sofas and settees and boxes full of various soft toys for visiting children to play with. Here the corridor looped back on itself.

Riddle carefully peered ahead but the corridor again just seemed to be an endless row of display cabinets. Where were these people, she thought?

Taking the lead she pressed on, aware of light in the distance which was just enough to hint at construction kits, steam engines, hobby horses, and coloured building blocks filling some of the cabinets they passed. Finally they emerged in a small gift shop whose dusty entrance windows afforded views over the town.

Riddle was mystified. Why herd them into this museum and then just fade away? In a flash she realised her attackers had been holding her attention, perhaps to give their friends more time to get away which meant they were not as far ahead of her as she'd thought and could still be caught.

She started to step towards the exit and then hesitated. It was very open out there and she didn't fancy being caught in a cross-fire if these people were still out there.

Turning back to her scout, she said: "Go outside and across to that cycle rack. Shout back what you see."

The scout was none too keen to do so but knew the penalty for disobedience. He licked his lips, stepped forward and slowly pushed open the exit doors, Riddle noticing the way fallen leaves had already been pushed back in a heap by someone before them.

It was increasingly obvious that all this had been planned. She wanted to disrupt that plan so, with her scout only half way towards the cycle rack, she stepped outside herself, ordering everyone else to follow her and then scatter. Nothing happened and as she looked around she was increasingly sure that nothing would. Why was that?

Suddenly she heard an engine start nearby and the sound of a vehicle being driven off. Tricked, she thought, we've been tricked! There had never been any intention to fight them, just draw them away from their transport. It would take at least fifteen minutes for her to get back to the bus, drive it here and get everyone on board to start a pursuit and in that time these people could have gone anywhere.

Furiously she tried to glimpse the vehicle below her, but she could see nothing of it as the sound faded back in the direction the gang had arrived from.

Hastily she ordered everyone to stay where they were while she went back for the bus. Riddle began to jog out of the car park and down the entrance road, weeds whipping at her legs. By the time she got out on the road and reached the ridge she was beginning to pant, unused to such strenuous exercise. The slope down to the castle helped, but her throat was so raw by the time she was half way down that she had to complete the rest of the way at a fast walk, all the time thinking about what she should do next.

The old bus didn't help when she got there. It took three attempts to start before Riddle could get the engine running and grind her way slowly back up to the ridge and then in to the museum. She left the engine running and got out to chivvy everyone on board, but there was a shock waiting for her.

Brody stepped forward and said: "Look what we've found!"

The group behind him parted and in among them stood Griff, his bearded faced twisted in pain from a leg with a bloody bandage.

CHAPTER SIXTEEN

MILES away the convoy had left Aberfoyle, passed the turn-off lane to the old hunting lodge and was descending towards Loch Lomond.

Dawn was in the lead van with Andrew McCain and Lauren when McCain pointed ahead at a large battered brown sign alerting drivers and tourists that they were approaching Turnbull House.

McCain turned to Dawn and said: "I just hope your man knows what he's doing. It's all very well to look at photos and plans of the place in my library but quite another to be here on the ground. Before the plague it was a ruin albeit a well managed ruin with tours, a gift shop and what have you. God knows what it will be like now with a few years of neglect."

Dawn said: "John wanted a place that you knew, that Ewan Fraser could get to quickly and that offered us a fighting chance on our terms not Riddle's."

Lauren had been against the plan from the start, particularly when she found out about the role Griff was being asked to play.

"If anything happens to Griff I'll never forgive myself for being talked into this," she told them. "Too much can go wrong."

It was Andrew McCain's local knowledge which had enabled John to give his plan a real chance of success.

McCain had told him: "Turnbull House might fit the bill for what you're after. It's a large ruin, partly restored, which became a tourist attraction. It's less than twenty miles from Loch Lomand Castle so, if Fraser agrees to help, he should be able to join us fairly quickly. I just hope the man I sent to ask him was convincing."

John had asked McCain a number of questions and learnt that some parts of Turnbull House were still in ruins and only a small amount of clearance and safety work had been done to make the cellars and tunnel under the ruin suitable for tours by tourists.

His plan was to draw Riddle and her gang into the ruin and then surround them with superior numbers from the two castles and John and Lauren's groups. It would then be surrender or die. No-one was in any doubt which one

Riddle would choose, but the hope was that enough of her gang would see sense.

Now debate was on the brink of becoming reality as McCain halted the convoy, sending the lorry load of food and the freezer van on to Loch Lomand Castle before leading everyone else up the side road to Turnbull House.

Vehicles were hidden back under trees down an old service road before everyone waited tensely for reinforcements.

Fraser was the first to arrive. He'd been a little sceptical at first about the message brought him by Alec Wilson, but a promise was a promise and he agreed to bring everyone he could. He was a lot more convinced after a brief chat with the driver he met on the way who said his lorry was loaded with food for Loch Lomand Castle and so was the freezer van behind him. He knew McCain would not have stripped his home unless the threat was real.

Now he and McCain were again shaking hands but this time there was more warmth to the gesture.

Dawn told Fraser what the plan was to deal with Riddle and, after a quick tour of the ruin, he offered a few suggestions which she took on board.

John's arrival in the hearse completed their forces and he swiftly brought Fraser and McCain up to date about Riddle's gang.

"Griff has been told to resist but to cave in at the first sign of any torture," he said. "All he has to do is reveal the existence of Loch Lomond Castle and the possibility of two food caches instead of one. If that doesn't hasten Riddle after us then nothing will. I want her keen, so keen that she puts her head in our noose before she thinks too much about it."

Lauren said: "I hope you're right, but the Riddle I know is just shrewd enough to smell a rat. We'll outnumber her but we'll be spread thinly. If she keeps her gang together and decides to fight as a group then she could steamroller her way out and escape."

"Then we'll have to make sure she's in too deep to do that before we spring our trap," said John.

The hearse was driven away out of sight before Lieutenant Mayhew positioned his soldiers into deep cover around an ivy-choked archway. To them fell the task of trying to turn Riddle and her gang back if they spotted something was wrong when they got inside and tried to flee.

"How long do you think we have?" asked Fraser.

"Perhaps an hour, maybe a little longer," said John, "and we need to make the best of it. Now show me the tunnel and these cellars and where we can get in and out of them."

A group of men including McCain, Fraser, Mayhew and John then set off into Turnbull House.

At first glance the structure looked solid. The gift shop was dusty but sound while a good part of the house had been restored with windows and doors intact and an historical display area created at the base of one corner turret. It was a different story with the far section of the house which was an overgrown ruin with tumbled timbers, plaster falling off corridor walls, large cracks in the stonework, rusting scaffolding and the tattered remains of tarpaulins where the plague had overtaken restoration. Roots were sinking into cracks and crevices as saplings took hold in drains or fought to grow in rubble while the most derelict section of the site had increasingly been taken over by ivy, bushes and grass.

They paused where restoration met ruin and McCain gestured to where stone steps led down into darkness from what seemed to have been a central entrance hall.

They descended two flights and found themselves in vaulted cellars. The only light came through small grubby ground floor windows set into the ceiling edge of the cellars whose floor had pools of water and walls dank with moisture, moss and a few ferns. The cellars were littered with the remains of wooden boxes and discarded furniture while they even found an old well. Its gaping stone-lined hole had a flimsy triangular warning sign in front with an exclamation mark on it while there was also a rusting notice encouraging tourists to toss a coin in and make a wish.

McCain led the way and tramped and splashed along until he reached another small set of steps just over half way along where he paused.

"These lead down to a tunnel," he said. "It was built to come out above a local river as a way of escape if the house were ever put under siege. Tourist tours used to come down to the cellars and tunnel but I've no idea if it's still passable."

John had been scanning every yard of the way they took including another set of steps at the far end of the cellar which he was told was a collapsed secondary entrance. He now turned and spoke as they walked back and climbed the stairs to the old ruined entrance hall.

He said: "We have to assume that if Riddle's lot get down this far then they've swallowed the bait, so we need to welcome them with a few surprises along the way."

His suggestions included a series of traps, deadfalls and tripwires. They might not cause many casualties, he said, but it would make the attackers cautious.

Men were gathered together and quickly told what he wanted and where he wanted it.

The next forty-five minutes were a hive of industry as the men worked to make the remains of Turnbull House a nightmare for the unwary.

Fraser brought his security expertise into play and teamed up with Lieutenant Mayhew to site the forces at their command in the best possible places for an ambush or a fighting retreat while Dawn and Lauren worked with Matilda and several others to erase all tyre tracks leading in to the service road.

John took time to talk to Fraser as he worked, telling him about the Australian Recovery Council and its plan to help get the country back on its feet.

"You and Mr McCain could be an integral part of that plan," said John. "Do you know of any other communities near you?"

"No," said Fraser, tying twine round a chunk of masonry. "You're the first fresh faces we've seen in quite a while."

"In that case your knowledge of the area will be crucial in trying to set up Recovery Councils in Scotland. We've flown over Glasgow and Edinburgh. Both showed signs of life."

"I worked in Glasgow, had my own security business there," said Fraser, "but the city was falling to pieces when I left. Gangs everywhere and a lot of looting."

"Then you'll know how important it is to bring back law and order, restore infrastructure and make a start on food production."

"Food production?" queried Fraser.

"Yes," said John. "The Recovery Council can help with some supplies, equipment and experts such as engineers and doctors but the sooner agriculture is put back on its feet then the better every surviving community will be."

"I hear what you say," said Fraser, "but there are going to be more like Riddle. Surely security has to take priority? No-one is going to grow tatties if all their work is lost when they are suddenly robbed of their crop."

"That's why the Recovery Council is advancing on a broad front," said John. "They sent hundreds of soldiers here, but local security will count for a lot. The soldiers can't be everywhere."

Fraser looked interested and thoughtful at the same time as he completed his work on the masonry and moved away to consider several baulks of timber near a fallen wall.

John felt he'd struck a chord with Fraser but only time would tell and they didn't have much of that spare at the moment.

He walked through the site and was about to go into the gift shop when a voice stopped him.

"I wouldn't do that if I was you," said Mayhew stepping from the shadows of an overgrown box hedge.

John looked at him and then suspiciously at the door he'd been about to open. Closer inspection revealed nothing obvious and he looked a question at Mayhew.

"If you turn the handle your day will get significantly worse," said Mayhew with a smile.

"What have you done to it?" asked John.

"Nothing too clever," said Mayhew. "Just a stout stick and a piece of fishing line."

"Which does what?" asked John warily.

Mayhew smiled and said: "Let's just say that if you go inside it could be a crushing experience."

John stepped back cautiously and said: "Fraser was working on masonry over there. Now this door. The place is rapidly becoming a death trap. You'd better let everyone know about it. We don't want to hurt our own people."

"Already passed the word," said Mayhew, looking at his watch. "I've also put a man a way down the road to tip us off if we get visitors."

John cursed at forgetting such an obvious action, but Mayhew said: "Don't beat yourself up about it. You can't be expected to think of everything and we're all in this together."

John thanked him and went looking for Dawn who he found working in a large restored hall full of information boards next to several dusty suits of armour and racks of ancient weaponry and small arms.

"How's it going?" he asked.

"We're working as fast as we can," she said. "The service road's done. Nothing to show we've driven down it. Now I'm trying to arrange a few surprises here. Can you see what I've done?"

John looked carefully around. He was wary after his recent experience at the gift shop, but even though he looked carefully around he could see no obvious dangers.

"OK, you've got me," he said. "What am I missing?"

"Try looking up," she said with a smile.

John did so, swore and almost fell over as he stumbled in his haste to change position. Above him near the door was an enormous wrought iron chandelier with a score of candles on it in a cobwebbed circle. The heavyweight construction was secured to the wall with a thin rusty chain which didn't look as if it could support itself never mind the chandelier. John gave the chain a nervous look.

"What have you done to it?" he asked in a quiet voice.

"Nothing yet," she said. "but if I tie a bit of rope with a quick release knot to the end of the chain then I'm hoping the first people to open that door are going to get about fifty kilos of metal on their heads."

John shuddered and said: "Warn our people about this and watch your step out there. You're not the only one with a nasty imagination. Mayhew's rigged the gift shop door so don't go in there! Stay close to the soldiers. I need to know where you are."

Dawn smiled and turned back to the chandelier as John set off to make a series of final checks on the disposition of their forces.

He found Matilda glaring at Duncan Weir near a section of fallen wall on an upper walkway where the restored section of Turnbull House met rusty scaffolding. They were arguing. Weir wanted her further back and she was giving him a piece of her mind to the effect that if he was frightened then he should be the one to be further back.

When John approached and asked what the problem was she rounded on him until he held his hands up and said: "All right, all right! You've made your point. You can stay here but, if you do, then he stays with you. Fair enough?"

Their faces stayed stiff then jerked in unwilling nods of assent. So much for the so-called weaker sex, he thought, and then remembered that their enemy was actually being ruthlessly led by a woman.

He shook his head and left to search out the rest. McCain, Fraser and their forces occupied opposite sections of the restored house commanding a good field of fire over the open area towards the old entrance hall and the ruined section.

The final group consisting of Lauren and her men had faded into the far side of the ruins and taken positions

behind fallen masonry and roof timbers, so he picked his
way gingerly over to them.

"All OK," John asked and Lauren nodded.

"Now remember. No heroics," he said. "If they get this far
then hold your position as noisily as you can. This is
rough ground and they won't fancy charging across it."

"We've done a bit of street fighting before," said Lauren
sweetly to which John smiled and said: "So you have, so
you have. Let's hope you don't have to do much more."

He went on to ask about possible lines of retreat and
Lauren told him she had already checked and there
seemed to be the heavily overgrown remains of a large
rockery garden behind them complete with a ruined
bandstand.

"As long as you can pull back if you have to," said John,
wishing them well and returning to stand in front of the
remains of the old entrance hall.

A slow look all around revealed a few of the defenders
but they'd be well hidden in good positions by the time
Riddle arrived. It was the best that could be done in a
short space of time.

He needed to take his position so he hurried away to a
point where the restored section of the house broke down
into stacks of stone, rusting cement mixers and
wheelbarrows and a weed-covered pile of sand.

Here an aluminium ladder lay jammed into fresh stonework for the restoration of a tower-turret. He climbed up and could see the sky through the open roof as he crouched behind a walkway wall looking towards the intact part of Turnbull House. It was a good vantage point, he thought, offering a view towards the main road yet with access both to the building and the ruin.

He settled down and began to wait, first with a sort of eagerness and then with doubt as more and more time passed. He'd estimated that they had a good hour before Riddle arrived, but when an hour and a half had gone by he began to worry.

The hearse was faster and more manoeuvrable than Riddle's bus, but they should have been here by now.

Just when he had almost decided to go out and check the main road he saw a soldier run into the large central courtyard, give a shrill whistle and then disappear into a doorway. Riddle was finally coming.

CHAPTER SEVENTEEN

A FIERCE blow rocked Griff's head and he spat out defiance and a wad of blood and saliva before glaring at the man in the greasy jacket who had hit him.

He stood facing Riddle surrounded by a ring of her gang members as she repeated her question.

"Where have they gone?" she asked, beginning to finger the pocket where she kept the two antique silver baby rattles.

Griff was seething with suppressed fury but he tried to look worried, his glance darting round those in front of him as he licked split lips and spat another gob of blood to the ground.

"I don't have time for this," said Riddle in a detached voice. "One last chance, where have the people from the castle gone?"

Griff deliberately hesitated then, when Riddle was on the point of speaking again, he said: "What happens to me if I tell you?"

"Why, we leave you here when we go," she said. "We're only interested in the food they took."

Griff tried to give the impression of a man making his mind up then said: "They're going to join forces with Loch Lomond Castle."

"Loch Lomond Castle?" said Riddle. "How many damn castles are there round here?"

Griff just looked at her, so Riddle said: "Where are they going to meet these forces?"

"I dunno," said Griff. "Some place along the road, some ruin or other. Mr McCain was talking about it. He seemed to know where it was."

"Who's McCain?" asked Riddle.

"He's the laird of the castle you've just been to," said Griff. "It's his family home."

"Not any more it isn't," said Riddle who thought for a moment and then asked: "How many men at each of these castles?"

"Fifteen to twenty all told," said Griff. "We had about eight or nine. I think Loch Lomond's got slightly more but I've not been there. It's just what my friends say who know the community there. It's a little bigger than Callander."

"All your food is gone," said Riddle accusingly.

"Well we weren't going to leave it were we," said Griff.

Riddle nodded in agreement. It was what she would have done. Leave nothing for anyone else, but what she'd found out did raise other questions.

"What about Loch Lomond? Do they have food stores?" she asked.

"Bound to I suppose," said Griff. "Our food filled three lorries and vans and we don't have as many people as they do. They'd have to have more stores than us. Everyone knows they've been foraging same as us."

He then stood there silently for a while, favouring his injured leg, Riddle lost in thought and seeming to have almost forgotten he was there.

Finally she tapped her teeth with a fingernail, gave him an appraising look and uttered two words.

"Take him," she said and strong hands closed on Griff's arms, pinning them to his sides.

"Hey, what's this?" he shouted. "You said you'd leave me behind when you left!"

"I was lying," said Riddle, "and so, I think, are you."

Griff's face became suffused with blood as he attempted to bluster a reply.

"Why would I lie?" he attempted.

"A good question," she said turning away, "and one I intend to find the answer to."

She ordered Burton to bind Griff's hands together and get everyone on the bus, slowly walking round to the driver's door as thoughts swirled about in her head.

Her previous raids in Edinburgh had been built on attacking signs of life glimpsed from her vantage point over the city. It was information seen with her own eyes, locations often revealed by smoke or movement that she could assess and plan an attack for, but this was different.

Here she was looking to launch a raid against a place she had never seen based solely on information from a man she had no cause to trust. No change there, she thought wryly, since she trusted no man.

On the face of it everything matched. She knew there had been people here, she knew they were armed and well organised and she knew they had already fooled her once, drawing her on and then fleeing when she couldn't immediately follow. That smacked of planning and if they could plan once then why not a second plan as well?

And this ruin her opponents were meeting at, why join forces there and not at Loch Lomond Castle where there was already a base? There was also the question of why they had left one of their number behind injured. To her it was a natural decision and in the past she had even taken it further and killed wounded people rather than be burdened with their care. Yet these people weren't her. They probably had feelings for the man which made it even more puzzling why they hadn't helped him escape unless he had somehow become separated from them.....or they had left him behind for a reason.

She thought about this as she opened the driver's door and climbed into the cab, waiting for a double bang on the partition behind to let her know everyone was on board.

Riddle started the engine and pulled slowly away to the road where she turned left and headed down into the town.

Perhaps she was reading too much into the situation, she thought, and the man was just trying to save his skin.

Behind her Griff was jammed into a window seat half way down the ground floor of the bus.

Not good, he thought, not good. When he accepted the task he had been given he knew he might be killed on the spot, but when Riddle began to question him his hopes had soared that she'd swallowed what he'd said only for those hopes to be dashed when she effectively called him a liar.

She wasn't totally sure but the chilling remark that she intended to find out left him under no illusion as to what he faced. Griff was braver than most men but torture had never been part of John's plan. He also realised that he had to stick to his guns. He'd lied about the amount of food so an attack would be even more tempting for Riddle and he'd lied about the number of people at the two castles because Riddle couldn't find that out until it was too late. John had coached him on these two crucial points. On everything else he had told the truth. He just had to stick with the plan. Riddle would instantly spot any deviation but would be forced to continue torturing him until she was sure what he was saying was the truth. He had to be consistent.

There was one other thing preying on Griff's mind. He hadn't been wounded in the fight. The bandage on his leg was soiled with deer blood from a Callander venison joint! If Riddle ever thought to check then the game would be up and he could end up praying for death.

He risked a careful glance round the bus and saw that some members of the gang were actually dozing off in their seats! Perhaps there might be a chance of escape, but his hopes were dashed by a sneering voice.

"Don't even think about it," said Brody. "They may be careless but I'm not. Her ladyship put me in charge of you. That means if you escape then I'm for the chop. The rattles will see to that."

"What rattles?" asked Griff. "What are you talking about?"

"Her rattles," Brody replied. "She keeps a couple of fancy silver baby rattles in her pocket. Anyone stepping out of line, anyone who becomes a liability, any special situation she has to decide on and out come the rattles. Bang! It's nearly always death, at least the times I've seen them used it's been death. Man or woman, old or young, makes no difference to Riddle. She'll kill you soon as look at you. I intend to live a long time so don't you go trying anything because I'll be watching you."

With that he subsided into his seat leaving Griff to realise that, if all the gang weren't as mad as Riddle, then a good few of them no longer bothered too much about what they did to stay alive.

Suddenly there was a lurch and a horrendous clashing of gears as Riddle brought the bus to a juddering halt, switched off the engine and got out.

The stop got the attention of everyone on the bus and people crowded the offside windows to peer out and see what was happening.

They watched, hands wiping the dirty glass when it steamed up from their breath, as Riddle walked away from the bus and squatted down to look at the surface of the road where it took a right turn into the A81.

She saw clear evidence of recent tyre marks scuffing the surface of the carriageway, the vehicle's track partially cutting the corner where it had mangled the grass and weeds steadily encroaching on to the macadam.

Standing up, Riddle began to walk briskly away from the bus until an impressive red sandstone bridge appeared to carry the road over the River Teith. There were enough muddy scrapes, wet tyre impressions and other signs along the way to convince Riddle that the vehicle hadn't doubled back and she made haste to return to the bus.

The gang shouted questions at her as she got close to them but Riddle ignored them all, climbed back in the cab and drove off slowly, eyes glued to the road ahead now she knew what she was looking for.

Her eyes were focussed on spotting any tell-tale signs that the vehicle she was pursuing had taken a turn off the road, but her mind was still wrestling with what her opponents might be planning.

If the captured man behind her in the bus could be believed then they were going to join forces at some ruin up ahead, but why? Surely this castle at Loch Lomond would be a better defensive position against her unless it had a weakness she didn't know about or the ruin some strength to work in favour of her opponents. She might have to ask the man a few more questions and her hand strayed to the pocket containing her two antique silver baby rattles.

The bus ground over the bridge, its buttresses cloaked in dead trees and mounds of rubbish washed down by the river, and then trees closed in around them.

Riddle felt a pang of a hunger, a reminder of her need for food, but she dismissed it. Back in the bus her followers were not so stoic.

"All this way for nothing!" said one man, other complaints rippling round the bus.

Griff's quiet appraisal of the gang showed him that if it was cowed by fear then it was ruled by its stomach. These were hungry men and Griff had seen similar situations in Edinburgh where ordinary people had torn each other apart for a can of meat. How long before hunger overcame fear and they rebelled against Riddle? He didn't know, but if Riddle thought she had everyone under her thumb then she was mistaken. These were thugs, likely murderers and rapists as well, and they would only follow as long as it suited them or until an opportunity arose to change their fortunes for the better at which point they were just as likely to round on Riddle and kill her.

He gently tested his bonds and found they had a little give in them, not enough to escape but perhaps enough that with some flexing he might be able to slip them off. It was something to do and take his mind off his predicament.

The road deviated, turning south west, and Riddle soon pulled up again to check for tyre marks and signs at another junction where the road came out of the trees and one side was flanked with ruined farmland. A tractor and trailer stood desolate in the middle of a field, weeds and brush almost reaching the top of its wheels.

This time signs of the hearse's passage were few and far between and Riddle had to search hard to find a few faint impressions. She got back in the bus and started them forward again, but it wasn't until they reached a small flooded section of the road and she could see wet tyre tracks coming out on the far side that she was sure her quarry was still on the road.

The character of the farmland changed and there was growing evidence of flooding, once rich pastureland now a marshy expanse with even a distant glimpse of highland cattle which lumbered off at the first sound of engine noise, their long horns twitching as they swiftly sought cover.

Two more junctions repeated the pattern of stop and check, each time Riddle finding enough to confirm their pursuit, but there came a time when a junction not only confirmed their pursuit of one vehicle but that a number of others had been along the same stretch as well, joining the route from the road to Aberfoyle.

It took Riddle a while to piece together what she was seeing but when she did she was furious at being duped for a second time. What they were following wasn't a rearguard but a decoy! The other vehicles must have left the castle much earlier and taken a different route to get here, but how? There was no other road on the map she had looked at, unaware of just how out of date it had been. She also realised that, had she known of the road, she might have been able to catch up to the food transports without the delay caused her by the fighting withdrawal of those in the vehicle ahead of her. She stamped her feet in frustration.

Furiously she went round to the bus platform, stepped up and went down the aisle to where Griff was sitting with his back to Brody.

"Bring him outside now." she told Brody, reaching into her pocket for the rattles. "And bring a rope!"

Brody dragged Griff upright and pushed him ahead and out on to the road where Riddle took a few steps away towards a large gnarled oak and turned to face him, holding the rattles in her hand and giving them a shake.

Griff watched in disbelief as she held the rattles up to one ear, appearing to listen to something that no-one else could hear. Then she spoke in a strangely harsh voice.

"No more twists, no more half-truths, no more lies. You get one chance and one chance only to answer my questions. Any time I think you are lying you get strung up."

She stabbed a finger at a thick branch overhanging the choked ditch at the side of the road and told the man with the rope to construct a noose and sling it over the branch.

When he'd done so to her satisfaction she said: "Right, first question. How far left to go to this ruin?"

By now half the bus had got out to watch what was happening. Griff sensed the violent eagerness in the watching men and women and realised that his life might literally hang by a thread.

He slowly licked his blood-caked lips and said: "I don't know for sure. I've never been there but I'd say about another ten miles."

Riddle looked hard at him for a moment and then said: "Is it by the road or off it."

Here he was on safer ground and he quickly said: "Off it up a side road. It might be signposted."

"Signposted?" said Riddle.

"Aye," said Griff. "When Mr McCain was talking about it he said before the plague came the place was being restored and used to be a tourist attraction."

So the food might now be just ahead of them within her reach, thought Riddle, but she had to be sure.

"Is the food being taken to this rendezvous at the ruin, on to Loch Lomond Castle or somewhere else?"

John had foreseen such a question. The food lorry and freezer van were already on their way to the castle, but he'd told Griff that if he was asked about them he was to lie and say all vehicles would meet at the ruin first for security and go on to the castle from there.

With a straight face and his heart in his mouth Griff said: "We were all supposed to meet at the ruin and go on together from there. More guards for the food."

Riddle studied his face, gave a single nod and said: "Right, string him up!"

Griff was stunned and he said: "It's the truth I tell you!" shock lending power to his voice.

Riddle seemed almost to ignore him, as if he were no longer there, and several grinning men stepped towards him, grabbing his arms and marching him towards the oak and under the bare bough, its girth now supporting a rope with a noose on the end.

"Everyone's going to the ruin!" shouted Griff, sweat starting to bead his forehead as Riddle stepped closer to watch proceedings.

The noose was placed over his head and he felt the rope begin to bite into his neck as the men took the strain and began to haul.

"For God's sake! I'm telling the truth!" choked Griff as pressure from the rope brought him up on tiptoe. Then his eyes bulged as the men hauled him clear of the ground and he began to swing in a chill breeze, his legs flailing at the air.

After what seemed like a lifetime the world suddenly whirled before his eyes and he found himself upside down in the ditch, his face thrust into weathered dead grass in which a disturbed beetle crawled along a strand and on to his nose.

Griff clawed at the rope with bound hands and his tortured lungs gave a great heave as he was able to breathe.

That had been close, so close that he had thought himself a dead man, but it seemed that Riddle had finally believed his story. Nothing else could have saved him.

The men used the rope to pull him out of the ditch, Griff trying to spare his raw neck as much as he could. When he gained the road he found Riddle standing in front of him.

"Maybe you are telling the truth. Difficult to lie when you're gasping on your last breath, but make no mistake. You're only alive in case I can make use of you at the ruin.

"Put him back in the bus," she said and a shove in his back sent Griff trudging back to the battered old vehicle.

He was halted by a triumphant voice which seemed to freeze every drop of blood in his veins.

"You seem to have lost your limp." said Riddle.

CHAPTER EIGHTEEN

MAISIE had just put a tray of oat biscuits in the oven and had gone to the sink to wash her hands.

She was tired and wanted to sit down for a while to rest her aching hip, but she knew the children playing in the drawing room would be after her soon for a story.

The baking had taken a lot out of her, but she loved to cook and knew that the oat biscuits would go down well when everyone came back from the tiger hunt.

She looked down to where her hands rubbed and dipped through bubbles in a bowl of warm water and remembered that she had to check on soap supplies and see if they needed to make some more. It was a steep learning curve. They were having to teach themselves new skills almost every day and it was important that the children were involved. The future was theirs and the key to that future was knowledge.

Shaking her hands dry, she looked up to find a towel and froze as a striped back flowed past just below window level. The tiger was here!

One desperate look at the kitchen door she had opened a crack to let out the smells of cooking and she knew she could never get there in time to close it.

Beginning to shake, Maisie used the big wooden dining table and chairs to help pull herself over to a door leading to a small sitting room, giving one agonised look at her walking stick propped up out of reach near the aga.

A stumble forced her to grab the doorframe, but she used her momentum to swing herself into the room before grabbing the door handle and pulling it closed. Her last sight of the kitchen was the outer door being warily pushed open to admit the great head and forequarters of the tiger. It caught a glimpse of Maisie before its silent snarl was cut off by the door closure.

For the moment she was safe, but as she dragged herself out into the hallway she only had thoughts for the children. Pain stabbed her hip as she limped heavily across to the drawing room and eased herself inside before shutting the door firmly and wedging a chair under the handle.

A chorus of delight greeted her arrival with a volley of requests for a story, but Maisie put her finger to her lips and said: "Stories later. For now we're going to play a special game of hide-and-seek and you all have to be very quiet."

She shuffled over to the other door and peered into an empty dining room, beckoning the children and again putting her finger to her lips as she shepherded them into a small sitting room containing Becky's baby, Tilly, who was fast asleep in a crib.

Maisie heart was thumping as she carefully scooped up the baby and handed her to Donna's daughter, Tess, who accepted the little bundle with a proud smile on her face.

"Now everybody listen," said Maisie. "We are going out of that door and up the stairs to the bathroom where we're going to hide and be quiet as mice."

"Mice are not very quiet," said Becky's son, Kevin. "They run around and squeak."

"Well none of us must make a sound or the dragon will get us," said Maisie.

Evie's daughters, Anne and Nancy, both said they were frightened of dragons but her son, Robert, scoffed and said there was no such thing.

"Dragons are stupid! Skull Man would kill them easy!" he went on, waving a toy figure of Skull Man in their faces.

Suddenly a rumbling growl came from the direction of the drawing room they had just left and the eyes of all the children widened in fear.

"Was that a dragon?" asked Nancy in a small voice.

"Let's not wait and find out," said Maisie shooing her charges out of the door which she swiftly closed behind her before urging them into the corridor, through a little hallway and up a wide wooden staircase to the first floor.

The children didn't have to be told twice and Maisie let them get a little way ahead of her before stepping over to the gun cabinet at the foot of the stairs, unlocking it and taking out the last remaining shotgun.

Memories flooded back of her clash last year with a gang who had attacked John's house in Launceston where she'd been staying. Didn't think I'd ever be using one of these again, she thought, grabbing a handful of cartridges which she thrust into the pocket of her apron before painfully following the children up the stairs.

Another growl came, this time punctuated by scraping noises, and Maisie frantically tried to drag herself on to the landing and at the same time fumble cartridges into the shotgun breech.

Just as she succeeded a darker shadow moved along the hall wall as the tiger found its way towards the foot of the stairs.

Maisie was already moving back to where the frightened children grouped in the bathroom door.

"Get inside! Get inside!" shouted Maisie, backing into the bathroom as the tiger found the staircase and in a split second bounded up it towards them.

Nancy was knocked over and burst into tears as Maisie tried to close the bathroom door with her left hand only for the shotgun in her right hand to become trapped between the door and the jamb.

In desperation she pulled first one trigger and then the other, the double explosion of sound causing the tiger to shy back from the thunderous noise which gave Maisie just enough time to jerk the shotgun barrel clear and slam and lock the door.

Her breath whistled through her teeth in relief as she managed one step before slumping down on the rim of the bath surrounded by wails of hunger from Tilly and cries and floods of tears from the children as they crowded round her.

Their cries turned to screams as the bathroom door creaked and groaned as a great weight came on the other side.

Maisie desperately fumbled in her apron pocket for spare cartridges only for little Anne, in an almost hysterical state, to knock her hand, spilling the cartridges on the floor.

"The dragon's going to eat us! The dragon's going to eat us!" she wailed as the door gave another ominous creak.

Maisie tried to comfort her and reach for the cartridges at the same time, but the toddler began to scream as wood split near the lock, the door shuddering under the pressure of the tiger's great weight as it tried to reach them. An intense growl caused pandemonium among the children who thought the "dragon" was breaking through.

A wild look round the bathroom revealed a clothes basket, a folding towel rail and a small swing bin but nothing of substance to prop against the door. In desperation Maisie considered the window as she found first one cartridge and then a second, shovelling them into the shotgun's breech and snapping it shut.

The window was narrow with diamond panes and a sturdy handle. She might be able to lift the children up and get them out through it but the aperture was too small for her even if she had been physically able to clamber up on to the sill.

So be it, she thought. She'd had a good life and there were worse ways to go than trying to save the lives of children.

The noise from the terrified youngsters in the confined space of the bathroom was shredding her nerves, so she shouted once and into the brief silence told them to go over to the toilet to one side of the window, backing slowly to join them as the tiger kept up its assault on the door.

Quickly she opened the window and saw a short section of roofing gently sloping down to a gutter. It would have to do.

Using her right arm to cradle the shotgun, Maisie told Tess to climb up on the toilet and then out of the window, steadying the fearful girl when she stepped up on to the window sill.

Another cracking sound dragged her gaze back to the door and she hastily snatched her hand away from Tess and used it to lift the shotgun as more screaming broke out among the children.

As if in a dream she heard the roaring arrival of the Landrover's engine followed by slamming doors and people shouting her name.

Rigidly focussed, she got another child on to the toilet and handed them up to Tess who had come back to the window to help.

Another child was handed up and another until only little Anne was left, her body almost catatonic with fear and her hands locked firmly in Maisie's skirt.

Still Maisie didn't look at her but instead spared a single glance at the window to check the other children were safe before lifting the shotgun in both hands and training it at the sagging lock.

Slowly she noticed the silence broken only by distant shouting and her name being repeated again and again.

The shouting came closer and closer until she could hear the clump of feet pounding up the stairs.

"Jesus! Look at the door!" came Jed's voice, followed by three knocks.

"You in there Maisie?" he asked.

"No, I've gone to my gymnastics class!" she said angrily. "Of course I'm in here and so are the children. Hang on a minute and I'll open the door."

She carefully broke the shotgun and removed the cartridges before putting it down and pulling back the slide which locked the door, but nothing happened.

Door and lock were in a sorry state from the tiger's battering and Jed had to put his shoulder to the frame and force the door open to get in.

The first thing Maisie saw was his white face as he stepped inside the bathroom and gave her a huge hug, little Anne continuing to blubber as Conrad and Roy crowded inside behind him and began to reach up to the window to lift the frightened children back inside from the roof.

Maisie took one look at the outside of the door raked by claw marks and burst into sobs which set off all the children, tears flooding as they tried to clutch at her for support.

"Quiet!" shouted Jed and startled tear-streaked faces jerked towards him.

"Maisie, is anyone hurt?" he asked and she was just able to mutely shake her head.

"Then where's the tiger?" he said.

Maisie wiped her eyes, ignored the wailing all around her and pulled herself together enough to say: "I don't know. One minute the damn thing was breaking in, the next it had gone."

Jed nodded and said: "Roy? Stay here and guard Maisie and the children. No one is to leave the bathroom until we've checked the house. The tiger could be anywhere. Conrad, Noah, with me. We'll check the bedrooms first."

The three men slowly and cautiously started down the bedroom corridor, checking each room. It was a nightmare task fraught with the chance of being ambushed. The animal could be behind each bed, lurking in each alcove they came to and every nerve they had was stretched to breaking point.

As they finished one section and started another they began to hear distant shouting as beaters and other marksmen arrived panting outside the manor.

By the time they descended again to the ground floor those who had outstripped the main hunt were starting to cautiously ease their way inside, but Jed told them to stay

outside and watch all doors and windows until he had
completed the search.

Ten minutes later and he pronounced the manor clear.
Somehow the tiger had fled without being seen and Jed
now set out the much more dangerous task of searching
the grounds of the manor where the advantage lay more
with the tiger.

Trapped inside it could have been cornered and killed, but
Jed knew only too well that among barns and outbuildings
the powerful animal could spring an attack from hiding
before they even had a hint it might be nearby.

More and more people were arriving back from the hunt
and Jed called as many of them together as he could.

"Has anyone seen the tiger?" he asked and when he got a
chorus of "Noes" and a general shaking of heads he
added: "In that case, if the tiger is still here it will be
somewhere round the barns or the open outhouses near
the road. It can't be towards the meadows and woods
because you've all just come from that direction.

"I want everyone to search in groups of five with at least
two guns to each group. No-one is to go into any open
building alone, no-one is to search anywhere on their
own. Anyone sees anything they are to fire a shot in the
air to alert the rest of us. Now spread out and keep your
eyes peeled."

Half a dozen groups quickly formed and moved off, an uneasy silence falling over Waterfall Manor. There were several nervous moments.

One man nearly triggered his rifle when a chicken shot into the open from under a pile of feed bags, clucking indignantly at being disturbed before strutting away and beginning to peck at the ground.

Another searcher saw the tiger near a large diesel fuel tank and almost raised his shotgun to fire only to realise he was looking at an old metal advertising sign screwed to a back wall featuring the Esso tiger!

Some open-sided barns were huge and contained a potentially lethal maze of vehicles, farm equipment, old furniture and even reclaimed building materials.

Jed's group were half way through one such building when the tiger struck, attacking them as they approached an intersection between a silage wagon and some old tables.

There was just a hint of a growl and it was on them, springing forward from the cover of a stack of roofing beams.

Cries of alarm came as everyone tried to throw themselves out of the way, but Jed found himself next to two old wardrobes and a stack of metal bedsteads which he could neither get under or on top of.

The tiger's body smashed into his shoulder and knocked him into the front of a wardrobe as the tiger landed lightly and turned to maul him, but no attack came.

Jed's body slid to one side, his impact triggering the wardrobe door which opened slowly towards the tiger whose snarl of anger turned into a roar of rage as it saw its own image in the mirrored door.

It caused the animal to hesitate for a few fatal seconds, convinced that it suddenly faced a rival tiger, and that was all it took for Lucas and Asher to aim and fire.

The tiger staggered, hit in the left shoulder and side, and when it turned to rend its attackers Jed recovered to loose both barrels into it at close range.

The blast tore into the tiger's spine, crippling its hind legs, but it was still far from dead. Two more blasts had to thunder out before its paws spasmed, clawing the dusty ground as its body slowly relaxed in death.

Jed lay on the ground, his shotgun half raised towards the great striped form in front of him.

Lucas carefully approached and gave the dead tiger a wary prod with the barrel of his shotgun before heaving a great sigh of relief.

"Nearly had you there!" he joked only to become concerned at the blood he saw trickling down the left shoulder of Jed's jacket.

Other people began to arrive as Lucas knelt and helped Jed to sit up, his shotgun sliding to the ground as his face twisted in pain and he tried to grip where a slash from the tiger's claws had laid his flesh open almost to the bone.

"Stay still," said Lucas, tearing a strip from Jed's jacket. "You won't bleed to death, but those cuts should be thoroughly washed."

"I'm alright," said Jed. "Stop fussing. The tiger's the one that's dead."

"And you will be too if you don't get some work done on that shoulder of yours. Tiger claws are notoriously filthy. God knows what you've got trudging around now in your bloodstream. You need anti-biotics and quick."

Jed seemed quite startled by what he said and made no objection when he was pulled to his feet and hustled round and down to the courtyard. He faced a host of questions as he was led through the sun room and round to the main kitchen where a grim-faced Becky sat him in a chair and got out a pair of scissors.

"You just couldn't stay safely out of the way, could you!" she said tersely, starting to snip through a seam to release the jacket sleeve. "You had to get involved, had to lead from the front, had to risk yourself."

At this point she gave the sleeve a brisk pull and tore it clear to a surprised yelp from Jed who eyed her cautiously as if she was going to tear his arm off as well.

"Now we're running round trying to prevent you getting blood poisoning or something worse. There are times I wish I'd married a mouse not a man," she said, angrily turning her attention to the remains of an old towel which she cut into a pad and began to carefully swab three open cuts which were still oozing blood.

When she finished doing that she turned to a small brown bottle and, taking another square of towel, dripped some of the contents of the bottle on to it.

"What's that?" asked Jed suspiciously as more people arrived in the kitchen to ask about the fate of the tiger.

"Disinfectant," said Becky succinctly. "Now shut up and hold still while I clean these cuts."

With that she gripped his arm with one hand and gave a first wipe of the wound with the other.

Breath hissed through Jed's teeth as a wave of fire engulfed his shoulder. It felt as if a thousand needles were being driven into his flesh and colour rapidly left his face to be replaced by a pinched white look as shock set in.

"Jesus!" said Jed, but Becky just poured more disinfectant on the towel pad and gave the cuts as thorough a cleaning as she could, Jed's arm turning rigid as his muscles clenched themselves in reaction against the pain.

Finally she picked up the largest sealed wound pad she could find among the supplies Jed had salvaged from the ruins of Derriford Hospital and tore it open. Carefully she peeled off the plastic coatings and smoothed it on over the cuts, pressing the sides to make sure the pad had stuck in place. She stepped back, gave her work a critical look and nodded once.

Jed unclenched his teeth, glanced at his shoulder and then looked up at his wife and said: "You enjoyed that!"

"I didn't," she said, "but maybe a bit of pain will make you listen when you won't pay attention to what I say."

"I didn't do this deliberately you know!" said Jed peevishly. "The tiger jumped us! The first I knew was being knocked over!"

"Who was it told everyone to keep their eyes peeled? You can't even follow your own advice!"

Everyone was relaxing now because they knew the tiger was dead, so the exchange between Becky and Jed took on a comic element for them and they began to laugh as nervous energy released itself.

Maisie, Roy and the children came into the overcrowded kitchen, the youngsters babbling about the "dragon" and Conrad and Victor shouted through the growing noise that people should get themselves a hot drink and then leave since it was now safe to start work again.

Someone brought Maisie her walking stick and she took it gratefully before sinking into a chair where she accepted a cup of tea with a smile.

Jed was mollified when Becky gave him a peck on the cheek before turning to accept Tilly from Tess. The baby was smacking its lips together and uttering regular screams of hunger which cut off and became snuffling sounds as Becky undid her blouse and pressed Tilly's mouth to a nipple before moving slowly away to a sitting room.

Mike came up and told Jed he would take a work party out to deal with the livestock and Jed replied that he wanted others sent out as well to survey fields near the ones used for haymaking to see which could be brought back into use next.

"You take it easy for a while," said Mike. "That was all just a bit too close for comfort."

He strode away, calling men and women to him, and Jed found himself being looked at by Maisie.

"I owe you an apology," he said. "It never occurred to me that the tiger might get round our beating line. I should have made sure you and the children were locked up safe and sound before we left."

"It did get a bit exciting here for a while!" said Maisie with a smile. "I'm too old now to be rushing up stairs away from tigers!"

"Well, I'm going to make it up to you with a special gift," said Jed, getting unsteadily to his feet and slowly walking out of the kitchen leaving a mystified Maisie behind him.

Jed made his way shakily outside via the sun room, his bare left arm chilling in a cold breeze which waved branches and sent a few stray leaves tumbling through the air.

By the time he reached the open barn containing the dead tiger his shoulder was beginning to throb in a steady rhythm.

Grimacing he tried to flex the muscles only to wince as he got a sharp reminder of the damage the tiger had done to him. Finding the big cat wasn't straightforward and twice he took a wrong turn, once into a cul-de-sac of stacked windows and doors and once down an alley of basins, baths, toilet bowls and cisterns which opened out near the entrance to a large walled garden.

Eventually he found his way to the tiger where he took out a razor-sharp clasp knife, cut two pieces from a roll of twine and trussed the tiger's front and back paws together. He then went away to an outbuilding full of tools where he selected a spade and a sturdy long handled hoe.

On his way back he grabbed Donald, Asher and Ryan, took them to the tiger and watched while they used the handle of the hoe to lift the body and carry it beyond the outbuildings and in through the gate of a heavily overgrown wheat field where he got the other two men to dig a pit near a hedge before they helped him carefully skin the tiger and roll up its skin. He had plans for that.

By the time they had finished the pit was ready and the tiger's body was unceremoniously dumped in to it and covered with earth. They then returned to the barns where Jed took several long pieces of wood and roughly pegged out the tiger's skin to let the hide dry, standing the frame to one side against a wall.

By now his head was spinning and he began to wonder if he should have spared his shoulder and given it a bit more time to recover.

Two hours later he had picked his way listlessly through a late lunch and worried Becky by saying he was going upstairs to lie down for a while as he didn't feel too good.

He was even worse when Becky looked in on him as evening fell. His face was flushed, his body hot and the flesh round the wound pad on his shoulder was starting to look red and angry.

Jed asked for water and Becky seized the opportunity to shell out two anti-biotic tablets from a foil sheet and get him to swallow them. Almost before she could tuck the sheets round him he rolled to one side and was violently sick on the floor. Swiftly she kept him on his side to prevent choking and then rushed out of the room, returning with a bowl, rags and two more anti-biotic tablets.

Carefully she wiped his face as his eyes closed and he sank back into the sheets, then she cleaned up the mess, scrubbing the carpet until it was clean before opening the bedroom window a crack despite the cold to let fresh air in. She spent a few minutes watching him, then placed the tablets on a bedside table and went downstairs to talk with Lydia, explaining that Jed had become ill and she was going to sit with him. Lydia promised to look in on them before she went to bed.

When Becky returned to the bedroom she found that Jed was burning up, his skin hot and dry to the touch. She eased him up on an elbow and trickled water into his mouth, forcing him to swallow the tablets despite his protests. This time he managed to keep them down but the effort cost him and he lay back on the sheets, one arm flapping weakly. Becky wiped his forehead with a damp cloth, keeping her worries to herself. She'd lost one husband before she met Jed. She didn't want to lose another.

News of Jed's condition spread through the manor and several people put their head round the door to ask how he was and wish him well.

Lydia took over for an hour to give Becky a break and a chance for a drink and a bite to eat, but she was soon back in the bedroom with a bowl of cold water and more rags which she used to sponge his body down in an attempt to help his fever.

It brought home to her how much they relied on the remnants of modern medicine. What would they do when they were all gone? The Recovery Council couldn't supply them indefinitely and it would be some years before even basic medicines were manufactured again.

All through the night she stayed with him, only breaking to feed Tilly and grab an hour's sleep towards morning when Jed stopped twisting about and became calmer.

As the day wore on she thought he seemed less flushed although a digital thermometer placed in his armpit still registered nearly 39C.

Lydia came in shortly after lunch, bullied her into eating a sandwich with a glass of milk and then got her to lie down and rest in another bedroom while she kept an eye on Jed.

The wound pad on his injured shoulder had already been changed once revealing angry, puffy flesh with a watery yellow discharge.

Now Lydia changed it again, flushing away the discharge with boiled water containing salt which brought moans from Jed although he didn't wake up. She was also able to get him to swallow two more anti-biotic tablets with small amounts of water without him vomiting.

By now there was an unnatural hush to daily life at the manor with everybody realising just how seriously ill Jed was.

Evening saw Becky jerk awake and stumble back to Jed's bedside, her eyes now heavily ringed with fatigue.

Lydia told her he seemed a little more settled but still hadn't woken up before slipping from the room as Becky sat down in an old armchair she had pulled up by the side of the bed.

It was a long night but Jed's fever broke as light began to filter through the bedroom curtains. Becky twice sponged his body with cold water and she was now convinced it felt cooler and there was none of the body twisting she had seen in him before.

She sat back to rest for a moment and the next thing she knew it was full light and she was being watched from the bed.

Jed's eyes were open although his sunken drawn face looked a pale shadow of his former healthy self.

Becky was out of the armchair immediately, placing the back of her hand on his forehead which felt cooler. She took the digital thermometer, placed it in Jed's armpit and was rewarded with a reading of 37.5C, not great but a lot better than it had been.

He cleared his throat and Becky carefully lifted his head and helped him take sips from a mug of water before easing his head back on the pillow.

Jed smiled at her and in a hoarse voice said: "You look terrible!"

It was too much for her and she burst into tears before hugging him which made Jed wince and Becky hastily babble "sorry" several times.

After that they just looked at each other for a while until Becky asked him if he was hungry.

"I wasn't until you asked me, but I could perhaps manage a bit of toast and some more water," he croaked.

Just then Lydia came in and, when she found out about the toast, she told Becky that she'd get something for them both and left.

When she'd gone Jed asked: "How long have I been asleep?"

"About two days," said Becky. "You were bad for a while but the anti-biotics seemed to help."

"That's good to know," said Jed. "Must still be a bit of life left in them yet."

"Jed, I've been thinking. We need to put medical supplies top of our list of questions when next we talk to Leo in London. Everything we've got is on the brink or already out of date. He may have new drugs but this country doesn't. We can't rely on him and the Recovery Council forever so we need to find out about manufacturing our own and, if it's possible, how many years it will take before we can do that."

"Well you won't get any arguments from me," said Jed, "but I'm no scientist. We'll need to chat to someone who is, perhaps arrange for some experts to come over on the next ship and help us start our own supply. Leo will know what's possible and what isn't and how to go about it."

When Jed made attempts to sit up and get out of bed, Becky pushed him back and said: "Take it easy.

"You're weak as a kitten and a day of rest won't make a blind bit of difference to the manor. It will all still be here waiting for you in the morning. I just hope John and Dawn are having an easier time of it than we are. They should be back in a few days if Scotland has gone well."

CHAPTER NINETEEN

GRIFF froze as Riddle walked slowly up and then round to stand in front of him. When she bent and unwrapped the bloody bandage on his leg and found there was no wound to go with it she straightened up and looked at him, eyes alight with malice.

"Not quite what you seem, are you," she said. "The question is, what else isn't as it seems? Perhaps there is no food, perhaps your friends have gone somewhere else."

"I've told you the truth," said Griff. "They're all meeting at the ruin."

"Well we'll see won't we," said Riddle, "and if they're not there then we'll have to have another little hanging, only this time you'll swing for good."

She smiled vacantly at him, her mind already on other things, and Griff shuddered. She was completely mad, he thought, hoping John would be ready for them when they came.

Several men hustled him back on board the bus and this time tied him to his seat as well while Riddle started the bus and drove slowly away.

Ten miles he'd said. Well she'd see about that, but one thing was for certain. She didn't trust him and if they were there then she had no intention of just walking in without a bit of insurance. She patted the rattles in her pocket and drove on.

The road was a lonely one, its stark countryside beautiful and rugged but empty of life. The occasional tumble of stones to mark a fallen hut or shelter was the only sign of human life and the road was so remote that they passed only one abandoned vehicle, its bonnet raised and a jumble of human bones and tattered clothing lying nearby on the side of the road. The plague had claimed a victim even here.

Riddle drove several miles, the road twisting and dipping as she went, until a large sign appeared. Faded lettering on battered metal proclaimed that Turnbull House was four miles away. She smiled and continued driving.

Another sign soon appeared, this one more ornate with a painted scene of a half-ruin and brief information that Turnbull House was a Scottish Heritage restoration project.

The sign also said the site was just one mile ahead, so Riddle slowed the bus and gradually brought it to a halt as soon as she saw a signpost appear ahead of her.

Getting out of the driver's cab, she came round and got inside the passenger section, walking forward to where Griff sat tied to his seat.

"Well now," she said. "Time to put your words to the test. Do you still say your friends are here?"

Griff just stared at her and then gave a brief nod to which Riddle smiled and said: "Then we'd better get you ready hadn't we. Must have you looking your best for the reunion!"

And with that she gave an order that had her men grinning and Griff's heart sinking with despair.

*   *   *

JOHN heard the sound of a large vehicle pull up in the distance and he tensed. Everything was set and it all depended on luring Riddle and her gang far enough into their trap that they could not get out of it.

He peered sharply towards the entrance. Still nothing, then his eyes narrowed as a single figure came into sight walking clumsily forward.

John couldn't make out features at first but as the distance closed he suddenly realised that the man he was looking at was Lauren's friend, Griff.

He seemed in some discomfort which John thought not surprising as he was carrying a huge chunk of stone attached to a taut rope wound into a noose round his neck.

Dawn was much closer and from her concealed position with Lieutenant Mayhew she saw Riddle's gang. They were following about thirty metres behind him and when they reached a fallen wall being rebuilt they split in two, half the force dividing to encircle the main house while the remaining members followed Riddle as she walked confidently up the entrance way behind Griff.

Dawn saw that he was exhausted, all his great strength being sapped by the stone he was carrying. His head was unnaturally stiff as he tried to prevent it being bowed over by the weight of the stone in his arms. Suddenly he shouted a warning.

"Watch out! They're circling behind you!" he managed and then just stood still, teeth bared with the effort of supporting his burden which Dawn saw appeared to be a piece of shaped masonry from the ruin.

Riddle's voice cut into the scene and said: "Listen to me! Your friend is in no position to help. You are surrounded, but all we want is the food. Give us that and we go away. No-one will be hurt."

Dawn whispered fiercely to Lieutenant Mayhew who appeared startled before looking closely at Griff as Dawn slipped away towards where she thought John was hidden.

"Don't believe her!" shouted Griff. "She'll kill you all if you give her the chance."

"That's not true," said Riddle, advancing to stand a few metres behind him as her men spread out into the open area between the two house wings.

"We're only interested in the food. A fight benefits no-one. Let us take the food and we'll just leave."

Dawn's progress down a dusty corridor lined with piles of planking, shovels and other tools ended suddenly when a hand clamped over her mouth as John dragged her behind a stack of bags containing plaster.

"What the hell are you doing here?" he asked. "I told you to stay with the soldiers so I knew where you were!"

"No time for that. You've got about two minutes to warn Lauren what's happening or she'll be ambushed."

"What is happening?" asked John.

"Lieutenant Mayhew is going to shoot Griff!" she replied and then hastily explained what she'd arranged. John

listened intently and told her to try and warn Fraser and
McCain before he rushed away in search of Lauren.

She managed to find Fraser and told him what to expect
but as she fled through a dusty room empty but for
cardboard historical figures she realised that there was no
time left to reach McCain. She paused by a window
overlooking the ruined central entrance hall to see what
would happen.

"Time's up," shouted Riddle. "Tell me where the food is
or face the consequences."

No sooner were the words out of her mouth than there
was the crack of a rifle shot and Griff fell to the ground to
shouts of rage from McCain and his men.

Riddle looked bemused by what had happened but
quickly ran for cover as her men fired at the house wing
containing McCain's group only to face withering return
fire from both McCain and Fraser's men.

Riddle screamed at her flanking forces to attack but they
faced problems of their own trying to thread a way
through piles of building materials and equipment to get
into unfamiliar buildings.

Their element of surprise was gone and when John and
Lauren split her group into two, each leading a section,
the battle fractured into a series of ambushes and hand to
hand combats.

Half a dozen gang members clambering about through stacks of oak beams, tiles and bricks behind the wing of the house where Fraser was fighting found an open side door which they cautiously approached.

Above them they heard the steady sounds of shotguns, rifles and pistols being fired, so they prepared to enter and look for a staircase to climb up and launch an attack. Instead it was they who were attacked from behind, John and his men sending shot after shot at them as the gang members milled about in confusion. By the time they threw themselves through the door they left behind two dead.

"I'm bleeding," moaned Burton, clutching a flesh wound in his left arm and ducking as a stray shot came in through the door and ricocheted off the stonework.

They crouched in a dim corridor down which Burton could see a newell post.

"Stairs are that way," he said pointing. "Let go give these bastards a taste of what they've given us."

The three remaining men with him nodded sharply in agreement and followed him down the corridor, but when they reached the post there were no stairs just a ladder propped up to the landing four metres above.

Burton gave the ladder a few careful tugs but it was sturdy enough and seemed to have been roped in place at the top, so he began to climb and the others moved in to follow him. They were approaching the top when there was a loud scraping noise as one of Fraser's men appeared and emptied a barrow load of bricks over them.

The bricks hurtling through the air had the impact of a grenade and there were screams from the men below as they were knocked off the ladder by the missiles raining down on them or the impact of those above falling and hitting them.

When two of Fraser's men darted down the ladder and pointed their guns into the clearing dust they found one man lying with his head at an unnatural angle where his neck had snapped, another unconscious and the final two moaning as they clutched limbs broken by the bricks or their fall.

"Tie them up," came Fraser's voice from the landing, "then one of you stay and guard them. The other can come back up here. We need all the help we can get."

The raiders had no better luck with the other wing of the house where McCain and his men were firing down at Riddle.

When the flanking force climbed in through an open window they found themselves in a large hall with shields, weapons and dusty information boards.

"Look!" said Oggie, standing next to a suit of armour. "It's bigger than I am. However did they fight in these?"

"Don't muck about there," said a man rejoicing in the name of Hanky because he was always wiping his nose. "Let's go and join the party."

He and the others moved towards an ornate door as Oggie bent over an information board and used his finger to slowly trace its words, marvelling as he discovered that some suits of armour could weigh more than ten gallons of beer!

Suddenly there was a clanking noise followed by a thunderous crash and some shrill screaming which went on and on.

Oggie stumbled through a cloud of dust to find a terrible scene in front of him. Somehow a giant chandelier had fallen on his friends, crushing them to the floor in a bloodied heap of bodies.

He hurried to try and lift the chandelier clear only for one of the bodies to scream and curse him for a fool as metal tore at a shattered leg, blood pumping past white bone. Bewildered, Oggie let go which only sparked more screams and cursing as metal smacked back into flesh.

There were cries for help but Oggie didn't know what he could do. Perhaps the lady would know and, happy at thinking things through, he set out to find Riddle.

Out in the open between the two wings it was hide or die for Riddle and her remaining men.

Some joined her as she ran forward towards the ruins while others broke back and tried to take shelter in buildings or hide behind walls and an ornamental well.

Those in the open included Griff who lay where he had fallen, crumpled in a heap across the huge chunk of masonry Riddle had forced him to carry.

She had wanted everyone in the ruins to focus on him while her flanking forces surrounded the site. Now it was her plan which was in ruins, he thought.

No-one was more surprised to be alive than he was, but if his body had been slowed by the great weight he carried then his mind had still been rapier quick. When a shot barked out severing the rope cruelly linking his neck to the chunk of masonry he lost no time in falling with the stone. At first he felt only the incredible relief of having his burden removed, but almost immediately he made sure his body and jacket covered the severed rope ends. To all intents and purposes he had been shot and he had no intention of moving while bullets whipped overhead or smacked into the ground near him.

Gathering himself he quietly waited for a lull and then surged to his feet and darted towards the safety of the Gift Shop door.

Near the Turnbull House entrance Lieutenant Mayhew and his soldiers were taking a terrible toll of those gang members who had tried to break back towards them.

Their position on and around an ivy-covered archway gave them a combination of height and an unobstructed field of fire which they made deadly use of.

Their first volley killed or wounded four gang members while others fell as they scrambled for cover anywhere they could find it. The exchange then fragmented into a sniping dual with the surviving gang members trying to locate and pick off the soldiers who soon found targets hard to come by as the attackers learnt to keep their heads down.

CHAPTER TWENTY

RIDDLE'S instinctive run for the cover of the ruins dragged half a dozen of her men with her and they dropped from sight where workmen had been restoring a stone framed window.

From there they began to pepper the windows in both wings of the house, forcing McCain, Fraser and their men to take extreme care when exposing themselves for a shot.

The result produced a staccato popping sound as marksmen tried to find a target or fired into cover they thought might conceal an enemy.

Riddle was thinking about easing her forces round to attack one wing of the house when Lauren's group fell on them like avenging angels, their memories full of the atrocities committed in Edinburgh.

They were in no mood to take prisoners and their first
volley into Riddle's position was immediately followed
by a charge, everyone screaming at the top of their voices
as they tried to close with their hated enemy.

Lauren led the way, darting through stacks of stone,
timber and bricks with just one thought in her mind, to
find Riddle and avenge her grandfather.

The fighting became fierce. With little or no time to
reload, combatants pulled knives and stabbed and thrust at
their opponent.

Richard, who had joined Lauren when Riddle abandoned
him for being late back to her bus, was in the thick of it
against his former comrades. He fired and missed at one
man and then retreated into a half rebuilt room to try and
reload. He was just ramming a cartridge into the breech of
his shotgun when a harsh voice behind told him: "Never
turn your back on the enemy!"

His attempt to swing and bring the shotgun to bear was
too slow and Brody rammed a knife into his heart,
Richard slumping to the ground where Brody spat on his
body and said: "Good riddance!"

The snarl on his face turned to a look of shock as a voice
behind him said: "You should practice what you preach."

The blast of a shotgun threw Brody against a stone wall
and he dropped lifeless to the ground as Steve stepped
into the room. He gave one glance at the body and then
knelt briefly beside Richard, closing his eyes and taking

his shotgun before rifling the pockets of both dead men for any spare ammunition.

He heard movement near the door and flattened himself against the remains of a wall only to heave a sigh of relief when Jack, one of Lauren's men, stepped cautiously inside.

"They both dead?" he asked.

"Aye," said Steve. "Where's Lauren?"

"God knows," said Jack. "Last I saw she was trying to find Riddle, but she could be anywhere. This ruin is like a maze."

They shared the cartridges Steve had found and Jack took Richard's shotgun, checking its load before the two men crept out of the room, darted their way past a stack of tiles and took cover behind a rusting cement mixer.

"See anything" whispered Jack only to throw himself to one side as two men jumped them from behind a stack of stones, hurling themselves forward with vicious-looking knives in their hands.

A split second later all four men were rolling about, locked together in hate as each strained to gain control of the deadly blades.

Jack succeeded in forcing his opponent's wrist back, the knife falling free as the man gave a cry of pain at his tortured muscles. Jack ignored him, snatching up the knife and plunging it into the man's stomach just as Steve shouted: "Watch yourself!"

Jack grabbed his shotgun and twisted round just in time to see Steve lying on the ground and the other man almost on him with a knife.

The man bared his teeth and slashed at Jack who leapt back, cannoning into a stack of oak beams as he attempted to bring his shotgun to bear.

Before he could recover the man was on him, but a killing thrust at Jack's stomach only pierced his jacket and the blade snapped off at the hilt when Jack tried to bull his way clear.

Instantly the man grabbed at the shotgun, both of them trying to twist it free enough to fire.

Jack swiftly realised the man was more powerful than he was and changed tactics, suddenly pushing where before he had pulled. The result sent the man stumbling back and he released his grip on the shotgun when he fell back over the body of his fellow gang member. Jack stepped swiftly forward as he tried to rise and fired a single barrel into him at close range. The man seemed to deflate and Jack took one brief look at him before dropping to his knees by Steve's side.

One glance was all it took to tell him that Steve was dying, his chest slick with blood pumping from a mortal wound.

"Nicely done," said Steve, then he coughed and blood ran from the corner of his mouth.

"Stay quiet," said Jack. He tried to take his jacket off to put behind Steve's head, but his friend weakly held up a hand to stop him.

"Too late for that," he said. "Are they both dead?" he asked and, when Jack nodded, he said: "So am I," his eyes glazing over and his body falling still as life slipped away.

Jack looked at his friend for a while, straightened his arms by his side and then moved off to continue searching for gang members.

A hundred metres away Griff's sprint had almost brought him to the Gift Shop door when a gang member stepped out from the edge of an overgrown box hedge, a pistol in one hand and a small hand axe in the other.

"Me first I think," he said with a smirk as a bullet spanged off nearby stonework. "Find your own bolthole."

And with a ferocious grin the man backed away, dropped his empty pistol and quickly twisted the door handle to step inside.

As he disappeared from view Griff heard a sudden scream cut off by a strange thumping noise. Bullets continued to whip through the air near him, so he hastily approached the door, but it stuck half way open when he tried to push it. Griff was forced to try and squeeze through the gap, the zipper of his jacket catching on the lock tongue, but he was able to stumble inside.

Lying on the floor inside was the gang member with the hand axe, his skull smashed horribly out of shape by a large stone with twine attached to it.

"I may have words with Health and Safety," muttered Griff, looking carefully around in case there were more booby traps. He couldn't see any and made his way through the shop, past a serving counter to a storage area door at the back which he opened. Inside were wide shelves full of dusty cardboard boxes of stock which he ignored, hunting about until he found the emergency exit door. Holding his breath he struck the release bar and pushed, the door grinding a bit but opening on to a small rear loading area with a large drift of rotting leaves in the corner of the building where it met an old wall.

His arms and legs still ached from carrying the huge stone Riddle had roped him to, but Griff was determined to rejoin Lauren if he could and made his way to the wall, peering over it towards the wing of the house held by McCain and his men.

Spotting an open window he vaulted the wall, wincing at the impact his feet made on landing, and jogged across to the side of the house where he quickly hauled himself through the window and jumped down to the floor of what seemed to be a large hall.

A piteous groan snapped his attention towards a door at the far end of the hall where there was a pile of rusty equipment. As he walked towards it he noticed several candles lying on the floor and then that there were half a dozen bodies lying under a giant metal chandelier. At least one person was still alive because the pile shifted slightly and a voice said: "For God's sake get this off me!"

Going closer Griff found several corpses and one man whose eyes watched him approach.

Griff knelt and the man said: "Can you shift this thing? Both my arms are broken so I can't move."

"Anyone else still alive here?" asked Griff moving round close to where the injured man lay.

"Don't know," said the man. "There was some screaming and shouting when it fell on us, but no-one's said anything for some time. Oggie was here but he's gone now."

"Who's Oggie?" ask Griff, scanning the chandelier to see if he might be able to move it.

"He's a little simple," said the man. "We sort of keep an eye on him."

Griff reached a decision, told the man to shout out if there was a problem and bent to grasp the edge of the chandelier, its rim spotted with candle wax.

He slowly heaved and straightened, his muscles bunching at the effort as they took on the weight of the chandelier which creaked as he lifted it. He attempted to drag it to one side but, although he managed to move it a little, the metalwork on the chandelier spokes caught in the corpses's clothing and he was forced to give up.

When he went back to the man he saw there was just enough space for him to be dragged out.

"I can get you out now," he said, "but it's going to hurt."

"Just do it," said the man gritting his teeth. "It can't hurt any more than it does now."

With that Griff nodded, reached down and carefully gripped the injured man under his armpits before slowly pulling him clear of the wreckage and propping him up to one side of an open door.

"That's the best I can do," said Griff. "I'll send help when I can."

The man nodded his thanks, closed his eyes in relief and said: "Fine. I'm going nowhere."

Cautiously Griff peered through the door, the muffled bang of firearms coming to him from above. Carefully he stepped down a corridor until he reached a simple oak staircase leading to the first floor. The stairs bent at ninety degrees half way up where a staircase post had its top carved into the shape of a thistle.

Griff began to climb, the stairs creaking at his weight, and had reached the half way landing where the stairs turned when a voice shouted at him to put his hands in the air. He froze and did so as Alec Wilson's face peered at him, the man shouting again which brought Duncan Weir swiftly to his side.

One look was all it took and Weir said: "That's Lauren Fane's man, Griff! We thought you were dead."

"I was, but I didn't like it" said Griff, lowering his hands and resuming his climb up the stairs.

When he got to the top he said: "How are you doing here? Have you seen Lauren?"

"No," said Weir smiling. "Just us piglets here trying to stop the wolves from huffing and puffing and blowing our house down."

"Well give me a gun and I'll help you," said Griff. "By the way, there's a man downstairs in some hall with two broken arms. He needs help."

"We'll get someone to him, but we're a bit busy at the moment. If you're offering we'll take all the help we can get. Step this way."

Meanwhile Lauren had lost sight of Riddle in the stacks of building materials. When they charged her position the gang leader had simply deserted her men and slipped away.

There were bodies everywhere and her face became bleak when she found Roddy lying face down beside a wall not far from the house wing where Fraser's men were fighting. He'd been shot in the back at close range.

There was nothing she could do for him and she began to turn away when there was the rasp of clothing on stone and she cursed herself for allowing her guard to drop.

"There you are," said John to her relief. "Been looking everywhere for you. Thought you'd want to know that Griff's here."

"Is he alright?" Lauren asked, stepping past John to peer cautiously round the corner of a stack of stones.

"I don't know," said John, "but Riddle had him roped to a piece of masonry and Dawn said she was going to get the good lieutenant to shoot it off him."

"Shoot it off him?!" Lauren practically shouted. "Is she mad?"

"A bit," said John, "but she told me Mayhew felt it was a pretty easy shot and it was Griff's only chance at escape. He was going nowhere carrying that rock."

"I'll kill him!" said Lauren, "but first I may kill you!"

John held his hands up palms outward and said: "Don't shoot the messenger! Griff knew what he was getting in to."

"You're all just a bunch of little boys aren't you!" raged Lauren as John followed her careful progress towards the wing where Fraser and his men were still firing the occasional shot.

"Where is he?" said Lauren, contemplating an open area between a fallen wall and the back of the wing.

"I don't know that either," said John. "It's been a bit hectic you know."

Lauren nodded and, after another searching look at the ground ahead, she darted out and across to the shelter of the building closely followed by John. They moved towards an open door past several dead gang members, Lauren glancing at the bodies and then at John who said: "Told you I'd been busy."

Lauren peered cautiously inside the door but the corridor ahead was clear and she slipped inside followed by John who said: "There's a ladder down there up to the first floor."

When they got there they found a jumble of bricks lying on the floor next to a corpse and three injured gang members who glared at them from where they lay tied up against a wall.

"That you John?" came a voice from the shadows and a man stepped out of an alcove containing a bust on a pedestal.

"Yeah, it's me," said John. "I see you've been entertaining visitors. Lauren, this is Woody."

Woody turned away as the gang members swore at them and complained about tight bonds, but they shut up when he pointed his shotgun at them.

"How are things going?" asked John.

"We're holding them," said Woody. "We may even be winning because they're not firing back so much."

"We've hit them hard outside and in," said John before their faces stilled when Lauren told them they had lost Richard, Steve and Roddy and there were probably more casualties she didn't know about.

Woody said: "We've one dead and three injured. Do you know how McCain is getting on?"

"No," said John. "Did Dawn reach you?" and when Woody said she had John nodded and said: "Then she's probably with McCain now."

Dawn was actually standing very still with Riddle's knife at her throat.

She had seen an apparently lifeless Griff fall to the ground and then immediately picked her way down to the ground floor only to run straight into Riddle. The gang leader had a knife in her face before she knew it, a trickle of blood starting from a nick on Dawn's jawline.

"Too early to leave the party," said Riddle, moving round to shield her body with Dawn's. "Lots of nasty people over there, so let's you and I go this way."

She pointed forward towards where restoration stopped at a crude timber door where the house ended and ruins began.

Having no choice, Dawn moved off, careful to make no sudden move which might open her throat on the razor-sharp blade. Riddle seemed as tightly drawn as a violin string, eyes darting everywhere and her wiry body taut with eagerness.

When they reached the door Riddle told her to open it a crack which Dawn did, pressing a simple latch below a warning sign that hard hats must be worn at all times during construction.

Riddle edged behind Dawn's shoulder and peered across to the ruined entrance and its dark hole where steps led down to the cellars.

"What's that over there?" asked Riddle, but Dawn remained silent.

Riddle face grew feral and she pressed the knife a little harder, Dawn gasping as a shallow cut opened on the side of her throat to trickle blood inside her shirt collar.

"Cellars," said Dawn. "There are steps leading down to cellars."

"There now," said Riddle. "That wasn't too hard was it? Let's you and me go and find ourselves some real shelter."

And with that she gripped Dawn's arm and forced her forward, keeping the knife tight against her throat as she propelled her captive across the open area and into shadow where they began to descend steps into darkness.

As they disappeared from sight there was movement behind them. Oggie looked on uncertainly. He had found the lady, but she had someone with her. It might be rude to disturb her. Perhaps he'd better wait.

CHAPTER TWENTY-ONE

ONCE underground, Riddle brought Dawn to a halt half way down the steps to allow her eyes to adjust to the gloom.

There was a dankness to the air that Riddle didn't like, but she was committed now and didn't hesitate, forcing Dawn further down the steps until they emerged on to the floor of the cellars.

Glimmers of light came from tiny windows overhead, enough to let Riddle see the tumbled nature of the scene in front of her.

Alcove sections which may once have held wine were now choked with roughly stacked pieces of old furniture and long forgotten household items while the floor was littered with broken boxes and an occasional piece of broken furniture.

Nobody had been down here for years, thought Riddle, as she pushed Dawn reluctantly forward.

Her eyes darted from side to side looking for an ambush. Instead she found reinforcements.

Bentley appeared suddenly from where he had been hiding behind a battered kitchen dresser. His face was crusted with blood from a head wound and he appeared slightly disorientated, but he still had a carving knife in his hand.

"Any more like you?" asked Riddle.

"No," said Bentley. "A good few of our lot are dead. I've seen the bodies. God knows where the rest are. Run off I suppose."

Riddle cocked her ear at distant popping sounds from above and said: "Well someone is still fighting up there which is more than can be said for you."

"I'm walking wounded I am!" whined Bentley indignantly. "I did my bit, then I got one in the head. I can't see too well now."

Riddle pursed her lips, thinking that in truth Bentley did look a bit rocky, but he'd do for guard duty.

"Keep an eye on this one," she said, pointing at Dawn. "I want to see where this place leads to."

Bentley nodded and moved closer to Dawn, leering at her when she moved further away from him into the cellars.

The ancient household goods abandoned everywhere struck some sort of chord with Riddle who paused frequently during her passage through the cellars to look at everything from a chipped floral jug to a bath chair and from broken marble-topped washstands to a cracked mirror which delighted her when she saw her face split in two.

Eventually she reached first the tunnel entrance and then the ruined far stone steps leading out of the cellars. She began to climb them and when she disappeared from sight Dawn focussed on trying to keep as much distance as possible between herself and Bentley, hoping for a chance to spring a surprise.

"Won't do you no good," he said, moving closer. "Sooner or later those rattles will come out and then instead of being dead scared you'll just be dead."

"I'm not scared," said Dawn. She needed to be much further into the cellars before Riddle came back and she again edged a little further away from Bentley.

"Have it your way," he said, following her past an empty wooden box of preserves and a broken hall stand. "She'll get rid of you in a heartbeat when it suits her. I've seen it happen a few times."

Dawn said nothing but continued to slip deeper into the cellars while up the far steps Riddle had been halted by a masonry fall.

She didn't think the collapse was man-made but more as if the weight of collapsed buildings above had finally proved too much for the ceiling supports which had fallen, bringing down everything above with them to create a jumble of beams, bricks and chunks of stone in a drift which completely blocked the way to the surface.

Riddle checked to make sure there was no way of escape that she might squeeze through then she returned to the bottom of the steps and began to walk back towards Dawn and Bentley.

She saw that they were much closer than they had been when she left them and she frowned.

Dawn saw her coming and realised it might be now or never to make her move, so she crabbed sideways towards a sagging chest of drawers. When Bentley again followed she suddenly changed tack and took two flowing steps towards him.

Bentley's face became wary and his hand brought the carving knife protectively up in front of him only for

Dawn to swerve away to one side and lash out with her foot.

There was a twang as twine snapped followed by a strange fluttering sound behind Bentley.

He whirled round to face the noise only for a hideous flapping ghostly figure with snarling teeth to fly through the air towards him.

Backing hurriedly away he gave a cry of fear which turned to a wailing scream of terror as the back of his legs met the flimsy rail surrounding the well and he plunged from sight, the warning sign with the exclamation mark sagging to one side as a section of railing collapsed.

The ghost now hung limply nearby, revealed as an old tablecloth with a mud-daubed face on it.

Dawn was stunned for a moment by the success of the trip wire trap and that was all it took for Riddle to arrive, backhand her in the face and knock her to the ground.

Keeping a close eye on Dawn as she got shakily to one knee, Riddle peered warily about, searching for any more traps, before approaching the well and cautiously looking down into it.

She called loudly and then once again, but there was no reply and Riddle was not one to waste time. Bentley was gone and that was that. She must make use of what she had.

Approaching a groggy Dawn, she dragged her roughly to her feet, gave her a shove and pointed down the cellars, emphasising her instruction to move on with a sharp wave of her kitchen knife.

Dawn wiped her mouth with the back of one hand, saw blood and bitterly cursed herself for not reacting faster and making an attempt to run back to the entrance.

She was beginning to realise that, mad though Riddle might be, she possessed a wiry strength out of all proportion to her size. The blow she had given had rocked Dawn and left her shocked at its power. If she got another chance at escape she had to bear that in mind.

The other woman gave her another push and Dawn reeled off along the uneven floor of the cellars, stumbling occasionally from dizziness and the rubbish she trod on.

She guessed what Riddle planned to do and resolved to try and break away when they emerged from the tunnel before the gang leader got to grips with the glare of being outside again.

Their careful walk through the cellars brought them to a large sign beneath which was a small dusty table with an overturned spike of ticket stubs on it.

The sign said: "TUNNEL TICKETS ONLY. ROUGH FOOTING. TAKE EXTRA CARE."

A faded painting accompanied the warning showing a man with a lamp guiding a small group of people along a rock-hewn passageway.

Riddle took one look at the painting and asked: "Do you have a torch?"

When Dawn shook her head she added: "Neither do I, so we'll have to make one won't we."

It didn't take Riddle long. First she herded Dawn further away from the tunnel and then she quickly scouted round and came up with two pieces of smashed planking and the remains of what looked like a curtain. Binding the material round the planking, she made two crude torches, removed a cigarette lighter from her pocket and lit the first torch which began to burn with an oily stinking smoke which made both women cough.

Riddle herded Dawn into the tunnel and soon their only illumination was the flickering sickly light from the smoky torch which sent shadows dancing across the craggy tunnel walls.

Progress slowed right down. The narrow tourist path was still there but it was now covered with loose stones through which a trickle of water ran which made the footing treacherous and they frequently stumbled.

The women soon reached a cross carved in the left wall of the tunnel beneath which a small niche had been hewn out. Inside was a glass vase with the dried remains of some flowers and the small stub of a candle. Riddle got her cigarette lighter out, flicked the wheel and lit the candle stub. Its soft light illuminated the niche and a hint of a breeze caused the flame to wobble, sending flickering shadows stuttering across the rock.

On they went, the tunnel slightly descending until the sound of rushing water became louder and louder and Dawn tried to prepare herself for another attempt to escape, realising it could be her last chance.

*   *   *

ABOVE them in the ruins a mopping up operation was taking place at Turnbull House.

The coalition forces of McCain, Fraser, John and Lauren had gained the upper hand and Riddle's gang was beaten, its surviving members trying to surrender or escape.

Oggie watched from a window as some of his friends were brought under armed guard and made to sit down against a wall.

Where was the lady, thought Oggie? He had hoped to ask her about the men who were hurt, but she had gone down some steps with another lady and although he had waited he hadn't seen her since. Perhaps his friends might know where she was.

His appearance from cover drew several shouts of warning and a hasty scattering of the guards until they realised he was only one man and unarmed.

John watched as a soldier intercepted the giant, pointed at the gang members by the wall and stood to one side as Oggie joined them and sat down where he began to ask if they had seen Riddle.

It was Oggie's elaborate pantomime gestures that drew John's attention and he wandered over within earshot.

It didn't take him long to grasp that Dawn's chandelier trap had reaped rich rewards and he was turning away to arrange what medical treatment they had for those who had been crushed when Oggie spoke again.

"I wanted to ask the lady what to do, but she went down with another lady and never came back up," said the giant, moving his fingers to indicate walking and then diving his hand down to mime descent.

John felt a chill run up his back and he spoke out.

"You there!" he said, pointing at Oggie. "Is the lady you are looking for called Riddle?"

Oggie looked confused so John tried again and said: "Is she your boss?"

This time Oggie's face cleared and he nodded and smiled, concentrating now on John who asked him. "And the other lady she was with, are they friends?"

Oggie thought for a moment and then said: "No, not friends. Other lady was with you."

His answer filled John with foreboding and he hastily sought out McCain who was having a bloody wound to his left hand cleaned by Matilda.

"Have you seen Dawn?" asked John and, when McCain shook his head, John's face turned grim.

"The women you brought with you from Callander, are they all accounted for?"

McCain began to answer but then looked at Matilda who finished tying a knot in a bandage and said: "They're all safe. Why do you ask?"

"Because I think Riddle's got Dawn down in the cellars. If she finds that escape tunnel then when she gets outside by the river she may just kill Dawn to be rid her."

Their concerned faces watched him as he began to run away from them towards the ruined main entrance where stone steps led underground.

*   *   *

FAR below him Riddle's first torch was guttering out and she paused long enough to light the second one from it before urging Dawn forward, their little circle of light bobbing downward through the darkness towards the noise of a river.

There was a trace of grit and sand underfoot now and the trickle of water on the narrow path had turned into a tiny stream as seepage from the walls drained away.

The water soaked their boots, causing the soles to skid and slide on the slippery rock surface as the rushing noise of the river came closer and closer.

Soon they could see a distant circle of light which slowly grew as they splashed along until Riddle threw her torch away for the last twenty metres, took a tighter grip on her knife and moved closer to Dawn. She didn't want to get rid of her hostage just yet.

Water lapped inside from the river for the final few paces of the tunnel and the level rose above their knees forcing care where they placed their feet in case a slip gave them a ducking.

Dense brambles and bushes came down close to the entrance as Dawn clambered up on to a small drift of pebbles and finally found herself on dry land again. Riddle stepped up beside her and they both looked around at where the tunnel emerged beneath an outcropping of rock topped with trees.

The land sloped up gently through bushes, small trees and deadfalls until a denser stand of oak took over, all the undergrowth and trees showing the first signs of spring with buds filling and an occasional splash of green among the bushes.

It was mid-afternoon and the light was fading. Riddle knew she was on her own now, so she gave the pocket with the antique silver baby rattles in it a pat and pushed Dawn forward along the bank of the river.

Even Riddle's stomach couldn't conceal the need for food and it rumbled in complaint as they followed the watercourse in a direction she judged would take her away from the ruin. The bus would have to be abandoned, of course. Other transport would have to be found but the first task was to get well clear of any pursuit from the ruin and find some sort of shelter for the night.

She was so taken up with her thoughts that she missed Dawn's hiss of breath and the slight check in her walk as her eyes spotted a single huge footprint in the river sand ahead.

It was enormous, bigger than her own boot prints, and it was very recent as water was still seeping into the indentations.

Hastily she scanned the immediate surroundings but she could see nothing through the chest-high undergrowth choking the edge of the river which was turning into a sharp bend below a small waterfall.

They walked on and, as the bank rose to skirt the falls, a huffing noise came followed by a low warning growl behind them.

Riddle wheeled at the sounds then hastily put Dawn between herself and any danger, peering left and right but unable to see what was making the noises.

Suddenly the bushes began to quake and an enormous grizzly bear burst out on to the foreshore and tore towards them.

Riddle took one look at the oncoming bear, smashed the haft of her knife into the back of Dawn's head and fled.

The blow crumpled Dawn and she collapsed motionless in a heap, but the bear ignored her and focussed instead on the fleeing Riddle, closing the distance to the gang leader with frightening speed.

Riddle just managed to reach the top of the bank near the waterfall when the bear caught up with her.

A single powerful blow from a wickedly clawed paw broke Riddle's jaw and smashed her skull, the impact hurling her off the bank and into the pool below the falls.

The bear turned with lightning speed and lumbered out on to the pool margin and then into the water itself, but a current from the falls swirled Riddle's lifeless body into deeper water and out of the bear's reach.

It patrolled the water's edge for a while but then lost interest and climbed back up the bank, huffing and sniffing as it shambled away upstream.

Seventy metres away Dawn lay unconscious on damp river stones as darkness began to deepen and the temperature to fall.

CHAPTER TWENTY-TWO

TWO soldiers had switched on a few battery lights inside several rooms, the windows bright squares in gathering darkness, as John pounded over the open area between the wings of Turnbull House.

The ruined main entrance and steps to the cellars came into sight and he slowed, unslung his Ruger rifle and breathed deeply to quieten his breathing before checking his surroundings as carefully as he could to make sure any remaining gang members weren't lying in wait.

The stone steps disappeared into darkness, so John reached into his breast pocket and took out the slim silver torch he used with the Ruger, clipped it to the barrel and switched it on. The beam sent shadows dancing across the walls as he swept it from side to side and began his descent.

Half way down the steps turned back on themselves at a landing with a painting screwed to the wall depicting how the cellars might have looked centuries before. The steps then continued their descent and John followed them down very carefully, aware that his light and the gritty sound of his footsteps was betraying his arrival to anyone who wished him harm.

Riddle certainly wished them all harm and John prayed that Dawn was alive, confidence in his tough wife shaken by the manic threat she faced which might do anything to anyone at any time. He also forced himself to push thoughts of their unborn baby to one side, trying to concentrate on the ground in front of him which he had only seen once before.

The bottom of the steps appeared and John checked left and right with his torch before stepping down into the cellars. He took a silent stride to his left behind a winged armchair collapsed on a broken leg then switched his torch off and waited. Five minutes went by without a sound other than vague noises filtering down from the clear-up operation above, so John felt his way several metres forward along a damp wall before stopping and switching his torch back on.

Everything looked like some atmospheric scene from a haunted house with the torch creating angled shadows as he moved it across an old bookcase with broken shelves, a chaise lounge with rusty springs poking through the upholstery and a carver chair missing one arm which was lying on its side.

Still he heard nothing and saw nothing, but his nose twitched at an acrid smell of burning which got stronger the further he went down the cellars.

When he got near a collapsed chest of drawers he saw that the dusty stone floor was heavily marked with mud and wet footprints, so he squatted to look at the scene.

John quickly identified Dawn's familiar army boot prints, a slightly smaller set of prints that he assumed were

Riddle's and a larger set he hadn't a clue about. Where had they come from and who did they belong to?

Again his torch swept the vicinity and he noticed the fallen warning sign near the gaping well hole.

Carefully he checked the ground and found the same mystery boot prints and a long scrape ending at the edge of the well. What had happened here, he thought, shining his torch around and then up.

The tablecloth with the ghostly face on it suddenly leapt into focus and John gasped and took an involuntary step back. Christ, how many more of these traps were there, he thought?

Cautiously he edged round the well and shone his torch on the floor beyond. The pool of light revealed more footprints, but there were only two sets not three. He looked back at the dark hole and realised that whoever owned the third set of boots had probably fallen down the well.

John turned and continued on down the cellars until he reached the tunnel entrance where he found more evidence of footprints, this time going past a small dusty table on which was an overturned spike with ticket stubs on it.

He remembered being told by McCain that long ago this tunnel had been hewn to provide an escape route in the event Turnbull House was ever put under siege and that the tunnel eventually came out on the banks of a river.

It had become part of a tourist attraction in modern times and this was the starting point for tunnel tours or it had been, he thought.

The acrid smell was very strong here and John shone his torch down the tunnel but there was nothing in sight, just rough hewn damp rock walls and a narrow path on the floor of the tunnel which led away into darkness beyond the range of his torch.

He pressed on, aware that time was passing, and he eventually reached a cross carved in the passage wall. Still he saw nothing but his nostrils caught a trace of candle smoke and when he stepped closer to the niche he saw a small puddle of wax with a tiny piece of wick in it. The wax was still faintly warm when he put his finger on it.

John's instincts kicked in and when he continued along the tunnel he was increasingly wary. He needed the light to see where he was going but it was both friend and enemy since it would betray his coming to anyone alert to pursuit.

Sounds of a river in the distance became increasingly louder and he slowed, halting altogether when the mouth of the tunnel was still twenty metres ahead of him.

He wasn't about to walk outside lit up by the torch, so he switched it off and waited until his night sight revealed the tunnel entrance as a lighter circle in the darkness.

Very slowly he allowed his feet to feel their way over the uneven surface, stumbling occasionally as a stone turned under his boot but feeling that the risk of injury was worth avoiding the risk of being shot by Riddle as he emerged from the tunnel.

He knew he stood at the entrance when one step sent deeper water surging up his leg. Carefully he eased to the left and soon found a bank of pebbles marking the river's edge. The crunching noise they made as he walked across them set his nerves on edge, but he knew he must be invisible in the darkness.

John realised that he had to take a chance and he began to risk the occasional beam of light from his torch, using it to orientate his way along the river's edge.

He recoiled in shock when one flick of the torch revealed a giant footprint superimposed on two sets of bootprints. Quickly he flicked off the Ruger's safety catch, but the only sound he could hear was the rush of water in the river and the sound of a nearby waterfall.

A few metres further on he practically fell over the body of his wife lying on a bed of stones. Again he listened and again he could hear nothing, so he removed the torch, shouldered his rifle and risked a longer burst of light.

It revealed she had no visible wound nor were there any holes or tears in her clothing. She almost looked as if she was asleep, thought John, switching the torch off and placing his fingers on her neck where he found a slow and steady pulse.

He missed the slight stir of her body and the first he knew that she was awake came when she said: "You've got cold fingers!"

Tears came to John's eyes and he gruffly said: "What do you expect? It's a cold night."

Then he gently lifted her to a sitting position and slowly hugged her until Dawn said: "Not so hard! My neck feels like it's been broken and badly mended."

Instantly he let her go and spent some time asking about any other injuries she might have, but Dawn said she was fine apart from a sore neck where Riddle had hit her.

"Speaking of Riddle, where is she?"

"I don't know," said John. "I followed your tracks, found a huge footprint and then found you. I haven't seen hide nor hair of Riddle."

"Maybe the bear got her," said Dawn.

"So that's what the footprint was," said John, unslinging his rifle again and looking out into the darkness.

"It was a grizzly," said Dawn, "and a big one at that. You can add it to your list of escaped wildlife."

"As long as it doesn't come back I don't care. We need to get you back to Turnbull. I want your head looked at. I can't do it here."

"What about Riddle?" asked Dawn.

"Five minutes, that's all," said John. "We leave then whether we find out what happened to her or not."

They didn't need five minutes. Their search ended quickly at the pool below the waterfall. The same currents which had swirled Riddle's body out of reach of the bear had now brought it back to lodge feet first on pebbles, the gang leader's hair waving slightly in the water as the torch beam showed her head rocking gently in the river current. They left her there and walked away, missing the swirl of current which moved Riddle's body just enough to reveal two antique silver baby rattles lying on the riverbed. She'd never hear them again.

Dawn was still a little shaky on the way back, but John took it slowly, helping her up the tunnel and then through the cellars to the stone steps beyond.

Their emergence from the ruined entrance went unnoticed until they stepped into a pool of light from the hall with the fallen chandelier where someone had taken a dusty oil lamp on display and lit it.

They were first challenged and then welcomed. John explained what had happened and Lauren took Dawn away and sat her down on a box in a small dusty room where she carefully checked her head.

After a few minutes she said: "Well, the skin isn't broken but you've got a lump there the size of an egg and I wouldn't be surprised if you've got mild concussion. I'm no expert but your pupils seem bigger than they should be."

"Riddle gave me a hefty whack," said Dawn, "but it's the last whack she'll ever give."

"She got off too lightly," said Lauren fiercely. "All the death and miscry she caused. The bitch should have been hung."

"Perhaps there's been enough death for one day," said Dawn. "I don't suppose you've anything to eat have you?"

Lauren stared at her for a moment and then burst out laughing.

"I keep forgetting you are eating for two! The baby still isn't really showing."

"I know it's there," said Dawn, "and recently I've felt more tired than I usually do."

"You should try and take it a little easier," said Lauren. "Get that man of yours to look after you."

"It's stopping him looking after me that I need," replied Dawn. "He's over-protective and it can get on your nerves!"

They both laughed and made their way to the hall where willing hands had pulled the chandelier back up into position to allow bodies to be removed.

Several soldiers had all the surviving prisoners under guard while others had set up a small field kitchen helped by the helicopter pilot, Captain Church

McCain and Fraser were working together, organising treatment for the wounded. Splints now helped the gang member with two broken arms, but help was not so easy for those with more serious wounds.

John estimated that the clash had involved more than seventy people. Nearly half of them were now dead, mostly gang members. Of all those who had followed Riddle less than a dozen had survived and some of those were not expected to live until morning.

Injuries ranged from head wounds, multiples fractures, gunshot and knife wounds to internal injuries which could only be guessed at. There was no hospital to call on and, apart from limited medical knowledge and field dressings possessed by the soldiers, no doctor or medical expert to call on apart from Dawn whose training had been cut short by the Red Plague.

Still she did her best, looking at every casualty McCain and Fraser sent her including some of their own casualties.

Fraser's group had two dead and four wounded, McCain had lost Alec Wilson and had three injured people, Lauren had several wounded and had lost Steve, Roddy and Richard and Lieutenant Mayhew had one soldier dead and two with flesh wounds.

Dawn patched, poked and prodded, paying as much attention to gang members as she did to those she knew.

One look at the prisoners they had under guard told her that two were unlikely to live until morning. They had been caught under the barrowload of bricks dumped on them when they tried to attack Fraser's positions in the house and had suffered severe internal injuries way beyond her ability to cope with. All she could do was try and make them as comfortable as she could.

Lauren and Matilda helped her with dressings, Lauren scolding Griff as she cleaned an angry weal on his neck where the rope holding the masonry he'd been forced to carry had bitten into his flesh.

"You just couldn't stay safe, could you!" she said, squeezing out rags which left a bowl of warm water tinged with pink.

Griff shied away as her hands rose again to his neck with a fresh rag but he was unceremoniously dragged back within reach for more dabs and wipes with the rags.

"Aren't you supposed to have a friendly bedside manner?" he said. "I only ask because you're rubbing more skin off me than the rope did!"

"Rubbish!" said Lauren, giving the wound a final wipe. "What do you want? A clean wound that will heal or an infection we're in no position to deal with?"

"Could I get a second opinion?" asked Griff and was promptly glared at by Lauren who then stormed off.

He seemed about to go after her when Matilda, who had been working nearby with Dawn said: "I'd leave her be for a while if I was you. Give her time to calm down. She was very worried."

Griff looked off warily in the direction Lauren had gone and said: "I'll never understand women if I live to be a hundred."

"You go after her now and you won't live until morning never mind reach a hundred," said Matilda. "She cares for you, probably even thought you were going to die. This bluster is just her way of showing she's glad you're all right."

"Blimey!" said Griff. "What does she do to people she doesn't like?"

"Ricky says she killed at least one gang member today," said Dawn as she joined them. "I'd step quietly for a bit. She'll calm down and come round."

Her face suddenly twisted in pain and she swayed, grasping Matilda's shoulder as the former madam looked at her with concern.

"What is it?" she asked. "Are you injured?"

Hastily Dawn looked about to make sure John wasn't within hearing distance, then she said: "I'm at least four months pregnant and........."

She broke off, unable to say more as her eyes filled with tears.

Matilda's face could have been carved from stone. As a madam in Glasgow she'd had more than one of her girls fall pregnant and lose the baby early on because a client got too rough. She was under no illusion about what Dawn faced. At best a nerve-wracking wait and at worst a stillborn birth, perhaps even death herself, so she put a bright face on.

"Don't talk like that," she said. "I'm sure the baby's fine. You haven't exactly had an easy time of it just recently. It's probably just your body's way of telling you to take it easy for a while."

Dawn nodded hopefully and allowed herself to be seated in an imposing oak chair near the treatment area.

By the time John left Mayhew after helping organise a rota for guard duty she was feeling much better and she rose when he walked into the hall.

"Time for some food I think," he said. "Care to join me?"

"Love to," said Dawn, hooking her arm through his and looking up at him with a smile as they left in search of the field kitchen.

Matilda watched them go. A nice couple, she thought, and they deserved a nice life together. What a pity life rarely obliged and, with that thought, she went to check on McCain's injured hand.

She found him deep in conversation with Fraser, emphasising a point with his left hand, the bloody bandage on it standing out in the harsh light of a battery lamp which was stood on the windowsill of a room being prepared as sleeping quarters. A small fire smoked in the grate.

Both men welcomed her and Matilda smiled at them before taking McCain's hand and checking that the bandage had no fresh blood on it. All seemed well, so she took a seat on a dusty ornately carved bench against one wall, relishing the opportunity for a brief rest.

The two men continued their conversation and she pieced together that they were discussing something John had talked about with both of them.

Setting up joint Recovery Councils for Glasgow and Edinburgh seemed to be the main topic of conversation and both men were not just interested in the idea but actively exploring ways to restore links between the two cities as quickly as possible.

Both agreed that the M8 was the key to doing so. If the motorway could be properly cleared and bridges and overpasses checked then that one artery would enable transport links to be established which would put both cities less than an hour apart.

Matilda listened for a while as Fraser talked about establishing security groups in each city and McCain about the need of government for the whole of Scotland, but it eventually proved too much for her.

It had been a long and stressful day and she decided to join John and Dawn, grab a bite to eat and then turn in for the night.

She found them sitting on a pile of timber near a glowing heap of coals flanked by bricks over which Lieutenant Mayhew and his men had laid a metal grid to serve as a cooking point.

John welcomed her and Dawn made space for her to sit before telling her that the cauldrons and pots she could see had come from Turnbull House's own kitchens.

"Waste not want not," said Dawn as John asked Matilda if she was hungry. When she said she was he left in search of a plate for her.

Dawn again waited until he was out of earshot and then whispered an entreaty for Matilda not to say anything to him about her pains.

"If it's nothing then he doesn't need to know and if it is something then there's nothing he can do."

Matilda nodded agreement and then asked her about what had happened with Riddle. When she found out about the bear she looked warily at the darkness.

"Do the sentries know about the bear?" she asked.

"John told them," replied Dawn, "but he's been talking with Duncan Weir? One of your men? He said he saw a bear recently. Apparently we are pretty safe at night because grizzlies are mostly active during the day."

"How does he come to know so much about grizzly bears?" Matilda asked .

"He doesn't," said Dawn. "Mr McCain has a small library and, when Weir was out foraging and caught a glimpse of a big animal, he spent ages going through wildlife books until he found a photograph which roughly matched what he'd seen. It seems that if we go down to the woods today we really could be in for a big surprise. Believe me, the glimpse I had of the bear before Riddle knocked me out....well, it was huge."

"Well, let's hope the bear has been reading the same books and leaves us alone!" said Matilda.

Both women laughed just as John returned with a plate of food for Matilda who was privately planning to have a few words with Weir.

"Nothing but the finest rations," he said, handing the plate to her. "Sorry there's no wine."

"Food is all I want although water to go with it would be nice."

John said they had boiled water over by the cooking area whenever she wanted it, but his mind was only half on what he was saying and he soon turned to Dawn, asked her how she was and if she had any headache.

"Stop fussing!" said Dawn. "I'm fine. Just a bit tired that's all."

"Sleeping quarters are being set up over there," said Matilda round a mouthful of food, pointing at a window limned in light. "I'd give it a while though. Mr McCain and Fraser are in there at the moment carving up Scotland!"

"Carving up Scotland?" queried John.

"Yes," said Matilda. "You're to blame for that. I was only with them a short while and all the talk was about joint Recovery Councils, security and roads. Come to think of it, if you want to go to sleep then now might be a very good time to go in there. Ten minutes was enough to get me nodding. You'll be fast asleep before you know it!"

All three of them laughed at her sally before John and Dawn said they were taking her advice, saying good-night and heading off in search of sleep.

Matilda watched them go and softly said: "Gently young man, gently."

Her attention turned back to finishing her food before she took the plate back to the cooking area, washed it and helped herself to a mug of water. She was still drinking it when she saw McCain and Fraser come out and go their separate ways, McCain coming over to join her.

"Not so cold tonight," he said. "I think Spring is finally on the way."

"Have you eaten?" asked Matilda and when he said he'd grabbed a bite, she asked him how his chat had gone with Fraser.

"It's strange," he replied. "All that time we spent at each other's throats and he's actually an interesting man. Do you know he once provided security for a hotel where that gangster Tommy Bridger was celebrating his birthday. Imagine that!"

"Well I never!" said Matilda, wondering what McCain would think if he knew Tommy Bridger had been one of the best customers at her brothel.

She drained her mug of water and said it was about time she went to bed, McCain saying he would turn in too.

They found the makeshift sleeping area nearly full already and decided to take their blankets and try some of the rooms down the corridor guided by a small dynamo torch that Matilda produced from her jacket pocket.

One door yielded an area with several information boards and a sofa covered in tapestry-style material. The boards said it used to be a sewing room where women gathered to socialise.

"Not much but it will do," said Matilda, sitting down and beginning to unlace her boots and undo the buckle on her trousers which slipped to the floor.

McCain looked round uncertainly, chose a corner and began to lay out his blanket watched by Matilda who had an amused smile on her face.

"What are you doing?" she asked.

"Getting ready for bed," replied McCain, taking his jacket off and folding it up for a pillow.

"No point being uncomfortable on the floor," said Matilda. "This sofa is big enough for both of us and we'll be warmer together."

She patted the cushions by her side and McCain thanked her for her courtesy, stumbling over his words as he collected his blanket and jacket, took off his boots and trousers and joined her on the sofa. Matilda let him settle and then lay down in front of him, adjusting the blankets so they were both covered before she switched off the torch.

"Good night," she said.

"Good night and thanks again for being so considerate," said McCain.

She had to bite her cheeks to keep from giggling, but when she tried to get comfortable and shifted position slightly against him she found that formality wasn't the only stiffness McCain was displaying.

It was decision time for Matilda and she had always been decisive. She shifted again only this time it was deliberate, rubbing herself casually against his erection which immediately grew even further. Better and better, she thought, and made no protest when his hand hesitantly sought the swell of her breast.

Pretty soon design and desire became one as McCain's fingers slipped inside her blouse and began to stroke her nipples which rapidly became erect. She responded, even encouraged him, as his hand moved down between her legs to find her wet and ready.

Matilda was in no mood for hesitancy now and backed slowly and deliciously on to his hardness which slid inside her.

There was a gasp from McCain and then she was moving rhythmically against him, her thrusts practised and sure until she heard a groan and felt him spasm inside her. She herself was some way from orgasm, but there was the rest of the night and she turned back into his arms and began to kiss him slowly.

Sentries were changed on rota during the night and John, who had insisted that Dawn stay in bed, later found himself on duty with Griff.

The burly man looked even bigger wrapped in a heavy coat as they peered into the gathering light which began to pick out timbers and the corner of a building. Mist had drifted in and everything was covered in a thin film of moisture, droplets of water condensing on Griff's beard.

Their spell on watch had been largely silent, but as it got lighter and lighter Griff asked: "Have you got much experience with women?"

Startled, John looked across at him and said: "A little, why?"

"Well, Lauren still won't talk to me. At first I thought it was me playing decoy with Riddle which she was against. Then I thought it was me nearly getting killed in the fight, but she still isn't speaking to me now."

John relaxed a bit and tried not to smile, aware that the other man was looking at him.

"I think you'll find she's just relieved," he said carefully.

"Relieved?" said Griff. "It doesn't feel like she's relieved, more like she's very hacked off!"

"That as well," said John, "but she's hacked off with herself not you. After all, she was against you being a decoy but it worked. Have you thought she might just be rationalising that with her feelings for you?"

"What feelings?" said Griff. "All she's done is tear me off a strip."

"But if she cares for you, cares for you a lot......."

"That's what Matilda said," and the bearded man shook his head.

"Do you like her?" asked John.

"Of course I like her," said Griff. "We've been through a lot together."

John smiled and said: "I mean, do you like her, really like her?" and Griff could only turn away and look out over the ruins.

"If you do like her then just wait. She'll come to you in her own time. Just be prepared to say it was your fault."

"But it wasn't my fault! I did what had to be done. I didn't exactly enjoy it you know!" said Griff.

"She doesn't see it that way," said John. "All she can see is that you nearly died, not what you nearly died for."

"I'm just getting more and more confused," said Griff.

"Don't be," said John. "Just give her time and the first chance you get, apologise. Women find it hard to be angry with someone who's agreeing with them. I know that much."

Griff didn't look convinced but said he'd give it a try and he thanked John for his advice as the two stood up and stretched when Fraser's men, Brennan and Ross, came to relieve them.

Dawn was half asleep and half awake when John returned to bed beside her.

"Is it morning?" she asked.

"Just about," said John, "but there's no rush. Breakfast will be a while yet."

"In that case I'll stay here," said Dawn, snuggling back under the blanket as he lay down beside her.

Down the corridor a slightly bemused McCain was waking up with his arms round Matilda. She had one thigh lazily draped over him and just the thought of their lovemaking during the night was arousing him again.

He tried to stifle his growing erection by slowly twisting away from her, but the movement woke Matilda and she gave a cat-like yawn and stretched before sliding her hand down between them.

"Good morning," she said throatily. "Is this for me?" and she gently began to stroke him.

All McCain could do was gasp in appreciation as she
drew his head down to her full breasts and urged him to
feast on their dark nipples, turning to pull him under her
as she slid on top and drew him inside her.

There had never been anything like this in his life before
and as her hips began to move languorously above him he
was determined to hang on to this wonderful woman for
as long as he could.

Matilda was enjoying herself. Who said you couldn't mix
business with pleasure? And this man was powerful, he
was the future and he wanted her. She could do worse
than encourage him, not that he needed much
encouraging! She moaned as he thrust deeply into her
again and again, Matilda driving him wild by leaning over
to brush her breasts against his face. Then she lost
concentration as she climbed towards orgasm, each of
them crying out as they shuddered to a climax and
collapsed together.

Things were a little cooler by the cook fire. Griff had
woken and come outside to warm up with a cup of tea
only to find himself joined by Lauren whose mouth
snapped shut on a yawn when she realised who the seated
figure was.

Stiffly she poured hot water into a mug, added a sachet of
coffee and retired to the other side of the flames to drink
it.

Neither said anything for a while and then both spoke at once, Griff trying to apologise and Lauren berating him for the risks he had taken.

When each realised what the other had said their roles were reversed, Griff becoming angry and defending what he had done and Lauren going quiet and mumbling something about him not doing it again.

Eventually Griff took a deep breath and went over to sit beside her, taking a nervous gulp from his own mug only to splutter out the scalding liquid and curse.

Lauren kept her face straight, reached into her pocket and handed him a piece of rag to wipe his beard.

He looked at her suspiciously but took it and patted away droplets of tea before handing it back to her.

"Thank you," he said, taking a more careful sip from his mug.

"You're welcome," said Lauren, the two sitting quietly together.

Just when the silence was becoming awkward they both apologised at the same time, suddenly laughing at the situation they found themselves in.

Lauren gently punched his arm and softly said: "John told me they were going to shoot the rock off to free you, but when I saw you lying there I thought they'd missed and I'd lost you."

"No chance," said Griff, absently fingering the rope weal on his neck only for Lauren to push his hand away.

"Leave it alone!" she said, gently pulling back the collar of his shirt and critically examining his injury.

"Crusting over nicely," she said.

"Well it itches a bit," said Griff, raising his hand but then dropping it when she gave him a look.

"It will be fine as long as you don't pick at it. It just needs time and a good airing."

"You make me sound like a stale sheet!" he said with a smile and this time Lauren laughed openly and hugged him. Maybe John was right, he thought, as he hugged her back.

More people were getting up and soon Captain Church and the soldiers were stoking the fire for breakfast, the scent of tinned bacon and cups of coffee drifting on the crisp morning air.

Talk was wide ranging and Fraser detailed how it might be best if he took the few surviving prisoners with him for safe keeping. Two more had died during the night and a third with a stomach injury didn't look well.

Lauren and Griff said they planned to start back for Edinburgh that day to tell everyone there what had happened, about Riddle's death and the plans for Recovery Councils in Glasgow and Edinburgh.

McCain, after getting a slight nod from Matilda, said that their party would be setting out for Callander later that morning, Fraser promising to send back the food transports when he returned to Loch Lomand Castle.

John said they would be spending the night at the old hunting lodge so Captain Church could check on his Arapaho helicopter at which McCain's face lit up with interest.

"A fine machine," he said, "but a bit out of my league."

Captain Church's face took on a look of surprise and he said: "Why, do you know about helicopters?"

"No," said McCain, "but I've got a little Beechcraft Venus which I fly occasionally. Small fry compared to your beast."

Church just stared at him, excitement growing on his face as he looked across at John. Then everyone seemed to be talking at once to the confusion of McCain.

"Whoa, whoa, whoa!" shouted John through the noise and everyone fell quiet.

He turned to a now bemused McCain and said: "I don't suppose you've got any Avgas?"

"I've a five thousand gallon tank at the airstrip, but it's barely half full now and I haven't flown for a while. Too dangerous."

"You've an airstrip?" said Church.

"Only a grass one," said McCain. "I'm a fair weather pilot. I like to go up and look at the mountains. Lovely country."

Church just stared at him like a thirsty man in a desert.

John said: "Would you be willing to provide us with fuel for the Arapaho?"

"Of course," said McCain. "Take as much as you like. Not much good to me at the moment until I can mow the strip for the summer. I might actually try and fly down and see Ewan if he can find me somewhere to land."

John shook his head in disbelief. He'd been trying to work out how long it would take to find an airport with Avgas that was still useable and here he was being presented with fuel practically on his doorstep!

"When might we be able to borrow a few gallons?" he asked McCain.

"Whenever you like," said McCain. "We should get back to Callander late this afternoon and I see no reason why I shouldn't be able to send you down a drum tomorrow morning. You can then fly up to the castle and refuel properly at your leisure."

And that was what they did.

Fraser left Turnbull House mid-morning with the prisoners after much talk of meeting up quickly with McCain for more discussion about the recovery councils. After some debate he left Oggie behind with John who felt his special needs could perhaps best be met at Waterfall with a fresh start in a fresh environment.

Lauren, Griff and their men left soon after in the hearse, promising to arrange as much support as they could to help get Edinburgh started on the road to a new life while McCain drove off shortly afterwards to arrange fuel for the helicopter.

Soon John, Dawn, Captain Church and the soldiers were the only ones left at Turnbull House as they finished packing their van transport with equipment including all the weapons salvaged from the battle with Riddle's gang.

When they finally bumped away to take the road back to the hunting lodge for the night it was after midday.

"Is the lady with the knife not coming?" asked Oggie to which John gently told him that she had gone away for a while. Oggie nodded and smiled at that, happy that he knew what was happening.

The lodge was still there, looming out of the gloomy trees when they pulled up outside later that afternoon.

Captain Church lost no time in hastening away to check on his precious machine and everyone else busied themselves unloading what they needed from the van to set up for the evening.

By the time night fell the first sentries were already on watch and a simple meal had been prepared and eaten.

There were so few of them now after the crush at Turnbull House that those not on sentry duty were able to sit round chatting at just two tables.

Church was excited at the prospect of getting back in the air again while Lieutenant Mayhew said he had made radio contact to give a brief report to Leo Anderson in London, promising a more thorough account once they had the helicopter airworthy.

John and Dawn had taken the room they'd slept in here before. They soon pleaded tiredness and left for an early night, the military men turning in not long after.

The next day they were all up early and soon welcomed an open backed van with two men in it and a drum of Avgas. The fuel was unloaded and carried through the trees to a green area of grass by a small river where Captain Church had performed a brilliant emergency landing what seemed like a lifetime ago.

John and Dawn helped soldiers carrying everything they were taking out to the two vans because Church wanted as little on board as possible and planned to make the first flight by himself on the grounds that if anything went wrong it was better for him to die than put all their lives and equipment at risk.

Fortunately the flushing of the fuel system and the refilling of tanks with fresh fuel made all the difference and the only unruly misbehaviour was a few stutters when Church initially fired up the engine.

Once he was satisfied that all the readings he was seeing from his instruments were what he expected to see, Church gave a cheery wave and lifted the Arapaho into the air for a quick five minute flight which ended with a feather-light landing back where he had started from.

He switched off and hopped out to join his smiling would-be passengers, telling Mayhew he could get everyone on board.

John had a brief word with McCain's men who wished them luck before they drove the two vans and their equipment off back to Callander Castle.

CHAPTER TWENTY-THREE

WHEN he climbed into the helicopter and slid the door closed John found his hand suddenly grasped by Dawn. She clung on, her face white, all through Church's start-up list, the growl of the engine firing and the gut-wrenching feeling as he took the machine into the air. Only then did she relax a bit.

Oggie had a huge smile on his face, peering out of the windows as the ground fell away beneath them as if it was all some treat specially arranged just for him.

The flight lasted barely ten minutes and the Arapaho was soon gently circling a small hangar near what had once been a grass air strip.

Lieutenant Mayhew pointed to a small group of people waving to them from the ground by the building and Church nodded before drifting the helicopter out and landing at the beginning of the runway.

The machine sank awkwardly into long tussocky grass beaten flat by the wash from the rotor blades, the engine died down and silence descended on the cabin.

John took one look at the overgrown runway and said: "I think Mr McCain will need to get his lawnmower out before he pays any social calls on Mr Fraser."

Everyone except Church climbed out, the pilot seemingly unwilling to let the Arapaho out of his sight now he had got it airworthy again.

McCain was waiting for them by the hangar when they walked up and he quickly shook hands with John and Dawn.

"Good to see you make it back here safely," he said. "If you come with me I'll show you where the fuel is."

With that he and two of his men walked inside the hangar past a little white and blue Beechcraft Venus and over to a series of workbenches. To one side stood a large fuel tank complete with fuel cocks, a black fuel hose and nozzle.

Several drums of fuel had already been filled and stood waiting.

"You can have as much as you want," said McCain. He pointed to a small two-wheel trolley and added: "Use that to carry the fuel drums."

When they got the first load of fuel out to the helicopter Captain Church insisted on inspecting it, but once he was satisfied they were soon topping up the Arapaho's tanks.

Towards the end of refuelling the head keeper, David Allen, came to the hangar and told McCain that the food lorry and vans had arrived back from Loch Lomond Castle and were being unloaded.

"Well at least I can offer you something to eat now," said McCain. "Will you stay overnight?"

John went away to consult with Captain Church who said he could complete a series of checks on the helicopter that afternoon and be ready to fly first thing in the morning weather permitting.

When John returned he told McCain: "It seems we can accept your kind offer. Captain Church needs a little time to go over his machine but is confident we can fly in the morning if the weather's OK."

"Splendid," said McCain and he sent Allen away with instructions for the kitchen so Poppy could start preparing a meal for them.

Lieutenant Mayhew said that if McCain didn't mind then he and his men would sleep in the hangar that night which could comfortably shelter them.

McCain was concerned for their comfort and offered Mayhew a bedroom for the night and his men some mattresses and the use of Callander's cellars, but Mayhew said he'd stay with his men, adding that they wanted to sleep near the helicopter so they could guard it.

"Hopefully there's nothing left to guard against," said McCain, but Mayhew said it didn't hurt to be careful and left to start helping his men set up for the night.

The afternoon passed agreeably for John and Dawn who took Oggie with them down to the castle where they were given two rooms. It didn't take long for them to settle in, but when they checked on Oggie they found him standing in almost the same place they had left him.

He was staring fascinated at an old film poster which had been framed and hung on the wall of his little bedroom.

When John and Dawn looked they discovered it was The Sword in the Stone, a cartoon feature about the young King Arthur and his wizard friend, Merlin.

Oggie was tracing the colourful words on the poster with his finger and smiling in delight at the illustrations of the dragon, squirrels, fish and wolf he could see in front of him.

When he noticed he was being watched Oggie smiled and said: "Very pretty, just like a book I had."

Gently they got him to take off his jacket and leave it in his room then come with them downstairs where Matilda took them to the kitchens and got them all a hot drink.

"I have a few things to arrange," she said, "but please feel free to wander round. Just treat Callander as your own."

With that she walked off briskly to continue organising the unloading of the food and its journey down to the cellars.

Oggie was very interested in Poppy's efforts to make bread and John and Dawn left him there happily getting his hands covered in flour.

They were soon sat in the library with McCain. John had a small glass of whisky in his hand but Dawn pleaded pregnancy and turned down McCain's offer of the peaty malt.

Both men soon fell to talking about recovery councils and the need to get infrastructure up and running again, so Dawn made her excuses and left them to it, wandering off to look at the many paintings and antiques she found in a drawing room, several reception and dining rooms and a large chilly ballroom with an enormous empty marble fireplace.

Another door she opened revealed a small music room with a desk in it behind which sat Matilda making notes in a writing book. She looked up and smiled when she saw Dawn.

"All well with your helicopter?" she asked.

"Yes, thank you," said Dawn. "Captain Church says we can leave tomorrow morning."

"You must be looking forward to getting home," said Matilda, putting her pen down and relaxing in her chair.

"More than you know," said Dawn. "I had another stabbing pain last night and the only doctors I know are at the other end of the country. I have some medical experience, enough to know something is not right, but not enough to identify what it is. You suggested it might just be my body's way of telling me I'd overdone it a bit. I wanted to believe that, but this second bout of pain is more than just being overtired."

"Aye, you may be right," said Matilda, "but in a couple of days you'll know for certain, one way or the other. Didn't you say there was a base now at Plymouth near where you live?"

"Yes," said Dawn," and I plan to knock on their door as soon as I can. This uncertainty is killing me. Thank God John doesn't know something might be wrong. He was bad enough when he found out I was pregnant. He'll be in pieces if I tell him something may be wrong with the baby."

Matilda looked at her briefly and then said: "I've only known your husband for a short while but he doesn't strike me as the type to go to pieces."

"Perhaps that was too strong," said Dawn, "but he is very protective and this is something he can't protect me from."

"True," said Matilda, "but I still wouldn't worry about it. Those doctors in Plymouth will check you over and put your mind at rest before you know it. Now let's you and me go and see how Poppy is getting on. It'll give you something else to think about."

Dawn smiled and said: "I think Poppy's already getting help. Oggie was very interested in her bread-making."

When they arrived at the kitchens their noses told them the bread was cooking and so was something else with a rich earthy aroma that sent saliva springing into their mouths.

Oggie was perched on a stool, a drift of flour on one cheek, watching Poppy peel and slice some potatoes.

He looked up at their entrance, smiled and said: "Bread!" and sniffed appreciatively. After a moment he added: "Also birds with long feathers," and he pointed to where a single long brilliantly coloured pheasant feather lay on the table.

Dawn and Matilda asked Poppy how she was getting on and if she needed any help to which she smiled and asked

if they'd mind laying the dining room table for about a
dozen people. There might be one or two more, she said,
if those who had been wounded felt like sitting up to table
rather than eating in their room.

Matilda nodded and took Dawn through to the dining
room and showed her where the cutlery was kept in a
sideboard while she uncorked two dusty bottles of wine to
let them breath.

She then took a glittering handful of small cut crystal
glasses and laid them on coasters by each setting.

"There's enough for a small glass each," she explained,
"but we have to be frugal now with our cellar. We have
less than a hundred cases left of quality wine and no
telling when we'll ever see more. We have slightly more
left of the ordinary wines but the same restriction holds
true. Good or plain, there won't be any deliveries from
France any time soon, so I'm using up wines in the order
of their shelf life. The only way really."

Just over half an hour later Poppy took a small mallet and
struck an antique gong in the shape of a shield to
announce that dinner was served.

Everyone took their places with McCain at the head of the
table, John and Dawn at his left and right and Matilda at
the bottom of the table facing them. Poppy and two men
served the starter quickly, a game pate with fresh bread.
They then ate their own portions before disappearing back
to the kitchen.

McCain got everyone laughing at his expense while they sipped their wine by regaling them with a story about a huge salmon he once caught. He told a good tale, drawing them in as the great fish was landed. Sadly when he put the net down on the river bank and bent to put his precious rod safely out of harm's way he was left speechless when he turned back to see his prize catch twisting and flexing its way back to the river and freedom!

He had perfect timing and the end of his story came as the door opened again and Poppy returned with heaped plates of the main course, pheasant in root vegetables with mashed potato and a rich gravy.

No-one had to be asked twice to eat that and there was a reverent silence broken only by the click of cutlery as they all did justice to her cooking.

There was no desert, but there was instant coffee and McCain offered a shot of brandy with it for those who wanted it. Dawn declined and John gave her a smile of commiseration and gallantly put his hand over his own coffee to decline as well.

People chatted for a while and then began to drift slowly off to bed, Oggie helping Poppy and the two men to clear the table and then wash up. A game developed between him and Poppy with Oggie picking up soap bubbles from the bowl and blowing them into the air until she called a halt, mopped up the water he had spilt and told him he should go to bed and she'd see him again in the morning.

He climbed the stairs in a happy frame of mind and turned in not far from where John and Dawn lay together.

"We must give Leo a full report tomorrow on all that's happened. I won't know where to start," she said.

"Stick to basics," he advised. "Tell him about our contact with Edinburgh, what we saw over Glasgow and how Fraser and McCain could help establish recovery councils."

"What about Riddle?"

"What about her?" said John. "She's the past. We're talking about the future."

And with that he clicked off their small bedside light, pulled her to him and prepared for sleep. His breathing soon deepened, but Dawn lay awake for a good while wondering what the future held for her and their baby.

Breathing in the master bedroom further down the corridor was shallow and a lot faster.

Matilda had allowed a decent length of time to pass and then put a thin dressing gown on and slipped down to McCain's bedroom door which she opened and eased inside.

His bedroom was dark except for a small oil lamp by an open book on a bedside table next to a gigantic oak columned four-poster bed. Sounds of someone brushing their teeth came from the en-suite bathroom and Matilda

quickly moved to the bed and sat down with a ripple of
her dressing gown folded provocatively to reveal one leg.

When McCain emerged from the bathroom with a pair of
pyjama bottoms in one hand he saw her and stopped in his
tracks.

She said nothing, just crooked a finger at him and he
slowly complied until he stood in front of her whereupon
she took the bottoms from his hand and simply dropped
them on the floor.

"You won't need those for a while," she said quietly,
walking the fingers of her right hand up his thigh and then
brushing them lightly across his stomach.

McCain groaned in delicious torment as her hand dropped
to stroke him, then she simply lay back on the bed and
held out her arms. McCain eagerly joined her and Matilda
drew his mouth to her's and kissed him wetly. Her legs
scissored his waist and pulled him into her, both gasping
at the exquisite contact as they began to rock together.

Matilda allowed him to dominate her at first, thrust
following thrust, but then she rolled him on to his back
and climbed on top, her breasts swinging gently as she
slowed things down. This night was about her pleasure
and she twisted and ground, kissed and nipped until she
felt herself grow hot as she quickened the pace of their
lovemaking and soared towards orgasm, crying out as
McCain thrust deep and erupted within her.

Even then she did not let go, gripping his hips with her thighs to keep him in her as sweat trickled between her breasts.

When she could speak she said: "Now you can put your pyjamas on!" at which they were shaken together by stifled laughter, their movement sparking bolts of pleasure which soon had them kissing passionately again.

By the time Matilda had pleasured herself again McCain was exhausted, a hank of damp hair plastered to his forehead as she reached across him to turn off the oil lamp. His last sight before the room was plunged into darkness was her right breast silhouetted against the light, its nipple slightly puckered. Then she was settling back, laying her head on his chest and preparing for sleep. He wondered idly if he had ever felt so relaxed as his eyes closed and he drifted happily off to sleep.

In the morning Callander was a hive of activity with the helicopter being loaded and John and Dawn taking the radio up on to the castle roof to make their report to Leo Anderson in London.

They paid particular attention to details of Edinburgh, the number of survivors and the way Lauren was going to try and rally support for a Recovery Council there which McCain was interested in being involved with.

They talked with him about Fraser and McCain, stressing Fraser's organisational skills and the fact he used to run a

security business in Glasgow which gave him unique
knowledge of the city and its surrounding area.

Anderson said he now had the bones of a Recovery
Council set up in London.

"We've already documented more than five thousand
survivors in the London area and more groups are
trickling in every day as word spreads and people hear our
speaker vans.

"The real problem will be re-establishing the
infrastructure. My experts tell me we'll have to make a
small start and build on that.

"Power, transport routes, perhaps a single circular tube
line to provide a link with districts and a huge emphasis
on getting land back into cultivation. People won't do
anything if they're hungry and this will be an agricultural
economy for a good while ahead."

"We've got that at Waterfall Manor," said John, "I think
Fraser and McCain realise that without staples such as
potatoes, wheat, barley and a few root crops then any
recovery is going to be difficult. They'll have to pool their
resources, decide on what needs to be done and then draw
up a list of priorities and stick to it."

"Do they have the manpower to make a go of it?" came
Anderson's crackling voice.

"Only time will tell," said Dawn, "but Edinburgh
certainly has hundreds still alive and we saw enough

smoke in Glasgow to suggest that the same may be true there. All they need are people to lead and organise them. You could do a lot worse than appoint Fraser to oversee Glasgow and McCain to organise Edinburgh. They know each other and have worked together. If these recovery councils are to work – and I mean really work – then there must come a time when the two cities work and trade together. If the leaders know and trust each other then that will be a big help."

"In that case," said Anderson, "I'll devote some thought to appointing them chairmen of two recovery councils, one for each city. I'll send them some radios so they can communicate more easily with each other.

"We've found a sizeable cargo ship which is seaworthy and we're going to use it to send up food, equipment and a party of experts with a Helios 3 fission reactor capable of powering both cities. They'll set it up and stay there until a viable electric power system can be established. There's bound to be some workable sub-stations they can interface with, but I'm told they can't just flip a switch and everything lights up! Checking everything will take a lot of time."

"We've got plenty of that," said John, "but Dawn and I would like to get home. Don't forget, you've given us duties there as well."

"That's fine," said Anderson, "but I want a full verbal report from you soon about your views on what you found in Scotland that can be recorded and kept for reference in London."

They signed off and then took the radio down and handed it over to Lieutenant Mayhew who was organising the loading of the helicopter with guidance from Captain Church. The pilot was eager to be back in the air.

Eventually it was time to make their good-byes. McCain and Matilda came up to the hangar with Duncan Weir to see them off.

Oggie's obvious happiness at Callander had seen McCain offer to take and look after him while Matilda gave Dawn a hug and quietly wished her and the baby well, urging her to let her know how the birth went.

Dawn promised she would and then followed John as he shook hands with McCain and climbed into the Arapaho and strapped himself in.

There was a blast of noise as Captain Church sent the rotor blades into a whirling disk above them followed by a jolt and a swimming sensation in their stomachs as he eased the helicopter into the sky.

McCain, Matilda and Weir became tiny waving figures below as the great machine wheeled once over the castle and clattered away south.

"Right," said McCain briskly. "Time we got moving. We've a lot of work to do and only about thirty years to do it in."

They began to stroll back towards the castle, McCain kicking at the long grass on the runway and making a mental note to get it cut.

Weir wanted to combine the walk back with a chat about restoring the greenhouse, developing a walled garden and even extending them both, Matilda following along quietly behind as she thought that, no matter what the circumstances, boys would always have their toys.

Miles away Church was relaxing a bit as he took the helicopter through 3,000ft and set a course towards Plymouth.

Gone were the jerks, bucks and loss of power caused by the contaminated fuel which had forced him to make an emergency landing by the forest river. In its place was a silk-like peaceful progress which to him was something to be savoured.

His passengers had a slightly different view of the flight. All were wearing earplugs or headsets to dampen the roar of the engine while the swooping feeling everyone was feeling from the helicopter's passage through the air was making Dawn feel sick.

John took one look at her white face and her fingernails digging into the upholstery of the seat and did his best to distract her.

He leaned close and shouted: "The further south we go the more you can see trees coming into leaf."

Spring was advancing now and John was able to point down at woodland where trees were fleshing themselves out in a new coat of green, but the villages and small towns they flew over were largely deserted, their outlines increasingly blurred by the countryside's gentle invasion.

For every place with a wisp of smoke, a vehicle moving or a hint of human activity they passed scores which were devoid of life. Streets were frozen tangles of rusting vehicles, playing fields and sports pitches were becoming small urban forests and everywhere there were signs of destructive fires, some of them appearing recent.

Captain Church flew them over the wilderness which had been the Lake District, water gleaming among the folded hills and the softened lines of dry stone walls, and then out over the Irish Sea where the sprawling areas of Liverpool and Manchester were dimly visible to the east.

They crossed the Welsh coast and Church lifted the Arapaho slightly to 5,000ft as Snowdonia slipped by to the west and by early afternoon they were crossing the Bristol Channel.

When they met the line of the old M5 motorway Church turned slightly at the outskirts of Exeter to fly across the rugged beauty of Dartmoor and on to Launceston and Waterfall Manor where he settled the machine on the landing area beyond the back of the buildings and allowed the rotor blades to whine down into stillness.

Their arrival had created a stir of excitement, but John and Dawn scarcely noticed. All they wanted to do was get out, stretch their legs and use a toilet.

A gaunt-faced Jed was among those waiting for them and he took their shoulder bags. Several children ran about them excitedly as they walked away from the helicopter having wished Lieutenant Mayhew a safe flight. He said he would stay with the Arapaho to organise a brief break for his men before they flew on to London.

"How did it go?" asked Jed, shifting their packs around on his shoulder with a grunt of effort.

John's eyes narrowed a bit at the difficulty Jed was having carrying the bags but he said nothing about it and replied: "Pretty good, pretty good. We had to sort out one or two things but by and large it went well. I'll tell you all about it over a cup of tea."

He broke off as they walked down through the buildings because Bruno threw himself forward uttering bark after bark, wagging his tail furiously and then rolling over so John could scratch his tummy.

"Well at least someone remembers you," said Dawn smiling.

"The little tinker nearly had my breakfast this morning!" said Jed.

John risked a quick glance and saw his friend had lost a lot of weight, his clothes now practically hanging off what had always been a sparse and wiry frame.

"By the look of it you're the one that needs feeding up not Bruno," he said.

"You aren't the only one with a tale to tell," said Jed with a smile. "It might even take several pints at the Manor Arms to do it justice!"

John raised a questioning eyebrow but Jed wouldn't be drawn as they stepped across the courtyard and through the sun room where he placed their packs near the bottom of the staircase and stepped into the kitchen.

Becky was in there trying to tempt Tilly with a little mashed potato and meat gravy, but the baby was having none of it and protested loudly until Becky opened her blouse and exposed a nipple for Tilly to suck on hungrily.

"Forgive me," said Becky coming over to kiss them both. "I'm trying her out with her first solids but I think it's still a little early for that."

Dawn reached out a finger and stroked Tilly's cheek but the baby was totally focussed on food and paid no attention.

"Sit you down, sit you down!" said Becky. "If you give me a moment I'll make you some tea."

"The only moment I need is a moment to use the loo or there's going to be a nasty accident here!" said John and he left hurriedly for the downstairs bathroom.

Becky laughed and turned to the aga where she put a kettle of water on to heat and took out two mugs. She put a precious teabag in John's and was about to do the same with Dawn's when she said: "Do you mind if I just have some of your chamomile?"

"Of course not," said a puzzled Becky. "Chamomile we have lots of, teabags are harder to get."

She turned away again and opened a cupboard, careful to avoid the door hitting Tilly, and took down a wire lever jar. When she opened it a strong herbal aroma filled the immediate area as she spooned out some of the aromatic flowers which she placed in a small teapot near Dawn's mug.

"Becky?" said Dawn as she sat down. "When you had Tilly did you ever have any pains beforehand?"

"You mean like labour pains?" said Becky, wiping a dribble of milk from the corner of Tilly's mouth as the baby's eyes began to droop into sleep.

"No, not labour pains," said Dawn. "More like a knife being stuck in your stomach and twisted."

Becky looked concerned and paused, her hand half way towards replacing the chamomile jar back in the cupboard. She glanced at Jed who could only shrug.

"You're not telling me it's happened to you are you?"

"Yes," said Dawn, "and not once but twice."

She broke off there and hastily put a finger over her lips as John returned to the kitchen.

"My turn now," she said gaily and quickly left for the bathroom as John sat down at the big table and smiled at Becky and Jed.

"It's good to be back," he said. "I've missed the place."

"We've missed you," said Becky and carefully picked up the kettle to send a stream of hot water into his mug and the little teapot which she stirred once before pushing a small jug of milk towards John.

"Was it a successful trip?"

"I think so," said John, picking his mug of tea up and blowing on it carefully.

"It was pretty much easy going apart from a mad murderess, a pitched battle in a ruined country house, a grizzly bear and having to crash land our helicopter."

Becky nodded slowly and said: "I know what you mean. Been pretty quiet here too apart from a tiger nearly killing Maisie and Jed."

John's face took on a slightly paler hue as he looked first at Becky and then at Jed as Dawn came back in and sat down next to him.

He paused a moment and then said hopefully: "I'm joking if you are."

"Uh, uh," said Becky. "Sounds like you've a story or two to tell, but so have we."

"Anybody hurt here?" asked John anxiously.

"Only the tiger," said Maisie shuffling into the kitchen and taking a seat after giving John a kiss. "Tickled Jed up a bit though!"

Becky gave her a look of exasperation and said: "She neglects to mention she saved the children and that Wild Bill Hiccup here got a slash in his shoulder which became so badly infected I thought he was going die."

That explained why Jed was looking so drawn and tired, thought John.

"Can't beat that," he said. "Our main problem was with human animals not wild ones."

"Well save all that for tonight when we can relax a bit," said Becky, moving out of Maisie's way as she opened an oven door to check the contents of several large baking trays producing some mouth-watering smells.

"Dinner will be in about an hour or so," she said closing the door and sitting down again.

"Time for me to change Tilly and put her down for a sleep," said Becky and left with the half comatose baby in her arms. Jed offered to go with her but she waved him back into his seat. "Keep your strength for getting up to bed!" she needled and Jed looked sheepish.

"What was all that about?" asked Dawn.

"Our Jed here has been mauled by a tiger," said Maisie.

"A tiger?!" said Dawn. "I thought those tracks John found were twenty miles away?"

"They were," said Jed, "but tigers can move about a fair bit and this one was a male. If the smaller set of tracks John saw was a female then we'd better hope they didn't mate. One tiger was bad enough but three or four could be a real headache particularly as the countryside is going back to the wild."

John took a mouthful of tea and said: "We're so busy trying to get the country going again that we've lost sight of the fact that the brakes have come off Nature. If there are carnivores about then it's going to make reclaiming farmland a bit more challenging than we bargained for while safeguarding our livestock could become a major problem.

"Forget for a moment that there might be more tigers, all we've done is react to animal escapes we know about because we've seen them. What about those escapes we don't know about? Other big cats, bears? I've seen what a grizzly can do in Scotland. We may have to change the whole way we farm to take new wildlife into account."

Jed looked thoughtful and said: "We're already starting to enclose some fields with security fencing we've taken from industrial estates, but we can't fence every field in. It's just not possible."

That's what I mean," said John. "We may reach a point where some of our livestock has to be taken out to graze during the day under guard and brought back to a secure area at night and that's going to be a real manpower headache."

There came a huge clatter from outside as the helicopter took off and began its flight to London just as Victor and Norma came in and began to bustle about the kitchen making preparations for the evening meal. They were serving beef, making the best use of what was left of the bullock the tiger had killed.

Soon both dining rooms were starting to fill with hungry people and it didn't take Dawn long to realise that several of the women were pregnant including Evie who said she and Mike hoped to marry later that year.

"Good luck with that," said Dawn. "Just make sure you get a bit of time to prepare!"

John blushed deeply at the reminder of how he'd sprung their own wedding on her last year. He'd nearly been divorced before he was married!

The meal was soon served and cleared away quickly so everyone could pack into the drawing room and hear about John and Dawn's experiences in Scotland.

There was a lot of chatter when Dawn told them about the signs of life they'd seen in Glasgow, the people they'd met from Edinburgh and the repetition there of the same looting and gang rule seen in so many other parts of the country.

John talked about how there could soon be recovery councils operating in the two Scottish cities and how Leo Anderson had told him about similar councils being set up in London and planned for Wales and Manchester to tie in with their own efforts in the South West. There was also silence when he passed on what Anderson had told him about a violent struggle for power going on in the Midlands and how he might have to send soldiers there to try and quell it. Not everywhere welcomed law and order, he said.

The children, already all too familiar with what a tiger was, had wide eyes when Dawn described the charging grizzly bear which had gone on to kill Riddle. There were "oohs!" at that and at John's description of crash-landing the helicopter and the battle at Turnbull House.

But it was his retreat through the Museum of Toys at Callander which created the most interest and he was peppered with questions by the children. How many toys were there? Had he brought any back with him? When could they go and see the museum?

John became a bit flustered and the adults grinned at his discomfiture before helping him out with questions about the castle, what Scotland was like and how many people up there might have survived the Red Plague.

Then it was Jed's turn to bring John and Dawn up to date with details of their hunt for the tiger. He was very modest and gave most of the credit for killing the beast to Lucas and Asher, everyone laughing when Becky said it was lucky for them that she'd married a big game hunter!

The evening seemed to pass in a flash and soon the children were being hurried off to bed. Everyone sat about chatting for a while but people eventually began to say "good-night" and drift off upstairs.

When John put his arm round Dawn as they lay down to sleep he found there was more there than he was used to.

"You're beginning to develop a baby bump!" he said, love and pride in his voice.

Dawn laughed and said: "You've only just noticed? I've been like that for a while now."

"Well, I've been distracted recently," said John. "No more lifting sacks of coal for you though!" he said.

Dawn smiled, but her thoughts became serious after he switched off the light. No stabbing pain now for a while. Perhaps it had been because she was over-tired just as Matilda had said. I really hope so, she thought, as she closed her eyes.

Several weeks went by and Waterfall Manor became busy with Spring work to clear and plant as many fields as they could. Some were stripped back and harrowed, others were ploughed and still more were selected for special attention to start growing wheat, barley, oats and potatoes from their precious seed stocks.

Donna masterminded the start of work to build a huge walled garden roughly a hundred metres by twenty metres, using bricks reclaimed from deserted builders' merchants in Launceston and the surrounding area.

It was a massive undertaking but, as Donna pointed out, they couldn't afford manpower to look after vegetables as well as animals, so the wall would repay their efforts by keeping animals out while mesh cages would keep birds away from their soft fruit.

Roy selected a relatively flat area for her near the landing site for the helicopter and then used an excavator to dig the foundation trench for the walls in a single day before filling it with rubble and cement poured in during the next week. Small teams worked at brick stacking and over the next fortnight Roy and four men laid so many for the wall that they could no longer see over the top and had to bring in towers to complete it to nearly four metres and put a cap on.

Entrances at each end had been calculated using two sets of ornate wrought iron gates removed from a park in Launceston while Donna got John to weld a few security fence sections together and create a secure area for her beehives between several wall buttresses.

She was in no hurry to start turning the ground over and spent an entire day planning what she wanted to grow and where she wanted it to be grown.

Donna wasn't the only one making plans and Dawn had one eye on the dairy at the abandoned farmhouse near where some farm machinery was kept.

More and more she and John were certain that they wanted to move back to their home in Launceston once the baby was born and let someone else have the farmhouse.

Dawn still had hopes to improve her medical expertise but her military experience was secondary now and she wanted something else to do as well. The dairy with its challenge of making butter, cream and cheese appealed to her. It was close to the manor and the town and she could reach it in a few minutes on a quad bike or a bicycle.

John indulged her more and more as her pregnancy advanced, frequently joining her at the dairy as she pottered about cleaning equipment or getting him to move things around more to her liking.

One morning John was called to repair a hedgecutter being used to peg back the unruly borders of fields and roads, so Dawn kissed him goodbye at the manor and once again made the brief quad bike trip to the dairy.

She had talked with Jed about the milk they produced and currently pasteurised at the manor, pointing out that she'd be able to do it much faster at the dairy once all its equipment had been checked and the baby was born.

Jed said it made sense to bring the dairy back into use. Hours had to be spent milking the few cows they had every day and laboriously pasteurising the milk. If she could get the dairy clean and viable it would make that job a lot easier by doing everything in one place, he said.

When she arrived at the dairy she parked outside the railed entrance walkway which funnelled the cows into the dairy to their milking points.

It was as she walked over to the door and reached up to take down the key from its lintel hideaway that the pain struck.

Her stomach convulsed and she screamed in agony, collapsing against the door and sliding down to crumple on to her back in long grass by the dairy wall. The pain was excruciating and this time it didn't go away.

She convulsed, her hands locked over her stomach, while her last thought before darkness took her was a prayer that she didn't lose the baby. She never saw the small rivulet of blood which snaked from her nose and ran down her face into one eye.

*　　*　　*

SCORES of miles away in Birmingham more blood was being spilt as the Wolves and the Blues clashed for control of the city of Birmingham.

Challenge had been issued by megaphone and the first skirmishes were taking place near tarnished remains of The Guardian, a bronze bull figure once hailed as one of the world's top public works of art.

Now one horn was snapped off and a man was impaled limply on the other.

CHAPTER TWENTY-FOUR

AWAY near the hayfields John was wiping oil from his fingers as he finished repairing the hedge cutter Zoe had been using with her tractor.

"Try it now," he told her and stood back as she engaged the blades and their fearful thrashing began to continue the swathe of destruction along the hedgerow.

John didn't like the machine but he hadn't found any of the old-style sliding blade hedge cutters which neatly snipped growth off but which were slower and more prone to break down.

He looked at his watch and saw that lunchtime wasn't that far away, so he carried all the tools back to his bicycle and put them in the rear pannier before cycling off back to the manor.

Everyone had got into the habit of a light lunch with the main meal taken at the end of the working day, so John grabbed himself some bread and butter, a hunk of cheese and a small slice of ham and took his plate and a mug of water to a table outside the sun room where he sat down and began to eat.

When he finished he took simple pleasure in just sitting there, listening to the cluck of the chickens, the distant noise of farm machinery and the clatter of cooking coming from the kitchen.

The weather was warm and he had the sleeves of his shirt rolled up, his biceps straining the material, enjoying the feel of sun on his face and skin. He was thinking about giving Puffin, his motor home, an overhaul that afternoon when his head turned at a shout from Victor.

"Have you finished?"

"Yes," said John. "I'll bring my plate back in a moment."

Victor joined him at the table and said: "Good weather's just what we need. You might as well enjoy it while it's here."

John nodded agreement as people began to trickle back to the manor to get their lunch.

"Where's Dawn?" asked Victor.

"At the dairy again," said John. "She doing too much, but she won't listen to any talk about taking it easy. I'm going to have a word with Becky. Maybe she'll listen to her."

"Good luck with that," said Victor and returned to the kitchen taking John's empty plate with him.

John brushed crumbs off the front of his shirt as others brought their food out into the sunshine, sitting on benches and low walls or joining him at the table.

He chatted with them for a while and then began to think about what he had to do with the Morelo that afternoon. It hadn't been used for a while and he wanted to keep its engine in good condition.

All the tools he needed were still in the family garage next to his home in Launceston barely a ten minute ride away so John took his time, finished his water and then got up and took the mug back into the kitchen. He told Conrad his plans for the afternoon and in return heard that Conrad was being sent out by Victor to check various deserted shops in Launceston for more cookware to cope with the numbers they were now having to provide meals for.

A lot of people were finishing their lunch and beginning to troop back to the fields or whatever afternoon job they had.

Still there was no sign of Dawn and her absence began to nag at John who stood at a window looking out at the road towards the direction she would come from.

"A watched kettle never boils," said Donna, handing her plate to Janice and walking over to join him but he appeared not to hear her.

"What are you doing this afternoon?" she asked and then had to ask again before she got his attention, John saying he was going to Launceston to work on the motor home.

"Good," said Donna. "I've got a billhook that needs sharpening. I want to coppice some hazel for the walled garden. I'm going to need bean and pea sticks and also some stakes for the tomatoes once work on repairing the greenhouse has finished."

"It's not a problem," he said. "Give me the billhook and I'll grind an edge on it. Only take a couple of minutes."

Donna glanced at the empty road and then at him before asking: "What are you looking for?"

"Dawn," he said, glancing at his watch. "She's late for lunch."

Now it was Donna's turn to be concerned and she said: "She's never late for lunch. All that "eating for two" talk."

"Five more minutes and I'm going out to the dairy," said John. "She might just have forgotten the time but, as you say, she never misses lunch."

The two of them stood and watched the road until John took one last look at his watch and began to leave.

"Wait, I'll come with you," said Donna. "You've got me worried now."

The two fetched their bicycles and were soon making the best speed they could through the choked lanes.

When they arrived at the barns and the machine sheds they turned up to the farmhouse and dairy, immediately seeing the quad bike parked outside.

John dismounted and just let his bicycle fall to the ground, striding towards the dairy and shouting: "Dawn? Dawn?" but he got no answer.

They reached the quad bike and Donna gave a cry of fear. She pointed at Dawn's body lying near the dairy door and began to run forward.

She had almost reached the figure lying slumped in long grass when she felt her shoulder grabbed and she was almost wrenched off her feet as John pulled her back.

"What are you doing?" shouted Donna, trying to pull herself free. "Have you gone mad?"

John didn't say anything, just kept hold of her and pointed at Dawn's face which had blood runnels coming from her nose, eye and the corner of her mouth.

Donna took a single look and froze, one hand rising to her mouth as her eyes opened wide with horror.

"Think where we've seen something like this before," said John grimly. "It might not be the Red Plague, but it looks a lot like it to me."

"What are we going to do?" asked Donna.

"You are going to do nothing," said John. "I want you to stay back while I check if Dawn is still alive."

"But if it is the plague you might catch it!" said Donna.

"If it is the plague we might both have caught it already, but there's no point you taking chances if you don't have to."

With that he pushed her a little further away then started to approach Dawn.

"John, you can't!" said Donna.

"Yes I can," said John. "This is the woman I love...my wife...my life. She has to be helped and I have to do it. Stay there in case I need you to do something but don't come any closer."

When John got near to Dawn he could see a slight rise and fall in her thin jacket as she breathed. Taking a deep breath, he reached down and put his fingers on her neck where he found a strong slow and steady pulse, her skin cool to his touch.

This in itself clashed with known Red Plague symptoms where victims exhibited a racing pulse and a fever.

"John?" came Donna's voice.

"She's alive," said John, frantically trying to recall what he knew about the plague but hadn't seen in action for more than three years.

Stricken people lasted perhaps two days but no more than three during which they bled heavily from mouth and nose before dying.

He could see Dawn clearly had blood tracks crusted from her nose and mouth with what seemed like more blood leaking from the corner of one eye, yet her body was showing none of the feverish reaction also associated with the Red Plague.

John loosened Dawn's clothing and turned her on her side before speaking to Donna.

"Listen closely to what I say because only you can help me. No-one else. I'm going to try and get Dawn on the quad bike, take her across to Launceston and put her in the motor home. Then I'm going to drive it towards the base hospital at Plymouth.

"What I need you to do is cycle back to the manor. Do not go inside. Shout to them from the road because, if it is the Red Plague, then you could be infected. Tell them what has happened and get Becky to radio Plymouth and tell the doctors there that I'm coming. I won't drive into the city, so they'll have to meet me in the open countryside. Make sure you get Becky to tell them that it may be the plague and they should come in full quarantine mode. If they confirm it is the plague then I'll take Dawn away somewhere quiet and stay with her until she dies. If that happens then I won't be coming back, so you have to tell Jed that he's to take charge and put the farmhouse and dairy off limits. That still leaves you with the hardest task. You have to deliver your message and then take yourself away for at least a week until you're sure you have no symptoms. I suggest you stay in my house. I'll switch the traps off and leave the door inside the garage open. There's enough food in the freezers for at least a month. Just make sure you tell Becky to alert Plymouth. It's the only hope we've got."

"John, you can't die!" said a now tearful Donna. "Perhaps Dawn has something else."

"Perhaps she does," said John desperately controlling himself, "but I watched both my parents die of plague and they looked pretty much like she does. Now get moving back to the manor. I've got work to do."

Donna stumbled away to their bicycles, picked up hers and, with one last anguished look at John, pedalled away towards Waterfall Manor.

John watched her go and then turned back to Dawn.

"Now you two. Let's see what I can do for you," and he bent over and got Dawn into a sitting position before hooking his arms behind her knees and shoulders and slowly lifting her up, grunting at the effort.

He turned and walked carefully to the quad bike and propped her gently in its seat before searching the panniers and pulling out a tow rope. He then searched her pockets for the ignition key.

When he found it he climbed on carefully in front of Dawn and wound the rope round them both, tucking her feet into his lap, feeling the bump of the baby in the small of his back. Then taking a deep breath he started the quad bike and set off for Launceston.

John died a dozen times on the way there. Each bump and jolt felt as if it was draining Dawn's life away, but he kept up a slow and steady pace. When he reached the main road he then accelerated along and in to town before turning off into Western Road and pulling up on the forecourt of his family's former garage business next to his house.

Taking time only to unlock the garage and its inner door to the house. John disabled the traps and alarms, grabbed some water and rushed outside to unlock Puffin, his Morelo motor home.

He carried Dawn from the quad bike up into the luxurious lounge area and used the rope to tie her to a leather recliner chair.

It then only took him a moment to leap forward into the driver's seat and turn the ignition key, but his face became stricken when all he heard was a grinding noise as the engine turned over weakly without firing.

Icicles of fear shot down John's back. He'd been due to give Puffin a service that very afternoon and now, when he needed it most, the motor home wouldn't start!

      *   *   *

MEANWHILE Donna had arrived at Waterfall Manor where her shouts soon brought people out, one of whom was Becky.

When they started to move towards her she shouted at them to stay where they were and told them what had happened, what John was doing and what he wanted them to do.

"Becky, you need to get on the radio and tell Plymouth that John is heading towards them with a pregnant woman who may have the Red Plague."

There were cries of fear at this news but Donna over-rode them and said: "Quiet! We don't have time for this. Tell Plymouth he will wait for them on the main road in open countryside well outside the city and that they should come in full quarantine gear."

She faced a barrage of questions from whether it really was the Red Plague to how Dawn had looked, but she only had the will to reassure them as best she could and tell them that she now had to go and quarantine herself in

John's house for at least a week. If she came back after that time they'd see she was alive, she said, and if she didn't come back.....well, they weren't to come looking for her because she'd be dead.

"Don't the doctors and Plymouth have some sort of vaccine with them for the plague?" asked Becky.

"I don't know" managed Donna, "but you need to stop talking and radio them about John. Maybe they'll tell you they do have a vaccine, but John said they wanted to test us all at some stage to find out why we're still alive. That doesn't sound to me as if they're certain they know all about immunity. Now I must go."

And with that she got back on her bicycle and pedalled off towards Launceston leaving tears and a chorus of "good lucks" ringing in her ears. She didn't hear them and also didn't see too well from the tears trickling down her own face.

Becky lost no time in getting on the radio to Plymouth, going through the sequences Dawn had taught her, and she was soon explaining what had happened to a base surgeon at Plymouth.

"The pregnant woman John Kane is bringing to you is his wife and she may have the Red Plague. He will stop well outside the city and wants you to meet him in open countryside. He says you should wear full quarantine gear."

After a tense but brief question and answer exchange a doctor told her: "We've got a mobile surgical team. Let's hope your driver heads for the Tamar Bridge. We'll come out of the city on the same road and keep driving until we meet him. Is her husband the only other contact?"

"No," said Becky. "There is one other woman but she has gone into isolation until you tell us what this thing is."

"Make sure she stays isolated until we say otherwise," said the doctor. "We have an experimental vaccine which is promising, but we haven't been able to properly test it. All the plague victims we've seen have been dead."

"Then let's hope it isn't plague," said Becky. "How quickly will you know?"

"Within a few hours of seeing her," said the doctor. "The tests we have are conclusive. There will be no room for doubt."

Becky prayed that Dawn had something else as she cut the radio call and went out to tell a crowd of people what was happening.

$$*\qquad\qquad*\qquad\qquad*$$

OVER in Launceston John tried the ignition again and this time was rewarded with a cloud of black smoke as the engine spluttered to life.

Never had anything sounded so good and he hastily engaged first gear and got Puffin moving towards

Plymouth, but after several miles he found himself dangerously split between focussing on the road in front while checking his interior mirror to see how Dawn was doing in the lounge.

He made himself concentrate on driving and more than half an hour passed without him seeing a soul. Then he caught movement in the distance and saw a large stocky army vehicle coming towards him along an empty stretch of road broken only by a distant house near a small copse of trees.

He slowed and the two vehicles met at the entrance of the driveway to the house where the Army vehicle turned round and men in containment suits lumbered rapidly over to the Morelo.

"Mr Kane I presume. I'm Major Freer," said one of them, standing below the driver's window. "Where is your wife?"

"She's roped in to a chair behind me," said John, the major walking round to the steps and then up inside the vehicle where he was soon examining Dawn.

"I don't like what I see," he said straightening up, "but it could be anything. We won't know until we've done some blood tests."

John nodded as two other surgical team members appeared carrying a folding stretcher which they put Dawn on to and carried her over to their vehicle.

Major Freer told John to stay in the motor home and said he would keep him informed as best he could.

An hour later and John had already made one mug of coffee and was thinking about a second when Major Freer appeared and waddled over to Puffin.

When he climbed slowly inside John felt ready to fly apart, but the major had a smile on his face and said: "She's stable, she's kept the baby and we don't think it's the Red Plague."

John almost collapsed with relief and was about to ask questions when the major held up both hands and said: "That's the good news. The bad news is that the baby is slightly twisted which would make an ordinary delivery harder. We have also had no success so far with getting your wife to regain consciousness."

"So what are you saying?" asked John.

"I'm saying we need to take her to the base hospital for more tests. Derriford Hospital is being worked on but it will be at least another six months to a year before it is capable of taking patients, so the base is the best place for her at the moment."

"Can I come?" asked John.

"Of course you can," said the major, "but don't be surprised if things stay pretty much as they are for a while. I want our initial blood test that it isn't Red Plague confirmed and I want to talk to a colleague of mine to discuss the options for a caesarean so we know what we're facing if it comes to that."

"A caesarean?" asked John.

"It's where we make an incision in your wife's tummy and bring the baby out through it."

"I know what a caesarean is!" said John. "What I want to know is, how much of a risk is it?"

"We would only do that in this case if the mother's health is a factor," said Major Freer. "That's what I want to discuss with my colleague, to find out if it is a factor."

"When will you know?" asked John.

"Well, I gather this young lady has only been unconsciousness for a few hours, so I imagine we'll discover that within a day, two days at the most."

John still looked crushed as the full significance of what he had been told registered with him.

He said he would follow behind and the major nodded agreement but told him not to leave the motor home when they arrived. He then returned to his vehicle, a combination ambulance and mini operating theatre, which drove slowly away with Dawn still on board.

It made the return journey to Plymouth at a steady pace and John found he could now bring the Morelo right into the city, barricades and other obstructions having been cleared on a single main route.

There was still the eerie atmosphere of driving through largely deserted streets as night came on, row after dark row of silent empty houses suddenly broken by lights and movement as they approached the new base in the port area.

When they finally pulled up it was at a simple checkpoint where a sergeant welcomed the major back, checked who they were and directed them on to a long low warehouse.

Dawn was quickly taken inside a plastic tunnel and John was told to park away from the building at the back of a loading area where Major Freer promised that food would be brought to him.

John followed his instructions and drove Puffin to the loading area where he switched off and looked around at the bustling military area which seemed to have everything from offices and stores to medical and canteen facilities.

A corporal approached with a covered metal meal tray which he placed near the motorhome door before stepping swiftly back. When John opened the door to get it the corporal repeated Major Freer's instruction not to leave the vicinity of the vehicle.

It was all a bit bewildering for John who collected the meal tray and took it into the motor home's lounge where he sat down and mechanically ate steak and kidney pie, with carrots and mashed potato. There was rice pudding for desert. It could have been blotting paper for all John noticed.

When he finished eating he resumed his seat behind the wheel and looked around at the coming and going of dozens of people.

I haven't seen this many people for years, he thought. Probably got survivors here as well.

Darkness slowly fell and after two hours Major Freer appeared and casually knocked on the Morello's door.

John had dozed off, but he started awake at the noise and immediately noticed that Freer was in uniform not a containment suit. He pressed a button, the door opened and Freer stepped up inside.

"I presume your just being in uniform is a good thing?" asked John.

Major Freer smiled and said: "Yes. Your wife definitely doesn't have Red Plague. She does have several very interesting things trudging round in her blood, but I'll come to that later

"Essentially your wife is fit and well and so is the baby. We think the bleeding may have been caused by her recent experiences in Scotland that your friend has told us a little about on the radio.

"Most minor trauma incidents during pregnancy do not affect mother or baby, but some do. As I've already said, your wife and unborn child both appear fine physically. She'll probably wake up in her own good time but we'd like to keep an eye on her for a day or so. My colleague says there is no need for a caesarean at this stage."

"So basically you're saying wait and see," said John.

"That's about the long and the short of it," said Major Freer. "We'll take good care of her and hopefully you'll be able to take her home soon.

"As for her blood test, she definitely has a different make-up than we were expecting, so we also want to test you and other members of your community. It may help us understand how you came to survive the plague."

He then took John into another section of the building and showed him an accommodation cubicle, a compact area with a single bed, a clothing rail with hangers and a small bedside cupboard. Communal toilets and showers were further down the corridor, he was told.

Major Freer then took him down to a casualty section, stood by while a sample of John's blood was taken for testing and then excused himself because of the press of other duties.

John returned to his cubicle and lay back on the bed where he soon fell into an exhausted sleep.

In the morning Major Freer said over breakfast that Dawn's vital signs were more active and that there were indications she was coming round.

Towards lunchtime there was a tannoy announcement for John who hurried to reception where Major Freer told him that Dawn had woken up.

"She's a bit disorientated about where she is," he said, "but apart from that she's fine for a mother in what we think is about the seventh month of pregnancy. You can only see her for a few minutes but, if she continues to improve, you can stay longer this afternoon."

He then led John to a ward with a dozen beds in it complete with an impressive array of equipment. Dawn was in the furthest bed partially screened by a curtain.

When she looked up and saw him she smiled and John said: "Mrs Kane I presume! How are you?"

"A little muzzy," said Dawn, hitching herself up on her pillows. "One minute I was reaching up for the dairy key and the next someone had stabbed me with a spear. That's the last I remember until waking up here which I'm told is the base in Plymouth."

"It is," said John. "You were very lucky we found you so quickly. No more gallivanting around for you. From now on you're going to get care, cosseting and lots of rest until baby is born."

Dawn smiled again and said: "Ooooh, I do like a bit of cosseting!" at which John blushed heavily.

"There'll be none of that sort of thing until we've got you safely home," he said, blushing even more when Dawn laughed.

"You have a dirty mind!" he said. "What I mean is, we have to think of the baby now. At least you look a lot better."

"I feel a lot better," said Dawn, "Major Freer thinks the pain and blackout may partially be a mental reaction to what happened to me in Scotland. He says the bleeding came when I fell over. I must have hit my nose and bitten my tongue."

"Well you can consider yourself watched from now on. I have to go, but I'm allowed back for a longer visit this afternoon if they think you're continuing to improve."

John kissed her and said good-bye before leaving in search of Major Freer who confirmed that he could take Dawn home the next day if all went well.

"Is there anything we can do for her when I get her home?" asked John.

"Just make sure she has a few essentials such as milk, vegetables, eggs and lean meat," the major said. "A good diet will help her a lot."

John said he'd make sure she was well looked after and asked the major to get a radio message to Waterfall so Donna could be given the good news and come out of quarantine.

He nodded and left John to find his way to the canteen for lunch, collecting him a few hours later for an afternoon visit to the ward.

The difference even just a few hours had made in Dawn was tremendous and she seemed to sparkle when John approached the bed, giving him a huge smile.

"How are you?" he asked.

"We are fine!" she said, patting the bulge in her stomach. "My nose and mouth are sore and I seem to have grazed my elbow, but I am more than ready to get out of here."

"Not just yet Mrs Kane," said Major Freer. "We have to keep you in overnight. If there is no relapse then you can go home tomorrow."

He left them to it and John and Dawn chatted happily about the baby, how much the Plymouth base had progressed since they were last there and what they were going to do when they got back to Waterfall.

It was early evening when John finally left to go in search of a meal after which he spent ten minutes checking Puffin over before grabbing a book from the motor home and taking it to his room where he relaxed and read for a while. When he was ready for sleep he grabbed a towel and went down to have a shower before he turned in.

Morning saw him up early and eager to get started on the journey home.

Dawn was brought out to the canteen and they had breakfast together before Major Freer waved them good-bye as they climbed into the motor home.

EPILOGUE

The journey back to Waterfall was uneventful, Dawn remarking on the way the roads to the Tamar Bridge had been cleared.

They were soon back in Launceston where John parked Puffin and carefully helped Dawn on to the quad bike he'd left there.

"At least I don't have to tie you to me with rope!" he said as they pulled away, Dawn wrapping her arms around him.

When they arrived at Waterfall Manor they were practically submerged by well-wishers including Donna who burst into tears and came over to hug Dawn.

Jed and Becky wished her well and John told them about the food the surgeons at Plymouth had said they should try to get Dawn to eat.

"I'm sure we can manage that," said Becky.

There was a babble of conversation as the little community of survivors enjoyed their evening meal together and everyone was interested to hear how much progress had been made in Plymouth.

"They're talking about having Derriford Hospital back up and running within a year," said John, "and Major Freer tells me that more ships are on the way here from Australia."

"I need to find out a bit about that," said Dawn.

John began to read the riot act to her about taking it easy, but Dawn gave him a kiss and said:"I'll be good, but I'm not an invalid.

"If I can't do manual work now then at least I can look after the radio which is no effort at all."

"You watch her," said Becky. "If you don't she'll be back at that dairy of hers before you know it."

Dawn stuck her tongue out at her and everyone laughed and began to drift to the sitting rooms to relax and talk.

That night as Dawn snuggled up to John she said: "Did you miss me?"

"Not at all," he said, trying to stop her stealing more than her share of the bedding.

She gave him a thump for his trouble, then stopped and said: "Baby says you should be nice to me."

John shot up in bed, the lamplight catching a worried expression on his face.

"You're not having more pains are you?" he asked.

Dawn smiled and said: "No, but little one is moving around a fair bit. Here, feel."

And she took his hand and placed it on her stomach where John suddenly felt movement beneath his fingers.

He smiled nervously and said: "Is that normal?"

"Perfectly normal I believe," said Dawn, "at least I think so."

But he'd caught the sly look in her eyes and didn't fall for her teasing, loftily turning his back on her and switching off the light.

In the morning Dawn woke to find John gone, but she wasn't alone for long when he returned with a breakfast tray for her.

"Nothing but the best for you," he said. "Fresh milk, eggs and bacon and toast with apple preserve."

Dawn smiled at him as he helped her use pillows to support her back before taking the tray

"Looks delicious," she said.

"Couldn't have your first morning back without giving you a treat. Just don't expect it every morning!" he said.

Despite what he said, John often brought her breakfast in bed as the coming days stretched into weeks and Dawn became more and more confined to the manor.

Then came the big day when John walked back for lunch after a morning spent repairing a tractor to find Dawn had gone into labour.

He no sooner stepped into the kitchen than he was hustled out, told what was happening and had Jed thrust at him with instructions to eat in the smaller kitchen.

"They wouldn't even let me wash my hands!" he told Jed.

"That's because they don't want you under their feet," said Jed. "Let's get you cleaned up and some food inside you. I don't think you'll be doing much work this afternoon."

The two of them then walked through to the other kitchen where John scrubbed his hands clean of oil and assembled himself a doorstep cheese sandwich with spring onions and tomatoes.

"Well, there's nothing wrong with your appetite!" said Jed.

"I'm nervous," said John, taking a huge bite from his sandwich. "That always makes me hungry."

"When you've finished we can always go for a beer. It's a little early but this is a special occasion."

"And it's going to stay a special occasion," said John. "You're not getting me into the state you were in when Tilly was born."

"That wasn't my fault!" said Jed indignantly. "You kept putting beer in front of me!"

"And you kept drinking it!" said John, tucking into a spring onion. "It took me weeks to get back into Dawn's good books because they all blamed me not you."

"Well then," said Jed. "This time they'll blame me!"

John considered this and then said: "Attractive though getting my own back is, I'm not getting drunk to achieve that."

"Don't drink beer then" said Jed. "We've still got some of the haymaking cider that Lucas made. Victor says it has a lovely flavour for cooking."

John slowly ate a tomato, looked at Jed and said: "Just one then and I mean just one."

He finished his sandwich, washed his hands again and the two of them risked a brisk peep at the hive of activity in the main kitchen before leaving quietly and heading for their little pub, the Manor Arms, which had been set up in a small stone outbuilding.

They were soon sat on stools at the tiny bar with Jed pouring from flip-top bottles of amber liquid which slid into their glasses without a bubble.

"Congratulations," said Jed, raising his glass to John and taking a mouthful. John nodded and took a sip from his own glass, allowing the cool dry flavour to slide down his throat.

They drifted into talk of Tilly's birth and how it had changed Jed's life and speculated on how the new baby would change John and Dawn's life.

Jed was convinced it would keep John closer to home, but John wasn't so certain because of their expanding community, the demands being made on him by Leo Anderson in London and the need to set up their own Recovery Council.

"The way I see it," he said, "is that we'll no sooner get our council up and running than it will be asked to liaise with those in London, Wales, the North and Scotland. And what about the Midlands? According to Anderson there's the makings of a nasty little war up there that he may have to send troops in to deal with. All the councils will be involved in discussion for that and we may have to supply men to help if only to provide proof that our community system works."

"Can't see it working with that lot," said Jed. "It all seems a bit feudal up there."

"We have to try and encourage them to see sense," said John. "We can't afford to waste lives on useless fighting when we've got a country to start rebuilding."

"Always the wider picture with you," said Jed with a smile. "Well good luck. I've a feeling Dawn may have a few words to say about that. Speaking of Dawn, I'll just pop over and see how things are going."

With that he left and John took a sip of his drink, wondering what the future was really going to be like.

Jed was soon back and said: "Early days yet I'm told. Could be hours before she gets close. Let me get you another drink."

He found two more bottles, but John waved his away and nursed what was left in his glass, hoping Dawn wasn't having too hard a time of it and that the delivery would be trouble-free.

Jed had brought back a handful of Maisie's biscuits and they munched them while waiting for news, but none came.

Eventually John said: "I think I'd better check again how things are going."

"No need," said Jed, taking a swallow from his glass. "Becky's in charge and she said she'd come and tell us when Dawn was getting near. We are strictly surplus to requirements. Another drink?"

John waved him away, got off his stool and began to pace up and down in the narrow little bar, muttering to himself.

"What was that?" said Jed.

"I said that I'll have to spend the next week getting the house ready. It will have to be properly cleaned and aired before the baby can go there, particularly the nursery."

"I'd wait until Dawn can be there," said Jed. "She'll only insist on changing what you've done. Women are like that."

"Are they now?" said Jed wryly. "I don't think Dawn will object to me cleaning the place up."

Just then there came a faint scream from the manor and John stumbled into a stool and nearly fell over.

"Was that what I think it was?" he said.

"Depends what you thought it was," said Jed. "Sounded to me like a party!" and he took a drink from his glass.

John looked at him suspiciously and said: "You're half cut already and I'm the one becoming a father!"

"I'm a little mellow tis true," said Jed, beaming at him, "but this is a speshul occasion. You're supposed to celebrate speshul occasions."

"Celebrate them yes," said John, looking warily at the cluster of bottles on the bar, "but not get unconscious! This stuff is lethal!"

Reaching a decision he pushed his glass away and began to walk towards the door followed by a swaying Jed who had to use both hands to put his glass on the bar.

"They wone like it," he said, stumbling along.

"I don't care if they don't like it," said John. "A man has a right to be at the birth of his child."

His words were followed by a thump as Jed slid bonelessly to the ground.

"Not again!" said John, picking him up and throwing him over one shoulder. He resumed his walk to the manor, dumping Jed in the kitchen where he told a startled Victor to sober him up.

He then climbed the stairs to where he and Dawn slept, the bedroom door being slightly open to reveal half a dozen women round the bed.

An ear-splitting shriek came followed by cries of encouragement from the women who now clustered even closer together.

John made to enter the room and then thought better of it. Perhaps he'd better check first, so he shouted: "How's it going? Is Dawn all right?"

There were some surprised shouts inside and suddenly Becky was out in the corridor with him.

"Didn't you get my message?" she hissed. "I said I'd send for you when she was getting close."

"I want to know how everything is going," said John stubbornly.

"Well everything is fine," said Becky. "Her contractions are coming faster but she still has a while to go yet. Do us all a favour and go and wait downstairs. You'll just be in the way up here and I promise to send for you when she nears time."

John nodded stiffly and suddenly found himself alone as Becky swiftly went back into the bedroom and closed the door behind her.

Nice to be wanted, thought John, as he stumped back down to the kitchen where he found Victor had propped Jed in a chair between the vegetable rack and a dresser where he was snoring loudly.

"How's it going up there?" he asked as John sat down at the kitchen table.

"All is well, so I'm told, but my presence is not required at the moment," said John.

"Sent you away with a flea in your ear did they!" said Victor. "Best you stay well out of the way or they'll have you doing something disgusting."

"Like what?" said John suspiciously.

"Don't ask me," said Victor. "Norma and I want children but we haven't been blessed yet. I can tell you one thing for nothing. If she does fall pregnant then I for one am staying right here until the very last moment."

John glowered at him so Victor said: "Relax and have another beer."

"We haven't been drinking beer," said John.

"Well you've been drinking something judging by the state Jed's in."

"It was hay making cider. Jed told me you said it had a lovely flavour."

"I did," said Victor, "but I also said it was so strong it could practically pour itself! How much have you had?"

"Not much. A bottle, perhaps two," said John. "Jed, as you can see, has had a little more."

"How much more?" said Victor.

"Four bottles, perhaps five."

"Five?!" said Victor. "No wonder he's out for the count! Becky will kill him!"

"I doubt that," said John. "She's in baby mode at the moment and according to her Dawn still has a while to go. Jed will be back in the land of the living by then."

He and Victor chatted desultorily for a while as the chef made preparations for Waterfall's main meal of the day that evening.

People came and went, John made himself a cup of herbal tea which seemed to relax him and Asher and Matthew came in to say the wheat, barley and oat fields were doing well and it also looked like they'd get a decent crop of potatoes.

Their words just washed over John and when the two men shot puzzled looks at Victor he just made a calming gesture with his hands, pointed upstairs and they nodded in understanding.

The manor was packed for the evening meal and still there was no news about Dawn.

Everyone was chatting about the birth, wondering if it would be a girl or a boy, until John could take it no more and said he was going to the library. When he got there he closed the door on all the chatter and simply sat in an armchair thinking.

Half an hour later the door opened and Jed walked in, wincing at the noise the door made when he shut it.

"Back with us now are you?" said John.

"My head feels like it's got a swarm of Donna's bees in it," said a white-faced Jed.

"You're lucky you sobered up before Becky found you," said John. "I don't suppose there is any news?"

"No," said Jed. "The best I can do for you is that it won't be long now."

"Means nothing," said John. "I've heard that at least twice already."

No sooner had the words left his lips than the door opened, Becky put her head inside and said: "Baby will be coming soon if you'd like to come up."

John shot out of his chair and swiftly followed Becky upstairs and into the bedroom where Dawn lay in bed, her legs parted and her face a mask of sweat.

"Hello love," he said and Dawn started to smile before her face writhed as another contraction hit her and she screamed in exertion.

"I can see baby's head," said Becky, leaning forward to wipe Dawn's face with a cloth. Push, push!"

And suddenly with one last effort from Dawn there was a squalling bundle being lifted clear, the umbilical cord was cut and the baby wrapped gently in towelling and placed in the arms of an exhausted Dawn.

John had watched the whole procedure with wide eyes and now stepped forward to kiss Dawn and the baby.

"You've a lovely healthy son," said Becky who looked very tired but pleased.

"We had a bit of trouble with the baby's placement but all's well that ends well."

John smiled proudly and took a seat as close to the bed as he could as Dawn parted the towelling to reveal a screwed up face, mouth opening and closing, little fingers flexing.

"Have you thought of a name?" asked Becky.

"Well, if it was a boy we were going to call him Phillip after my father, so Phillip it is," said John.

Dawn smiled agreement as some of the women washed her clean and took the baby briefly so she could put on a fresh nightgown.

It wasn't too long before a steady trickle of well-wishers began to knock on the door to see the baby.

More than a dozen packed into the bedroom as some of the women who had been helping with the birth left and others arrived with fresh hot water, flannels and towels.

Among those visiting was Maisie who stumped into the room, John giving his seat up for her so she could see the baby properly.

"Handsome little fellow isn't he!" she said.

No-one had a chance to respond because a chorus of screams rang out from those near the door as people suddenly pushed and shoved each other in their efforts to get further into the room.

"What the hell....." said John, fighting his way through the crush towards the door only to recoil sharply when he saw what was there.

The tiger was back, lips curled over its great teeth as the huge striped body filled the doorway!

Then Jed stood up, the tiger skin fell off his shoulders and he said: "Surprise! This is for you Maisie. Told you I'd have a gift for you. Oh, and congratulations to you John and you Dawn."

A stunned silence greeted his words before a roar of exasperation washed over him and people beat him over the head with towels or simply gave him a piece of their mind.

John shook his head in disbelief and weakly stepped back to the bed where he sat down, Dawn rocking their baby as it voiced its displeasure at all the noise.

"Foolish man!" said Maisie. "What do I want with a tiger skin rug? Bad enough that I had to chase off a real one without bringing it back inside!"

Everyone was laughing now nerves had settled while outside a moon shone down as night fell, cloaking Waterfall Manor in silver.

*   *   *

More than thirty miles away the tigress was leading her three cubs on the eastern edge of Dartmoor.

The cubs were playing, stalking each other among undergrowth flanking the path the tigress was following through a deserted village.

Her head raised every now and again as she tested the air. She had killed a deer two days ago but the cubs needed fresh meat and she would have to kill again.

THE END

Printed in Great Britain
by Amazon

83347800R00253